EDGAR HUNTLY;
or,
MEMOIRS OF A SLEEP-WALKER

with Related Texts

Charles Brockden Brown

EDGAR HUNTLY;
or,
MEMOIRS OF A SLEEP-WALKER

with Related Texts

Edited, with an Introduction and Notes, by
Philip Barnard and Stephen Shapiro

Hackett Publishing Company, Inc.
Indianapolis/Cambridge

13 12 11 10   2 3 4 5 6

For further information, please address
  Hackett Publishing Company, Inc.
  P.O. Box 44937
  Indianapolis, IN 46244-0937

  www.hackettpublishing.com

Cover design by Abigail Coyle
Text design by Carrie Wagner
Composition by Professional Book Compositors
Printed at Victor Graphics, Inc.

The text of *Edgar Huntly; or, Memoirs of a Sleep-Walker* included in this edition was provided by the University of Virginia Library's Electronic Text Center.

Library of Congress Cataloging-in-Publication Data

Brown, Charles Brockden, 1771–1810.
  Edgar Huntly, or, Memoirs of a Sleep-walker ; with Related Texts / Charles Brockden Brown ; edited, with an introduction and notes, by Philip Barnard and Stephen Shapiro.
    p. cm.
  Includes bibliographical references.
  ISBN-13: 978-0-87220-853-7 (pbk. : alk. paper)
  ISBN-10: 0-87220-853-2 (pbk. : alk. paper)
  ISBN-13: 978-0-87220-854-4 (cloth : alk. paper)
  ISBN-10: 0-87220-854-0 (cloth : alk. paper)
  1. Young men—Fiction. 2. Murder—Investigation—Fiction. 3. Sleepwalking—Fiction. 4. Dementia—Fiction. 5. Wilderness areas—Fiction. 6. Delaware Indians—Fiction. 7. Philadelphia (Pa.)—History—18th century—Fiction. 8. Psychological fiction. I. Barnard, Philip, 1951– II. Shapiro, Stephen, 1964– III. Title. IV. Title: Edgar Huntly. V. Title: Memoirs of a sleep-walker.
PS1134.E34 2006
813'.2—dc22

2006016441

CONTENTS

ACKNOWLEDGMENTS

We thank the Department of English, University of Kansas, and the Department of English and Comparative Literary Studies, University of Warwick, for support throughout the preparation of this volume. The College of Liberal Arts and Sciences at Kansas provided support in the form of a sabbatical leave used for the research and preparation of this edition. The staffs of the University of Kansas Libraries and The Spencer Research Library rare book collection have been helpful sources of textual materials. The indefatigable and exacting Lydia Ash has provided patient help with managing documents and computer support.

For access to and help with their digitized text of the first edition (1799) of *Edgar Huntly*, we acknowledge and thank the University of Virginia Libraries and their Early American Fiction Collection project. Mike Furlough of Virginia Library's Digital Research and Instructional Services, in particular, has facilitated our use of this resource.

We are indebted to the community of scholars who work on Brown and early modern culture, and to colleagues in the Charles Brockden Brown Society, whose insights and advice have helped form our ideas about and approach to *Edgar Huntly*. This and all future editions of *Edgar Huntly* are indebted to the organization and analysis of textual data provided by S. W. Reid and Sydney J. Krause in the Kent State Bicentennial Edition of 1984. Alfred Weber's editions of Brown's essays and short fiction have also been invaluable for our work. Special thanks are due to colleague Mark Kamrath, who read and advised on early versions of the notes.

For guidance and support with the editorial process at Hackett, we thank Rick Todhunter and Carrie Wagner.

Personal thanks, gratitude, and Woldwinite relations of reason and desire link us to Anne Schwan, Cheryl Lester, and Julia Barnard.

INTRODUCTION

> "It was dangerous to awaken a *somnambulist* on the brink of a precipice."

> —Mary Wollstonecraft, *An Historical and Moral View of the Origin and Progress of the French Revolution* (1794, I:275)

When *Edgar Huntly; or, Memoirs of a Sleep-Walker* first went on sale in late summer 1799—the first of its three volumes was published in August or early September—it was the fourth of Charles Brockden Brown's novels to be published in book form in the space of twelve months. By 1801 two more would be published as books; one more would be serialized; yet another was lost. *Edgar Huntly* is thus one of the peaks in an extraordinary burst of novel writing that is still the best-known aspect of Brown's prolific literary career, and a remarkable achievement by any standards.

Brown's novels are intellectually ambitious works that present the reader with considerable formal and conceptual complexity, and *Edgar Huntly* is no exception. As this Introduction will suggest, *Edgar Huntly* draws on and refers in detail to eighteenth-century medical theories and doctrines of sensibility, British radical-democratic social theory, theories of the novel, revolution debates of the 1790s, politicized Celtic folktales, and a wide swath of recent history, from Anglo-French imperial wars to Irish revolutionary uprisings, Quaker-Indian frontier relations, and struggles between Pennsylvania Quakers and other immigrant groups. Brown's dark tale of somnambulism and frontier violence combines the explosive political atmosphere of the revolutionary and counterrevolutionary 1790s with the brutality of settler-Indian conflict in Pennsylvania extending back through the eighteenth century. It relates both these theaters of conflict, Old World revolutionary wars and New World Indian wars, to the global reach of Anglo-French imperialism and commerce, and to the shock of the (early) modern in the widest sense, from North America and Ireland to the Asian subcontinent. Dramatically organized around one individual's unconscious or sleepwalking fall into murderous frontier violence in backcountry Pennsylvania, the novel's actions are nevertheless connected to global political and economic transformations that still shape our world and bodies today. Although the novel leaves the reader with a gloomy picture of the challenges facing its protagonist at the end of the revolutionary era and beginning of the commercial and expansionist nineteenth century, it nonetheless holds out the hope that we are not doomed to repeat the social traumas of the past and may progressively come to understand the collective forces that condition our individual lives.

This Introduction will orient the reader to the world of *Edgar Huntly* by providing some tools for understanding Brown and his novel. We will outline and provide background for the novel's primary themes in order to draw the reader's attention to them and open them up for discussion. A sketch of Brown's life and the late 1790s context, and a discussion of his understanding of novels as instruments of political education and enlightenment, will provide general background. Information on central motifs—sleep-walking, Quaker-Irish-Indian violence on the Pennsylvania frontier, questions about gender and sexuality, and Brown's use of gothic and folk motifs like human-animal transformation—will lead to a discussion of how the novel develops and explores its primary social, psychological, and political concerns.

Brown's Life and the Context of the 1790s

Brown was born into a Philadelphia Quaker merchant family on January 17, 1771. Philadelphia—the capital of the newly formed United States during the 1790s and then the largest, most culturally and politically diverse city in North America—was his home for most of his life. Beginning in the mid-1790s and particularly during the intense 1797–1800 period when Brown was writing his novels, however, he also lived in New York and moved in a cosmopolitan circle of young upper-class intellectuals who circulated and debated the latest medical-scientific, political, and cultural information, and produced writings on a wide variety of subjects.

Growing up a Philadelphia Quaker (members of The Religious Society of Friends are commonly known as Quakers or Friends), Brown was shaped by that community's history of dissenting relations to mainstream Protestant and Anglo-American culture and by the history of William Penn's Pennsylvania. From its founding as a Quaker colony in 1682 to Brown's lifetime, Pennsylvania experienced a number of basic historical transformations that Brown addressed in his writings: the rapid commercial expansion of Philadelphia as a wealthy trading center that enriched and often bankrupted its Quaker merchant elite; the gradual erosion of Quaker political power and community unity as other immigrant and ethno-religious groups came to outnumber Quakers in Pennsylvania; and the history of conflicts in the Pennsylvania backcountry or frontier, where Anglo-French imperial contests like the Seven Years War (1756–1763; the French and Indian War is the North American theater of this conflict) pitted Quakers against Indians on the one hand and other European immigrant groups (particularly the Irish) on the other. Brown had a classical education at the elite Friends Latin School in Philadelphia and taught at the Friends Grammar School briefly in the early 1790s, but he did not, like male friends in his New York circle, attend a university, since Quakers and other dissenters in the United States and England did not patronize the educational institutions that served dominant Protestant groups. Additionally, progressive traditions and doctrines concerning egalitarianism and equal authority for women in the Quaker community contributed to Brown's lifelong commitment to female education and equality. Quaker doctrines of nonviolence figure dramatically in the background of *Edgar Huntly*, since the novel's protagonist is a Quaker farmer who casts these beliefs aside to become an Indian-killing machine in the second half of his story. Although Brown's adult years led him from his Philadelphia origins to the intellectual world of the radical Enlightenment, his Quaker background nonetheless marks his development in fundamental ways. Interestingly, after having grown up as Quakers in the increasingly diversified Philadelphia of the late eighteenth century, Brown and all his siblings married non-Quakers. Brown was formally expelled from the Quaker meeting in Philadelphia when he married Elizabeth Linn, daughter of a Presbyterian minister, in 1804.

Growing up the fourth of five brothers and seven surviving siblings total in a merchant family,[1] Brown's life was marked by the instability and crises of mercantile and revolutionary Philadelphia. It is notable that the two main forms of commerce that figure in *Edgar Huntly* are land acquisition and development (then called "land conveyancing"), and the circum-Atlantic import-export commerce that was the main business of Philadelphia's port, for Brown's father and older brothers had checkered, up-and-down careers in these two areas. As expansionism and the transformation of frontier land into private property created vicious cycles of settler-Indian violence and revenge attacks in this period, imperial conflicts (primarily between England and France), the 1790s revolutions in France and Haiti, and rebellion in Ireland enriched Philadelphia's import-export trade and filled its streets with political refugees and immigrants of every stripe and color. Brown's father Elijah was imprisoned and briefly banished from Philadelphia in 1777–1778, during the American Revolution, as a Quaker whose religious neutrality made him suspect to both royalists and revolutionaries. In 1784 he was humiliatingly imprisoned for debt. Through all this, the father struggled to continue in business, working primarily as a land broker and conveyancer (a real estate agent). Brown's oldest brothers Joseph and James—like the merchant Weymouth in this novel—were buying interest shares in ocean ventures as early as the 1780s and traveled frequently to Europe, the Middle East, and the Caribbean as merchant importers.[2] Brown himself became a reluctant partner in their import-export firm, James Brown and Co., from late 1800 to the firm's dissolution in 1806.[3] In 1801, Brown reflected on the loss of Indian tribal lands when his brother James bought 20,000 acres of property on the Pennsylvania frontier.[4] Thus *Edgar Huntly*'s dramatics of disputed land claims, violent conversions of tribal land into private property, inheritances, risky export investments, and sudden financial failures are drawn not just from Brown's wider knowledge of the world around him, but from his own family business background.

---

[1] Kafer's *Charles Brockden Brown's Revolution* provides the numbers we use here—that is, five brothers and two sisters who survived to adulthood, plus three siblings who died at birth or in early infancy (45; 210, note 36; 221, note 25).

[2] Warfel, *Charles Brockden Brown,* 16–18. The oldest brother Joseph died in 1807 in Flanders, Holland, while on a Weymouth-like business voyage.

[3] See the accounts of Brown family business interests in Warfel, *Charles Brockden Brown,* 16–18, 23, 204; Clark, *Charles Brockden Brown,* 108–9, 194–95; and Kafer, *Charles Brockden Brown's Revolution,* 26–37; 45–46; 162; 214, note 15.

[4] Krause, "Penn's Elm and *Edgar Huntly*," 473–75. See this text, from the "Memorandums Made on a Journey Through Part of Pennsylvania" in this volume's Related Texts.

Although his family intended for him to become a lawyer, Brown abandoned his Philadelphia law apprenticeship in 1793 and moved toward the circle of young, New York–based intellectuals who helped launch his literary career and, with Brown as one of their group, enacted progressive Enlightenment ideals of conversation, intellectual inquiry, and companionship.[5] The key figure in this group was Elihu Hubbard Smith (1771–1798), a Yale-educated physician who met Brown in Philadelphia in 1790 and who formed part of the model for the character Waldegrave in *Edgar Huntly*. Like Waldegrave in this novel, Smith was an abolitionist and deist[6] dedicated to progressive ideals; when he died prematurely, while he and Brown were roommates, during a yellow fever epidemic in 1798, the deist writings he left behind were perceived as scandalous. The New York group included a number of young male professionals who called themselves The Friendly Club, along with female relatives and friends who were equally invested in progressive intellectual exchange and enlightened models for same-sex and other-sex companionship. This progressive model of companionship based on "reason and desire" (Teute) expressed through a "republic of letters" is a crucial context for Brown's astonishing burst of novel writing between 1798 and 1800. As one of this circle, Brown developed his knowledge of like-minded British radical-democratic writers of the period—above all William Godwin and Mary Wollstonecraft (whose books were already in Brown's household as a youth, before he met Smith)—as well as physiological theories of sense perception and moral philosophy drawn from the Scottish Enlightenment (notably Erasmus Darwin), the French Naturalists, and other streams of Enlightenment thought. The circle's interest in similar groups of progressive British thinkers was strong enough that they established contact with scientist Erasmus Darwin (who corresponded with Smith) and novelist Thomas Holcroft (who corresponded with Dunlap). Thus Brown's interest in European developments led him to participate in a network of like-minded endeavors, but his progressive, modernizing ideals meant that he felt little or no need to emulate Europe or the past as a superior culture.

If Brown's intellectual circle in New York constitutes one part of the context for his burst of novel writing, the other crucial element in this context is the explosive political atmosphere of the revolutionary 1790s as the decade culminated in the antirevolutionary backlash of 1797 1799. As the decade long process of the French

---

[5] For discussions of this circle, see Teute, "A 'Republic of Intellect'" and "The Loves of the Plants." The diaries of William Dunlap and Elihu Hubbard Smith provide detailed records of Brown's activities and relations within this circle.

[6] Deism is a progressive eighteenth-century response to Christianity. It affirms the existence of a supreme being but rejects revelation, supernatural doctrines, and any notion of divine intervention in human affairs. Reason and science, rather than revelation and dogma, are the basis for religious belief. Late eighteenth-century writers often adopt a deistic stance as part of their general secular and rationalist critique of earlier institutions. Deism is associated with natural religion and the well-known metaphor of the deity as a clock-maker who creates the universe but makes no further intervention in it. Many leaders of the American revolutionary generation were deists, most notably Benjamin Franklin and Thomas Jefferson. See Walters, *Rational Infidels*.

Revolution (including the Haitian Revolution of 1791–1804 and the failed Irish uprisings of 1796–1798) drew to its close in the late 1790s, a severe reaction against the progressive ideals of the revolutionary era spread through the Atlantic world and was especially powerful in England, Germany, and the recently formed United States. During the administration of the second U.S. president, John Adams (1796–1800), the ruling Federalist party presided over a hysterical, authoritarian response to real and imagined threats of revolutionary subversion and potential conflict with France.[7] Enacting the now-infamous Alien and Sedition Acts (1798), for example, the Federalists made it illegal to criticize the Adams administration and legitimated the arrest and deportation of those deemed "dangerous" state enemies (i.e., French and Irish radicals). Paranoid countersubversive fantasies about conspiracies led by mysterious groups like the Illuminati, as well as elite panic about ideals of female equality and universal democracy that arose and circulated widely during the revolutionary years, contributed to this crisis.[8] Although these excesses led to the election of their Democratic-Republican opponent Jefferson in 1800, the larger early romantic, culturally conservative wave of which they were a part put an end to the revolutionary era and laid the foundations for the more staid cultural order of the nineteenth century. Mysterious and threatening Brownian characters like *Edgar Huntly*'s Clithero Edny—a deranged Irish refugee whose story is a gothic condensation of recent Irish class and revolutionary struggles—draw on and respond to the countersubversive myths of this crisis period.

Brown's efforts to establish himself as a writer were impressive indeed. After several years of experimentation with literary narratives that remained unfinished, Brown's novelistic phase began with the 1798 feminist dialogue *Alcuin* and continued unabated through the composition of eight novels by 1801. In addition to these novels, Brown was editing the New York *Monthly Magazine* and published many essays and short stories throughout this period. As noted earlier, the four gothic novels for which Brown is best known—*Wieland, Ormond, Arthur Mervyn*, and *Edgar Huntly*—were all published between September 1798 and September 1799 (a continuation of *Arthur Mervyn* appeared in summer 1800), and there was a period in 1798 when all four were under way at once. Although commentators have seen Brown as a writer who renounced his literary and progressive political ideals when he stopped publishing novels in 1801, a more plausible explanation for his subsequent shift toward other forms of writing is that his novels did not make money; the particular conditions that fueled the intense novelistic burst between 1798 and 1800 changed (who could sustain such a rhythm of production?); and he became interested in new literary outlets. Like his older counterpart Godwin in England, Brown

---

[7] See the discussions of this backlash and its implications in Cotlar, "The Federalists' Transatlantic Cultural Offensive of 1798"; Fischer, *The Revolution of American Conservatism;* and Miller, *Crisis in Freedom.*

[8] On the countersubversive fantasies that were a basic element of this crisis, see Hofstadter, *The Paranoid Style;* Rogin, *Ronald Reagan, the Movie;* and Davis, *The Fear of Conspiracy.*

moved away from the novel because he felt it no longer offered an effective mode of argumentation in the increasingly conservative cultural and political environment that emerged after 1800. Had Brown lived longer, he might conceivably have returned to novel writing, as Godwin did in the later 1810s.

Brown's later literary career builds continuously on the novels and earlier writings. Between 1801 and his death from tuberculosis in 1810, Brown edited *The Literary Magazine* (1803–1807), a literary and cultural miscellany that renewed his experience with the earlier *Monthly Magazine* and which he filled with his own essays and fiction, and *The American Register* (1807–1809), a historical and political periodical that featured Brown's "Annals of Europe and America," a contemporary political history of the Napoleonic era. In addition, he wrote a novel-length, experimental historical fiction known as *The Historical Sketches* (1803–1806) that was published posthumously, a now-lost play, and several lengthy, quasi-novelistic pamphlets on expansion into the Louisiana territory and Jefferson's embargo policies (1803, 1809). Seen as a whole, these writings continue Brown's career-long concern with the link between historical and fictional ("romance") writing and extend the earlier program of "reason and desire" that makes writing an instrument of progressive, educational principles in the public sphere. Rather than dramatizing the ways individuals are shaped by social pressures, as he did in his novels, the later Brown explores forms of historical narrative and the larger historical world that made up the allusive backdrop of the earlier fiction. The critical perspective on global webs of imperialism and colonialism that is mostly implicit in the life-stories of characters in *Edgar Huntly* and his other novels, for example, becomes explicit and is explored in detail in the later histories and essays.[9]

The Woldwinite Writers and Brown's Novelistic Method

The world of Brown's novels—with their gothic emotional intensities, disorienting psychosocial violence, and imbedded plots and subplots—may be difficult to sort out on first encounter. Understanding some basics about Brown's primary intellectual and political sources and his well-defined novelistic method, however, can help the reader understand features of Brown's novels that otherwise seem difficult to grasp. This information also sheds light on basic critical questions about how to understand Brown's use of narrative point of view, which helps us consider the key issue of whether Brown is speaking directly through his narrator or, rather, implying a distanced and critical view of the narrator's ideas and actions.

Unlike many authors of eighteenth-century fiction, Brown had a well-developed methodology and set of themes for writing novels. His method draws on and further develops the ideas of the British radical-democratic writers of the period. Brown's

---

[9] On Brown's later commentary on the imperialist backdrop of *Edgar Huntly*, see Kamrath, "American Exceptionalism and Radicalism."

enthusiastic reception of these Woldwinite[10] (Anglo-Jacobin) writers—above all Mary Wollstonecraft, William Godwin, Thomas Holcroft, Robert Bage, Helen Maria Williams, and Thomas Paine—undergirds his entire literary project after the mid-1790s. The British Dissenter culture of highly educated middle-class professionals and the clubs and academies from which these writers emerge is the wider context of Brown's own Philadelphia Quaker community. Thus Brown comes to be exposed to the Woldwinite writers through his father's copies of their works even before Brown moved into the New York circle and explored these writers' works in greater detail.[11]

The Woldwinite agenda rests on three basic arguments that draw together the main strands of knowledge and critique in the late, radical Enlightenment. Drawing on well-established eighteenth-century arguments and themes such as associative sentiment (the idea that emotions are communicated from one individual to another and may be used to encourage constructive, progressive behavior), these three arguments sum up this group's rejection of the prerevolutionary order and the group's conviction that social progress may be achieved by altering dominant ways of thinking through peaceful cultural means such as literature. First, the social order of the old regime (monarchy and feudalism) is to be rejected, because it is artificial and illegitimate, violating the natural equality of humanity by imposing coercive hierarchies of caste and faith. Second, a new social order will need to operate in more rational and constructive ways, for the old regime maintained its domination through an obscurantist mythology of territorialized race, priestly tricks, and a politics of secret plots, conspiracies, and lies. Third, the illustration of progressive behavior will multiply to generate larger social transformation, because society works through chains of associative sentiment. These cultural relays will have progressive results since the illustration of virtuous behaviors and results will spread through imitation, as one person learns new and improved ways of acting by observing others. Proceeding from these assumptions, the Woldwinites' critique leads to their antistatism, their distrust of institutions, and their use of cultural forms such as literature to advance their program. Because they believe in the natural propulsion of cooperative behavior and the guidance of critical reason, these writers see social change

---

[10] We use the term "Woldwinite" to highlight, through an abbreviation of Wollstonecraft and Godwin, this group's special place among the British radical democrats of the 1790s. The term "Godwinians" erases the crucial role of Wollstonecraft and other women in this group, a role that was particularly important for Brown and many other writers. Similarly, these British writers are also discussed as "Jacobins" or "Anglo-Jacobins," names used by their enemies to link them to the most authoritarian and destructive faction of the French Revolution, but the group explicitly rejected the Jacobin position in favor of the kind of progressive cultural politics that Brown adapts from the group. For studies of literary Woldwinism, see Clemit, *The Godwinian Novel;* Kelly, *The English Jacobin Novel* and *English Fiction of the Romantic Period;* Butler, *Jane Austen and the War of Ideas;* and Tompkins, *The Popular Novel in England.* This passage condenses arguments from Shapiro, *The Culture and Commerce of the Early American Novel.*

[11] For the Woldwinite writings in Brown's household, see Warfel, *Charles Brockden Brown,* 17–18, 27; Clark, *Charles Brockden Brown,* 16; Kafer, *Charles Brockden Brown's Revolution,* 46, 66–72.

as resulting from the amplification of transformed local and interpersonal or intersubjective relations. Thus, as we say today, the personal is political.

In their assumption that global historical change begins from the bottom up with the premeditated transformation of relations among a small circle, the Woldwinites are an early instance of cultural avant-gardism that aims to develop means of worldly social revolution through arts and manners rather than political parties or state institutions. In contemporary terms, the Woldwinites introduce a relatively straightforward, albeit limited, idea of environmental or social construction, the notion that individuals are shaped or conditioned by their social environments. The Woldwinites' ideas about social construction are limited, because they position themselves as innocent participants, do not recognize the dilemmas implicit in their own social program (particularly its assumptions about sentiment, benevolence, and associative imitation, e.g.), and direct their critique at the hierarchical inequalities of the old regime while neglecting the emergent structures of liberal capitalism. Brown adopts their environmentalist argument but also, as a second-wave Woldwinite, recognizes that their ideas about social construction and action are incomplete. His fiction attempts to think through these limitations and their implications in ways that we will explore in greater detail when we turn to the plot of *Edgar Huntly.*

Building on these basic Woldwinite ideas, Brown's fictional method is articulated in several key essays on narrative technique and the social role of the novel that appear at the height of his novelistic phase, most notably the manifesto-like "Walstein's School of History" (Aug.–Sept. 1799) and "The Difference between History and Romance" (April 1800).[12] To summarize this method, we can say that Brown's fiction combines elements of history and the novel to place his characters in extreme conditions of social distress as a means of engaging a wider audience into considerations of progressive behavior. His novels explore how common, disempowered subjects respond to damaging social conditions caused by defects in dominant ideas and practices. Through their interconnected patterns of socially conditioned behavior, dramatic suspense, and gothic intensities, Brown's fictions urge readers to reflect on how to overcome corruption in order to construct a more "virtuous," equal, and fulfilling society.

This approach begins with Brown's understanding of the relation between historical and fictional writing. History and fiction, he argues, are not different because one deals with factual and the other with fictional materials. Rather, history and fiction are intrinsically connected as two sides of one coin, because history describes and documents the results of actions, while fiction investigates the possible motives that cause these actions. Fictions are thus narrative experiments that tease out possible preconditions for historical events or behaviors and that reason through social problems presented as hypothetical situations. Whereas history describes events, romance analyzes and projects the probable causes, conditions, and preconditions of events. The "Walstein" essay builds on this distinction and develops a three-fold plan for

---

[12] These essays are included in the Related Texts at the end of this volume.

novel writing. As critics have noted, the plan outlined in this essay gives us an accurate account of Brown's motivation for writing fiction and of how he builds his novels. The historian Walstein first combines history and romance in such a way as to promote "moral and political" engagement while rejecting universal truths in order to stress the situatedness of engaged political response in noble and classical figures such as Cicero. Walstein's pupil Engel then modernizes and develops the theory by adding that a romance, to be effective in today's world, must be addressed to a wide popular audience and draw its characters not from the elite but from the same lower-status group that will read and be moved by the work. History and romance alike must address issues and situations familiar to their modern audience, notably the common inequalities arising from relations of sex and property. Thus a modern piece of literature will insert ordinary individuals like Edgar Huntly, rather than elite characters like Cicero, into situations of stress over contemporary conflicts involving money and erotic desire. Finally, a thrilling style and form are crucial and necessary, since a romance capable of moving its audience to considerations of progressive action must, as Brown writes, "be so arranged as to inspire, at once, curiosity and belief, to fasten the attention, and thrill the heart." In this manner, Brown's method uses the twists and turns of his plots and their many embedded narratives as ways to illustrate and think through interrelated social problems. The first edition (1799) of *Edgar Huntly* illustrates the method outlined in "Walstein" quite literally; while Edgar's tale is that of a common individual struggling with shared inequalities of sex and property, the novel's third volume also included "The Death of Cicero," a Walstein-like narrative that illustrates the shortcomings of a classical, elite protagonist.[13]

Sleep-Walking on the Frontier

Sleep-walking and cycles of frontier violence and revenge supply the spectacular plot points and dramatic motifs in *Edgar Huntly*. As Brown develops them, these motifs connect outward to an implicit commentary on the revolutionary and colonial struggles of the eighteenth-century, and inward to observations on how individual consciousness and forms of collective interaction are shaped by these conditions.

In accordance with the latest medical works of the period, Brown understood sleep-walking in terms of the associative physiology of sentiment and sensibility, and as a socially generated symptom of emotional damage. In the moral and psychological theories of the Enlightenment, physical responsiveness to external stimuli is a basic link in the associative chain of sentiments and emotions that drives human interaction. Physical symptoms are thus signs of breakdowns in an individual's response to social networks. As Edgar observes in Chapter 2, after his sentimentalized response to Clithero's sleep-walking: "The incapacity of sound sleep denotes a mind sorely wounded" (11). Along with his roommate Elihu Hubbard Smith and other members

---

[13] See "The Death of Cicero," in Weber, ed., *Somnambulism and Other Stories,* 117–33.

of his New York circle, Brown read Erasmus Darwin's *Zoönomia; or, The Laws of Organic Life* (1794). This medical-biological study is important for *Edgar Huntly,* because it provides Brown with his basic understanding of madness as a disorder of the senses and, more particularly, because it provides the novel's understanding of sleep-walking, *Somnambulismus,* as a disease "of volition" that is one example of this disorder.[14] Darwin sees the dissociation of volition and outward stimuli in sleep-walking as fundamentally akin to the same problem in the ailments he refers to as "reverie" and "sentimental love"; whereas a pathological level of dissociation in sleep-walking is manifested in "the exertions of the locomotive muscles," reverie and sentimental love concern "the exertions of the organs of sense." Darwin explains that in all these states—sleep-walking, reverie, and sentimental love (or "erotomania")—the body is engaged in "violent voluntary exertions of ideas to relieve pain."

With Elihu Hubbard Smith's help, Brown collected information about and examples of sleep-walking that he put to use in a series of narratives from 1797 to 1805. In 1796, for example, Smith showed Brown the "History of the Sleepless Man of Madrid" in Benjamin Gooch's *Practical Treatise on Wounds and Other Chirurgical Subjects* (1767). In June 1798 Brown published queries in the Philadelphia *Weekly Magazine* requesting information from the public on sleep-walking and other physiological-psychological phenomena that he would dramatize in his novels. One month later, in July, just months before he died in Brown's presence, Smith recorded in his diary an incident of somnambulism that he learned about during a trip home to Connecticut and notes, "This will do for C. B. Brown."[15] Earlier that year, in March and April 1798, Smith, William Dunlap, and other friends were already reading and discussing Brown's initial use of somnambulism in his first (and now lost) novel, *Sky-Walk; or, The Man Unknown to Himself.*[16] The one fragment of the novel that was published to promote its appearance suggests that somnambulism in that story is a symptom of intolerable anxieties concerning debt and social status.[17] Elements of the lost *Sky-Walk* reappeared in both *Edgar Huntly* in 1799 and the tale "Somnambulism. A fragment," published in 1805. A substantive difference between *Sky-Walk* (based on the little information that survives) and *Edgar Huntly* seems to be Brown's later concern, which we will discuss later, with the effects of imperialism and global commerce. These concerns come to the fore in *Edgar Huntly,* but they are not evident in the earlier material nor in first-wave Woldwinite writings, which affirm a cosmopolitan program but never ask how it might be destroyed by commercial empire and landgrabs. Scholars explore the precise interrelation of these somnambulism narratives, but the way that sleep-walking, reverie, and sentimental love are combined in all three plots demonstrates Brown's fundamental interest in

---

[14] See the excerpts from Darwin's *Zoönomia* in Related Texts.

[15] Smith, *Diary;* July 1, 1798 (454).

[16] The surviving fragment of and other information on this novel are included in Related Texts.

[17] On the thematic links between *Sky-Walk* and *Edgar Huntly,* see Hinds, "Charles Brockden Brown's Revenge Tragedy"; and Krause, "Historical Essay."

the links between psychic distress and social networks, and illustrates how his narratives reference the medical and moral-philosophical research of the progressive Enlightenment.

Along with the basic motif of sleep-walking, the Delaware Indians that appear in *Edgar Huntly* are probably the most frequently discussed aspect of the narrative, partly because this is the first American novel to dramatize frontier violence between settlers and first peoples. This novel is therefore a critical point in the long history of representations of Euro-Indian conflict in America, extending back to the earliest contact narratives and forward to the movie genre of the western. In recent years there has been considerable critical debate over how to interpret Brown's portrayal of settler-Indian relations. Some commentators maintain that Brown's novel is an early example of Manifest Destiny or expansionist ideology at the turn of the nineteenth century and suggest that it offers a frankly or covertly racist, xenophobic perspective on settler-Indian relations.[18] After all, the novel's initially peaceful protagonist does become a vicious Indian-killer by the end of his story. Earlier commentators, in particular, often identify Brown with his protagonists even though Brown's novelistic method makes this kind of author-character identification difficult to justify and, quite to the contrary, works in many more and less obvious ways to situate both author and reader at a critical distance from the novel's characters and actions. All of Brown's novels require the reader to dis-identify with and take a critical perspective on their protagonists.

Our discussion in what follows generally takes the view that Brown is critical of the patterns of imperialism, expansionism, and racialism that he depicts in *Edgar Huntly*. Besides questions about whether or not Brown can be identified with his narrators and protagonists, many thematic aspects of *Edgar Huntly* and a considerable body of scholarship suggest that the novel's frontier violence is framed by a critical perspective on the history of Quaker-Indian relations and the wider processes of imperial dispossession and displacement that surround them. In fact, Brown's staging of settler-Indian relations not only frames Edgar's actions within a critical account of frontier violence, but it also arguably makes this novel an implicit critique and rejection of late eighteenth-century Quaker political tracts and captivity narratives, which were written to present the Quaker community's self-interested interpretation of ongoing multiethnic frontier conflicts.

This framing begins with the most basic elements of the plot's setting and geography. The site of Waldegrave's murder, a locale that returns throughout the first half of the narrative, is the giant Elm that is one of the leitmotifs of the plot. This Elm is the place where Edgar's friend Waldegrave was mysteriously murdered, the place that first joins him to Clithero, and the obsessive point around which the novel's sleep-walking proliferates. As Edgar notes on his first approach to it:

---

[18] For readings of *Edgar Huntly* as a prototypical expansionist and Indian-hating novel, see Weidman, "White Man's Red Man"; Newman, "Indians and Indian-Hating in *Edgar Huntly*"; and the influential interpretations in Slotkin, *Regeneration through Violence,* and Gardner, "Alien Nation." This interpretation is taken up by numerous recent discussions.

> I descried through the dusk the widespread branches of the Elm. This tree, however faintly seen, cannot be mistaken for another. The remarkable bulk and shape of its trunk, its position in the midst of the way, its branches spreading into an ample circumference, made it conspicuous from afar. My pulse throbbed as I approached it. (8)

Scholars beginning with Daniel Edwards Kennedy in the 1930s have suggested that this Elm, with its centrality to sleep-walking and frontier violence, condenses into a single image the long history of betrayal and violence in eighteenth-century Quaker-Indian relations. The Elm itself refers to the Treaty Elm, which, according to legend, marked the site of the founding of Pennsylvania in 1682, the spot where William Penn may (or may not) have negotiated a treaty of peace between Quakers and the Lenni Lenape (Delaware) Indians, who have recently lost their tribal lands in *Edgar Huntly*. This Treaty Elm was still a tourist attraction in the Philadelphia of Brown's time and featured in many well-known images, from fabrics and plates to Benjamin West's 1771 historical painting *Penn's Treaty with the Indians*.[19]

The geographical setting of *Edgar Huntly*'s action, in the "Forks" of the Delaware, where the fictional Elm links the novel's Anglo settlements Solebury and Chetasco with the wilderness area called Norwalk, ties the dubious legend of the Treaty Elm to the harsh realities of Quaker land-grabbing and the infamous Walking Purchase Treaty that was an instrument of fraud in seizing Delaware tribal lands. In the Walking Purchase Treaty of 1737, agents of William Penn's sons dishonestly maintained that they would resurvey a tract of land that they claimed was sold to Penn by the Delawares fifty years earlier, a tract defined as the amount that could be walked at a normal pace, along a winding river and under ordinary conditions, in a day and a half. Ordinarily this might amount to twenty or twenty-five miles, but a path was cleared in advance and hired walkers with a support team worked continuously to cover sixty-four miles, in a straight line, in the allotted time. In this manner the Delawares were defrauded of about 1,200 square miles of tribal territory in what is now northern Bucks, Lehigh, and Northampton counties in Pennsylvania.[20] Historian Francis Jennings describes the calculated misrepresentations and outright deceptions of the 1737 land-conveyancing documents as "a feat of prestidigitation on the level of a carnival shell game."[21] The forcible removal of the Delawares took several more years and was only accomplished after the Iroquois-Quaker negotiation of 1742, when Canasatego and the Iroquois declared the Delawares "women" and evicted them from their lands on behalf of Anglo-Quaker commercial interests. Canasatego, who flew a British flag in front of his home, addressed the Delawares in forceful terms:

---

[19] For a full discussion of the novel's material on Penn's Elm, see Krause, "Penn's Elm and *Edgar Huntly.*"

[20] On the Walking Purchase Treaty and the topography of *Edgar Huntly*, see Krause, "Penn's Elm and *Edgar Huntly*"; and Kafer, *Charles Brockden Brown's Revolution*, 173–83.

[21] Jennings, "The Scandalous Indian Policy of William Penn's Sons," 37.

We conquer'd You, we made Women of you, you know you are Women, and can no
more sell Land than Women. . . . This Land that you Claim is gone through Your Guts.
You have been furnished with Cloaths and Meat and Drink . . . and now You want it
again like [the] Children you are. . . . This String of Wampum serves to forbid You . . .
for ever medling in Land Affairs.[22]

This dispossession and its gendered language seem relevant to *Edgar Huntly,* for the
novel's main Indian character Old Deb is presented as a female personification of
the Delaware people and their removal from land stolen by Quakers in a notorious
fraud.[23] Solebury, the settlement where Edgar lives, is the name of an actual town in
this area, as is Abingdon, mentioned as the settlement where Edgar's fiancée Mary is
located. Chetasco, the non-Quaker settlement near Solebury in this novel, is a fictional name, but it suggests an anagram of Chester County, the county just west of
Philadelphia and southwest of the Forks, where Brown's father (as well as his fictional
character Arthur Mervyn) grew up.

Before settler-Indian conflicts were mythologized in novels, a long tradition of influential captivity narratives presented the settler view of these conflicts and of the
cycles of violence and revenge that accompanied colonial expansionism. Captivity
narratives are first-person, supposedly autobiographical accounts of European
colonists who were captured by and lived as prisoners among Indians. In them, the
captive—often a pious, female settler like the nameless girl that Edgar rescues from
the Delaware war party in this novel—appears as an innocent victim of barbaric Indian aggression, and, in this manner, the larger white community is made to appear
innocent of hostile intention and action in the overall picture of settler-Indian conflict. As Joanna Brooks puts it, "The captivity narrative formula utilized a story of individual suffering to mask the implication of the colonial subject in the broader
machinations of English imperialism. It isolated and allegorized the war experiences
of individual colonists to articulate a colonial white identity that was innocent of
history."[24] Brown was certainly aware of these narratives and draws on them for the
novel's general emphasis on captivity, which is experienced in one form or another by
most of its characters (Sarsefield, Wiatte, Clithero, Edgar, and the nameless girl
Edgar rescues), but Brown's use of these narratives tends to critically reverse or invert

---

[22] Hazard, *Minutes of the Provincial Council,* 4:660. For Canasatego, see Starna, "The Diplomatic
Career of Canasatego." Starna examines Canasatego's part in the 1742 council on pages 148–52.
Brown's great-uncle William Brown, a close friend of his father Elijah, was present at a later 1756
negotiation when Delaware chieftain Teedyuscung told the Quakers he was attacking Anglo settlers
because of the Walking Purchase fraud. This great-uncle apparently helped raise money to buy off
the Delawares at that juncture; see Kafer, *Charles Brockden Brown's Revolution,* 174–76 and 236,
note 13.

[23] See Hinds, "Deb's Dogs," and Sivils, "Native American Sovereignty and Old Deb." For the "tumultuous social and cultural transformations and adaptations" that followed the Walking Purchase
Treaty, see Harper, "Delawares and Pennsylvanians after the Walking Purchase."

[24] Brooks, "Held Captive by the Irish," 33.

their customary function of shifting responsibility for historical violence onto native peoples. If Brown draws on the 1787 "Panther" captivity narrative, for example, as some scholars have suggested, he also seems to reject its emphasis on Native American irrationality by ending his novel with a rational explanation for the Delaware war party as resistance to the encroachment of white settlers.[25]

In the late eighteenth century, Pennsylvania Quakers published a new wave of captivity narratives and other tracts that argued that Quakers were innocent of frontier violence, because other settler groups, above all the "wild Irish," were victimizing Indians and Quakers alike. These writings built on a long history of Anglo-Quaker disregard for the Irish and painted Quakers as reasonable, pacifist actors in relation to both the Irish and the Indians.[26] In the aftermath of English colonialism in Ireland and massive Irish immigration to Pennsylvania, Anglo-Quakers viewed the Irish—particularly those from the same northern (Ulster) Protestant areas of Ireland as this novel's character Clithero—not just as a rival immigrant people, but as barbaric ethno-racial others every bit as "savage" and threatening as Indians; "the very scum of mankind," as one contemporary put it.[27] This history of distrust rose to a boiling point in the aftermath of the French and Indian War, when large numbers of lower-class Irish immigrants, in incidents like the violent Paxton Boys uprising (1763–1764), challenged Quaker authority on the Pennsylvania frontier. In the pamphlet war that followed the Paxton uprising, illustrated here by the excerpts from Franklin and Barton,[28] the Philadelphia Anglo-Quaker elite sought to shift responsibility for frontier violence onto Irish settlers, characterizing them as "White Christian Savages" (Franklin) who were destroying Penn's legacy of harmonious Quaker-Indian relations. Similarly, in Chapter 27 of this novel, the manner in which Edgar blames Deb's anger on the Chetasco settlers—shifting responsibility for provoking the Delaware raids onto this other group—seems to reference the Quaker community's attempts to blame Irish backcountry settlers for conflicts that go back to the original Quaker colonization and landgrabs.[29]

At the moment Brown was writing *Edgar Huntly*, these antagonisms were intensified yet again by the Irish revolutionary uprisings of 1796–1798 and the arrival of

[25] See the "Panther" captivity narrative, included in this volume's Related Texts.

[26] See Brooks' entire discussion of the Quakers' neo-captivity narratives in her article "Held Captive by the Irish." Brooks sees *Edgar Huntly* as the "apotheosis" of these Irish-blaming narratives (41), but obviously we are suggesting, here and in the last part of this Introduction, that the novel critically reverses or inverts these narratives on several levels.

[27] See Griffin, *The People with No Name*, 99–124.

[28] See the excerpts from Franklin and Barton's pamphlets in this volume's Related Texts. For more on the Paxton uprising, see Griffin, *The People with No Name*, 157–73; Kafer, *Charles Brockden Brown's Revolution*, 173–83; White, *The Backcountry and the City*, 105–21; and Camenzind, "Violence, Race, and the Paxton Boys."

[29] For a wider account of the cultural impact of these backcountry conflicts in the period, see White, *The Backcountry and the City*.

fresh waves of Irish revolutionaries and émigrés in both Philadelphia and the back-country frontier, where they mixed with Indians and took part in multiethnic Indian-African-European communities extending from western Pennsylvania into the "middle ground" of the Great Lakes area.[30] Thus it is highly significant that *Edgar Huntly* sets its action in the aftermath of the French and Indian Wars (the narrative reminds us that Edgar's uncle participated in the most disastrous chapter of that conflict) and leads its reader to understand profound similarities, rather than differences, between Edgar, his Irish doppelgänger Clithero Edny, and, ultimately, the Indians themselves. As we will note later, Edgar comes to resemble Clithero more and more as the tale progresses: both are tutored by the English colonialist Sarsefield, both are driven by intolerable social pressures to sleep-walk, and both are pressured toward marriage to the same inheritor of the British-imperial class system. Like the Indians they outdo in barbarity, both are driven to violence in cycles of displacement that the novel takes pains to link with wider Anglo-French imperial struggles extending from Pennsylvania to what is now Pakistan and India.

Rather than scapegoating Irish or Indian "savages" and revolutionaries as a means of avoiding the history of Quaker responsibility in settler-Indian violence, Brown's novel acknowledges Quaker violence (quite literally in the savage exploits of Edgar and his warrior uncle) and seems to make its Quaker and Irish figures into doubles for one another, exploring how cycles of frontier violence are driven by larger social structures and conflicts. Clithero initially appears to the reader as a Northern Irish other, just as Edgar initially appears as an enlightened, pacifist Anglo-Quaker. But the entire novel works in obvious and more subtle ways to outline the social and historical forces that transform these men into something very different than what they initially seem to be, and to explore the structures that lead them to their "unconscious" explosions of violence. Edgar's romantic renaming of the Indian Old Deb as a Celtic Queen Mab repeats the racial dynamics of Indian- and Irish-hating, but rather than figuring Indians like Deb as barbaric others, the novel emphasizes the historic responsibility, barbaric violence, and projective scapegoating of its Anglo-Quaker protagonist.

Enlightenment Benevolence and the Rejection of Gothic Revenge

In the introductory "To the Public" that begins *Edgar Huntly* by rejecting "Gothic castles and chimeras" as "puerile superstition and exploded manners," Brown is insisting that every age requires its own literary forms and cultural codes. For Brown, a

---

[30] For information on the "middle ground" from western Pennsylvania to the Great Lakes and the mixed communities of Indians, Irish, escaped slaves, and other European settlers there, see White, *The Middle Ground;* Dowd, *A Spirited Resistance;* Jennings, *Empire of Fortune;* and Linebaugh, "The Red-Crested Bird and Black Duck."

modern-looking world struggling to achieve enlightenment neither needs to nor should continue the traditional narrative structures that hearken to its collective adolescence. In "Romances," an essay published a few years after *Edgar Huntly,* Brown argues that because every period produces its "*own* conceptions of truth and nature," the tales of the ancient Greeks and Romans and even those of the fifteenth and sixteenth centuries can no longer motivate contemporary readers.[31] The "gradual revolution of human manners and national taste" necessitates new cultural and literary forms. Since all narratives must inescapably represent the "manners and sentiments" of "the age in which the works were written," the "works that suited former ages are now exploded by us," just as our own productions will be "exploded in their turn" by ensuing generations.

With this claim about the necessary linkage between standards of taste, the historical transformation of social structures, and the alteration of literary forms and conventions, Brown stands as one of the early proponents of a pragmatic, modernist perspective. Like Thomas Paine's dictum that the dead should not legislate for the living, Brown's frank refusal of the need to revere established literary genres or consecrate a tradition of great writers insists that cultural productions should not be judged according to universalizing standards or transcendental ideals, as Kantian and romantic aesthetics argue, but according to the terms and debates of their own historical context and struggles.

Early modern Europe was regulated by aristocratic feudal regimes, materialized by fortressed manors ("Gothic castles"), and the dogma of institutionalized, Catholic mysticism ("puerile superstition"). Brown's point in "exploding" the old cultural forms linked to this past is that in an age, like the eighteenth century, when the rising middle class seeks to replace the artificial status divisions of aristocratic blood-lineages and priestly superstition with a new society based on republican-liberal equality and skeptical reason, writers must craft new tales that articulate these democratic desires and help the reader acculturate into his or her actually existing social environment. If authors continue to use the "exploded manners" and locales of an increasingly obsolete early modern society, they hold back the collective maturation of modern society by confusing it with specters of a thankfully vanquished past. In an essay "On the Effects of Theatric Exhibitions," written shortly before *Edgar Huntly,* Brown condemns Shakespeare's plays for crippling their viewer's analytical development.[32] Being "foreign to the experience of men of the present times and of middling classes," using "a language as unintelligible as Greek, and raving about thrones and mistresses," Shakespeare presents "mistaken notions of virtue and duty" to the modern bourgeoisie. "Theatres are, in themselves, capable of being converted into schools of the purest wisdom and philanthropy," but not if they regressively insist on staging the mentality of a historically superseded society.

---

[31] This essay is included in this volume's Related Texts.

[32] See the excerpt from this essay in this volume's Related Texts.

Conversely, Brown sees his own writing as participating in the action of progressive social transformation. While scholars frequently observe that *Edgar Huntly* and Brown's other novels inaugurate U.S. gothic writing as a genre that often recalls the past, these novels are also postgothic in the sense that they seek to leave the premodern behind. The horror resonating in their subterranean passages echoes the challenges of escaping archaic behavior that is not only unsuitable to the contemporary moment but also degrades their reader's ability to properly understand the ongoing revolution in social manners in the late eighteenth century. As Edgar Huntly attempts to explain what has happened to him, he repeatedly emphasizes the newness of events and scenes that cannot easily be compared to traditional themes. The problem Edgar indicates is that contemporary readers lack codes of reference that might provide a moral compass to guide their actions. Hence, the main plot points of sleep-walking, performances of exaggerated shame, or frontier confusion provide metaphors for the uncertainty of tumbling forward into a modern, postfeudal society that both requires and produces new modes of social consciousness and new forms of human interaction.

Nowhere is *Edgar Huntly*'s investigation into the event threshold of modernity more explicit than in the novel's dogged rejection of the kind of historical continuity manifested in vicious cycles of revenge blood-feuds. For Brown and many of his contemporaries, the resolution of conflict through honor codes requiring automatized violence, typified by the aristocratic duel, is an atavistic throwback to feudal clan antagonisms, a tragic failure to seek legitimate, rationalized, and modern forms of justice in the courtroom. The bloodthirsty obsession with vengeance through retribution, mutilation, and murder sets off an unending series of retaliations that lock humanity into patterns of vengeance that stunt its moral progress. The main cause of Clithero Edny's problems in Ireland is the challenge of breaking free from his own internalized notions of the landed gentry's immemorial prestige. Clithero's difficulty is that he cannot liberate his mind from the shackles of subordination to notions of inborn lineage. He cannot bring himself to imagine the possibility that his relationship to his landed mistress's niece Clarice could possibly be a partnership of equals.

Clithero's psychological obstacle here is that he understands all too well how challenges to the status boundaries of aristocratic bloodlines will be met with the personal violence embodied by Clarice's father, Arthur Wiatte. Wiatte personifies the gentrified old order's refusal to suffer the dishonor of treating the urban middle class as its equal. In Chapter 5, Wiatte forces his sister Euphemia to break off her engagement with the bourgeois surgeon Sarsefield and then vows revenge on her for having undermined blood allegiances in favor of the middle-class courtroom determinations of justice. Wiatte returns from exile to set off a new round of spontaneous violence in Chapters 7 and 8, as Wiatte is killed by Clithero while attempting to murder him. The inheritance of violence, and the violence generated by the social codes of aristocratic inheritance, continues to unfold when Clithero attempts a kind of allegorical clan revenge by deciding to murder Wiatte's sister and daughter, insanely claiming that this murder will spare Lorimer the pain of learning about her brother's death. *Edgar Huntly* charts other instances of revenge acts that are nightmarishly projected through the generations, notably the vicious cycles of settler-Indian violence in the book's second half. Edgar's blood-lust against the Delawares who killed his parents (Chapters 17–19), and the plot of Delaware Indian Old Deb against the white settlers for their failure to respect her identity as defined by premodern claims of land-blood status (Chapters 20 and 27), are mirror images of this process. Similarly, Edgar's uncle's fatal desire to retaliate on the Delawares for the deaths of his army comrades in the disaster of Braddock's defeat thirty years prior to the novel's action (Chapter 24) offers another instance of the risks involved in continuing to hold onto past injuries and construct an identity grounded in victimization and dishonor.[33]

Brown does not, however, seem to argue for an extreme position of rupture from the past, for simply forgetting or repressing the feeling of having suffered historical wrongs. Edgar begins his tale, in Chapter 1, traumatized by the unresolved mystery of his friend Waldegrave's murder. His hurt at the loss is made more severe by the collective amnesia of the Solebury settlers, who quickly lose interest in attempting to discover the agent of Waldegrave's death. As we first see Edgar walking at night, while the settlers are in bed, this movement toward sleep-walking may allegorize his psychological stasis in being both alive and dead because of his inability to bring Waldegrave's death to satisfying closure. Hence the Elm that is the site of Waldegrave's death becomes a geographical fetish that increasingly magnetizes Edgar's movements as he enacts repeated open-air performances of mental and physical trauma. Brown seems to be dramatizing the way that the past's crimes and misdemeanors continually resurface to shape the present if left unresolved.

If the wrongs of the past cannot be simply forgotten, Brown uses *Edgar Huntly* to claim that the misdeeds of the past need to be confronted and worked through before they can be dissolved and consigned to the trashheap of history. For this revolution to succeed, however, it must forgo the dubious satisfaction of violent revenge. When Edgar insists on questioning Clithero, who he believes has murdered Waldegrave, the purpose of the meeting is not to demand a duel, but to talk through the past in a dispassionate fashion. Edgar insists that his responsibility is two-fold. The ethical need to excavate the crimes of the past is yoked to the need to comfort, rather than denounce, the agent of Waldegrave's murder. Edgar assumes that in every act of violence, the perpetrator is also damaged and needs therapeutic relief as much as the associates of the primary victim. Partly motivated by the pacifist principles of his Quaker upbringing, Brown also recognizes that conflict resolution through violence (through war or the death penalty) psychologically damages the victor brandishing the sword of justice. Edgar abandons his desire for a fear-driven revenge and instead proposes a project of benevolent compassion for Clithero as he seeks to comfort the Irishman both physically and psychologically. Edgar's purpose in returning to Norwalk in Chapters 9–12 is not to secure Clithero and deliver him to public judgment, but to provide food and water so that Clithero can himself come to terms with his actions.

---

[33] For more on revenge in the novel, see Hinds, "Charles Brockden Brown's Revenge Tragedy."

In this program of compassion, Edgar, and Brown, are guided by two assumptions. First, demonizing Clithero will only tear away at the fabric of society as it introduces practices whereby others can, in turn, be destroyed. This argument can be more forcefully seen with a figure seemingly inspired by Brown's fiction: the creature in Mary Shelley's *Frankenstein* (1818). In the years before Mary Shelley wrote one of the most influential works of gothic fiction, she and her husband actively set about reading all of Brown's fiction that they could find. While she later admitted that she disliked Americans for their cultural brashness, the sole exception to her aversion was Brown, whom she wished she had had a chance to meet. Mary Shelley seems to have been an especially discerning reader of Brown, for she perceives how Brown's "freaks," the marginal figures like Clithero here or Carwin in the novel *Wieland*, are monstrous primarily because they have been denied inclusion within the conviviality and mutuality of dominant society. Shelley's creature seeks out comfort in the home of the blind man, who may "overlook" his physical difference from the white English but is then driven off into mad revenge when he is denied this compassion. With Shelley's novel, we see a brilliant continuation of Brown's antirevenge tragedy in *Edgar Huntly*.[34]

The second assumption behind Edgar's benevolence appears as he seeks to engage Clithero in conversation that will calm and cure Clithero's mental distress. In keeping with widely accepted doctrines of eighteenth-century sentimental pathology, that were exemplified by naturalists like Erasmus Darwin and that were the mainstay of medical practice among Brown's physician friends, Brown believes that mental illness is caused by an imbalance in the body's senses that deranges our apparatus of cognition. The chief therapy for this dysfunction is reasonable dialogue that reduces the intemperate anger or "madness" that is the origin of insanity. In ways that prefigure psychoanalysis's faith in the talking cure, Brown's character believes that without the therapeutic sedative of conversation, the body's wild senses will overwhelm the individual. Edgar repeatedly comments on the rate of his heartbeat and respiration in order to gauge the state of his physical calmness and emotional balance, which if lost will result in mental incoherence.

Edgar's insistence on the power of sympathy in the act of reconciliation is a programmatic renunciation of aristocratic manners. He enacts this through a radical internalizing of the other's experiences so as to understand the conditions and cognitive lifeworld of those who have wronged him. It is a truism that male-authored gothic tales frequently involve the narrator's paranoid sense that he is being pursued by an omniscient, inscrutable double or doppelgänger, plotting his humiliation and downfall. In conventional gothic narratives, this phantom menace must be destroyed at all costs. The reverse is the case in *Edgar Huntly*. Edgar progressively *doubles* Clithero, rather than the other way around. Sleep-walking, starvation, bodily laceration and disarray, the reburial and resurfacing of private letters, marriage plans frustrated by the return of an enigmatic stranger, and locked cabinets are all devices associated

[34] For a discussion of the Shelleys and Brown, see Shapiro, "I Could Kiss Him One Minute."

with Clithero that Edgar progressively duplicates. As Edgar actively and progressively doubles Clithero, Brown suggests that the only way to escape from a permanent war of revenge is to put ourselves literally in the position of the other so as to experience the dynamics of power confrontations from the perspective of our antagonist. Only by gaining a complete understanding of the perspective of the other can we dissolve a culture of trauma and move beyond the cyclical violence intrinsic to premodern, unenlightened societies. This gesture seems to act as Brown's initial revision of his belief in the power of sentiment. Rather than expecting that Edgar's deeds will be repeated by others, the novel suggests that his act of virtue will only succeed if he recognizes the human condition and perspective of others.

Failed Benevolence?

Until Chapter 16, slightly more than halfway through *Edgar Huntly,* Brown gives little indication that his narrative will include the events that dominate nearly all criticism on the text: the action surrounding the Delaware Indian warpath. Because the Indian action looms so large in discussions of the narrative, the coherence of the tale until this point and its implied trajectory must be emphasized. Until Chapter 16, *Edgar Huntly* has clearly marked themes and a predictable conclusion. Edgar refuses the impulse of gothic revenge against Clithero so that rational benevolence can replace the vengeful and backward-looking passions produced by prebourgeois, aristocratic society. Edgar's refusal of landed interests does not, however, imply the embrace of commercial ones, as seen by his readiness to forgo Mary Waldegrave's inheritance.

An abrupt break occurs, though, as Edgar awakens in a pit that is guarded by armed Delaware Indians on the warpath. From this point, the theme of mutuality and compassion is not only marginalized but also seemingly refuted and thoroughly denied. The hardly vigorous Edgar, who "never delighted" in hunting's "carnage and blood" (84), begins devastating Delaware Indians with a spontaneous dispatch that few who knew the youth could have predicted. If Edgar assumes that calm reflection, interpersonal dialogue, and mute sympathy can resolve the bad feelings surrounding the mystery of Waldegrave's murder, all these assumptions are upended by the narrative's deflationary, mournful conclusion. Clithero is saved from self-starvation in Norwalk, but this rescue is only physical, as he remains mentally traumatized, and even this respite will be momentary. Clithero may be repaired from the bodily damage he suffers during his anorexic retreat into Norwalk and at the hands of the Delawares, but he remains defiantly morose, alienated, and psychologically damaged. By *Edgar Huntly*'s end, Clithero may have been exonerated from Waldegrave's murder, but only so that he can incriminate himself once again by apparently rushing to assassinate Euphemia Lorimer. Edgar's plans for nursing Clithero back to health go for naught as the Irishman ultimately commits suicide to evade the social death of permanent institutionalization. Edgar's notion that male mutuality and sympathy could replace long-standing resentments fails, and he ends the narrative as marginal a figure as he was when we first see him walking at night. The resolution of the mystery of Waldegrave's murder has not brought him lasting mental composure, closure, or integration within the settler community. Throughout the tale, Edgar dreams about the return of his tutor Sarsefield in utopian terms; he hopes to reestablish a caring community among friends. Yet when Edgar shouts with joy on seeing the older man again, in Chapter 24, Sarsefield brusquely refuses to reciprocate and gaze on, embrace, or speak warmly to him. Instead, Sarsefield comes with a prearranged plan that Edgar should marry Clarice Lorimer, although Edgar has never seen or communicated with Clarice (he has only heard of her from Clithero's tale, not Sarsefield) and remains engaged to Mary Waldegrave. If taken seriously, Sarsefield's plan to marry Edgar and Clarice forces Edgar to choose between (the sister of) Waldegrave and (the daughter-in-law of) Sarsefield in a way that makes relations with one old friend incompatible with the other. This gesture of exclusion continues with Sarsefield's merciless refusal of his surgical expertise to a mangled Clithero, a vengeful denial that even Edgar considers "inhuman" (179). When Sarsefield sees that Edgar nevertheless seeks to help Clithero, he rushes away in a stunning denial of human compassion and betrayal of medical ethics. Edgar later recounts Clithero's tale in order to still Sarsefield's maddened "fury" and heart-throbbing "vehemence" (178). Even in this more rational, composed state, Sarsefield reiterates his unwillingness to give medical assistance that might prolong Clithero's life.

The failure of compassion and benevolence to succeed in an American society no longer ruled by aristocratic social codes raises *Edgar Huntly*'s main sociological question: what is the modern spring of action that leads to the psychological dysfunction represented by Clithero's continuing madness, Edgar's anomie, and Sarsefield's brutality? In staging this question, Brown shifts the plot's mystery away from the initial riddle of who murdered Waldegrave to ask a more global question about the contemporary conditions that generate social aggression.

In this turn to the greater mystery about the state of collective damage, Brown's writing differs in important ways from the dominant pattern of most later detective fiction written for an assumed bourgeois reader. In conventional detective fictions, the riddle of assigning guilt to a perpetrator must be resolved in such a way that the dominant social interests that structure the underlying tensions leading to the crime are left unexplored and able to proceed with their agendas unquestioned. The burden of sanitizing the tensions of collective inequalities by translating them into the simple answer of an individual's guilt, leaving the existing social order blissfully unaware of its constitutional defects, is carried by the figure of the detective, who bears these contradictions on his body and mind. Like the eccentric, drug-addled Sherlock Holmes, the detective is frequently himself alienated from sustaining relationships and congeniality, deeply cynical, and psychologically damaged in ways that lead to drug or alcohol abuse when the pressure of maintaining the fiction of society's innocence and the criminal's sole guilt becomes too difficult to bear.

Brown does something similar with *Edgar Huntly*'s physical and psychic transformation after Chapter 16, in the story of the Delaware war party. But instead of shifting responsibility onto a guilty individual, Brown, in keeping with his plan for novel writing, leads the reader toward an awareness of the collective forces that condition individual responses. As *Edgar Huntly* moves from a tale that is primarily centered on Clithero's struggles to one about settler-Indian conflicts, Brown traces out what he considers to be the primary current threat to reforming domestic society through "the magic of sympathy, the perseverance of benevolence" (76). He indicates his answer to this question with the motif of sympathy for the damaged male body. Nearly all of the male characters' bodies are starved and wear the marks of torture and distress, manifested in worry lines, wounds, scarring, and other symptoms. When Edgar meets Clithero for their conversation, the latter's face is "pale and wan, and his form emaciated and shrunk" (24), and the worry lines of his sorrows later "dignify and solemnize his features" (76). When Edgar emerges from the forest, his "countenance was wan and haggard" and his body lacerated and bleeding (130). The merchant Weymouth appears as "sallow and emaciated," prematurely aged and facially marked by "deep traces of the afflictions he had endured" (103). Sarsefield, likewise, has become "rugged" looking as a result of "vicissitude and hardship, rather than of age" (43).

Men's bodies are preternaturally worn out in *Edgar Huntly* as a result of two interlinked global events. The initial cause for physical decay is the international pursuit of commercial gain. Edgar sees Weymouth's premature decay as the result of entrepreneurial adventures that send men "over every sea and every land in pursuit of that wealth which will not screen them from disease and infirmity, which is missed much oftener than found, and which, when gained, by no means compensates them for the hardships and vicissitudes endured in the pursuit" (104). Edgar's pessimism about the personal value of long-distance commerce is then tied to a larger critique of global relations.

From the perspective of many commentators, *Edgar Huntly* is an exceptionally American tale about the events, history, and psychology of the frontier. Its action is set in 1787, the year the U.S. constitution was ratified and thus year one of the national institution; in this sense, the novel casts a skeptical light on the founding narratives of Pennsylvania (in the Treaty Elm) and the United States (in the constitution) alike.[35] But beyond this traditional focus on events in the United States alone, the reader may consider the way the novel connects its action with a global network of forces and struggles. Edgar's review of male infirmity illustrates how the men's trauma usually results from a captivity experience that has its roots within a larger geography of border disputes between Europeans and nonwhite populations as a result of infra-European imperial conflicts. Sarsefield's body has been damaged not simply because he has had to seek his fortune outside Europe, but because he was imprisoned by Asian Indian forces who were themselves caught up in the Seven Years War between the British and French over which nation would colonize India and profit from its resources and trade. On the other side of this global war between English and French imperial rivals, Edgar's uncle suffers wounds in the British general Braddock's disastrous defeat by French and North American Indian forces.

---

[35] See Grabo's Introduction to the 1988 edition of *Edgar Huntly*.

Braddock's defeat sets off a new wave of settler-Indian antagonism, and one consequence of these struggles is Old Deb's anger at her people's removal from their ancestral lands in the Forks of the Delaware. Deb's desire for revenge sets off the raiding party that leads to Waldegrave's death as retaliation for the collective wrongs done to the Delaware people. In response to Waldegrave's death, Edgar then suffers "the insanity of vengeance and grief" (6). As Sarsefield's double-barreled musket from the Bengal campaign turns up to be used by Edgar against the Delawares, Brown seems to suggest that the two Indian frontiers—one in North America, the other in South Asia—are linked because both belong to the same environment of conflicts between imperial powers mediated through native populations.

The cause of male suffering, then, appears to be the commercial desire for gain that creates the need for conflict between European nations that enlist local aboriginal populations in their disputes. With *Edgar Huntly,* Brown extends the Woldwinite critique against the old regime by turning that group's progressive analysis toward a new object: the sentimental-liberal assumptions of laissez-faire commerce, exemplified by Adam Smith's *The Wealth of Nations* (1776). For Brown, the logical consequence of this emerging economic philosophy leads inevitably to conflict between nations in ways that re-create early modern cycles of revenge in a new, commercial mode. The eighteenth-century proponents of a "free" market, exemplified by Smith and other writers of the Scottish Enlightenment, assumed that exchanging goods, commercial exchange and circulation, was the defining, intrinsically progressive characteristic of humanity and civilization. Trade, for these writers, can only continue to exist if the buyer and seller learn how to satisfy each other's needs so as to ensure the satisfaction of their own self-interest. Exchange is not only about fulfilling the financial needs of traders; it also generates a surplus value of sympathetic mutuality as each successful trade generates more confidence in business and cooperative networks. This surplus is then directed outward as traders continually seek to expand their activities and search out new, foreign markets within which to trade. Thus, for Adam Smith, the moral community generated among strangers through business ultimately expands to encompass the entire globe, revolutionizing all societies as trade magnetizes, and improves cultural standards and trust between different peoples.

As *Edgar Huntly* collapses back into moody isolation, Brown's implicit argument seems to suggest that international free trade, as an index to the rising middle class, does not lead to benevolence but introduces a new, modern feeling of revenge in the entrepreneurial competition that generates new forms of global antagonism, which, in turn, spark local emergencies. From this perspective, Brown's narrative can be read as one of the first anti-imperialist fictions, as *Edgar Huntly* assumes that the desire for profit leads to overseas conflict between those seeking to gain from business, and that this conflict both deranges the mind and eviscerates the body. As Brown shifts the tale's mystery from the whodunit of Waldegrave's murder to the deeper question of why benevolence fails, he indicates his realization that a postaristocratic commercial society will not erase or overcome the sociocultural deficiencies of the prior age. Instead, these passions will be reformulated to create new forms of destructive behavior, typified by Sarsefield's inhumanity. The codes of aristocratic honor-violence are transformed and now appear in commercial terms, spread through imperialism, which sets off contemporary cycles of revenge that will be transmitted across generations in ways that will also deform the inheritors of those struggles.

In the end, Brown's treatment of Edgar's violence and Indian fighting may have more to do with large-scale social and economic relations than with notions about the intrinsic savagery of the human soul. Brown's narrative can be read as showing how global conditions of competition for profit position local agents in situations where they commit acts that appear to be spontaneous but, in reality, respond to and represent global conflicts and transformations.[36] With *Edgar Huntly,* Brown dramatizes the social relations of bourgeois-led imperialism, which turns its carriers into heartless men, like the returned Sarsefield, or randomized agents of violence, like Edgar.

Subordination and Sexuality: Male-Female Relations

Responding to the conservative counterrevolution of the late 1790s, when the egalitarian aspirations of the radical Enlightenment were turned back, *Edgar Huntly* charts the defeat of women's autonomy. By the narrative's end, the tale's women have been stripped of control over their finances and locked within positions of infantile subordination to men. Euphemia Lorimer's fortune may have given her the ability to challenge aristocratic hierarchies by marrying Sarsefield, but in so doing she loses control of her wealth to him. The Delaware Old Deb's claims, moral and otherwise, to sovereignty over her ancestral lands have been negated, and she must flee the region to escape punishment. Euphemia Lorimer's daughter Clarice is presented to Edgar as an object that Sarsefield feels empowered to transfer at will, and Edgar's sisters are saved from death only to find that they have been made homeless and impoverished by their uncle's death. Other minor female characters include the abused wife of the drunken Selby and the unnamed female hostage that Edgar rescues and returns to her father's authority. To say that women's ability to transcend gender limitations is severely diminished in this narrative would be an understatement.

The question here, then, is why a Wollstonecraftian feminist like Brown would write a fiction that is so unrelentingly pessimistic about female empowerment. What are the social factors that constrain women? In line with Wollstonecraft's *Vindication of the Rights of Woman,* Brown primarily represents women's disempowerment by the impositions that men place on their access to knowledge and opportunities for education and rational improvement. The novel's male characters assume a paternalist, disciplinary right to censor the information women need in order to participate in enlightened discussion. It is not the case that women are essentially less mature than men, but that the male characters structurally infantilize the women. Lorimer's twin

---

[36] See Brown's 1804 "Memorandums Made on a Journey Through Part of Pennsylvania" in this volume's Related Texts. There he reflects again on these issues and portrays resourceful and witty Indians who adjust to commercial expansionism and play on and reverse the stereotypes of frontier whites.

brother prohibits her from choosing Sarsefield as her intended partner, and, when she asserts her rights by refusing to provide an alibi for Wiatte, he vows punishing revenge. From this point on, all the male characters, regardless of their actual rank, assume for Lorimer, because of her gender, that she cannot be trusted to hear the truth about Wiatte's return, his murder, or Clithero's movements.

Edgar also reinforces the imposition of female ignorance. Like Clithero, who seeks to protect a text by burying it, Edgar in Chapter 13 wants to hide Waldegrave's deist letters from Mary, his fiancée and Waldegrave's sister. Edgar has been transcribing these letters for Mary's benefit but paternalistically denies her the complete acquisition of her brother's letters, just as he ensures that she does not gain his inheritance. Because Edgar assumes that Mary's religious convictions are merely intuitive, he believes that they cannot withstand the subtleties of Waldegrave's arguments. Consequently, he decides to give Mary edited copies of Waldegrave's letters so that she reads only their "narrative or descriptive" elements, but not the analytical or deductive passages.

The male imposition of female childishness continues with Old Deb. As noted earlier in the discussion of the novel's historical background, Deb seems to personify the historical "feminization" and subordination of the Delawares after the Walking Purchase fraud of 1737 and the Quaker-Iroquois-Delaware negotiations of 1742. Within the context of her own people in this novel, Deb has authority to speak before the tribe's general council and possesses a powerful "eloquence" that sways their collective decisions (137). Yet to Edgar and the other white settlers, she is inscrutable, incoherent, and tolerated as semi-mad. Her language is likened to her dogs' barking: "Her voice was sharp and shrill, and her gesticulations were vehement and grotesque" (137). Deb appears to the settlers as a primitive figure, a barbaric and uncultivated creature unfamiliar with the higher stages of human refinement.

The novel's male characters express their assumed patriarchy as they insist that the novel's women are incapable of negotiating the complexities of a modern commercial economy, an inability exacerbated as the women are refused equal access to means of knowledge and channels of self-education. While Edgar is willing to give the men he encounters the benefit of sympathy, he does not always do the same with women. He readily signs over Mary Waldegrave's fortune, abandons the female hostage in Deb's hut where she is rediscovered by the Delaware warriors, joins in the collective denial of Old Deb's intelligence, and refuses to stay longer at the drunken Selby's, where he might comfort the crying, abused wife. *Edgar Huntly*'s geography is fundamentally a man's world.

Friendship and Sexuality: Male-Male Relations

In recent decades, studies of the gothic tradition have explored the centrality of psychosexual dynamics—particularly anxieties about same-sex relations, whether erotic or merely social—in the novels of this period. As this scholarship has brought new insights into Brown's engagement with issues concerning gender and sexuality in general, the importance of same-sex dynamics in his writings has also attracted scholarly attention. If *Edgar Huntly* dramatizes a man's world, it also expresses hopes and anxieties about new models for behavior between men.

During the eighteenth century, new spaces and opportunities for male-male relationships began to emerge throughout western Europe and its Atlantic colonies. The rise of commercial cities swollen with hinterland immigrants like Clithero created zones where old status relationships between men began to be put aside. The nascent bourgeoisie fashioned realms where they could meet, discuss, and make trades outside of the regal state's supervision. In semipublic places where one could enter for a small admission fee—typified by rapidly spreading new institutions like coffee houses—the middle class developed new, more egalitarian patterns of social interaction between men who looked to overcome older ethnic or regional identities in order to take part in the larger, corporate identity of the urban, middling classes. As part of their refusal of older clan-blood and lord-serf hierarchies, the bourgeoisie forged new conceptions of male friendship, mutuality, and benevolence in terms that encouraged and legitimated modern social relations. "Friendship," in particular, was a theme of endless reflection as the term shifted from a sense of obligation to one's kinship group or political allies to a new state of chosen emotional affinity wherein men would protect and nurture each other in the emerging world of competitive commerce.

This long reconfiguration of male manners opened up a new spectrum of possibilities regarding the possible interrelations of emotion and sexuality.[37] As new institutions, ideas, and behaviors emerged during the eighteenth century, there also arose both the material conditions for and conceptions of homoerotic community, along with modern fears and anxieties about these relations, particularly fears about how association with the passion of male-male sexuality might undermine the middle-class man's public status. Recent scholarship has begun to uncover the eighteenth-century world of homoerotic contact in streets, pubs, and harbor underworlds, and cultural historians have become more sensitive to the semicovert symbolic codes and narrative devices in which male-male desire was represented before the late twentieth century.[38]

With its emphasis on means of communication between men that use tone and gesture, rather than explicit speech, and a self-conflicted tension between private actions and public role, *Edgar Huntly* seems to evoke many late eighteenth-century homoerotic themes. In Erasmus Darwin's medical text *Zoönomia; or the Laws of Organic Life,* mentioned earlier as Brown's primary source on sleep-walking, Darwin lists the stages of the disease sentimental love (erotomania) as reverie, which causes sleep-walking, the desire for solitude in mountains and forests, and, lastly, "furious or

---

[37] See Trumbach, *Sex and the Gender Revolution.*

[38] See Higgs, *Queer Sites;* Norton, *Mother Clap's Molly House;* and Bray, *Homosexuality in Renaissance England.* For discussions of early American sexuality and male friendship, see Godbeer, *Sexual Revolution in Early America;* Crain, *American Sympathy;* Arnebeck, *Through a Fiery Trial;* and Foster, *Long before Stonewall.*

melancholy insanity; and suicide, or revenge."[39] Because Clithero performs each of these symptoms in the order that Darwin mentions, the reader can see how Brown's use of this sequence implies that Clithero's perturbed state is the result of an unresolved conflict of love. But love for whom?[40] When Edgar confronts Clithero and accuses him of murdering Waldegrave, the latter responds with his autobiography in lieu of an explicit confession. Clithero's testimony, in Chapters 4–8, begins as a story about conflicted love as he struggles to repress a socially transgressive desire for a woman above his class position, the niece of his landowning, aristocratic employer Euphemia Lorimer. As Clithero's superior, Lorimer raises Clithero above his peasant origins and grants him permission to disregard the erotic prohibitions of older hierarchies. This lovefest between classes, however, is damaged by the eruption of violence and vengeance in the unexpected return of Lorimer's exiled brother Arthur Wiatte, who seems to represent the latent power and brutality of the old order's codes of rank and status.

Clithero has every reason to fear and despise Wiatte as Lorimer's antagonist and a formidable obstacle to his marriage to Clarice, Wiatte's daughter. Yet Wiatte also magnetizes Clithero in ways that suggest a covert attraction. From this perspective, the first section of Clithero's tale about the erotic drive to overcome divisions between peasant and noble may also be said to introduce a symbolic language for overcoming the felt prohibitions about sexual relations between men of different status, such as Clithero and Wiatte. Clithero's emotional difficulties in the first (male-female) instance become even more extreme and conflicted in the second (male-male). Clithero's murder of Wiatte, from this perspective, could also be read as suggesting an emotional panic in which Clithero attacks Wiatte in order to reject and displace a subliminal attraction. As Clithero is trapped between mutually incompatible modes of masculinity, his sleep-walking might also, on this level, be taken as a metaphor for his being caught in between two states of identity, much as later gothic fiction uses figures of vampires, werewolves, and specters to allegorize homoerotic identity.

Clithero continues to be tormented by his actions in Ireland (his five-chapter narrative is the longest segment in the novel), and he uses the site of Waldegrave's death at the Elm to agonize over the events and aftermath of Wiatte's death. Unlike Clithero, however, Edgar is more eager to realize the possibilities of positive male-male relations in Norwalk. Almost all of Edgar's interaction with Clithero occurs when the two are alone together in this isolated space. Thus when Edgar first sees Clithero at the Elm, it is not entirely clear whether he is surprised because he discovers someone else there, or because that someone else is a muscular, half-naked man.

Edgar Huntly often uses descriptions of spatial and geographical borders as a symbolic map for psychic ones regarding male-male sexual identities. Edgar and Clithero's concern that biographical documents remain buried or locked within

---

[39] See this excerpt from Darwin's *Zoönomia* in this volume's Related Texts.

[40] The following passage condenses arguments from Shapiro, "Man to Man."

secret boxes may suggest what is today called "the closet," the self-protecting, self-tormenting state of enclosing one's felt desires. The world of *Edgar Huntly* is a world where men closely observe each other's bodies and faces in public for signs of experience that are not otherwise spoken aloud. Although it will later become the site of frontier violence, Norwalk initially appears to Edgar as a space for intimate emotional and possibly physical relations between men, where the pain of erotic repression can be overcome. The doubled aspect of Norwalk, as a space where homoeroticism becomes potentially empowered and contested, illuminates meanings latent within the Delaware Indian sequence. From this perspective, the Indian fighting recodes earlier tensions in Ireland as the Euphemia-Wiatte-Clithero triangle reappears in the conflict between Old Deb, the male Delawares, and Edgar. If the male Delawares appear more like nightmarish phantoms than humans, this may partly be because Brown also uses them as a medium to represent struggles over male-male relations. That Edgar's first and last sightings of Delaware warriors occur when he's emerging from sleep and in bed suggests that the entire Indian episode may also function as a dreamscape in which the matter of homoeroticism is displaced and projected onto the question of settler-Indian conflict. Edgar's weird rationalizations for killing Delawares at close range, when no other course of action seems possible, replicates Clithero's alibi for "spontaneously" and "unconsciously" assassinating Wiatte ("as if by spontaneous energy," 51). As another case in which Edgar replicates or doubles Clithero's actions so as to help understand the latter's experience, the entire Indian war segment seems to reiterate Clithero's biography in an alternative locale that might—but does not—provide a happier ending.

If the theme of male-male relations initially seems foreign to the more obvious issues in *Edgar Huntly*, the significance of the issue for Brown becomes a bit plainer to see if we look briefly at how it recurs in some of his other writings. The homoerotic inflection in this novel seems to be connected, for example, with similar themes in Brown's *Memoirs of Stephen Calvert,* a novel he published serially in 1799–1800, immediately after finishing *Huntly. Stephen Calvert* begins with a Clithero-like narrator who lives among Indians in the Great Lakes' "middle ground" area and seeks protective isolation and refuge on the frontier. The narrator claims that he is seeking to escape the danger of love, and the nature of the attraction is implied when Calvert relates how he suddenly became uninterested in his fiancée and how his bachelor cousin prohibited the marriage until Calvert could learn more about his true self. Calvert then becomes entranced by a mysterious woman and proposes to her, only to be told that she is already fleeing from a man she married in Europe. In the first American literary account of male homosexuality, this unattainable female character explains to Calvert that she had assumed her husband's lack of sexual contact with her was due to competition from a female mistress. She is then shocked to discover him having sex with another man. Because this story is embedded within the larger narrative of Calvert's self-discovery, it suggests that Calvert himself may be implicated within its dynamics.

Edgar Huntly's narrative, however, ends on a pessimistic note as Norwalk's grounds of male mutuality turn into a gory battlefield. Clithero remains entombed within self-loathing and fits of uncontrollable aggression, and Edgar ends the novel perhaps even more alienated from the other whites than he began it. The implication here is that any new models and opportunities for male companionship that may have opened up at the end of the eighteenth century are closing back down again. The narrative's structural disempowerment of women likewise suggests that failure in one sphere of gender equality will translate into failure in other spheres of sexual liberty. Both projects appear to be overwhelmed by the tale's end with the rise of Sarsefield as a representative of the new bourgeois order. Sarsefield insists that his relation to Clithero Edny (and Edgar) can only be understood as the domestic and unequal relation to a father-in-law, rather than the civic and cooperative relation of equals or comrades, and likewise that Lorimer and Clarice give up the rights to manage their own fortunes in favor of the middle-class version of patriarchy that Sarsefield now inhabits. The larger theme—how the project of benevolence as a means of overcoming early modern revenge codes is blocked by the rise of global imperialism—thus takes on additional significance when placed in context of the narrative's depiction of male-male and male-female relations. Brown draws out connections that illuminate the ways in which overseas adventures and counterattacks on non-Christians also work to justify denying new kinds of sexual and gender equality in the modern world. In *Edgar Huntly,* Brown charts an emerging bourgeois structure of feeling that meshes together global capitalism, the restriction of women and men into a cult of middle-class domesticity, and imperial wars.

In magazine writings after *Edgar Huntly,* Brown continued to stage the tension between celebrating male-male desire and its social disapproval. In Brown's "On the Odes of Anacreon,"[41] the issue emerges in a debate between a prurient narrator and Tom R– about the merits of the Greek poet. An enraptured Tom praises the poet's cadence, imagery, and celebration of love. The narrator, on the other hand, sees Anacreon's poetry as lascivious and worse, because "this poetry appears not to have even *woman* for its object." Responding to a poet who celebrates drunkenness and a passion for novel experience that confounds cross-gender sexuality, the narrator exclaims, "Fough! The very thought excites nausea. Between disgust and abhorrence, my stomach sickens," and instead recommends a therapeutic reading course of Edward Moore's moral fables (130). The narrator's violent speech and complacent hypocrisy in saying that he likes to "praise [him]self" for lacking "conceit or arrogance" is Brown's way of suggesting to the reader that this condemnation of Anacreon is small-minded and should not be taken seriously.

Brown's intention to satirize this narrator's moral smugness is clear in a slightly later (June 1805) piece considering the relative merits of the Persian poet Hafiz, whose lyrics "are generally dedicated to love and wine."[42] Brown comments that editions of Hafiz's poetry struggle to hide the male object choice of the poem's addressee and notes that "English translators," particularly, give "a very different sense from that

---

[41] "On the Odes of Anacreon," *Literary Essays* (December 1803): 129–31.

[42] "Of Persian Poetry and Hafiz," *Literary Essays* (June 1805): 148–53.

conveyed by the text," changing the genders within the poems so that "the 'angel-faced cup-bearer' and 'infidel boy' are converted into damsels and nymphs of paradise." Brown ultimately finds Hafiz's poetry lacking, but on account of its poor versification and rhyme, not because of the main themes concerning love and "the object, *either male or female*, of another appetite" (151).

By the early years of the nineteenth century, Brown's associates began having an internal debate about the ideas they held in the 1790s. In "The Traveler," a series of columns written in the *Literary Magazine and American Register* in 1803–1804, Brown's associates return to debate the meaning of male friendship.[43] While "I.O." claims that male friendship is not scripturally forbidden, "W.D."—who is likely Brown's close associate and later biographer William Dunlap—replies with support for these male relations but then argues for puerile friendship, in the sense that relations between men ought to be replaced in time with a man's relationship to a woman.

The homoerotic themes in *Edgar Huntly* and its oblique defense of male-male sexuality, by absence of its condemnation, does not immediately mean that Brown himself felt that these erotic impulses defined his identity. They merely show his awareness of the pressures and public opposition surrounding homoeroticism. Yet readers of Brown's biography may wonder at the possible link, especially considering his argument that novel readers need to train themselves to be careful and astute observers who can "supply the intermediate links" between a text's "*obvious parts*" and a meaning that the surface narrative "wishes to *conceal*" (171).[44]

A standard reading of Brown sees him rejecting a law career over disgust for its willful obscurities and gothic language. Brown's decision to abandon a law career may also have something to do with how this decision synchronizes with the end of a personal friendship with another male law clerk, W. W. Wilkins. In emotionally saturated letters to Wilkins, Brown charts out their intimacy and describes how Wilkins suddenly breaks off from Brown. Afterward, Brown wandered for several years without regular employment. His later friendship with medical student and literary editor Elihu Hubbard Smith brought Brown back into society and encouraged him to focus his literary ambitions. Yet during this time, Brown alternates between rarely communicating with Smith and sending depressed, suicidal letters full of self-loathing and hinting of secret crimes. Smith, finally, tells Brown to either explain himself openly or be quiet. To our ears, at the beginning of the twenty-first century, Brown's letters sound the ambivalent tones of someone flirting with leaving the closet.

Because critics and historians still debate how to read the period's discourses of male friendship, and the degree to which male friendship acts as a code for some men to express a new sense of collectivity around homoerotic desire, readers ultimately will have to decide for themselves whether they see *Edgar Huntly* as a text of sexual longing or as an expression of progressive hopes for male companionship in a period that allowed greater emotional intensities between friends than is the case today.

---

[43] See the excerpts from "The Traveler" in this volume's Related Texts.

[44] "Remarks on Reading," *Literary Essays* (March 1806): 165–71.

Gothic Inversions: Lycanthropy and Imperialism

Finally, let us look a bit more closely at the ways Brown uses the iconography of gothic and folk traditions. Scholars have noted the ways the novel develops parallels between its panthers, dogs, and Indians.[45] Edgar regards panthers and Indians alike as savage others who threaten the Anglo-Quakers of Solebury, and the dogs that accompany Old Deb provide a third link in this associative chain of animalistic savagism. As he dramatizes these associations in *Edgar Huntly,* Brown seems be drawing on recent transformations of this imagery in late eighteenth-century Ireland and America.[46]

When Edgar makes his first detour to the site of Waldegrave's murder, in Chapter 1, he discerns a presence that would "have been unnoticed" by any other "casual observer" (8). While the reader might initially assume that this obscure movement is a fantasy or symptom of Edgar's distress, Edgar insists that "this apparition was human" (8). He insists that the movement is not a figment of his imagination and thus rejects the possibility that he has encountered the kind of ghost, ghoul, or supernatural spirit that appears in generic gothic or "terrific" novels (see Brown's discussion of "terrific" novels in the Related Texts). In keeping with the antisupernatural mode of narrative he announced in the novel's preface, Brown refuses to allow Edgar's discovery of Clithero at the murder site to descend into a gothic mode of explanation. Yet while Brown dismisses supernatural gothic causes, he nevertheless plays on the reader's familiarity with gothic imagery and conventions. In the initial scenes concerning Clithero, for example, Brown suggestively floats the possibility that Clithero is not merely a sleep-walker, whose nocturnal movements are forgotten in the light of day, but possibly a lycanthrope, a were-beast who shape-shifts across the borderlines between human and animal as he crosses the borderlines between Solebury and Norwalk.

This possibility is literalized when Edgar searches for Clithero and instead encounters an American panther. When Edgar first follows Clithero into Norwalk in Chapter 2, Clithero watches Edgar enter a cave. After he abandons his pursuit at the cave mouth and waits for Clithero to reappear, a mysterious panther emerges instead (16). The story's visual exchange of man for animal is suggested again when Edgar returns to the cave, after hearing Clithero's tale, in Chapter 10. After traversing the cave's interior chambers by crawling on all fours, Edgar emerges into the "desolate and solitary grandeur" of Norwalk's gothic chasms and projectures, where he sees "as if by some magical transition . . . an human countenance," "an human creature" that is Clithero (72). At this point Clithero appears to be in a "trance" and has undergone

---

[45] See for example Hinds, "Deb's Dogs," or the suggestion of "a strange change of identity between man and animal" in Slotkin, *Regeneration through Violence* (384).

[46] For an earlier discussion of some ways that Brown uses gothic motifs to explore countersubversive anxieties about the Ulster Irish and Native Americans, see Gibbons, "Ireland, America, and Gothic Memory."

a shocking metamorphosis that leaves him unusually hirsute: "his arms, bosom and cheek were overgrown and half-concealed by hair" (72). When Edgar returns to the scene the following day, in Chapter 11, to leave food for a sleeping Clithero ("buried in profound slumber," 75), he cuts down a tree to bridge the chasm that separates them. Returning to the spot for a third time in Chapter 12, Edgar again encounters and escapes the threatening panther that appears in Clithero's place (84). This will not be the last encounter, for in Chapter 16's central cave episode, Edgar awakes in a pit to face a second panther, which he kills and savagely devours to slake his ravenous hunger and thirst. Similar gothic human-animal associations then finally appear in Chapter 20 with the Delaware Old Deb/Queen Mab. From her first appearance Deb is surrounded by snarling dogs—"three dogs, of the Indian or wolf species" (137)—who might be thought of as transmutated Delaware warriors, later restored to human form so that they can enact Deb's vengeance against the colonizing white settlers.

Readers may therefore wonder why Brown's novel rejects the supernatural as a narrative device for modern readers yet simultaneously uses plot devices that seem to allude to tales of human transformation into werewolves and were-cats. The answer may lie in how Brown uses recent eighteenth-century adaptations of folkloric traditions and early accounts of colonial conquest and metamorphosis as he crafts an anti-imperialist message. The idea that the Irishman Clithero might be a shape-shifter alludes to a tradition beginning with one of the earliest Conquest of Ireland narratives, the medieval *Topographia Hibernica* by Gerald of Wales. This narrative links werewolf transformations to Irish resistance and traditions about the legendary figure of Queen Mab that Brown will reference in *Edgar Huntly*. In this historical-allegorical account of the English conquest of Ireland, Gerald relates the story of a priest traveling from Ulster toward Meath. Stopping at night in a wood on the borders of Meath, he is asked by a speaking wolf to provide last rites for his dying wife, who is also a human transmogrified into the shape of a wolf. This tale of wolflike natives seeking grace through Christian absolution helps allegorize Gerald's larger ideological goal, which is to justify English conquest as a civilizing discipline imposed on a backwards and bestial Irish population. In a later version, Gerald has the male werewolf prophesy that the English will continue to dominate Ireland so long as the colonizers refuse to adopt the "depraved habits" of the colonized.[47]

Gerald's story is part of a "werewolf renaissance of the twelfth century," in which accounts of lycanthropy appeared widely, but this account of Irish werewolves significantly differs from most others in that it unusually focuses on a *female* werewolf. This representation of an older female werewolf has specific political meanings in stories about the domination of the Irish.[48] Catharine Karkov explains that Gerald's account draws on the "pseudohistorical tales of early Ireland," where "the sovereignty of Ireland was personified as an old woman often roaming the wilderness." Consequently, the dying female werewolf "can also be understood as a personification of Ireland and

[47] Bynum, *Metamorphosis and Identity,* 15–16.

[48] Ibid., 94.

[the] passing from the old to a new [imperial English] order." If "the old woman was traditionally associated with land and sovereignty in the Irish tales, the wolf was traditionally associated with the warrior and outlaw figures whose violent activities were highlighted in Gerald's *Topographia* as being typical of the Irish."[49] The chief exemplum of this old female personifying Ireland is the legendary Queen Mab of the Ulster cycle tales, who presides over the warrior figures, the *fiana*, who foreshadow the later Fenian resistance to English domination.

Gerald's fantastical demonization of the Irish through ethnographic history eventually became a textual site of anti-imperialist resistance as Irish scholars, like John Lynch in *Cambrensis Eversus* (1662), vigorously rejected Gerald's condescending accounts of an Irish people lacking civility and civilization before the English conquest. This refutation was reaffirmed and amplified in Brown's era when Protestant Irish (Ulster) scholars sought to reclaim preconquest, pagan Irish culture as a means of bridging the divide between Catholics and Protestants and mounting a united Irish resistance to British rule. The Protestant scholars who spearheaded this political Gaelic antiquarianism established the Royal Irish Academy in 1785 in order to develop Celtic studies as a substitute for the kind of English colonizer's history that began with Gerald's account. Rather than using history as a means of legitimizing imperialism, these Irish Protestant scholars represented preconquest Ireland as a more civilized place than it would become after English conquest. In this manner they challenged the sociological historians of the Scottish Enlightenment, such as Adam Smith and Adam Ferguson, who argued that the English incorporation of Scotland brought modern commerce and progressive civilization to "north Britons."[50] Like Brown, Smith and Ferguson's Irish contemporaries have a darker and more pessimistic view of the civilizing mission of imperialism. In 1802, three years after Brown wrote *Edgar Huntly,* Irish radical John Dunne addressed the Royal Irish Academy. Returning from North America, where he lived among Indians in the "middle ground" of the Great Lakes, Dunne told the Royal Irish Academy an allegorical story about an Indian woman who discovers that her husband is, in fact, a werewolf. If Dunne's 1802 story of Indian werewolves is an allegory for Irish and mixed-race resistance, as historian Peter Linebaugh has argued, then Dunne is connecting Indian characters with a centuries-old theme of Irish lycanthropy in such a way as to parallel Native Americans with the Irish as mutual victims of English commercial empire.[51]

Brown seems similarly aware of contested narratives of lycanthropes as imperial subjects in *Edgar Huntly,* when, like Dunne, he uses savage-animal allusions to link or parallel Clithero, the Indian "Queen Mab," and her male Delaware tribesmen as American fenians. If Brown alludes to gothic motifs of human transformation,

[49] Karkov, "Tales of the Ancients."

[50] Kidd, "Gaelic Antiquity and National Identity."

[51] Linebaugh, "The Red-Crested Bird and Black Duck."

however, he does so to throw charges of Irish-Indian bestiality back onto the imperialists. For the animalistic flesh-eaters in this novel are neither Clithero nor the Delawares, but Edgar as the representative of an invading Anglo presence. When Edgar awakens in the pit, he kills a panther that is suggestively encoded as a substitute for both Clithero and the Delaware "savages," and feasts upon its "yet warm blood and reeking fibres" (112). When he becomes ravenously thirsty afterward, he leaves the pit to enter into a phase of mindless, semiautomatized Indian-killing. When this episode is read allegorically and in the context of the narrative history of conquest, it therefore suggests Brown's anti-imperialist meaning that the real werewolves are not the native peoples but the so-called civilized Europeans who are bestially invading and devouring aboriginal peoples' lands (whether Celtic or Delaware).

To this image of the triangular relations between the Quaker Edgar, the Irish Clithero, and the Delaware Deb, Brown adds one more generic twist. As noted earlier in this Introduction, Joanna Brooks has discussed the ways that Pennsylvania Quakers began revising the genre of Indian captivity narratives in the late eighteenth century so as to represent backcountry Protestant Irish as savages threatening metropolitan Quaker civilization and its innocent pacificism. In this light, we can see again that Brown's description of the Quaker Edgar as the one actually acting like a lycanthrope confronts his own Quaker community with their complicity as they financially benefit from English imperial rule over the Pennsylvania frontier while absenting themselves from the dirty work and moral responsibility for killing and "removing" Indians.[52] As we have noted, numerous critics suggest that Brown's novel in fact exemplifies the impulses that animate colonialism and imperialism. The manner in which Brown draws here on his contemporaries' research and reevaluation of a long iconographic history resulting from colonizing invasions and settler plantations may suggest, on the contrary, that Brown crafts *Edgar Huntly* as one of the first anti-imperialist narratives, as a story that inverts and deflates the myth that Anglo invasion is a culturally beneficial and socially progressive act.

---

[52] Brooks, "Held Captive by the Irish."

A NOTE ON THE TEXT

Edgar Huntly; or, Memoirs of a Sleep-Walker was first published in late 1799 by Hugh Maxwell, in three volumes, in Philadelphia. This first Philadelphia edition (A) was followed by a London edition in 1803 (E), which corrected most of A's obvious errors in spelling and punctuation. The Kent State Bicentennial Edition (B), published in 1984, is the modern scholarly text of the novel and provides a "Textual Essay" and "List of Emendations" that document copy-text variants and explain the relation of A and E to the scholarly text.

This Hackett edition, like the Grabo Penguin edition of 1988, returns to the 1799 text of A as its copy-text, incorporates the corrections of E when they are not themselves problematic, and regularizes the first edition's irregular dashes and ellipses. We have neither modernized nor regularized spellings or place names, since these present no problem for the contemporary reader. Like other modern editions, we have eliminated the volume divisions of the 1799 edition, the repetition of the title over each chapter heading, and certain typographical details like the use of italics for the "To the Public" preface.

Unlike the Grabo edition, however, the present Hackett edition accepts the five substantive emendations in B that correct the sense of A and E when it is obviously mistaken. These are:

103.15: *funds* for *friends* (153.32 in B)
146.23: *halloos* for *hollows* (220.38 in B)
152.34: *locks* for *looks* (230.22 in B)
163.24: *my Uncle's* for *Inglefield's* (245.22 in B)
190.04: *effected* for *affected* (286.02 in B)

For a complete discussion of the novel's textual history and all variants, see the textual essay, notes, and appendices by S. W. Reid in the Kent State edition.

EDGAR HUNTLY;

OR,

MEMOIRS

OF A

SLEEP-WALKER.

BY THE AUTHOR OF ARTHUR MERVYN,
WIELAND,—ORMOND, &c.

VOL. I.

PHILADELPHIA:
PRINTED BY H. MAXWELL, No. 3 LETITIA COURT,
AND SOLD BY THOMAS DOBSON, ASBURY DICKINS,
AND THE PRINCIPAL BOOKSELLERS.
....
1799.

TO THE PUBLIC

The flattering reception that has been given, by the public, to Arthur Mervyn,[1] has prompted the writer to solicit a continuance of the same favour, and to offer to the world a new performance.

America has opened new views to the naturalist and politician, but has seldome furnished themes to the moral painter. That new springs of action, and new motives to curiosity[2] should operate; that the field of investigation, opened to us by our own country, should differ essentially from those which exist in Europe, may be readily conceived. The sources of amusement to the fancy and instruction to the heart, that are peculiar to ourselves, are equally numerous and inexhaustible. It is the purpose of this work to profit by some of these sources; to exhibit a series of adventures, growing out of the condition of our country, and connected with one of the most common and most wonderful diseases or affections of the human frame.[3]

One merit the writer may at least claim; that of calling forth the passions and engaging the sympathy of the reader, by means hitherto unemployed by preceding

---

[1] The first part of Brown's previous novel, *Arthur Mervyn; or, Memoirs of the Year 1793,* appeared in May 1799. *Edgar Huntly*'s first volume appeared in August 1799. A second part of *Arthur Mervyn* subsequently appeared in summer 1800.

[2] "Springs of action" and "curiosity" are key words in eighteenth-century debates about history and the pursuit of knowledge. By using these terms, Brown is invoking attitudes and concerns that are widespread during the late Enlightenment.

"Springs of action" refers to a search for the causes and conditions of events and behaviors that are both individual and social. Brown belongs to the broad spectrum of period writers who believe the two are interlinked; he believes that if we can understand personal actions, we can also perceive the causes of social events and changes. In this sense, Brown offers *Edgar Huntly* as both the story of an individual and that of representative conflicts in his social world.

"Curiosity" has an ambivalent meaning. It reflects the Enlightenment desire to learn, but it can also lead to unchecked excess. This is what happens to the protagonist of William Godwin's novel *Caleb Williams* (1794), a key source for Brown's approach to novel writing. Curiosity in this sense is also central to Brown's novel *Arthur Mervyn.*

[3] "Wonderful," in this usage, means something marvelous to behold, something inexplicable that excites the emotions of the beholder, and something that one desires to know or learn about; this is a disease that excites the faculty of wonder and imagination. Throughout his fiction, Brown uses contemporary medical concepts and terms to link "wonderful" diseases or symptoms in this sense to social phenomena. In *Zoönomia; or, the Laws of Organic Life* (1794), the medical text that Brown refers to here and in other works, Erasmus Darwin discusses sleep-walking as a "wonderful disease." See the excerpts from *Zoönomia* in this volume's Related Texts.

authors. Puerile superstition and exploded manners; Gothic castles and chimeras,[4] are the materials usually employed for this end. The incidents of Indian hostility, and the perils of the western wilderness, are far more suitable; and, for a native of America to overlook these, would admit of no apology. These, therefore, are, in part, the ingredients of this tale, and these he has been ambitious of depicting in vivid and faithful colours. The success of his efforts must be estimated by the liberal and candid reader.

C. B. B.

---

[4] "Chimera" is another key word for Brown, meaning "an unreal creature of the imagination, a mere wild fancy; an unfounded conception" (OED). Brown uses it as an adjective to mean delusive, irrational, mistaken conclusions based on false premises or the illogical linkage of cause and effect.

In rejecting "chimeras," Brown rejects the traditional use of castles, ghosts, and other supernatural accessories of European gothic tales, suggesting that his use of the gothic will focus on conditions in the modern world.

EDGAR HUNTLY;
OR, MEMOIRS OF A SLEEP-WALKER

Chapter I

I SIT down, my friend, to comply with thy request.[1] At length does the impetuosity of my fears, the transports of my wonder permit me to recollect my promise and perform it. At length am I somewhat delivered from suspence and from tremors. At length the drama is brought to an imperfect close, and the series of events, that absorbed my faculties, that hurried away my attention, has terminated in repose.

Till now, to hold a steadfast pen was impossible; to disengage my senses from the scene that was passing or approaching; to forbear to grasp at futurity; to suffer so much thought to wander from the purpose which engrossed my fears and my hopes, could not be.

Yet am I sure that even now my perturbations are sufficiently stilled for an employment like this? That the incidents I am going to relate can be recalled and arranged without indistinctness and confusion? That emotions will not be re-awakened by my narrative, incompatible with order and coherence? Yet when I shall be better qualified for this task I know not. Time may take away these headlong energies, and give me back my ancient sobriety: but this change will only be effected by weakening my remembrance of these events. In proportion as I gain power over words, shall I lose dominion over sentiments; in proportion as my tale is deliberate and slow, the incidents and motives which it is designed to exhibit will be imperfectly revived and obscurely pourtrayed.

O! why art thou away at a time like this. Wert thou present, the office to which my pen is so inadequate would easily be executed by my tongue. Accents can scarcely be too rapid, or that which words should fail to convey, my looks and gestures would suffice to communicate.[2] But I know thy coming is impossible. To leave this spot is equally beyond my power. To keep thee in ignorance of what has happened would justly offend thee. There is no method of informing thee except by letter, and this method, must I, therefore, adopt.

---

[1] Edgar's use of the archaic and familiar pronouns "thee," "thou," and "thy" in the opening paragraphs marks him as a Quaker. He uses these forms in this opening passage and periodically thereafter (e.g., in Chapters 3, 11, 13, and 15–21), and only in addressing his fiancée Mary Waldegrave, as he is doing in this opening passage. At certain moments he also uses the more distanced "you" to address Mary—for example, in the last sentence of his narrative in Chapter 27. The use of "friend" in the story's first sentence also hints at Edgar's background with the Quakers, or Society of Friends.

[2] "My looks and gestures would suffice to communicate": throughout his narrative, Edgar emphasizes physical codes of meaning or body language in "looks and gestures." Sight, sound, and gesture will often be used in contrast to explicit meaning.

How short is the period that has elapsed since thou and I parted, and yet how full of tumult and dismay has been my soul during that period! What light has burst upon my ignorance of myself and of mankind! How sudden and enormous the transition from uncertainty to knowledge!—

But let me recall my thoughts: let me struggle for so much composure as will permit my pen to trace intelligible characters. Let me place in order the incidents that are to compose my tale. I need not call on thee to listen. The fate of Waldegrave was as fertile of torment to thee as to me. His bloody and mysterious catastrophe equally awakened thy grief, thy revenge, and thy curiosity. Thou wilt catch from my story every horror and every sympathy which it paints. Thou wilt shudder with my forboding and dissolve with my tears. As the sister of my friend, and as one who honours me with her affection, thou wilt share in all my tasks and all my dangers.

You need not be reminded with what reluctance I left you. To reach this place by evening was impossible, unless I had set out early in the morning, but your society was too precious not to be enjoyed to the last moment. It was indispensable to be here on Tuesday, but my duty required no more than that I should arrive by sun-rise on that day. To travel during the night, was productive of no formidable inconvenience. The air was likely to be frosty and sharp, but these would not incommode one who walked with speed. A nocturnal journey in districts so romantic and wild as these, through which lay my road, was more congenial to my temper than a noon-day ramble.

By night-fall I was within ten miles of my uncle's house. As the darkness increased, and I advanced on my way, my sensations sunk into melancholy. The scene and the time reminded me of the friend whom I had lost. I recalled his features, and accents, and gestures, and mused with unutterable feelings on the circumstances of his death.

My recollections once more plunged me into anguish and perplexity. Once more I asked, who was his assassin? By what motives could he be impelled to a deed like this? Waldegrave was pure from all offence. His piety was rapturous. His benevolence[3] was a stranger to remisness or torpor. All who came within the sphere of his influence experienced and acknowledged his benign activity. His friends were few, because his habits were timid and reserved, but the existence of an enemy was impossible.

I recalled the incidents of our last interview, my importunities that he should postpone his ill-omened journey till the morning, his inexplicable obstinacy; his resolution to set out on foot, during a dark and tempestuous night, and the horrible disaster that befel him.

The first intimation I received of this misfortune, the insanity of vengeance and grief into which I was hurried, my fruitless searches for the author of this guilt, my midnight wanderings and reveries beneath the shade of that fatal Elm, were revived

---

[3] "Benevolence" is tied to "sympathy," "sensibility," and "sentiment" throughout the novel. The novel frequently contrasts the therapeutic effect of benevolence with the destructive passion for revenge. For more on this topic, see note 1.9 on sympathy, sensibility, and sentiment, and the discussion of the novel's themes of benevolence and revenge in the Introduction.

and re-acted. I heard the discharge of the pistol, I witnessed the alarm of Inglefield, I heard his calls to his servants, and saw them issue forth, with lights and hasten to the spot whence the sound had seemed to proceed. I beheld my friend, stretched upon the earth, ghastly with a mortal wound, alone, with no traces of the slayer visible, no tokens by which his place of refuge might be sought, the motives of his enmity or his instruments of mischief might be detected.

I hung over the dying youth, whose insensibility forbade him to recognize his friend, or unfold the cause of his destruction. I accompanied his remains to the grave, I tended the sacred spot where he lay, I once more exercised my penetration and my zeal in pursuit of his assassin. Once more my meditations and exertions were doomed to be disappointed.

I need not remind thee of what is past. Time and reason seemed to have dissolved the spell which made me deaf to the dictates of duty and discretion. Remembrances had ceased to agonize, to urge me to headlong acts, and foster sanguinary[4] purposes. The gloom was half dispersed and a radiance had succeeded sweeter than my former joys.

Now, by some unseen concurrence of reflections, my thoughts reverted into some degree of bitterness. Methought that to ascertain the hand who killed my friend, was not impossible, and to punish the crime was just. That to forbear inquiry or withold punishment was to violate my duty to my God and to mankind. The impulse was gradually awakened that bade me once more to seek the Elm; once more to explore the ground; to scrutinize its trunk. What could I expect to find? Had it not been an hundred times examined? Had I not extended my search to the neighbouring groves and precipices? Had I not pored upon the brooks, and pryed into the pits and hollows, that were adjacent to the scene of blood?

Lately I had viewed this conduct with shame and regret; but in the present state of my mind, it assumed the appearance of conformity with prudence, and I felt myself irresistably prompted to repeat my search. Some time had elapsed since my departure from this district. Time enough for momentous changes to occur. Expedients that formerly were useless, might now lead instantaneously to the end which I sought. The tree which had formerly been shunned by the criminal, might, in the absence of the avenger of blood, be incautiously approached. Thoughtless or fearless of my return, it was possible that he might, at this moment, be detected hovering near the scene of his offences.

Nothing can be pleaded in extenuation of this relapse into folly. My return, after an absence of some duration, into the scene of these transactions and sufferings, the time of night, the glimmering of the stars, the obscurity in which external objects were wrapped, and which, consequently, did not draw my attention from the images of fancy, may, in some degree, account for the revival of those sentiments and resolutions which immediately succeeded the death of Waldegrave, and which, during my visit to you, had been suspended.

---

[4] "Sanguinary": "bloody" or "bloodthirsty" (OED). Here, the word refers to the desire for mortal revenge.

You know the situation of the Elm,[5] in the midst of a private road, on the verge of Norwalk,[6] near the habitation of Inglefield, but three miles from my uncle's house. It was now my intention to visit it. The road in which I was travelling, led a different way. It was requisite to leave it, therefore, and make a circuit through meadows and over steeps. My journey would, by these means, be considerably prolonged, but on that head I was indifferent, or rather, considering how far the night had already advanced, it was desirable not to reach home till the dawn.

I proceeded in this new direction with speed. Time, however, was allowed for my impetuosities to subside, and for sober thoughts to take place. Still I persisted in this path. To linger a few moments in this shade; to ponder on objects connected with events so momentous to my happiness, promised me a mournful satisfaction. I was familiar with the way, though trackless and intricate, and I climbed the steeps, crept through the brambles, leapt the rivulets and fences with undeviating aim, till at length I reached the craggy and obscure path, which led to Inglefield's house.

In a short time, I descried through the dusk the wide-spread branches of the Elm. This tree, however faintly seen, cannot be mistaken for another. The remarkable bulk and shape of its trunk, its position in the midst of the way, its branches spreading into an ample circumference, made it conspicuous from afar. My pulse throbbed as I approached it.[7]

My eyes were eagerly bent to discover the trunk and the area beneath the shade. These, as I approached, gradually became visible. The trunk was not the only thing which appeared in view. Somewhat else, which made itself distinguishable by its motions, was likewise noted. I faultered and stopt.

To a casual observer this appearance would have been unnoticed. To me, it could not but possess a powerful significance. All my surmises and suspicions, instantly returned. This apparition was human, it was connected with the fate of Waldegrave, it led to a disclosure of the author of that fate. What was I to do? To approach unwarily would alarm the person. Instant flight would set him beyond discovery and reach.

I walked softly to the road-side. The ground was covered with rocky masses, scattered among shrub-oaks and dwarf-cedars, emblems of its sterile and uncultivated

---

[5] "The Elm" becomes a crucial focal point in the novel and refers, for readers of the 1790s, to the famous Treaty Elm where, according to legend, William Penn founded Pennsylvania by signing a treaty of peace with the Delaware Indians. As the site of the murder of Edgar's friend Waldegrave (whose name means "grave in the forest") and a central point around which the novel's sleep-walking is organized, this Elm is thus a more sinister image and an implicit reflection on the history of Pennsylvania. For more, see the discussion of the Elm in the Introduction.

[6] "Norwalk" will be the name of the wilderness area where much of the novel's action takes place. Edgar explains more about the area in Chapter 2 and Chapter 9. The wilderness area Norwalk (with overtones of walking and negation) will be opposed throughout the novel to the white settlements Solebury (with overtones of "soul" burial, or social blindness and denial) and Chetasco. Thus the novel's dualistic landscape seems to underline its oppositions between irrational and rational action, savage revenge and benevolence, and so on.

[7] Edgar frequently comments on his pulse, blood circulation, or beating heart as a way of indicating his state of physical and mental balance.

state. Among these it was possible to elude observation and yet approach near enough to gain an accurate view of this being.

At this time, the atmosphere was somewhat illuminated by the moon, which, though it had already set, was yet so near the horizon, as to benefit me by its light. The shape of a man, tall and robust, was now distinguished. Repeated and closer scrutiny enabled me to perceive that he was employed in digging the earth. Something like flannel was wrapt round his waist and covered his lower limbs. The rest of his frame was naked. I did not recognize in him any one whom I knew.

A figure, robust and strange, and half naked,[8] to be thus employed, at this hour and place, was calculated to rouse up my whole soul. His occupation was mysterious and obscure. Was it a grave that he was digging? Was his purpose to explore or to hide? Was it proper to watch him at a distance, unobserved and in silence, or to rush upon him and extort from him by violence or menaces, an explanation of the scene?

Before my resolution was formed, he ceased to dig. He cast aside his spade and sat down in the pit that he had dug. He seemed wrapt in meditation; but the pause was short, and succeeded by sobs, at first low, and at wide intervals, but presently louder and more vehement. Sorely charged was indeed that heart whence flowed these tokens of sorrow. Never did I witness a scene of such mighty anguish, such heart-bursting grief.

What should I think? I was suspended in astonishment. Every sentiment, at length, yielded to my sympathy.[9] Every new accent of the mourner struck upon my heart with additional force, and tears found their way spontaneously to my eyes. I left the spot where I stood, and advanced within the verge of the shade. My caution had forsaken me, and instead of one whom it was duty to persecute, I beheld, in this man, nothing but an object of compassion.

My pace was checked by his suddenly ceasing to lament. He snatched the spade, and rising on his feet began to cover up the pit with the utmost diligence. He

[8] The presence of the Delaware Indians who will play a central role in the second half of the novel seems foreshadowed by Clithero's first appearance, "robust and strange, and half naked," and wearing something like a loincloth.

[9] "Sympathy" and its cognates "sensibility" and "sentiment" are important, well-defined concepts in eighteenth-century literature and culture, particularly in the Anglophone world and France. Like "benevolence," "sympathy," "sensibility," and "sentiment" identify an emotional-physical connection with or response to other individuals, often interpreted as an intrinsically egalitarian connection that replaces feudal-aristocratic modes of deference with new, more modern models for interpersonal behavior. The politics of sympathy was fiercely debated by both the left and right during the revolutionary period, and progressive Woldwinite writers like Brown treated the concept in a variety of ways both positive and negative. Edgar's insistence here on benevolence and emotionalized states of sympathy with Clithero and others continues throughout the narrative. To understand the general importance of this motif, consider that the earliest U.S. novel, published in 1789 by author William Hill Brown (no relation to Charles Brockden Brown), was titled *The Power of Sympathy*. For more on this topic, see the discussion of benevolence in the Introduction.

seemed aware of my presence, and desirous of hiding something from my inspection. I was prompted to advance nearer and hold his hand, but my uncertainty as to his character and views, the abruptness with which I had been ushered into this scene, made me still hesitate; but though I hesitated to advance, there was nothing to hinder me from calling.

What, ho! said I. Who is there? What are you doing?

He stopt, the spade fell from his hand, he looked up and bent forward his face towards the spot where I stood. An interview and explanation were now methought unavoidable. I mustered up my courage to confront and interrogate this being.

He continued for a minute in his gazing and listening attitude. Where I stood I could not fail of being seen, and yet he acted as if he saw nothing. Again he betook himself to his spade, and proceeded with new diligence to fill up the pit. This demeanour confounded and bewildered me. I had no power but to stand and silently gaze upon his motions.

The pit being filled, he once more sat upon the ground, and resigned himself to weeping and sighs with more vehemence than before. In a short time the fit seemed to have passed. He rose, seized the spade, and advanced to the spot where I stood.

Again I made preparation as for an interview which could not but take place. He passed me, however, without appearing to notice my existence. He came so near as almost to brush my arm, yet turned not his head to either side. My nearer view of him, made his brawny arms and lofty stature more conspicuous; but his imperfect dress, the dimness of the light, and the confusion of my own thoughts, hindered me from discerning his features. He proceeded with a few quick steps, along the road, but presently darted to one side and disappeared among the rocks and bushes.

My eye followed him as long as he was visible, but my feet were rooted to the spot. My musing was rapid and incongruous. It could not fail to terminate in one conjecture, that this person was *asleep*. Such instances were not unknown to me, through the medium of conversation and books. Never, indeed, had it fallen under my own observation till now, and now it was conspicuous and environed with all that could give edge to suspicion, and vigour to inquiry. To stand here was no longer of use, and I turned my steps toward my uncle's habitation.

Chapter II

I HAD food enough for the longest contemplation. My steps partook, as usual, of the vehemence of my thoughts, and I reached my uncle's gate before I believed myself to have lost sight of the Elm. I looked up and discovered the well-known habitation. I could not endure that my reflections should so speedily be interrupted. I, therefore, passed the gate, and stopped not till I had reached a neighbouring summit, crowned with chesnut-oaks and poplars.

Here I more deliberately reviewed the incidents that had just occurred. The inference was just, that the man, half-clothed and digging, was a sleeper: But what was the cause of this morbid activity? What was the mournful vision that dissolved him in tears, and extorted from him tokens of inconsolable distress? What did he seek, or what endeavour to conceal in this fatal spot? The incapacity of sound sleep denotes a mind sorely wounded. It is thus that atrocious criminals denote the possession of some dreadful secret. The thoughts, which considerations of safety enables them to suppress or disguise during wakefulness, operate without impediment, and exhibit their genuine effects, when the notices of sense are partly excluded, and they are shut out from a knowledge of their intire condition.

This is the perpetrator of some nefarious deed. What but the murder of Waldegrave could direct his steps hither? His employment was part of some fantastic drama in which his mind was busy. To comprehend it, demands penetration into the recesses of his soul. But one thing is sure; an incoherent conception of his concern in that transaction, bewitches him hither. This it is that deluges his heart with bitterness and supplies him with ever-flowing tears.

But whence comes he? He does not start from the bosom of the earth, or hide himself in airy distance. He must have a name and a terrestrial habitation.[1] It cannot be at an immeasurable distance from the haunted Elm. Inglefield's house is the nearest. This may be one of its inhabitants. I did not recognize his features, but this was owing to the dusky atmosphere and to the singularity of his garb. Inglefield has two servants, one of whom was a native of this district, simple, guileless and incapable of any act of violence. He was, moreover devoutly attached to his sect.[2] He could not be the criminal.

The other was a person of a very different cast. He was an emigrant from Ireland,[3] and had been six months in the family of my friend. He was a pattern of sobriety and

---

[1] By insisting that the figure must be human, must "have a name and a terrestrial habitation," Edgar rejects the conventional gothic possibility that he has seen a ghost or some other kind of supernatural apparition.

[2] "Sect": this is the first indication that Clithero is not a Quaker like the other settlers in Solebury.

[3] For readers in 1799, Clithero's Irishness connects him with both the long history of Quaker-Irish-Indian conflict on the Pennsylvania frontier, and with the counterrevolutionary paranoia concerning Irish émigré revolutionaries in the late 1790s. Because he comes from the north of Ireland (see Chapter 4, note 4.2), and is not identified as Catholic, the reader is to assume that Clithero is a

11

gentleness. His mind was superior to his situation. His natural endowments were strong, and had enjoyed all the advantage of cultivation. His demeanour was grave, and thoughtful, and compassionate. He appeared not untinctured with religion, but his devotion, though unostentatious, was of a melancholy tenor.

There was nothing in the first view of his character calculated to engender suspicion. The neighbourhood was populous. But as I conned over the catalogue, I perceived that the only foreigner among us was Clithero.[4] Our scheme was, for the most part, a patriarchal one.[5] Each farmer was surrounded by his sons and kinsmen. This was an exception to the rule. Clithero was a stranger, whose adventures and character, previously to his coming hither, were unknown to us. The Elm was surrounded by his master's domains. An actor there must be, and no one was equally questionable.

The more I revolved the pensive and reserved deportment of this man, the ignorance in which we were placed respecting his former situation, his possible motives for abandoning his country and chusing a station so much below the standard of his intellectual attainments, the stronger my suspicions became. Formerly, when occupied with conjectures relative to the same topic, the image of this man did not fail to occur; but the seeming harmlessness of his ordinary conduct, had raised him to a level with others, and placed him equally beyond the reach of suspicion. I did not, till now, advert to the recentness of his appearance among us, and to the obscurity that hung over his origin and past life. But now these considerations appeared so highly momentous, as almost to decide the question of his guilt.

But how were these doubts to be changed into absolute certainty? Henceforth this man was to become the subject of my scrutiny. I was to gain all the knowledge, respecting him, which those with whom he lived, and were the perpetual witnesses of his actions, could impart. For this end I was to make minute inquiries, and to put

---

Protestant Irishman. The great majority of the poor, Scots-Irish immigrants to the Pennsylvania backcountry of the eighteenth century were northern, Protestant "Ulster" Irish; and most of the United Irishmen, the Irish revolutionaries who were arriving in the United States and notably Philadelphia in the late 1790s, were Protestant as well. For more, see the discussion of Clithero and his tale in the Introduction.

[4] This is the first appearance of Clithero's name. "Clitheroe" is the name of a town in Lancashire, England. The character's last name, "Edny," is an anagram for "deny" and sounds similar to "Edgar." Thus a phonetic similarity between "Edgar" and "Edny" echoes the way Edgar increasingly doubles and comes to resemble Clithero in the course of the novel.

[5] Beginning with this mention of Solebury's "patriarchal" social system and throughout the remainder of the narrative, Brown emphasizes the patriarchal, paternalistic norms and structures of his society, drawing attention to tensions and conflicts concerning patriarchal norms in the revolutionary period. Note the references to fathers and paternal authority throughout the narrative. This emphasis also reminds the reader that the frontier property in the novel is owned and farmed by local settler-inhabitants and not absentee landlords. Large-scale landlord ownership was a norm in the period—for example, on Euphemia Lorimer's Irish estate (in Clithero's tale) or in the contemporary United States in parts of New York State (where it provoked armed resistance by tenants) or on southern plantations (where it provoked slave rebellions).

seasonable interrogatories. From this conduct I promised myself an ultimate solution of my doubts.

I acquiesced in this view of things with considerable satisfaction. It seemed as if the maze was no longer inscrutable. It would be quickly discovered who were the agents and instigators of the murder of my friend.

But it suddenly occurred to me, For what purpose shall I prosecute this search? What benefit am I to reap from this discovery? How shall I demean myself when the criminal is detected? I was not insensible, at that moment, of the impulses of vengeance, but they were transient. I detested the sanguinary resolutions that I had once formed. Yet I was fearful of the effects of my hasty rage, and dreaded an encounter, in consequence of which, I might rush into evils which no time could repair, nor penitence expiate.

But why, said I, should it be impossible to arm myself with firmness? If forbearance be the dictate of wisdom, cannot it be so deeply engraven on my mind as to defy all temptation, and be proof against the most abrupt surprise? My late experience has been of use to me. It has shewn me my weakness and my strength. Having found my ancient fortifications insufficient to withstand the enemy, what should I learn from thence but that it becomes me to strengthen and enlarge them?

No caution indeed can hinder the experiment from being hazardous. Is it wise to undertake experiments by which nothing can be gained, and much may be lost? Curiosity is vicious,[6] if undisciplined by reason, and inconducive to benefit.

I was not, however, to be diverted from my purpose. Curiosity, like virtue, is its own reward. Knowledge is of value for its own sake, and pleasure is annexed to the acquisition, without regard to any thing beyond. It is precious even when disconnected with moral inducements and heart-felt sympathies, but the knowledge which I sought by its union with these was calculated to excite the most complex and fiery sentiment in my bosom.

Hours were employed in revolving these thoughts. At length I began to be sensible of fatigue, and returning home, explored the way to my chamber without molesting the repose of the family. You know that our doors are always unfastened, and are accessible at all hours of the night.

My slumbers were imperfect, and I rejoiced when the morning light permitted me to resume my meditations. The day glided away, I scarcely know how, and as I had rejoiced at the return of morning, I now hailed, with pleasure, the approach of night.

My uncle and sisters having retired, I betook myself, instead of following their example, to the *Chesnut-hill.* Concealed among its rocks, or gazing at the prospect, which stretched so far and so wide around it, my fancy has always been accustomed to derive its highest enjoyment from this spot. I found myself again at leisure to recall the scene which I had witnessed during the last night, to imagine its connection with the fate of Waldegrave, and to plan the means of discovering the secret that was hidden under these appearances.

---

[6] "Vicious": meaning "depraved, immoral, bad" (OED), "vicious" is used here in the sense of selfish, nonbenevolent behavior.

Shortly, I began to feel insupportable disquiet at the thoughts of postponing this discovery. Wiles and stratagems were practicable, but they were tedious and of dubious success. Why should I proceed like a plotter? Do I intend the injury of this person? A generous purpose will surely excuse me from descending to artifices? There are two modes of drawing forth the secrets of another, by open and direct means and by circuitous and indirect. Why scruple to adopt the former mode? Why not demand a conference, and state my doubts, and demand a solution of them, in a manner worthy of a beneficent purpose? Why not hasten to the spot? He may be, at this moment, mysteriously occupied under this shade. I may note his behaviour; I may ascertain his person, if not by the features that belong to him, yet by tracing his footsteps when he departs, and pursuing him to his retreats.

I embraced this scheme, which was thus suggested, with eagerness. I threw myself, with headlong speed, down the hill and pursued my way to the Elm. As I approached the tree, my palpitations increased, though my pace slackened. I looked forward with an anxious glance. The trunk of the tree was hidden in the deepest shade. I advanced close up to it. No one was visible, but I was not discouraged. The hour of his coming was, perhaps, not arrived. I took my station at a small distance, beside a fence, on the right hand.

An hour elapsed before my eyes lighted on the object of which they were in search. My previous observation had been roving from one quarter to another. At last, it dwelt upon the tree. The person whom I before described was seated on the ground. I had not perceived him before, and the means by which he placed himself in this situation had escaped my notice. He seemed like one, whom an effort of will, without the exercise of locomotion,[7] had transported hither, or made visible. His state of disarray, and the darkness that shrouded him, prevented me, as before, from distinguishing any peculiarities in his figure or countenance.

I continued watchful and mute. The appearances already described took place, on this occasion, except the circumstance of digging in the earth. He sat musing for a while, then burst into sighs and lamentations.

These being exhausted, he rose to depart. He stalked away with a solemn and deliberate pace. I resolved to tread, as closely as possible, in his footsteps, and not to lose sight of him till the termination of his career.

Contrary to my expectation, he went in a direction opposite to that which led to Inglefield's. Presently, he stopped at bars,[8] which he cautiously removed, and, when he had passed through them, as deliberately replaced. He then proceeded along an obscure path, which led across stubble fields, to a wood. The path continued through the wood, but he quickly struck out of it, and made his way, seemingly at random, through a most perplexing undergrowth of bushes and briars.

I was, at first, fearful that the noise, which I made behind him, in trampling down the thicket, would alarm him; but he regarded it not. The way that he had selected, was always difficult; sometimes considerable force was requisite to beat down obstacles;

---

[7] "Without the exercise of locomotion": without consciously walking there.

[8] "Bars": fence gates.

sometimes, it led into a deep glen, the sides of which were so steep as scarcely to afford a footing; sometimes, into fens, from which some exertions were necessary to extricate the feet, and sometimes, through rivulets, of which the water rose to the middle.

For some time I felt no abatement of my speed or my resolution. I thought I might
proceed, without fear, through breaks and dells, which my guide was able to penetrate. He was perpetually changing his direction. I could form no just opinion as to
my situation or distance from the place at which we had set out.

I began at length to be weary. A suspicion, likewise, suggested itself to my mind,
whether my guide did not perceive that he was followed, and thus prolonged his
journey in order to fatigue or elude his pursuer. I was determined, however, to baffle
his design. Though the air was frosty, my limbs were bedewed with sweat and my
joints were relaxed with toil,[9] but I was obstinately bent upon proceeding.

At length a new idea occurred to me. On finding me indefatigable in pursuit, this
person might resort to more atrocious methods of concealment. But what had I to
fear? It was sufficient to be upon my guard. Man to man, I needed not to dread his
encounter.

We, at last, arrived at the verge of a considerable precipice. He kept along the edge.
From this height, a dreary vale was discoverable, embarrassed with the leafless stocks
of bushes, and encumbered with rugged and pointed rocks. This scene reminded me
of my situation. The desert[10] tract called Norwalk, which I have often mentioned to
you, my curiosity had formerly induced me to traverse in various directions. It was in
the highest degree, rugged, picturesque and wild. This vale, though I had never before viewed it by the glimpses of the moon, suggested the belief that I had visited it
before. Such an one I knew belonged to this uncultivated region. If this opinion were
true, we were at no inconsiderable distance from Inglefield's habitation. Where, said
I, is this singular career to terminate?

Though occupied with these reflections, I did not slacken my pursuit. The stranger
kept along the verge of the cliff, which gradually declined till it terminated in the valley. He then plunged into its deepest thickets. In a quarter of an hour he stopped
under a projecture of the rock which formed the opposite side of the vale. He then
proceeded to remove the stalks, which, as I immediately perceived, concealed the
mouth of a cavern. He plunged into the darkness, and in a few moments, his steps
were heard no more!

Hitherto my courage had supported me, but here it failed. Was this person an assassin, who was acquainted with the windings of the grotto, and who would take advantage of the dark, to execute his vengeance upon me, who had dared to pursue him
to these forlorn retreats; or was he maniac, or walker in his sleep? Whichever supposition were true, it would be rash in me to follow him. Besides, he could not long remain in these darksome recesses, unless some fatal accident should overtake him.

---

[9] "Relaxed with toil": exhausted and worn out with toil, "rendered soft and feeble" (OED).

[10] "Desert": uncultivated, uninhabited area. This eighteenth-century sense of "desert" is closer to
"wilderness" in twenty-first-century English.

I seated myself at the mouth of the cave, determined patiently to wait till he should think proper to emerge. This opportunity of rest was exceedingly acceptable after so toilsome a pilgrimage. My pulse began to beat more slowly, and the moisture that incommoded me ceased to flow. The coolness which, for a little time, was delicious, presently increased to shivering, and I found it necessary to change my posture, in order to preserve my blood from congealing.

After I had formed a path before the cavern's mouth, by the removal of obstructions, I employed myself in walking to and fro. In this situation I saw the moon gradually decline to the horizon, and, at length, disappear. I marked the deepenings of the shade, and the mutations which every object successively underwent. The vale was narrow, and hemmed in on all sides by lofty and precipitous cliffs. The gloom deepened as the moon declined, and the faintness of star-light was all that preserved my senses from being useless to my own guidance.

I drew nearer the cleft at which this mysterious personage had entered. I stretched my hands before it, determined that he should not emerge from his den without my notice. His steps would, necessarily, communicate the tidings of his approach. They could not move without a noise which would be echoed to, on all sides, by the abruptnesses by which this valley was surrounded. Here, then, I continued till the day began to dawn, in momentary expectation of the stranger's reappearance.

My attention was at length excited by a sound that seemed to issue from the cave. I imagined that the sleeper was returning, and prepared therefore to seize him. I blamed myself for neglecting the opportunities that had already been afforded, and was determined that another should not escape. My eyes were fixed upon the entrance. The rustling increased, and presently an animal leapt forth, of what kind I was unable to discover.[11] Heart-struck by this disappointment, but not discouraged, I continued to watch, but in vain. The day was advancing apace. At length the sun arose, and its beams glistened on the edges of the cliffs above, whose sapless stalks and rugged masses were covered with hoar-frost. I began to despair of success, but was unwilling to depart, until it was no longer possible to hope for the return of this extraordinary personage. Whether he had been swallowed up by some of the abysses of this grotto, or lurked near the entrance, waiting my departure, or had made his exit at another and distant aperture, was unknown to me.

Exhausted and discouraged, I prepared, at length, to return. It was easy to find my way out of this wilderness by going forward in one direction, regardless of impediments and cross-paths. My absence I believed to have occasioned no alarm to my family, since they knew not of my intention to spend the night abroad. Thus unsatisfactorily terminated this night's adventures.

---

[11] "An animal leapt forth . . .": a panther has emerged from the cave in Clithero's place. This panther will reappear in Chapter 12 to threaten Edgar, and its presumed mate will encounter Edgar in Chapter 16's central cave scene. In these scenes, the panthers progressively develop as "savage" symbols of the violent otherness of Clithero and the Delaware Indians who appear in the novel's second half. For more on the iconographic connection between these animals, Clithero, and the Delawares, see the Introduction.

Chapter III

THE ensuing day was spent, partly in sleep, and partly in languor and disquietude. I incessantly ruminated on the incidents of the last night. The scheme that I had formed was defeated. Was it likely that this unknown person would repeat his midnight visits to the Elm? If he did, and could again be discovered, should I resolve to undertake a new pursuit, which might terminate abortively, or in some signal disaster? But what proof had I that the same rout would be taken, and that he would again inter himself alive in the same spot? Or, if he did, since his reappearance would sufficiently prove that the cavern was not dangerous, and that he who should adventure in, might hope to come out again in safety, why not enter it after him? What could be the inducements of this person to betake himself to subterranean retreats? The basis of all this region is *limestone;* a substance that eminently abounds in rifts and cavities. These, by the gradual decay of their cementing parts, frequently make their appearance in spots where they might have been least expected. My attention has often been excited by the hollow sound which was produced by my casual footsteps, and which shewed me that I trod upon the roof of caverns. A mountain-cave and the rumbling of an unseen torrent, are appendages of this scene, dear to my youthful imagination. Many of romantic structure[1] were found within the precincts of Norwalk.

These I had industriously sought out; but this had hitherto escaped my observation, and I formed the resolution of sometime exploring it. At present I determined to revisit the Elm, and dig in the spot where this person had been employed in a similar way. It might be that something was here deposited which might exhibit this transaction in a new light. At the suitable hour, on the ensuing night, I took my former stand. The person again appeared. My intention to dig was to be carried into effect on condition of his absence, and was, consequently, frustrated.

Instead of rushing on him, and breaking at once the spell by which his senses were bound, I concluded, contrary to my first design, to wait his departure, and allow myself to be conducted whithersoever he pleased. The track into which he now led me was different from the former one. It was a maze, oblique, circuitous, upward and downward, in a degree which only could take place in a region so remarkably irregular in surface, so abounding with hillocks and steeps, and pits and brooks as *Solebury.* It seemed to be the sole end of his labours to bewilder or fatigue his pursuer, to pierce into the deepest thickets, to plunge into the darkest cavities, to ascend the most difficult heights, and approach the slippery and tremulous verge of the dizziest precipices.

---

[1] "Romantic structure": the descriptions of wilderness settings throughout the novel make use of eighteenth-century aesthetic categories, notably the romantic, the picturesque, and the sublime. Here the aesthetic overtones of the term "romantic" are applied directly to the landscape. "Romantic" also implies a response based in the senses or in reverie, rather than in calculated thought. See the Introduction and Related Texts for more on reverie, and its relation to sleep-walking and sentimental love in Erasmus Darwin's *Zoönomia.*

I disdained to be outstripped in this career. All dangers were overlooked, and all difficulties defied. I plunged into obscurities, and clambered over obstacles, from which, in a different state of mind, and with a different object of pursuit, I should have recoiled with invincible timidity. When the scene had passed, I could not review the perils I had undergone without shuddering.

At length my conductor struck into a path which, compared with the ruggedness of that which we had lately trodden, was easy and smooth. This track led us to the skirt of the wilderness, and at no long time we reached an open field, when a dwelling appeared, at a small distance, which I speedily recognized to be that belonging to Inglefield. I now anticipated the fulfilment of my predictions. My conductor directed his steps towards the barn, into which he entered by a small door.

How were my doubts removed! This was no other than Clithero Edny. There was nothing in his appearance incompatible with this conclusion. He and his fellow servant occupied an apartment in the barn as a lodging room. This arduous purpose was accomplished, and I retired to the shelter of a neighbouring shed, not so much to repose myself after the fatigues of my extraordinary journey, as to devise farther expedients.

Nothing now remained but to take Clithero to task; to repeat to him the observations of the two last nights; to unfold to him my conjectures and suspicions; to convince him of the rectitude of my intentions, and to extort from him a disclosure of all the circumstances connected with the death of Waldegrave, which it was in his power to communicate.

In order to obtain a conference, I resolved to invite him to my uncle's to perform a certain piece of work for me under my own eyes. He would, of course, spend the night with us, and in the evening I would make an opportunity of entering into conversation with him.

A period of the deepest deliberation was necessary to qualify myself for performing suitably my part in this projected interview. I attended to the feelings that were suggested in this new state of my knowledge. I found reason to confide in my newly acquired equanimity. Remorse, said I, is an ample and proper expiation for all offences. What does vengeance desire but to inflict misery? If misery come, its desires are accomplished. It is only the obdurate and exulting criminal that is worthy of our indignation. It is common for pity to succeed the bitterest suggestions of resentment. If the vengeful mind be delighted with the spectacle of woes of its own contriving, at least its canine hunger is appeased,[2] and thenceforth, its hands are inactive.

On the evening of the next day, I paid a visit to Inglefield. I wished to impart to him the discoveries that I had made, and to listen to his reflections on the subject. I likewise desired to obtain all possible information from the family respecting the conduct of Clithero.

---

[2] "If the vengeful mind be delighted . . . at least its canine hunger is appeased": by comparing revenge to the predatory behavior of hungry dogs, Edgar foreshadows the dogs who will accompany the Delaware Indian Old Deb and her embodiment of her clan's desire for revenge. See also the note concerning the appearance of Deb and her dogs in Chapter 20 (note 20.4).

My friend received me with his usual kindness. Thou art no stranger to his character; thou knowest with what paternal affection I have ever been regarded by this old man; with what solicitude the wanderings of my reason and my freaks of passion, have been noted and corrected by him.[3] Thou knowest his activity to save the life of thy brother, and the hours that have been spent by him, in aiding my conjectures as to the cause of his death, and inculcating the lessons of penitence and duty.

The topics which could not but occur at such a meeting, were quickly discussed, and I hastily proceeded to that subject which was nearest my heart. I related the adventures of the two preceding nights, and mentioned the inference to which they irresistably led.

He said that this inference coincided with suspicions he had formed, since our last interview, in consequence of certain communications from his house-keeper. It seems the character of Clithero, had, from the first, exercised the inquisitiveness of this old lady. She had carefully marked his musing and melancholy deportment. She had tried innumerable expedients for obtaining a knowledge of his past life, and particularly of his motives for coming to America. These expedients, however profound and addressful,[4] had failed. He took no pains to elude them. He contented himself with turning a deaf ear to all indirect allusions and hints, and, when more explicitly questioned, with simply declaring that he had nothing to communicate worthy of her notice.

During the day he was a sober and diligent workman. His evenings he spent in incommunicative silence. On sundays, he always rambled away,[5] no one knew whither, and without a companion. I have already observed that he and his fellow servant occupied the same apartment in the barn. This circumstance was not unattended to by Miss Inglefield. The name of Clithero's companion was Ambrose. This man was copiously interrogated by his mistress, and she found him by no means so refractory as the other.

Ambrose, in his tedious and confused way, related that soon after Clithero and he had become bed-fellows,[6] the former was considerably disturbed by restlessness and talking in his sleep. His discourse was incoherent. It was generally in the tone of expostulation, and appeared to be intreating to be saved from some great injury. Such phrases as these "have pity"; "have mercy," were frequently intermingled with groans, and accompanied with weeping. Sometimes he seemed to be holding conferences with some one, who was making him considerable offers on condition of his

---

[3] "The wanderings of my reason and my freaks of passion, have been noted and corrected by him": this language implies that Clithero's (and Edgar's) sleep-walking and physical discomposure in Norwalk are resolvable errors, not permanent, intrinsic faults.

[4] "Addressful": skillful, clever, adroit.

[5] "On sundays, he always rambled away . . .": another indication that Clithero does not belong to the same Christian sect as the villagers, since he is left free from their religious meetings.

[6] "Bed-fellows": in this period servants and farmhands did not necessarily have the luxury of their own bed and had to share.

performing some dangerous service. What he said, in his own person, and in answer to his imaginary tempter, testified the utmost reluctance.

Ambrose had no curiosity on the subject. As this interruption prevented him at first from sleeping, it was his custom to put an end to the dialogue, by awakening his companion, who betrayed tokens of great alarm and dejection, on discovering how he had been employed, he would solicitously inquire what were the words that he had uttered; but Ambrose's report was seldom satisfactory, because he had attended to them but little, and because he begrudged every moment in which he was deprived of his accustomed repose.

Whether Clithero had ceased from this practice, or habit had reconciled his companion to the sounds, they no longer occasioned any interruption to his slumber.

No one appeared more shocked than he at the death of Waldegrave. After this event his dejection suddenly increased. This symptom was observed by the family, but none but the house-keeper took the trouble to notice it to him, or build conjectures on the incident. During nights, however, Ambrose experienced a renewal of his ancient disturbances. He remarked that Clithero, one night, had disappeared from his side. Ambrose's range of reflection was extremely narrow. Quickly falling asleep, and finding his companion beside him when he awoke, he dismissed it from his mind.

On several ensuing nights he awakened in like manner, and always found his companion's place empty. The repetition of so strange an incident at length incited him to mention it to Clithero. The latter was confounded at this intelligence. He questioned Ambrose with great anxiety as to the particulars of this event, but he could gain no satisfaction from the stupid inattention of the other. From this time there was a visible augmentation of his sadness. His fits of taciturnity became more obstinate, and a deeper gloom sat upon his brow.

There was one other circumstance, of particular importance, mentioned by the house-keeper. One evening some one on horseback, stopped at this gate. He rattled at the gate, with an air of authority, in token of his desire that some one would come from the house. Miss Inglefield was employed in the kitchen, from a window of which she perceived who it was that made the signal. Clithero happened, at the same moment, to be employed near her. She, therefore, desired him to go and see whom the stranger wanted. He laid aside his work and went. The conference lasted above five minutes. The length of it excited in her a faint degree of surprise, inducing her to leave her employment, and pay an unintermitted attention to the scene. There was nothing, however, but its duration that rendered it remarkable.

Clithero at length entered, and the traveller proceeded. The countenance of the former betrayed a degree of perturbation which she had never witnessed before. The muscles of his face was distorted and tremulous. He immediately sat down to his work, but he seemed, for some time, to have lost all power over his limbs. He struggled to avoid the sight of the lady, and his gestures, irresolute, or misdirected, betokened the deepest dismay. After some time, he recovered, in some degree, his self-possession; but, while the object was viewed through a new medium, and the change existed only in the imagination of the observer, a change was certainly discovered.

These circumstances were related to me by Inglefield and corroborated by his house-keeper. One consequence inevitably flowed from them. The sleep-walker, he who had led me through so devious a tract, was no other than Clithero. There was, likewise, a strong relation between this person and him who stopped at the gate.[7] What was the subject of discourse between them? In answer to Miss Inglefield's interrogatories, he merely said that the traveller inquired whither the road led, which at a small distance forward, struck out of the principal one. Considering the length of the interview it was not likely that this was the only topic.

My determination to confer with him in private acquired new force from these reflections. Inglefield assented to my proposal. His own affairs would permit the absence of his servant for one day. I saw no necessity for delay, and immediately made my request to Clithero. I was fashioning an implement, I told him, with respect to which I could not wholly depend upon my own skill. I was acquainted with the dexterity of his contrivances, and the neatness of his workmanship. He readily consented to assist me on this occasion. Next day he came. Contrary to my expectation, he prepared to return home in the evening. I urged him to spend the night with us; but no: It was equally convenient, and more agreeable to him, to return.

I was not aware of this resolution. I might, indeed, have foreseen, that, being conscious of his infirmity, he would desire to avoid the scrutiny of strangers. I was painfully disconcerted, but it occurred to me, that the best that could be done, was to bear him company, and seize some opportunity, during this interval, of effecting my purpose. I told him, that since he would not remain, I cared not if, for the sake of recreation, and of a much more momentous purpose, I went along with him. He tacitly, and without apparent reluctance, consented to my scheme, and accordingly, we set off together. This was an awful crisis. The time had now come, that was to dissipate my uncertainty. By what means should I introduce a topic so momentous and singular? I had been qualified by no experience for rightly conducting myself on so critical an emergency. My companion preserved a mournful and inviolable silence. He afforded me no opening, by which I might reach the point in view. His demeanour was sedate, while I was almost disabled, by the confusion of my thoughts, to utter a word.

It was a dreadful charge that I was about to insinuate. I was to accuse my companion of nothing less than murder. I was to call upon him for an avowal of his guilt. I was to state the grounds of my suspicions, and desire him to confute, or confirm them. In doing this, I was principally stimulated by an ungovernable curiosity; yet, if I intended not the conferring of a benefit, I did not, at least, purpose the infliction of evil. I persuaded myself, that I was able to exclude from my bosom, all sanguinary or vengeful impulses; and that, whatever should be the issue of this conversation, my equanimity would be unsubdued.

---

[7] "There was, likewise, a strong relation between this person and him who stopped at the gate": the novel never explains who this stranger was or why his visit causes Clithero such anxiety.

I revolved various modes of introducing the topic, by which my mind was engaged. I passed rapidly from one to another. None of them were sufficiently free from objection, to allow me to adopt it. My perplexity became, every moment, more painful, and my ability to extricate myself, less.

In this state of uncertainty, so much time elapsed, that the Elm at length appeared in sight. This object had somewhat of a mechanical influence upon me. I stopped short, and seized the arm of my companion. Till this moment, he appeared to have been engrossed by his own reflections, and not to have heeded those emotions, which must have been sufficiently conspicuous in my looks.

This action recalled him from his reverie. The first idea that occurred to him, when he had noticed my behaviour, was, that I was assailed by some sudden indisposition.

What is the matter, said he, in a tone of anxiety: Are you not well?

Yes, replied I, perfectly well; but stop a moment; I have something to say to you.

To me? answered he, with surprise.

Yes, said I, let us turn down this path, pointing at the same time, to that along which I had followed him the preceding night.

He now partook, in some degree, of my embarrassment.

Is there any thing particular? said he, in a doubting accent. There he stopped.

Something, I answered, of the highest moment. Go with me down this path. We shall be in less danger of interruption.

He was irresolute and silent, but seeing me remove the bars and pass through them, he followed me. Nothing more was said till we entered the wood. I trusted to the suggestions of the moment. I had now gone too far to recede, and the necessity that pressed upon me, supplied me with words. I continued.

This is a remarkable spot. You may wonder why I have led you to it. I ought not to keep you in suspence. There is a tale connected with it, which I am desirous of telling you. For this purpose I have brought you hither. Listen to me.

I then recapitulated the adventures of the two preceding nights. I added nothing, nor retrenched any thing. He listened in the deepest silence. From every incident, he gathered new cause of alarm. Repeatedly he wiped his face with his handkerchief, and sighed deeply. I took no verbal notice of these symptoms. I deemed it incumbent on me to repress nothing. When I came to the concluding circumstance, by which his person was identified, he heard me, without any new surprise. To this narrative, I subjoined the inquiries that I had made at Inglefield's, and the result of those inquiries. I then continued in these words.

You may ask why I subjected myself to all this trouble? The mysteriousness of these transactions would have naturally suggested curiosity in any one. A transient passenger would probably have acted as I have done. But I had motives peculiar to myself. Need I remind you of a late disaster? That it happened beneath the shade of this tree? Am I not justified in drawing certain inferences from your behaviour? What they are, I leave you to judge. Be it your task, to confute, or confirm them. For this end I have conducted you hither.

My suspicions are vehement. How can they be otherwise? I call upon you to say whether they be just.

The spot where we stood was illuminated by the moon, that had now risen, though all around was dark. Hence his features and person were easily distinguished. His hands hung at his side. His eyes were downcast, and he was motionless as a statue. My last words seemed scarcely to have made any impression on his sense. I had no need to provide against the possible suggestions of revenge. I felt nothing but the tenderness of compassion. I continued, for some time, to observe him in silence, and could discover no tokens of a change of mood. I could not forbear, at last, to express my uneasiness at the fixedness of his features and attitude.

Recollect yourself. I mean not to urge you too closely. This topic is solemn, but it need not divest you of the fortitude becoming a man.

The sound of my voice startled him. He broke from me, looked up, and fixed his eyes upon me with an expression of affright. He shuddered and recoiled as from a spectre. I began to repent of my experiment. I could say nothing suitable to this occasion. I was obliged to stand a silent and powerless spectator, and to suffer this paroxysm to subside of itself. When its violence appeared to be somewhat abated, I resumed.

I can feel for you. I act not thus, in compliance with a temper that delights in the misery of others. The explanation that I have solicited is no less necessary for your sake than for mine. You are no stranger to the light in which I viewed this man. You have witnessed the grief which his fate occasioned, and the efforts that I made to discover, and drag to punishment his murderer. You heard the execrations[8] that I heaped upon him, and my vows of eternal revenge. You expect that, having detected the offender, I will hunt him to infamy and death. You are mistaken. I consider the deed as sufficiently expiated.

I am no stranger to your gnawing cares. To the deep and incurable despair that haunts you, to which your waking thoughts are a prey, and from which sleep cannot secure you. I know the enormity of your crime, but I know not your inducements. Whatever they were, I see the consequences with regard to yourself. I see proofs of that remorse which must ever be attendant on guilt.

This is enough. Why should the effects of our misdeeds be inexhaustible? Why should we be debarred from a comforter? An opportunity of repairing our errors may, at least, be demanded from the rulers of our destiny.

I once imagined, that he who killed Waldegrave inflicted the greatest possible injury on me. That was an error, which reflection has cured. Were futurity laid open to my view, and events, with their consequences unfolded; I might see reason to embrace the assassin as my best friend. Be comforted.[9]

He was still incapable of speaking; but tears came to his relief. Without attending to my remonstrances, he betrayed a disposition to return. I had, hitherto, hoped for some disclosure, but now feared that it was designed to be withheld. He stopped not

---

[8] "Execrations": curses.

[9] "I might see reason to embrace the assassin as my best friend. Be comforted": Edgar links rationality and progress with cooperation and distances himself from the passion of revenge.

till we reached Inglefield's piazza. He then spoke, for the first time, but in an hollow and tremulous voice.

You demand of me a confession of crimes. You shall have it. Some time you shall have it. When it will be, I cannot tell. Something must be done, and shortly.

He hurried from me into the house, and after a pause, I turned my steps homewards. My reflections, as I proceeded, perpetually revolved round a single point. These were scarcely more than a repetition, with slight variations, of a single idea.

When I awoke in the morning, I hied, in fancy, to the wilderness. I saw nothing but the figure of the wanderer before me. I traced his footsteps anew, retold my narrative, and pondered on his gestures and words. My condition was not destitute of enjoyment. My stormy passions had subsided into a calm, portentous and awful. My soul was big with expectation. I seemed as if I were on the eve of being ushered into a world, whose scenes were tremendous, but sublime. The suggestions of sorrow and malice had, for a time, taken their flight, and yielded place to a generous sympathy, which filled my eyes with tears, but had more in it of pleasure than of pain. That Clithero was instrumental to the death of Waldegrave, that he could furnish the clue, explanatory of every bloody and mysterious event, that had hitherto occurred, there was no longer the possibility of doubting. He, indeed, said I, is the murderer of excellence, and yet it shall be my province to emulate a father's clemency, and restore this unhappy man to purity, and to peace.

Day after day passed, without hearing any thing of Clithero. I began to grow uneasy and impatient. I had gained so much, and by means so unexpected, that I could more easily endure uncertainly, with respect to what remained to be known. But my patience had its limits. I should, doubtless, have made use of new means to accelerate this discovery, had not his timely appearance made them superfluous.

Sunday being at length arrived, I resolved to go to Inglefield's, seek an interview with his servant, and urge him, by new importunities, to confide to me the secret. On my way thither, Clithero appeared in sight. His visage was pale and wan, and his form emaciated and shrunk. I was astonished at the alteration, which the lapse of a week had made in his appearance. At a small distance I mistook him for a stranger. As soon as I perceived who it was, I greeted him with the utmost friendliness. My civilities made little impression on him, and he hastened to inform me, that he was coming to my uncle's, for the purpose of meeting and talking with me. If I thought proper, we would go into the wood together: and find some spot, where we might discourse at our leisure, and be exempt from interruption.

You will easily conceive with what alacrity I accepted his invitation. We turned from the road into the first path, and proceeded in silence, till the wildness of the surrounding scenery informed us, that we were in the heart of Norwalk. We lighted on a recess, to which my companion appeared to be familiar, and which had all the advantages of solitude, and was suitable to rest. Here we stopped. Hitherto my companion had displayed a certain degree of composure. Now his countenance betokened a violent internal struggle. It was a considerable time before he could command his speech. When he had so far effected the conquest of his feelings, he began.

Chapter IV

YOU call upon me for a confession of my offences. What a strange fortune is mine! That an human being, in the present circumstances, should make this demand, and that I should be driven, by an irresistable necessity to comply with it! That here should terminate my calamitous series! That my destiny should call upon me to lie down and die, in a region so remote from the scene of my crimes; at a distance, so great, from all that witnessed and endured their consequences!

You believe me to be an assassin. You require me to explain the motives that induced me to murder the innocent. While this is your belief, and this the scope of your expectations, you may be sure of my compliance. I could resist every demand but this.

For what purpose have I come hither? Is it to relate my story? Shall I calmly sit here, and rehearse the incidents of my life? Will my strength be adequate to this rehearsal? Let me recollect the motives that governed me, when I formed this design. Perhaps, a strenuousness may be imparted by them, which, otherwise, I cannot hope to obtain. For the sake of those, I consent to conjure up the ghost of the past, and to begin a tale that, with a fortitude like mine, I am not sure that I shall live to finish.

You are unacquainted with the man before you. The inferences which you have drawn, with regard to my designs, and my conduct, are a tissue of destructive errors. You, like others, are blind to the most momentous consequences of your own actions. You talk of imparting consolation. You boast the benificence of your intentions. You set yourself to do me a benefit. What are the effects of your misguided zeal, and random efforts? They have brought my life to a miserable close. They have shrouded the last scene of it in blood. They have put the seal to my perdition.

My misery has been greater than has fallen to the lot of mortals. Yet it is but beginning. My present path, full as it is of asperities, is better than that into which I must enter, when this is abandoned. Perhaps, if my pilgrimage had been longer, I might, at some future day, have lighted upon hope. In consequence of your interference, I am forever debarred from it. My existence is henceforward to be invariable. The woes that are reserved for me, are incapable alike of alleviation or intermission.

But I came not hither to recriminate. I came not hither to accuse others but myself. I know the retribution that is appointed for guilt like mine. It is just. I may shudder at the foresight of my punishment and shrink in the endurance of it; but I shall be indebted for part of my torment to the vigour of my understanding, which teaches me that my punishment is just. Why should I procrastinate my doom and strive to render my burthen more light? It is but just that it should crush me. Its procrastination is impossible. The stroke is already felt. Even now I drink of the cup of retribution. A change of being cannot aggravate my woe. Till consciousness itself be extinct, the worm that gnaws me will never perish.

Fain would I be relieved from this task. Gladly would I bury in oblivion the trans-actions of my life: but no. My fate is uniform. The dæmon[1] that controuled me at first is still in the fruition of power. I am entangled in his fold, and every effort that I make to escape only involves me in deeper ruin. I need not conceal, for all the conse-quences of disclosure are already experienced. I cannot endure a groundless imputa-tion, though to free me from it, I must create and justify imputations still more atrocious. My story may at least be brief. If the agonies of remembrance must be awakened afresh, let me do all that in me lies to shorten them.

I was born in the county of Armagh.[2] My parents were of the better sort of peasants, and were able to provide me with the rudiments of knowledge. I should doubtless have trodden in their footsteps, and have spent my life in the cultivation of their scanty fields, if an event had not happened, which, for a long time, I regarded as the most fortunate of my life; but which I now regard as the scheme of some infernal agent and as the primary source of all my calamities.[3]

My father's farm was a portion of the demesne of one who resided wholly in the metropolis, and consigned the management of his estates to his stewards and retain-ers. This person married a lady, who brought him great accession of fortune. Her wealth was her only recommendation in the eyes of her husband, whose understand-ing was depraved by the prejudices of luxury and rank, but was the least of her at-tractions in the estimate of reasonable beings.

They passed some years together. If their union were not a source of misery to the lady, she was indebted for her tranquility to the force of her mind. She was, indeed, governed, in every action of her life by the precepts of duty, while her husband lis-tened to no calls but those of pernicious dissipation. He was immersed in all the vices that grow out of opulence and a mistaken education.

---

[1] "Daemon": Clithero's reference to a demon or spirit suggests that he holds onto an irrational, backward notion that madness is caused by supernatural possession, rather than Edgar's conviction that mental illness is a medical matter than can be addressed and managed rationally.

[2] "I was born in the county of Armagh": County Armagh is the area around the city of Armagh in Ulster, Northern Ireland. Large numbers of Irish settlers emigrated to eighteenth-century Pennsyl-vania from this area, mainly belonging to Presbyterian and other dissenting Protestant groups. Ar-magh was also the site of some of the most bitter sectarian struggles of the Irish 1790s, leading to the founding of the Catholic Defender Movement and the Orange Order. In 1795 the "Armagh Out-rages" triggered the expansion of the United Irishmen, the most important organization in the failed Irish rebellion of 1796–1798. Many United Irishmen fled Ireland to Philadelphia and backcountry Pennsylvania. In the late twentieth century, the southern part of County Armagh, because of its his-tory of struggle against British rule, became the most militarized region in western Europe.

[3] "The primary source of all my calamities": Clithero is born into an Irish peasant family whose so-cial subordination is determined by the feudal land and rank system of the period. The early part of his story emphasizes his inferior "rank," "station," and "condition" as a servant in the extended household of his patroness Lorimer. His story and complex problems are predicated on his position in the late-feudal class structure of Ireland and in the colonial system of land exploitation England has imposed on Ireland. For more on Clithero's tale, see the Introduction.

Happily for his wife his career was short. He was enraged at the infidelity of his mistress, to purchase whose attachment, he had lavished two thirds of his fortune. He called the paramour, by whom he had been supplanted, to the field. The contest was obstinate, and terminated in the death of the challenger.[4]

This event freed the lady from many distressful and humiliating obligations. She determined to profit by her newly acquired independence, to live thence-forward conformable to her notions of right, to preserve and improve, by schemes of economy, the remains of her fortune, and to employ it in the diffusion of good. Her plans made it necessary to visit her estates in the distant provinces.

During her abode in the manor of which my father was a vassal, she visited his cottage. I was at that time a child. She was pleased with my vivacity and promptitude, and determined to take me under her own protection. My parents joyfully acceded to her proposal, and I returned with her to the capital.

She had an only son of my own age. Her design, in relation to me, was, that I should be educated with her child, and that an affection, in this way, might be excited in me towards my young master, which might render me, when we should attain to manhood, one of his most faithful and intelligent dependents. I enjoyed, equally with him, all the essential benefits of education.[5] There were certain accomplishments, from which I was excluded, from the belief that they were unsuitable to my rank and station. I was permitted to acquire others, which, had she been actuated by true discernment, she would, perhaps, have discovered to be far more incompatible with a servile station. In proportion as my views were refined and enlarged by history and science, I was likely to contract a thirst of independence, and an impatience of subjection and poverty.

When the period of childhood and youth was past, it was thought proper to send her son, to improve his knowledge and manners, by a residence on the continent. This young man was endowed with splendid abilities. His errors were the growth of his condition. All the expedients that maternal solicitude and wisdom could suggest, were employed to render him an useful citizen. Perhaps this wisdom was attested by the large

---

[4]"Terminated in the death of the challenger": Lorimer's first husband, in other words, is an aristocrat who wasted much of Lorimer's fortune, which became his in marriage, on wasteful extravagance and mistresses. His acts illustrate both the vices of the feudal aristocracy and the gender system that gives him ownership and legal authority over his wife's person and wealth. His death in a duel over a mistress is a final illustration of both problems. Many novels of the period, from Samuel Richardson's *Clarissa* (1748) to Brown, use dueling, already archaic in this period, as an example of the decadence of the landed aristocracy. Dueling exemplifies a regressive, irrational, aristocratic determination of justice by force, rather than modern, middle-class adjudication through law. In his *Enquiry Concerning Political Justice* (1793), a crucial text for Brown (see the Related Texts in this volume), William Godwin writes that dueling "was originally invented by barbarians for the gratification of revenge."

[5] "All the essential benefits of education . . .": the job of tutoring a noble's children was a common, and more lucrative and secure, source of employment for eighteenth-century intellectuals than a university professorship. Many influential figures of the period, such as John Locke and Adam Smith, were private tutors.

share of excellence which he really possessed; and, that his character was not unblemished, proved only, that no exertions could preserve him from the vices that are inherent in wealth and rank, and which flow from the spectacle of universal depravity.[6]

As to me, it would be folly to deny, that I had benefited by my opportunities of improvement. I fulfilled the expectation of my mistress, in one respect. I was deeply imbued with affection for her son, and reverence for herself. Perhaps the force of education was evinced in those particulars, without reflecting any credit on the directors of it. Those might merit the name of defects, which were regarded by them as accomplishments. My unfavorable qualities, like those of my master, were imputed to my condition, though, perhaps, the difference was advantageous to me, since the vices of servitude are less hateful than those of tyranny.

It was resolved that I should accompany my master in his travels, in quality of favourite domestic. My principles, whatever might be their rectitude, were harmonious and flexible. I had devoted my life to the service of my patron. I had formed conceptions of what was really conducive to his interest, and was not to be misled by specious appearances. If my affection had not stimulated my diligence, I should have found sufficient motives in the behaviour of his mother. She condescended to express her reliance on my integrity and judgment. She was not ashamed to manifest, at parting, the tenderness of a mother, and to acknowledge that, all her tears were not shed on her son's account. I had my part in the regrets that called them forth.

During our absence, I was my master's constant attendant. I corresponded with his mother, and made the conduct of her son the principal theme of my letters. I deemed it my privilege, as well as duty, to sit in judgment on his actions, to form my opinions without regard to selfish considerations, and to avow them whenever the avowal tended to benefit. Every letter which I wrote, particularly those in which his behaviour was freely criticised, I allowed him to peruse. I would, on no account, connive at, or participate in the slightest irregularity. I knew the duty of my station, and assumed no other controul than that which resulted from the avoiding of deceit, and the open expression of my sentiments. The youth was of a noble spirit, but his firmness was wavering. He yielded to temptations which a censor less rigorous than I would have regarded as venial, or, perhaps laudable. My duty required me to set before him the consequences of his actions, and to give impartial and timely information to his mother.

He could not brook a monitor. The more he needed reproof, the less supportable it became. My company became every day less agreeable, till at length, there appeared a necessity of parting. A seperation took place, but not as enemies. I never lost his respect. In his representations to his mother, he was just to my character and services. My dismission was not allowed to injure my fortune, and his mother considered this event merely as a new proof of the inflexible consistency of my principles.

---

[6] "The vices that are inherent in wealth and rank . . . universal depravity": as with the aforementioned "prejudices of luxury and rank" (six paragraphs earlier), Clithero's language implies that the nonegalitarian idea that money and aristocratic titles make some people superior to others is not simply a matter of prejudice but inevitably leads to corrupt behavior.

On this change in my situation, she proposed to me to become a member of her own family. No proposal could be more acceptable. I was fully acquainted with the character of this lady, and had nothing to fear from injustice and caprice. I did not regard her with filial familiarity, but my attachment and reverence would have done honour to that relation. I performed for her the functions of a steward. Her estates in the city were put under my direction. She placed boundless confidence in my discretion and integrity, and consigned to me the payment, and in some degree, the selection and government of her servants. My station was a servile one, yet most of the evils of servitude were unknown to me. My personal ease and independence were less infringed than that of those who are accounted the freest members of society. I derived a sort of authority and dignity from the receipt and disbursement of money. The tenants and debtors of the lady were, in some respects, mine. It was, for the most part, on my justice and lenity that they depended for their treatment. My lady's household establishment was large and opulent. Her servants were my interiors and menials. My leisure was considerable, and my emoluments[7] large enough to supply me with every valuable instrument of improvement or pleasure.

These were reasons why I should be contented with my lot. These circumstances alone would have rendered it more eligible than any other, but it had additional, and far more powerful recommendations, arising from the character of Mrs. Lorimer, and from the relation in which she allowed me to stand to her.

How shall I enter upon this theme? How shall I expatiate upon excellencies, which it was my fate to view in their genuine colours, to adore with an immeasurable and inextinguishable ardour, and which, nevertheless, it was my hateful task to blast and destroy? Yet I will not be spared. I shall find in the rehearsal, new incitements to sorrow. I deserve to be supreme in misery, and will not be denied the full measure of a bitter retribution.

No one was better qualified to judge of her excellencies. A casual spectator might admire her beauty, and the dignity of her demeanour. From the contemplation of those, he might gather motives for loving or revering her. Age was far from having withered her complexion, or destroyed the evenness of her skin; but no time could rob her of the sweetness and intelligence which animated her features. Her habitual beneficence was bespoken in every look. Always in search of occasions for doing good, always meditating scenes of happiness, of which she was the author, or of distress, for which she was preparing relief, the most torpid insensibility was, for a time, subdued, and the most depraved smitten by charms, of which, in another person, they would not perhaps have been sensible.

A casual visitant might enjoy her conversation, might applaud the rectitude of her sentiments, the richness of her elocution, and her skill in all the offices of politeness. But it was only for him, who dwelt constantly under the same roof, to mark the inviolable consistency of her actions and opinions, the ceaseless flow of her candour, her cheerfulness, and her benevolence. It was only for one who witnessed her behaviour at all hours, in sickness and in health, her management of that great instrument

---

[7] "Emoluments": salary or profit from one's position.

of evil and good, money, her treatment of her son, her menials, and her kindred, rightly to estimate her merits.

The intercourse between us was frequent, but of a peculiar kind. My office in her family required me often to see her, to submit schemes to her consideration, and receive her directions. At these times she treated me in a manner, in some degree, adapted to the difference of rank, and the inferiority of my station, and yet widely dissimilar from that, which a different person would have adopted, in the same circumstances. The treatment was not that of an equal and a friend, but still more remote was it from that of a mistress. It was merely characterised by affability and condescention,[8] but as such it had no limits.

She made no scruple to ask my council in every pecuniary affair, to listen to my arguments, and decide conformably to what, after sufficient canvassings and discussions, should appear to be right. When the direct occasions of our interview were dismissed, I did not of course withdraw. To detain or dismiss me was indeed at her option, but, if no engagement interfered, she would enter into general conversation. There was none who could with more safety to herself have made the world her confessor; but the state of society in which she lived, imposed certain limitations on her candour. In her intercourse with me there were fewer restraints than on any other occasion. My situation had made me more intimately acquainted with domestic transactions, with her views respecting her son, and with the terms on which she thought proper to stand with those whom old acquaintance or kindred gave some title to her good offices. In addition to all those motives to a candid treatment of me, there were others which owed their efficacy to her maternal regard for me, and to the artless and unsuspecting generosity of her character.

Her hours were distributed with the utmost regularity, and appropriated to the best purposes. She selected her society without regard to any qualities but probity and talents. Her associates were numerous, and her evening conversations embellished with all that could charm the senses or instruct the understanding. This was a chosen field for the display of her magnificence, but her grandeur was unostentatious, and her gravity unmingled with hautiness. From these my station excluded me, but I was compensated by the freedom of her communications in the intervals. She found pleasure in detailing to me the incidents that passed on those occasions, in rehearsing conversations and depicting characters. There was an uncommon portion of dramatic merit in her recitals, besides valuable and curious information. One uniform effect was produced in me by this behaviour. Each day, I thought it impossible for my attachment to receive any new accessions, yet the morrow was sure to produce some new emotion of respect or of gratitude, and to set the unrivalled accomplishments of this lady in a new and more favourable point of view. I contemplated no change in my condition. The necessity of change, whatever were the alternative, would have been a subject of piercing regret. I deemed my life a cheap sacrifice in her

---

[8] "Condescention": in this usage, to be condescending has a positive sense of treating someone of lower social rank as one's equal, not the negative sense of implying one's superiority to another.

cause. No time would suffice to discharge the debt of gratitude that was due to her. Yet it was continually accumulating. If an anxious thought ever invaded my bosom it arose from this source.

It was no difficult task faithfully to execute the functions assigned to me. No merit could accrue to me from this source. I was exposed to no temptation. I had passed the feverish period of youth. No contagious example had contaminated my principles. I had resisted the allurements of sensuality and dissipation incident to my age. My dwelling was in pomp and splendour. I had amassed sufficient to secure me, in case of unforeseen accidents, in the enjoyment of competence. My mental resources were not despicable, and the external means of intellectual gratification were boundless, I enjoyed an unsullied reputation. My character was well known in that sphere which my lady occupied, not only by means of her favourable report, but in numberless ways in which it was my fortune to perform personal services to others.

Chapter V

MRS. LORIMER had a twin brother. Nature had impressed the same image upon them, and had modelled them after the same pattern. The resemblance between them was exact to a degree almost incredible. In infancy and childhood they were perpetually liable to be mistaken for each other. As they grew up nothing to a superficial examination appeared to distinguish them but the sexual characteristics. A sagacious observer would, doubtless, have noted the most essential differences. In all those modifications of the features which are produced by habits and sentiments, no two persons were less alike. Nature seemed to have intended them as examples of the futility of those theories, which ascribe every thing to conformation and instinct, and nothing to external circumstances; in what different modes the same materials may be fashioned, and to what different purposes the same materials may be applied. Perhaps the rudiments of their intellectual character as well as of their form, were the same; but the powers, that in one case, were exerted in the cause of virtue, were, in the other, misapplied to sordid and flagitious purposes.

Arthur Wiatte, that was his name, had ever been the object of his sister's affection. As long as he existed she never ceased to labour in the promotion of his happiness. All her kindness was repaid by a stern and inexorable hatred. This man was an exception to all the rules which govern us in our judgments of human nature. He exceeded in depravity all that has been imputed to the arch-foe of mankind. His wickedness was without any of those remorseful intermissions from which it has been supposed that the deepest guilt is not entirely exempt. He seemed to relish no food but pure unadulterated evil. He rejoiced in proportion to the depth of that distress of which he was the author.

His sister, by being placed most within the reach of his enmity, experienced its worst effects. She was the subject on which, by being acquainted with the means of influencing her happiness, he could try his malignant experiments with most hope of success. Her parents being high in rank and wealth, the marriage of their daughter was, of course, an object of anxious attention. There is no event on which our felicity and usefulness more materially depends, and with regard to which, therefore, the freedom of choice and the exercise of our own understanding ought to be less infringed, but this maxim is commonly disregarded in proportion to the elevation of our rank and extent of our property.[1]

---

[1] "The elevation of our rank and extent of our property": Lorimer, in other words, is a landed aristocrat. This section of Clithero's story explains how Lorimer's parents and brother Arthur Wiatte oppose her initial desire to marry Sarsefield, a character who will be introduced in Chapter 6. The "imbecility" (in two paragraphs) of the parents and malice of the brother affirm the feudal-aristocratic and patriarchal principle that marriage is not an affective union of individuals but an alliance between noble families or bloodlines, arranged to maximize the power and property of each party to the agreement. In Clithero's story, the brother's status as an evil twin, the opposite of Lorimer's virtues, situates him as an embodiment of the most rapacious and tyrannical aspects of the feudal social system.

The lady made her own election,[2] but she was one of those who acted on a comprehensive plan, and would not admit her private inclination to dictate her decision. The happiness of others, though founded on mistaken views, she did not consider as unworthy of her regard. The choice was such as was not likely to obtain the parental sanction, to whom the moral qualities of their son-in-law, though not absolutely weightless in the balance, were greatly inferior to the considerations of wealth and dignity.

The brother set no value on any thing but the means of luxury and power. He was astonished at that perverseness which entertained a different conception of happiness from himself. Love and friendship he considered as groundless and chimerical, and believed that those delusions, would, in people of sense, be rectified by experience; but he knew the obstinacy of his sister's attachment to these phantoms, and that to bereave her of the good they promised was the most effectual means of rendering her miserable. For this end he set himself to thwart her wishes. In the imbecility and false indulgence of his parents he found his most powerful auxiliaries. He prevailed upon them to forbid that union which wanted nothing but their concurrence, and their consent to endow her with a small portion of their patrimony to render completely eligible. The cause was that of her happiness and the happiness of him on whom she had bestowed her heart. It behoved her, therefore, to call forth all her energies in defence of it, to weaken her brother's influence on the minds of her parents, or to win him to be her advocate. When I reflect upon her mental powers, and the advantages which should seem to flow from the circumstance of pleading in the character of daughter and sister, I can scarcely believe that her attempts miscarried. I should have imagined that all obstacles would yield before her, and particularly in a case like this, in which she must have summoned all her forces, and never have believed that she had struggled sufficiently.

Certain it is that her lot was fixed. She was not only denied the husband of her choice, but another was imposed upon her, whose recommendations were irresistible in every one's apprehension but her own. The discarded lover was treated with every sort of contumely. Deceit and violence were employed by her brother to bring his honour, his liberty, and even his life into hazard. All these iniquities produced no considerable effect on the mind of the lady. The machinations to which her love was exposed, would have exasperated him into madness, had not her most strenuous exertions been directed to appease him.

She prevailed on him at length to abandon his country, though she thereby merely turned her brother's depravity into a new channel. Her parents died without consciousness of the evils they inflicted, but they experienced a bitter retribution in the conduct of their son. He was the darling and stay of an ancient and illustrious house, but his actions reflected nothing but disgrace upon his ancestry, and threatened to bring the honours of their line to a period in his person. At their death the bulk of

---

[2] "Election": Lorimer wants to choose, to elect, her husband on the grounds of personal affinity, rather than to preserve aristocratic bloodlines or the family's wealth and property.

their patrimony devolved upon him. This he speedily consumed in gaming and riot.[3] From splendid, he descended to meaner vices. The efforts of his sister to recall him to virtue were unintermitted and fruitless. Her affection for him he converted into a means of prolonging his selfish gratifications. She decided for the best. It was no argument of weakness that she was so frequently deceived. If she had judged truly of her brother, she would have judged not only without example, but in opposition to the general experience of mankind. But she was not to be forever deceived. Her tenderness was subservient to justice. And when his vices had led him from the gaming table to the highway, when seized at length by the ministers of law, when convicted and sentenced to transportation,[4] her intercession was solicited, when all the world knew that pardon would readily be granted to a supplicant of her rank, fortune, and character, when the criminal himself, his kindred, his friends, and even indifferent persons implored her interference, her justice was inflexible:[5] She knew full well the incurableness of his depravity; that banishment was the mildest destiny that would befall him; that estrangement from ancient haunts and associates was the condition from which his true friends had least to fear.

Finding intreaties unavailing, the wretch delivered himself to the suggestions of his malice, and he vowed to be bloodily revenged on her inflexibility. The sentence was executed. That character must indeed be monstrous from which the execution of such threats was to be dreaded. The event sufficiently shewed that our fears on this head were well grounded. This event, however, was at a great distance. It was reported that the fellons, of whom he was one, mutinied on board the ship in which they had been embarked. In the affray that succeeded it was said that he was killed.

---

[3] "Riot": wanton or licentious personal behavior.

[4] "Transportation" : transportation was a British system of banishing or deporting convicted felons to penal colonies and work details overseas. This form of punishment was particularly common in the eighteenth century; it relieved pressure on expensive and overcrowded English prisons and was regarded as a humane alternative to capital punishment. Transportation was institutionalized as a form of punishment in 1717, and initially most convicts were transported to North America, particularly to the colony of Georgia, although penal colonies were also established in the West Indies, in particular Jamaica and Barbados. The beginning of the American Revolution in 1775 halted transportation to North America, and the destination of choice soon became New South Wales, Australia, where convicts were located beginning in 1788. Transportation from Ireland to New South Wales, however, did not begin until 1791. Since the timeline presented in Chapter 7 (see note 7.3) indicates that Arthur Wiatte's transportation occurred around 1776 or 1777—assuming that Brown is concerned with this level of detailed reference—this episode of transportation would have occurred at the moment when the outbreak of the American Revolution was upsetting the system and requiring new destinations for its convicts.

[5] "Her justice was inflexible": Lorimer refuses to intercede on behalf of her brother and thereby rejects the priority of the patriarchal and feudal codes that govern her family. Rejecting the honor codes of the old regime and the rights of the eldest son (primogeniture, the right of succession of the first-born) in this manner, Lorimer becomes a modernizing master of the family's property and her own destiny until she later marries Sarsefield and surrenders her wealth and independence to his husbandly control. This is why her brother Wiatte vows "to be bloodily revenged" in the next paragraph and returns to exact this revenge in Chapter 7.

Among the nefarious deeds which he perpetrated was to be numbered the seduction of a young lady, whose heart was broken by the detection of his perfidy. The fruit of this unhappy union was a daughter. Her mother died shortly after her birth. Her father was careless of her destiny. She was consigned to the care of an hireling, who, happily for the innocent victim, performed the maternal offices for her own sake, and did not allow the want of a stipulated recompence to render her cruel or neglectful.

This orphan was sought out by the benevolence of Mrs. Lorimer and placed under her own protection. She received from her the treatment of a mother. The ties of kindred, corroborated by habit, was not the only thing that united them. That resemblance to herself, which had been so deplorably defective in her brother, was completely realized in his offspring. Nature seemed to have precluded every difference between them but that of age. This darling object excited in her bosom more than maternal sympathies. Her soul clung to the happiness of her *Clarice,* with more ardour than to that of her own son. The latter was not only less worthy of affection, but their separation necessarily diminished their mutual confidence.

It was natural for her to look forward to the future destiny of *Clarice.* On these occasions she could not help contemplating the possibility of a union between her son and niece. Considerable advantages belonged to this scheme, yet it was the subject of hope rather than the scope of a project. The contingencies were numerous and delicate on which the ultimate desirableness of this union depended. She was far from certain that her son would be worthy of this benefit, or that, if he were worthy, his propensities would not select for themselves a different object. It was equally dubious whether the young lady would not think proper otherwise to dispose of her affections. These uncertainties could be dissipated only by time. Meanwhile she was chiefly solicitous to render them virtuous and wise.

As they advanced in years, the hopes that she had formed were annihilated. The youth was not exempt from egregious errors. In addition to this, it was manifest that the young people were disposed to regard each other in no other light than that of brother and sister. I was not unapprised of her views. I saw that their union was impossible. I was near enough to judge of the character of Clarice. My youth and intellectual constitution made me peculiarly susceptible to female charms. I was her play-fellow in childhood, and her associate in studies and amusements at a maturer age. This situation might have been suspected of a dangerous tendency. This tendency, however, was obviated by motives of which I was, for a long time, scarcely conscious.

I was habituated to consider the distinctions of rank as indelible.[6] The obstructions that existed, to any wish that I might form, were like those of time and space, and as, in their own nature, insuperable.[7]

---

[6] "Indelible": that which cannot be removed or erased. For Clithero, feudal status distinctions were material realities, not ideological fictions or social categories that could be challenged or changed. The past tense of the sentence seems to imply that he no longer thinks this way.

[7] "The obstructions that existed . . . were . . . insuperable": in this passage and the remainder of the chapter, Clithero's anxiety about his social status comes to the fore. The possibility of a union with Clarice produces rising tension between his attraction to the young heiress and the social status she

Such was the state of things previous to our setting out upon our travels. Clarice was indirectly included in our correspondence. My letters were open to her inspection, and I was sometimes honoured with a few complimentary lines under her own hand. On returning to my ancient abode, I was once more exposed to those sinister influences which absence had, at least, suspended. Various suitors had, meanwhile, been rejected. Their character, for the most part, had been such as to account for her refusal, without resorting to the supposition of a lurking or unavowed attachment.

On our meeting she greeted me in a respectful but dignified manner. Observers could discover in it nothing not corresponding to that difference of fortune which subsisted between us. If her joy, on that occasion, had in it some portion of tenderness, the softness of her temper, and the peculiar circumstances in which we had been placed, being considered, the most rigid censor could find no occasion for blame or suspicion.

A year passed away, but not without my attention being solicited by something new and inexplicable in my own sensations. At first I was not aware of their true cause; but the gradual progress of my feelings left me not long in doubt as to their origin. I was alarmed at the discovery, but my courage did not suddenly desert me. My hopes seemed to be extinguished the moment that I distinctly perceived the point to which they led. My mind had undergone a change. The ideas with which it was fraught were varied. The sight, or recollection of Clarice, was sure to occasion my mind to advert to the recent discovery, and to revolve the considerations naturally connected with it. Some latent glows and secret trepidations were likewise experienced, when, by some accident, our meetings were abrupt or our interviews unwitnessed; yet my usual tranquility was not as yet sensibly diminished. I could bear to think of her marriage with another without painful emotions, and was anxious only that her choice should be judicious and fortunate.

My thoughts could not long continue in this state. They gradually became more ardent and museful. The image of Clarice occurred with unseasonable frequency. Its charms were enhanced by some nameless and indefinable additions. When it met me in the way I was irresistibly disposed to stop and survey it with particular attention. The pathetic cast of her features, the deep glow of her cheek, and some catch of melting music, she had lately breathed, stole incessantly upon my fancy. On recovering from my thoughtful moods, I sometimes found my cheeks wet with tears, that had fallen unperceived, and my bosom heaved with involuntary sighs.

These images did not content themselves with invading my wakeful hours; but, likewise, incroached upon my sleep. I could no longer resign myself to slumber with the same ease as before. When I slept, my visions were of the same impassioned tenor.

There was no difficulty in judging rightly of my situation. I knew what it was that duty exacted from me. To remain in my present situation was a chimerical project.

---

represents, and his realization that the immense difference in their status (the one a peasant, the other an aristocrat, albeit the illegitimate daughter of a disgraced felon) may pose an insurmountable obstacle to any hope of union.

That time and reflection would suffice to restore me to myself was a notion equally falacious. Yet I felt an insupportable reluctance to change it. This reluctance was owing, not wholly or chiefly to my growing passion, but to the attachment which bound me to the service of my lady. All my contemplations had hitherto been modelled on the belief of my remaining in my present situation during my life. My mildest anticipations had never fashioned an event like this. Any misfortune was light in comparison with that which tore me from her presence and service. But should I ultimately resolve to separate, how should I communicate my purpose? The pain of parting would scarcely be less on her side than on mine. Could I consent to be the author of disquietude to her? I had consecrated all my faculties to her service. This was the recompence which it was in my power to make for the benefits that I had received. Would not this procedure bear the appearance of the basest ingratitude? The shaddow of an imputation like this was more excruciating than the rack.

What motive could I assign for my conduct? The truth must not be told. This would be equivalent to supplicating for a new benefit. It would more become me to lessen than increase my obligations. Among all my imaginations on this subject, the possibility of a mutual passion never occurred to me. I could not be blind to the essential distinctions that subsist among men. I could expatiate, like others, on the futility of ribbonds and titles, and on the dignity that was annexed to skill and virtue; but these, for the most part, were the incoherences of speculation, and in no degree influenced the stream of my actions, and practical sentiments. The barrier that existed in the present case, I deemed insurmountable. This was not even the subject of doubt. In disclosing the truth, I should be conceived to be soliciting my lady's mercy and intercession; but this would be the madness of presumption. Let me impress her with any other opinion than that I go in search of the happiness that I have lost under her roof. Let me save her generous heart from the pangs which this persuasion would infallibly produce.

I could form no stable resolutions. I seemed unalterably convinced of the necessity of separation, and yet could not execute my design. When I had wrought up my mind to the intention of explaining myself on the next interview, when the next interview took place my tongue was powerless. I admitted any excuse for postponing my design, and gladly admitted any topic, however foreign to my purpose.

It must not be imagined that my health sustained no injury from this conflict of my passions. My patroness perceived this alteration. She inquired with the most affectionate solicitude, into the cause. It could not be explained. I could safely make light of it, and represented it as something which would probably disappear of itself, as it originated without any adequate cause. She was obliged to acquiesce in my imperfect account.

Day after day passed in this state of fluctuation. I was conscious of the dangers of delay, and that procrastination, without rendering the task less necessary, augmented its difficulties. At length, summoning my resolution, I demanded an audience. She received me with her usual affability. Common topics were started; but she saw the confusion and trepidation of my thoughts, and quickly relinquished them. She then noticed to me what she had observed, and mentioned the anxiety which these appearances had given her. She reminded me of the maternal regard which she had always manifested towards me, and appealed to my own heart whether any thing could be said in vindication of that reserve with which I had lately treated her, and urged me as I valued her good opinion, to explain the cause of a dejection *that was too visible.*

To all this I could make but one answer: Think me not, Madam, perverse or ungrateful. I came just now to apprise you of a resolution that I had formed. I cannot explain the motives that induce me. In this case, to lie to you would be unpardonable, and since I cannot assign my true motives, I will not mislead you by false representations. I came to inform you of my intention to leave your service, and to retire with the fruits of your bounty, to my native village, where I shall spend my life, I hope, in peace.

Her surprise at this declaration was beyond measure. She could not believe her ears. She had not heard me rightly. She compelled me to repeat it. Still I was jesting. I could not possibly mean what my words imported.

I assured her, in terms still more explicit, that my resolution was taken and was unalterable, and again intreated her to spare me the task of assigning my motives.

This was a strange determination. What could be the grounds of this new scheme? What could be the necessity of hiding them from her? This mystery was not to be endured. She could by no means away with it. She thought it hard that I should abandon her at this time, when she stood in particular need of my assistance and advice. She would refuse nothing to make my situation eligible. I had only to point out where she was deficient in her treatment of me and she would endeavour to supply it. She was willing to augment my emoluments in any degree that I desired. She could not think of parting with me; but, at any rate, she must be informed of my motives.

It is an hard task, answered I, that I have imposed upon myself. I foresaw its difficulties, and this foresight has hitherto prevented me from undertaking it; but the necessity by which I am impelled, will no longer be withstood. I am determined to go; but to say why, is impossible. I hope I shall not bring upon myself the imputation of ingratitude; but this imputation, more intolerable than any other, must be borne, if it cannot be avoided but by this disclosure.

Keep your motives to yourself, said she. I have too good an opinion of you to suppose that you would practice concealment without good reason. I merely desire you to remain where you are. Since you will not tell me why you take up this new scheme, I can only say that it is impossible there should be any advantage in this scheme. I will not hear of it I tell you. Therefore, submit to my decree with a good grace.

Notwithstanding this prohibition I persisted in declaring that my determination was fixed, and that the motives that governed me would allow of no alternative.

So, you will go, will you, whether I will or no? I have no power to detain you? You will regard nothing that I can say?

Believe me, madam, no resolution ever was formed after a more vehement struggle. If my motives were known, you would not only cease to oppose, but would hasten my departure. Honour me so far with your good opinion, as to believe that, in saying this, I say nothing but the truth, and render my duty less burthensome by cheerfully acquiescing in its dictates.

I would, replied my lady, I could find somebody that has more power over you than I have. Whom shall I call in to aid me in this arduous task?

Nay, dear madam, if I can resist your intreaties, surely no other can hope to succeed.

I am not sure of that, said my friend, archly: there is one person in the world whose supplications, I greatly suspect, you would not withstand.

Whom do you mean? said I, in some trepidation.

You will know presently. Unless I can prevail upon you, I shall be obliged to call for assistance.

Spare me the pain of repeating that no power on earth can change my resolution.

That's a fib, she rejoined, with increased archness. You know it is. If a certain person intreat you to stay, you will easily comply. I see I cannot hope to prevail by my own strength. That is a mortifying consideration, but we must not part, that is a point settled. If nothing else will do, I must go and fetch my advocate. Stay here a moment.

I had scarcely time to breathe, before she returned, leading in Clarice. I did not yet comprehend the meaning of this ceremony. The lady was overwhelmed with sweet confusion. Averted eyes and reluctant steps, might have explained to me the purpose of this meeting, if I had believed that purpose to be possible. I felt the necessity of new fortitude, and struggled to recollect the motives that had hitherto sustained me.

There, said my patroness, I have been endeavouring to persuade this young man to live with us a little longer. He is determined, it seems, to change his abode. He will not tell why, and I do not care to know, unless I could shew his reasons to be ground-less. I have merely remonstrated with him on the folly of his scheme, but he has proved refractory to all I can say. Perhaps your efforts may meet with better success.

Clarice said not a word. My own embarrassment equally disabled me from speaking. Regarding us both, for some time, with a benign aspect, Mrs. Lorimer resumed, taking an hand of each and joining them together.

I very well know what it was that suggested this scheme. It is strange that you should suppose me so careless an observer as not to note, or not to understand your situation. I am as well acquainted with what is passing in your heart as you yourself are, but why are you so anxious to conceal it? You know less of the adventurousness of love than I should have suspected. But I will not trifle with your feelings.

You, Clithero, know the wishes that I once cherished. I had hoped that my son would have found, in this darling child, an object worthy of his choice, and that my girl would have preferred him to all others. But I have long since discovered that this could not be. They are nowise suited to each other. There is one thing in the next place desirable, and now my wishes are accomplished. I see that you love each other, and never, in my opinion, was a passion more rational and just. I should think my-self the worst of beings if I did not contribute all in my power to your happiness. There is not the shadow of objection to your union. I know your scruples, Clithero, and am sorry to see that you harbour them for a moment. Nothing is more unworthy of your good sense.

I found out this girl long ago. Take my word for it, young man, she does not fall short of you in the purity and tenderness of her attachment. What need is there of tedious preliminaries! I will leave you together, and hope you will not be long in coming to a mutual understanding. Your union cannot be completed too soon for my wishes. Clarice is my only and darling daughter. As to you Clithero, expect henceforth that treatment from me, not only to which your own merit intitles you, but which is due to the husband of my daughter. —With these words she retired and left us together.

Great God! deliver me from the torments of this remembrance. That a being by whom I was snatched from penury and brutal ignorance, exalted to some rank in the intelligent creation, reared to affluence and honour, and thus, at last, spontaneously endowed with all that remained to complete the sum of my felicity, that a being like this—but such thoughts must not yet be—I must shut them out, or I shall never arrive at the end of my tale. My efforts have been thus far successful. I have hitherto been able to deliver a coherent narrative. Let the last words that I shall speak afford some glimmering of my better days. Let me execute without faltering the only task that remains for me.

Chapter VI

HOW propitious, how incredible was this event! I could scarcely confide in the testimony of my senses. Was it true that Clarice was before me, that she was prepared to countenance my presumption, that she had slighted obstacles which I had deemed insurmountable, that I was fondly beloved by her, and should shortly be admitted to the possession of so inestimable a good? I will not repeat the terms in which I poured forth, at her feet, the raptures of my gratitude. My impetuosity soon extorted from Clarice, a confirmation of her mother's declaration. An unrestrained intercourse was thenceforth established between us. Dejection and languor gave place, in my bosom, to the irradiations of joy and hope. My flowing fortunes seemed to have attained their utmost and immutable height.

Alas! They were destined to ebb with unspeakably greater rapidity, and to leave me, in a moment, stranded and wrecked.

Our nuptials would have been solemnised without delay, had not a melancholy duty interferred. Clarice had a friend in a distant part of the kingdom. Her health had long been the prey of a consumption. She was now evidently tending to dissolution. In this extremity she intreated her friend to afford her the consolation of her presence. The only wish that remained was to die in her arms.

This request could not but be willingly complied with. It became me patiently to endure the delay that would thence arise to the completion of my wishes. Considering the urgency and mournfulness of the occasion, it was impossible for me to murmur, and the affectionate Clarice would suffer nothing to interfere with the duty which she owed to her dying friend. I accompanied her on this journey, remained with her a few days, and then parted from her to return to the metropolis. It was not imagined that it would be necessary to prolong her absence beyond a month. When I bade her farewell, and informed her on what day I proposed to return for her, I felt no decay of my satisfaction. My thoughts were bright and full of exultation. Why was not some intimation afforded me of the snares that lay in my path? In the train laid for my destruction, the agent had so skilfully contrived that my security was not molested by the faintest omen.

I hasten to the crisis of my tale. I am almost dubious of my strength. The nearer I approach to it, the stronger is my aversion. My courage, instead of gathering force as I proceed, decays. I am willing to dwell still longer on preliminary circumstances. There are other incidents without which my story would be lame. I retail them because they afford me a kind of respite from horrors, at the thought of which every joint in my frame trembles. They must be endured, but that infirmity may be forgiven, which makes me inclined to procrastinate my suffering.

I mentioned the lover whom my patroness was compelled, by the machinations of her brother, to discard.[1] More than twenty years had passed since their separation.

---

[1] "I mentioned the lover whom my patroness was compelled . . . to discard": this is Sarsefield, the man Lorimer's parents and brother prevented her from marrying in Chapter 5 and who will be in-

His birth was mean and he was without fortune. His profession was that of a surgeon. My lady not only prevailed upon him to abandon his country, but enabled him to do this by supplying his necessities from her own purse. His excellent understanding was, for a time, obscured by passion; but it was not difficult for my lady ultimately to obtain his concurrence to all her schemes. He saw and adored the rectitude of her motives, did not disdain to accept her gifts, and projected means for maintaining an epistolary intercourse during their separation.

Her interest procured him a post in the service of the East-India company.[2] She was, from time to time, informed of his motions. A war broke out between the Company and some of the native powers. He was present at a great battle in which the English were defeated.[3] She could trace him by his letters and by other circumstances thus far, but here the thread was discontinued, and no means which she employed could procure any tidings of him. Whether he was captive, or dead, continued, for several years, to be merely matter of conjecture.

---

troduced by name in Chapter 7. The narrative makes it clear that Sarsefield's "mean" birth "without fortune" (noted in the next sentences) was the reason Lorimer's family opposed the union.

[2] "In the service of the East-India company": Lorimer arranges a position for her lover Sarsefield with the East India Company, a powerful colonialist institution that ruled India in the service of British imperialism. The company was transformed from a joint-stock company to a large-scale ruling institution after the Battle of Plessey in 1757, just before Sarsefield begins working for it; the Battle of Plessey marked England's victory over France in India and was a turning point in the Seven Years War, a global imperial conflict that included the French and Indian War in North America. During the 1760s and 1770s, the years when the novel has Sarsefield working for the East India Company, the organization presided over a highly exploitative system of tax collection and a ruinous famine, had to be rescued from insolvency by the British government, and was established as an extension of British Parliament by the Regulating Act of 1773. In 1786 the first governor-general of India was replaced by the same Lord Cornwallis whose defeat at Yorktown in 1781 marked the end of hostilities in the American Revolution. Like the Second Anglo-Mysore War evoked in the next sentence, the East India Company situates Sarsefield and the novel's action in the larger arena of British imperialism and commerce.

[3] "A war broke out . . . the English were defeated": this is the Second Anglo-Mysore War, 1780–1784, between England (in the form of its surrogate the East India Company) and the Indian kingdom of Mysore. Because Mysore was an ally of France, Anglo-French conflict over the American Revolution (still ongoing in 1780) was a major factor in the outbreak of hostilities. The basic question in the conflict was whether England or France would colonize India. This war is linked to the American Revolution as part of the period's larger conflict between the two imperial powers. The "great battle in which the English were defeated" is the battle on September 10, 1780, at Arcot, near Madras, in which Haidar Ali defeated a British army under Colonel William Baillie. This battle is now remembered as a key episode of Indian resistance to British imperialism, the most serious military defeat the British ever experienced in India. In the context of this novel, this mention also echoes the British general Braddock's disastrous defeat in the French and Indian War. See Chapter 24 (note 24.3), where Sarsefield recalls that Edgar's uncle fought in that battle. Thus Sarsefield and Edgar's uncle are functionaries and soldiers who are formed by and still bear the suffering and wounds they incurred in the service of British imperialism.

On my return to Dublin, I found my patroness engaged in conversation with a stranger. She introduced us to each other in a manner that indicated the respect which she entertained for us both. I surveyed and listened to him with considerable attention. His aspect was noble and ingenious, but his sun-burnt and rugged features bespoke a various and boisterous pilgrimage. The furrows of his brow were the products of vicissitude and hardship, rather than of age. His accents were fiery and energetic, and the impassioned boldness of his address, as well as the tenor of his discourse, full of allusions to the past, and regrets that the course of events had not been different, made me suspect something extraordinary in his character.

As soon as he left us, my lady explained who he was. He was no other than the object of her youthful attachment, who had, a few days before, dropped among us as from the skies. He had a long and various story to tell.[4] He had accounted for his silence by enumerating the incidents of his life—He had escaped from the prisons of Hyder,[5] had wandered on foot, and under various disguises, through the northern district of Hindoostaun.[6] He was sometimes a scholar of Benares, and sometimes a disciple of the Mosque. According to the exigencies of the times, he was a pilgrim to Mecca or to Jagunaut.[7] By a long, circuitous, and perilous route, he at length arrived at the Turkish capital.[8] Here he resided for several years, deriving a precarious subsistence from the profession of a surgeon. He was obliged to desert this post, in consequence of a duel between two Scotsmen. One of them had embraced the Greek religion, and was betrothed to the daughter of a wealthy trader of that nation. He perished in the conflict, and the family of the lady not only procured the execution of his antagonist, but threatened to involve all those who were known to be connected with him in the same ruin.

His life being thus endangered, it became necessary for him to seek a new residence. He fled from Constantinople with such precipitation as reduced him to the lowest

---

[4] "He had a long and various story to tell": Sarsefield's travels during his twenty-year separation from Lorimer, outlined in this passage, make him familiar with the extent and the workings of the British empire in the late eighteenth century. He travels through Ireland, India (his time with the British East India Company and in captivity), Central Asia and Saudi Arabia, Turkey, Greece, Italy, and North America. For more on Sarsefield and imperialism, see Kamrath, "American Expectionalism and Radicalism," 376–78.

[5] "He had escaped from the prisons of Hyder": after the British defeat at Arcot, mentioned earlier, Sarsefield endured captivity in the prisons of the Indian commander Haidar (or Hyder) Ali.

[6] "He . . . had wandered on foot . . . through the northern district of Hindoostaun": Hindustan was the name given to the region that now covers Pakistan, northern India, and Bangladesh. Since Sarsefield escaped from southern India, he has walked northward.

[7] "To Mecca or to Jagunaut": after escaping from prison, Sarsefield disguises himself first as a Hindu and then as a Muslim as he travels through the holy cities of Hinduism (at Benares, the holiest city of Hinduism on the Ganges, and at Jagannath-Puri) and Islam (at Mecca, in what is now Saudi Arabia). "Jagunaut" is Brown's spelling of Jagannath or Jagannath-Puri, a holy city in India, the seat of Lord Jagannath (one of the forms of Vishnu) in Puri. See Kamrath, "American Exceptionalism and Radicalism."

[8] "The Turkish capital": Constantinople, or modern Istanbul.

poverty. He had traversed the Indian conquests of Alexander, as a mendicant. In the same character, he now wandered over the native country of Philip and Philopoemen. He passed safely through multiplied perils, and finally, embarking at Salonichi,[9] he reached Venice. He descended through the passes of the Apennine into Tuscany. In this journey he suffered a long detention from banditti, by whom he was waylaid. In consequence of his harmless department, and a seasonable display of his chirurgical skill, they granted him his life, though they, for a time restrained him of his liberty, and compelled him to endure their society. The time was not misemployed which he spent immured in caverns and carousing with robbers.[10] His details were eminently singular and curious, and evinced the acuteness of his penetration, as well the steadfastness of his courage.

After emerging from these wilds, he found his way along the banks of the Arno to Leghorn.[11] Thence he procured a passage to America, whence he had just returned, with many additions to his experience, but none to his fortune.

This was a remarkable event. It did not at first appear how far its consequences would extend. The lady was, at present, disengaged and independent. Though the passion which clouded her early prosperity was extinct, time had not diminished the worth of her friend, and they were far from having reached that age when love becomes chimerical and marriage folly. A confidential intercourse was immediately established between them. The bounty of Mrs. Lorimer soon divested her friend of all fear of poverty. At any rate, said she, he shall wander no further, but shall be comfortably situated for the rest of his life. All his scruples were vanquished by the reasonableness of her remonstrances and the vehemence of her solicitations.

A cordial intimacy grew between me and the newly arrived. Our interviews were frequent, and our communications without reserve. He detailed to me the result of his experience, and expatiated without end on the history of his actions and opinions. He related the adventures of his youth, and dwelt upon all the circumstances of

---

[9] "He now wandered over the native country of Philip and Philopoemen . . . embarking at Salonichi": that is, after Sarsefield traveled through India and the eastern parts of the empire of Alexander the Great, he traveled through Macedonia and Greece. Macedonia was the home of Alexander and his empire-making father Philip II of Macedon (382–336 BCE); Philopoemen was a Greek general (253–184 BCE) who resisted the extension of Roman empire into Greece about a century later. Both are warriors who struggle over empire. Salonichi is Thessalonica or modern Saloniki, the principal seaport of Macedonia. In May 1799, while he was writing *Edgar Huntly*, Brown published "Thessalonica: A Roman Story," a tale that dramatizes Roman imperial violence in that city.

[10] Sarsefield's second captivity is with robbers or "banditti." The plot device of being captured by a band of robbers and forced to work for them was already a generic cliché and widely used during the Enlightenment. Friedrich Schiller used the theme to great effect in his play *The Robbers* (1781). Similarly, the protagonist of William Godwin's *Caleb Williams* (1794) falls in with robbers who teach him about injustices of the British social and legal system.

[11] "Arno to Leghorn": in Tuscany, Sarsefield follows the Arno River to Leghorn, or Livorno, a port city from which he can sail to America.

his attachment to my patroness. On this subject I had heard only general details. I continually found cause, in the course of his narrative, to revere the illustrious qualities of my lady, and to weep at the calamities to which the infernal malice of her brother had subjected her.

The tale of that man's misdeeds, amplified and dramatised, by the indignant eloquence of this historian, oppressed me with astonishment. If a poet had drawn such a portrait I should have been prone to suspect the soundness of his judgment. Till now I had imagined that no character was uniform and unmixed, and my theory of the passions did not enable me to account for a propensity gratified merely by evil, and delighting in shrieks and agony for their own sake.[12]

It was natural to suggest to my friend, when expatiating on this theme, an inquiry as to how far subsequent events had obliterated the impressions that were then made, and as to the plausibility of reviving, at this more auspicious period, his claims on the heart of his friend. When he thought proper to notice these hints, he gave me to understand that time had made no essential alteration in his sentiments in this respect, that he still fostered an hope, to which every day added new vigour, that whatever was the ultimate event, he trusted in his fortitude to sustain it, if adverse, and in his wisdom to extract from it the most valuable consequences, if it should prove prosperous.

The progress of things was not unfavourable to his hopes. She treated his insinuations and professions with levity; but her arguments seemed to be urged, with no other view than to afford an opportunity of confutation; and, since there was no abatement of familiarity and kindness, there was room to hope that the affair would terminate agreeably to his wishes.

---

[12] "Delighting in shrieks and agony for their own sake": the pained sounds caused here by Wiatte's cruelty foreshadow similar sounds later emitted by the panthers and Delaware Indians in Norwalk.

Chapter VII

CLARICE, meanwhile, was absent. Her friend seemed, at the end of a month, to be little less distant from the grave than at first. My impatience would not allow me to wait till her death. I visited her, but was once more obliged to return alone. I arrived late in the city, and being greatly fatigued, I retired almost immediately to my chamber.

On hearing of my arrival, Sarsefield hastened to see me.[1] He came to my bed-side, and such, in his opinion, was the importance of the tidings which he had to communicate, that he did not scruple to rouse me from a deep sleep. . . .[2]

At this period of his narrative, Clithero stopped. His complexion varied from one degree of paleness to another. His brain appeared to suffer some severe constriction. He desired to be excused, for a few minutes, from proceeding. In a short time he was relieved from this paroxysm, and resumed his tale with an accent tremulous at first, but acquiring stability and force as he went on.

On waking, as I have said, I found my friend seated at my bed-side. His countenance exhibited various tokens of alarm. As soon as I perceived who it was, I started, exclaiming—What is the matter?

He sighed. Pardon, said he, this unseasonable intrusion. A light matter would not have occasioned it. I have waited, for two days past, in an agony of impatience, for your return. Happily, you are, at last, come. I stand in the utmost need of your council and aid.

Heaven defend! cried I. This is a terrible prelude. You may, of course, rely upon my assistance and advice. What is it that you have to propose?

Tuesday evening, he answered, I spent here. It was late before I returned to my lodgings. I was in the act of lifting my hand to the bell, when my eye was caught by a person standing close to the wall, at the distance of ten paces. His attitude was that of one employed in watching my motions. His face was turned towards me, and happened, at that moment, to be fully illuminated by the rays of a globe-lamp that hung over the door. I instantly recognized his features. I was petrified. I had no power to execute my design, or even to move, but stood, for some seconds gazing upon him. He was, in no degree, disconcerted by the eagerness of my scrutiny. He seemed perfectly indifferent to the consequences of being known. At length he slowly turned his eyes to another quarter, but without changing his posture, or the sternness of his

---

[1] "Sarsefield hastened to see me": after the introduction of this character in Chapters 5 and 6, this is the first appearance of his name. The name "Sarsefield" has associations with Irish patriotism and Ireland's long struggles against British imperialism: Patrick Sarsfield (1655–1693) was a celebrated Irish Jacobite (Catholic) commander, who fought alongside James II and French generals in Ireland in the late 1680s and later against the British in France. A minor character with the name "Sarsefield" (also a warrior) appears in Chapter 27 of Brown's novel *Ormond; or, The Secret Witness*, which appeared in early 1799, only a few months before *Edgar Huntly*.

[2] "Did not scruple to rouse me from a deep sleep": Clithero's growing anxieties are linked to sleep disturbances.

looks. I cannot describe to you the shock which this encounter produced in me. At last I went into the house, and have ever since been excessively uneasy.

I do not see any ground for uneasiness.

You do not then suspect who this person is?

No. . . .

It is Arthur Wiatte. . . .

Good heaven! It is impossible. What, my lady's brother?

The same. . . .

It cannot be. Were we not assured of his death? That he perished in a mutiny on board the vessel in which he was embarked for transportation?

Such was rumour, which is easily mistaken. My eyes cannot be deceived in this case. I should as easily fail to recognize his sister, when I first met her, as him. This is the man, whether once dead or not, he is, at present, alive, and in this city.

But has any thing since happened to confirm you in this opinion?

Yes, there has. As soon as I had recovered from my first surprise, I began to reflect upon the measures proper to be taken. This was the identical Arthur Wiatte. You know his character. No time was likely to change the principles of such a man, but his appearance sufficiently betrayed the incurableness of his habits. The same sullen and atrocious passions were written in his visage. You recollect the vengeance which Wiatte denounced against his sister. There is every thing to dread from his malignity. How to obviate the danger, I know not. I thought, however, of one expedient. It might serve a present purpose, and something better might suggest itself on your return.

I came hither early the next day. Old Gowan the porter is well acquainted with Wiatte's story. I mentioned to him that I had reason to think that he had returned. I charged him to have a watchful eye upon every one that knocked at the gate, and that if this person should come, by no means to admit him. The old man promised faithfully to abide by my directions. His terrors, indeed, were greater than mine, and he knew the importance of excluding Wiatte from these walls.

Did you not inform my lady of this?

No. In what way could I tell it to her? What end could it answer? Why should I make her miserable? But I have not done. Yesterday morning Gowan took me aside, and informed me that Wiatte had made his appearance, the day before, at the gate. He knew him, he said, in a moment. He demanded to see the lady, but the old man told him she was engaged, and could not be seen. He assumed peremtory and haughty airs, and asserted that his business was of such importance as not to endure a moment's delay. Gowan persisted in his first refusal. He retired with great reluctance, but said he should return to-morrow, when he should insist upon admission to the presence of the lady. I have inquired, and find that he has not repeated his visit. What is to be done?

I was equally at a loss with my friend. This incident was so unlooked for. What might not be dreaded from the monstrous depravity of Wiatte? His menaces of vengeance against his sister still rung in my ears. Some means of eluding them were indispensable. Could law be resorted to? Against an evil like this, no legal provision had been made. Nine years had elapsed since his transportation. Seven years was the period of his exile.[3] In returning, therefore, he had committed no crime. His person could not be lawfully molested. We were justified, merely, in repelling an attack. But suppose we should appeal to law, could this be done without the knowledge and concurrence of the lady? She would never permit it. Her heart was incapable of fear from this quarter. She would spurn at the mention of precautions against the hatred of her brother. Her inquietude would merely be awakened on his own account.

I was overwhelmed with perplexity. Perhaps if he were sought out, and some judgment formed of the kind of danger to be dreaded from him, by a knowledge of his situation and views, some expedient might be thence suggested.

But how should his haunts be discovered? This was easy. He had intimated the design of applying again for admission to his sister. Let a person be stationed near at hand, who, being furnished with an adequate description of his person and dress, shall mark him when he comes, and follow him, when he retires, and shall forthwith impart to us the information on that head which he shall be able to collect.

My friend concurred in this scheme. No better could, for the present, be suggested. Here ended our conference.

I was thus supplied with a new subject of reflection. It was calculated to fill my mind with dreary forbodings. The future was no longer a scene of security and pleasure. It would be hard for those to partake of our fears, who did not partake of our experience. The existence of Wiatte, was the canker that had blasted the felicity of my patroness. In his reappearance on the stage, there was something portentous. It seemed to include in it, consequences of the utmost moment, without my being able to discover what these consequences were.

That Sarsefield should be so quickly followed by his Arch-foe; that they started anew into existence, without any previous intimation, in a manner wholly unexpected, and at the same period. It seemed as if there lurked, under those appearances, a tremendous significance, which human sagacity could not uncover. My heart sunk within me when I reflected that this was the father of my Clarice. He by whose cruelty her mother was torn from the injoyment of untarnished honour, and consigned to infamy and an untimely grave: He by whom herself was abandoned in the helplessness of infancy, and left to be the prey of obdurate avarice, and the victim of wretches who traffic in virgin innocence: Who had done all that in him lay to devote her youth to guilt and misery. What were the limits of his power? How may he exert the parental prerogatives?[4]

To sleep, while these images were haunting me, was impossible. I passed the night in continual motion. I strode, without ceasing, across the floor of my apartment. My

---

[3] "Seven years was the period of his exile": since the novel's action occurs in 1787 and Clithero's tale is in the past of the narrative, Wiatte's absence of nine years means that his transportation occurred in the mid-1770s, probably in 1776 or 1777.

[4] "Parental prerogatives": Clarice is Wiatte's illegitimate daughter, so Wiatte's old-regime patriarchalism and desire for revenge against Lorimer now presents a threat to plans for a marriage between Clithero and Clarice.

mind was wrought to an higher pitch than I had ever before experienced. The occasion, accurately considered, was far from justifying the ominous inquietudes which I then felt. How then should I account for them?

Sarsefield probably enjoyed his usual slumber. His repose might not be perfectly serene, but when he ruminated on impending or possible calamities, his tongue did not cleave to his mouth, his throat was not parched with unquenchable thirst, he was not incessantly stimulated to employ his superfluous fertility of thought in motion. If I trembled for the safety of her whom I loved, and whose safety was endangered by being the daughter of this miscreant, had he not equal reason to fear for her whom he also loved, and who, as the sister of this ruffian, was encompassed by the most alarming perils? Yet he probably was calm while I was harassed by anxieties.

Alas! The difference was easily explained. Such was the beginning of a series ordained to hurry me to swift destruction. Such were the primary tokens of the presence of that power by whose accursed machinations I was destined to fall.[5] You are startled at this declaration. It is one to which you have been little accustomed. Perhaps you regard it merely as an effusion of phrenzy. I know what I am saying. I do not build upon conjectures and surmises. I care not indeed for your doubts. Your conclusion may be fashioned at your pleasure. Would to heaven that my belief were groundless, and that I had no reason to believe my intellects to have been perverted by diabolical instigations.

I could procure no sleep that night. After Sarsefield's departure I did not even lie down. It seemed to me that I could not obtain the benefits of repose otherwise than by placing my lady beyond the possibility of danger.

I met Sarsefield the next day. In pursuance of the scheme which had been adopted by us on the preceding evening, a person was selected and commissioned to watch the appearance of Wiatte. The day passed as usual with respect to the lady. In the evening she was surrounded by a few friends. Into this number I was now admitted. Sarsefield and myself made a part of this company. Various topics were discussed with ease and sprightliness. Her societies were composed of both sexes, and seemed to have monopolized all the ingenuity and wit that existed in the metropolis.

After a slight repast the company dispersed. This separation took place earlier than usual on account of a slight indisposition in *Mrs. Lorimer.* Sarsefield and I went out together. We took that opportunity of examining our agent, and receiving no satisfaction from him, we dismissed him, for that night, enjoining him to hold himself in readiness for repeating the experiment to-morrow. My friend directed his steps homeward, and I proceeded to execute a commission, with which I had charged myself.

A few days before, a large sum had been deposited in the hands of a banker, for the use of my lady. It was the amount of a debt which had lately been recovered. It was lodged here for the purpose of being paid on demand of her or her agents. It was my

---

[5] "That power by whose accursed machinations I was destined to fall": Clithero identifies the onset of his madness at this point. It is connected to his sleep disturbances and will be manifested in the onset of sleep-walking that he recounts in Chapter 8.

present business to receive this money. I had deferred the performance of this engagement to this late hour, on account of certain preliminaries which were necessary to be adjusted.

Having received this money, I prepared to return home. The inquietude which had been occasioned by Sarsefield's intelligence, had not incapacitated me from performing my usual daily occupations. It was a theme, to which, at every interval of leisure from business or discourse, I did not fail to return. At those times I employed myself in examining the subject on all sides; in supposing particular emergencies, and delineating the conduct that was proper to be observed on each. My daily thoughts were, by no means, so fear-inspiring as the meditations of the night had been.

As soon as I left the banker's door, my meditations fell into this channel. I again reviewed the recent occurrences, and imagined the consequences likely to flow from them. My deductions were not, on this occasion, peculiarly distressful. The return of darkness had added nothing to my apprehensions. I regarded Wiatte merely as one against whose malice it was wise to employ the most vigilant precautions. In revolving these precautions nothing occurred that was new. The danger appeared without unusual aggravations, and the expedients that offered themselves to my choice, were viewed with a temper not more sanguine or despondent than before.

In this state of mind I began and continued my walk. The distance was considerable between my own habitation and that which I had left. My way lay chiefly through populous and well frequented streets. In one part of the way, however, it was at the option of the passenger either to keep along the large streets, or considerably to shorten the journey, by turning into a dark, crooked, and narrow lane.[6] Being familiar with every part of this metropolis, and deeming it advisable to take the shortest and obscurest road, I turned into the alley. I proceeded without interruption to the next turning. One night officer, distinguished by his usual ensigns, was the only person who passed me. I had gone three steps beyond when I perceived a man by my side. I had scarcely time to notice this circumstance, when an hoarse voice exclaimed—"Damn ye villain, ye're a dead man!"

At the same moment a pistol flashed at my ear, and a report followed. This, however, produced no other effect, than, for a short space, to overpower my senses. I staggered back, but did not fall.

The ball, as I afterwards discovered, had grazed my forehead, but without making any dangerous impression. The assassin, perceiving that his pistol had been ineffectual, muttered, in an enraged tone,—This shall do your business—At the same time, he drew a knife forth from his bosom.

I was able to distinguish this action by the rays of a distant lamp, which glistened on the blade. All this passed in an instant. The attack was so abrupt that my thoughts could not be suddenly recalled from the confusion into which they were thrown. My

---

[6] "A dark, crooked, and narrow lane": the description of a street in Dublin echoes the mazy, disorienting pathways in Norwalk as if to suggest that Clithero remains caught in the same mental topography he experienced in Ireland.

exertions were mechanical. My will might be said to be passive, and it was only by retrospect and a contemplation of consequences, that I became fully informed of the nature of the scene.

If my assailant had disappeared as soon as he had discharged the pistol, my state of extreme surprise might have slowly given place to resolution and activity. As it was, my sense was no sooner struck by the reflection from the blade, than my hand, as if by spontaneous energy, was thrust into my pocket. I drew forth a pistol—

He lifted up his weapon to strike, but it dropped from his powerless fingers. He fell and his groans informed me that I had managed my arms with more skill than my adversary. The noise of this encounter soon attracted spectators. Lights were brought and my antagonist discovered bleeding at my feet. I explained, as briefly as I was able, the scene which they witnessed. The prostrate person was raised by two men, and carried into a public house, nigh at hand.

I had not lost my presence of mind. I, at once, perceived the propriety of administering assistance to the wounded man. I dispatched, therefore, one of the by-standers for a surgeon of considerable eminence, who lived at a small distance, and to whom I was well known. The man was carried into an inner apartment and laid upon the floor. It was not till now that I had a suitable opportunity of ascertaining who it was with whom I had been engaged. I now looked upon his face. The paleness of death could not conceal his well known features. It was Wiatte himself who was breathing his last groans at my feet! . . .

The surgeon, whom I had summoned, attended; but immediately perceived the condition of his patient to be hopeless. In a quarter of an hour he expired. During this interval, he was insensible to all around him. I was known to the surgeon, the landlord and some of the witnesses. The case needed little explanation. The accident reflected no guilt upon me. The landlord was charged with the care of the corse till the morning, and I was allowed to return home, without further impediment.

Chapter VIII

TILL now my mind had been swayed by the urgencies of this occasion. These reflections were excluded, which rushed tumultuously upon me, the moment I was at leisure to receive them. Without foresight of a previous moment, an entire change had been wrought in my condition.

I had been oppressed with a sense of the danger that flowed from the existence of this man. By what means the peril could be annihilated, and we be placed in security from his attempts, no efforts of mind could suggest. To devise these means, and employ them with success, demanded, as I conceived, the most powerful sagacity and the firmest courage. Now the danger was no more. The intelligence in which plans of mischief might be generated, was extinguished or flown. Lifeless were the hands ready to execute the dictates of that intelligence. The contriver of enormous evil, was, in one moment, bereft of the power and the will to injure. Our past tranquility had been owing to the belief of his death. Fear and dismay had resumed their dominion when the mistake was discovered. But now we might regain possession of our wonted confidence. I had beheld with my own eyes the lifeless corpse of our implacable adversary. Thus, in a moment, had terminated his long and flagitious career. His restless indignation, his malignant projects, that had so long occupied the stage, and been so fertile of calamity, were now at an end!

In the course of my meditations, the idea of the death of this man had occurred, and it bore the appearance of a desirable event. Yet it was little qualified to tranquilise my fears. In the long catalogue of contingencies, this, indeed, was to be found; but it was as little likely to happen as any other. It could not happen without a series of anterior events paving the way for it. If his death came from us, it must be the theme of design. It must spring from laborious circumvention and deep laid stratagems.

No. He was dead. I had killed him. What had I done? I had meditated nothing. I was impelled by an unconscious necessity. Had the assailant been my father the consequence would have been the same. My understanding had been neutral. Could it be? In a space so short, was it possible that so tremendous a deed had been executed? Was I not deceived by some portentous vision? I had witnessed the convulsions and last agonies of Wiatte. He was no more, and I was his destroyer!

Such was the state of my mind for some time after this dreadful event. Previously to it I was calm, considerate, and self-collected. I marked the way that I was going. Passing objects were observed. If I adverted to the series of my own reflections, my attention was not seized and fastened by them. I could disengage myself at pleasure, and could pass, without difficulty, from attention to the world within, to the contemplation of that without.

Now my liberty, in this respect, was at an end. I was fettered, confounded, smitten with excess of thought, and laid prostrate with wonder![1] I no longer attended to my

---

[1] "Now my liberty, in this respect, was at an end. . . . I was laid prostrate . . . with wonder": this paragraph provides the first indication of Clithero's somnambulism. Note that the term "wonder" has a

steps. When I emerged from my stupor, I found that I had trodden back the way which I had lately come, and had arrived within sight of the banker's door. I checked myself, and once more turned my steps homeward.

This seemed to be an hint for entering into new reflections. The deed, said I, is irretreivable. I have killed the brother of my patroness, the father of my love.

This suggestion was new. It instantly involved me in terror and perplexity. How shall I communicate the tidings? What effect will they produce? My lady's sagacity is obscured by the benevolence of her temper. Her brother was sordidly wicked. An hoary ruffian, to whom the language of pity was as unintelligible as the gabble of monkeys. His heart was fortified against compunction, by the atrocious habits of forty years:[2] he lived only to interrupt her peace, to confute the promises of virtue, and convert to rancour and reproach the fair fame of fidelity.

He was her brother still. As an human being, his depravity was never beyond the health-restoring power of repentance. His heart, so long as it beat, was accessible to remorse. The singularity of his birth had made her regard this being as more intimately her brother, than would have happened in different circumstances. It was her obstinate persuasion that their fates were blended. The rumour of his death she had never credited. It was a topic of congratulation to her friends, but of mourning and distress to her. That he would one day reappear upon the stage, and assume the dignity of virtue, was a source of consolation with which she would never consent to part.

Her character was now known. When the doom of exile was pronounced upon him, she deemed it incumbent on her to vindicate herself from aspersions founded on misconceptions of her motives in refusing her interference. The manuscript, though unpublished, was widely circulated. None could resist her simple and touching eloquence, nor rise from the perusal without resigning his heart to the most impetuous impulses of admiration, and enlisting himself among the eulogists of her justice and her fortitude. This was the only monument, in a written form, of her genius. As such it was engraven on my memory. The picture that it described was the perpetual companion of my thoughts.

Alas! It had, perhaps, been well for me if it had been buried in eternal oblivion. I read in it the condemnation of my deed, the agonies she was preparing to suffer, and the indignation that would overflow upon the author of so signal a calamity.

I had rescued my life by the sacrifice of his. Whereas I should have died. Wretched and precipitate coward! What had become of my boasted gratitude? Such was the zeal that I had vowed to her. Such the services which it was the business of my life to perform. I had snatched her brother from existence. I had torn from her the hope

clinical sense here, echoing Brown's language in the preface, "To the Public," when he writes that the novel will feature "one of the . . . most wonderful diseases . . . of the human frame"; see the note on this vocabulary on page 3 (note 3). Brown's language here is drawn from the medical writings of Erasmus Darwin and other eighteenth-century medical and biological scientists. See the excerpts from Darwin on somnambulism in Related Texts.

[2] Wiatte is forty years old when Clithero kills him.

which she so ardently and indefatigably cherished. From a contemptible and dastardly regard to my own safety I had failed in the moment of trial, and when called upon by heaven to evince the sincerity of my professions.

She had treated my professions lightly. My vows of eternal devotion she had rejected with lofty disinterestedness. She had arraigned my impatience of obligation as criminal, and condemned every scheme I had projected for freeing myself from the burthen which her beneficence had laid upon me. The impassioned and vehement anxiety with which, in former days, she had deprecated the vengeance of her lover against Wiatte, rung in my ears. My senses were shocked anew by the dreadful sounds "Touch not my brother. Wherever you meet with him, of whatever outrage he be guilty, suffer him to pass in safety. Despise me: abandon me: kill me. All this I can bear even from you, but spare, I implore you, my unhappy brother. The stroke that deprives him of life will not only have the same effect upon me, but will set my portion in everlasting misery."

To these supplications I had been deaf. It is true I had not rushed upon him unarmed, intending no injury nor expecting any. Of that degree of wickedness I was, perhaps, incapable. Alas! I have immersed myself sufficiently deep in crimes. I have trampled under foot every motive dear to the heart of honour. I have shewn myself unworthy the society of men.

Such were the turbulent suggestions of that moment. My pace slackened. I stopped and was obliged to support myself against a wall. The sickness that had seized my heart penetrated every part of my frame. There was but one thing wanting to complete my distraction. . . . My lady, said I, believed her fate to be blended with that of Wiatte. Who shall affirm that the persuasion is a groundless one? She had lived and prospered, notwithstanding the general belief that her brother was dead. She would not hearken to the rumour. Why? Because nothing less than indubitable evidence would suffice to convince her? Because the counter-intimation flowed from an infallible source? How can the latter supposition be confuted? Has she not predicted the event?

The period of terrible fulfilment has arrived. The same blow that bereaved *him* of life, has likewise ratified her doom.

She has been deceived. It is nothing more, perhaps, than a fond imagination. . . . It matters not. Who knows not the cogency of faith? That the pulses of life are at the command of the will? The bearer of these tidings will be the messenger of death. A fatal sympathy will seize her. She will shrink, and swoon, and perish at the news!

Fond and short-sighted wretch! This is the price thou hast given for security. In the rashness of thy thought thou said'st, Nothing is wanting but his death to restore us to confidence and safety. Lo! the purchase is made. Havock and despair, that were restrained during his life, were let loose by his last sigh. Now only is destruction made sure. Thy lady, thy Clarice, thy friend, and thyself, are, by this act, involved in irretrievable and common ruin!

I started from my attitude. I was scarcely conscious of any transition. The interval was fraught with stupor and amazement. It seemed as if my senses had been hushed in sleep, while the powers of locomotion were unconsciously exerted to bear me to my chamber.[3] By whatever means the change was effected, there I was. . . .

I have been able to proceed thus far. I can scarcely believe the testimony of my memory that assures me of this. My task is almost executed, but whence shall I obtain strength enough to finish it? What I have told is light as gossamer, compared with the insupportable and crushing horrors of that which is to come. Heaven, in token of its vengeance, will enable me to proceed. It is fitting that my scene should thus close.

My fancy began to be infected with the errors of my understanding. The mood into which my mind was plunged was incapable of any propitious intermission. All within me was tempestuous and dark. My ears were accessible to no sounds but those of shrieks and lamentations. It was deepest midnight, and all the noises of a great metropolis were hushed. Yet I listened as if to catch some strain of the dirge that was begun. Sable robes, sobs and a dreary solemnity encompassed me on all sides. I was haunted to despair by images of death, imaginary clamours, and the train of funeral pageantry. I seemed to have passed forward to a distant era of my life. The effects which were to come were already realized. The foresight of misery created it, and set me in the midst of that hell which I feared.

From a paroxysm like this the worst might reasonably be dreaded, yet the next step to destruction was not suddenly taken. I paused on the brink of the precipice,[4] as if to survey the depth of that phrensy that invaded me; was able to ponder on the scene, and deliberate, in a state that partook of calm, on the circumstances of my situation. My mind was harrassed by the repetition of one idea. Conjecture deepened into certainty. I could place the object in no light which did not corroborate the persuasion that, in the act committed, I had ensured the destruction of my lady. At length my mind, somewhat relieved from the tempest of my fears, began to trace and analize the consequences which I dreaded.

The fate of Wiatte would inevitably draw along with it that of his sister. In what way would this effect be produced? Were they linked together by a sympathy whose influence was independent of sensible communication? Could she arrive at a knowledge of his miserable end by other than verbal means? I had heard of such extraordinary co-partnerships in being and modes of instantaneous intercourse among beings locally distant. Was this a new instance of the subtlety of mind? Had she already endured his agonies, and like him already ceased to breathe?

Every hair bristled at this horrible suggestion. But the force of sympathy might be chimerical. Buried in sleep, or engaged in careless meditation, the instrument by

---

[3] "The powers of locomotion were unconsciously exerted to bear me to my chamber": the onset of Clithero's somnambulism is described in quasi-clinical terms drawn from Erasmus Darwin's *Zoönomia*.

[4] "I paused on the brink of the precipice . . .": note the frequent use of cliff edges—precipices, projectures, and so on—throughout the novel to describe psychosocial crisis points. The novel's topography and landscape reflect its central concerns.

which her destiny might be accomplished, was the steel of an assassin. A series of events, equally beyond the reach of foresight, with those which had just happened, might introduce, with equal abruptness, a similar disaster. What, at that moment, was her condition? Reposing in safety in her chamber, as her family imagined. But were they not deceived? Was she not a mangled corse? Whatever were her situation, it could not be ascertained, except by extraordinary means, till the morning. Was it wise to defer the scrutiny till then? Why not instantly investigate the truth?

These ideas passed rapidly through my mind. A considerable portion of time and amplification of phrase are necessary to exhibit, verbally, ideas contemplated in a space of incalculable brevity. With the same rapidity I conceived the resolution of determining the truth of my suspicions. All the family, but myself, were at rest. Winding passages would conduct me, without danger of disturbing them, to the hall from which double staircases ascended.[5] One of these led to a saloon above, on the east side of which was a door that communicated with a suit of rooms, occupied by the lady of the mansion. The first was an antichamber, in which a female servant usually lay. The second was the lady's own bed-chamber. This was a sacred recess, with whose situation, relative to the other apartments of the building, I was well acquainted, but of which I knew nothing from my own examination, having never been admitted into it.

Thither I was now resolved to repair. I was not deterred by the sanctity of the place and hour. I was insensible to all consequences but the removal of my doubts. Not that my hopes were balanced by my fears. That the same tragedy had been performed in her chamber and in the street, nothing hindered me from believing with as much cogency as if my own eyes had witnessed it, but the reluctance with which we admit a detestable truth.

To terminate a state of intolerable suspense, I resolved to proceed forthwith to her chamber. I took the light and paced, with no interruption, along the galleries. I used no precaution. If I had met a servant or robber, I am not sure that I should have noticed him. My attention was too perfectly engrossed to allow me to spare any to a casual object. I cannot affirm that no one observed me. This, however, was probable from the distribution of the dwelling. It consisted of a central edifice and two wings, one of which was appropriated to domestics, and the other, at the extremity of which my apartment was placed, comprehended a library, and rooms for formal, and social, and literary conferences. These, therefore, were deserted at night, and my way lay along these. Hence it was not likely that my steps would be observed.

I proceeded to the hall. The principal parlour was beneath her chamber. In the confusion of my thoughts I mistook one for the other. I rectified, as soon as I detected my mistake. I ascended, with a beating heart, the staircase. The door of the antichamber was unfastened. I entered, totally regardless of disturbing the girl who

---

[5] "Winding passages . . . from which double staircases ascended": the layout of Lorimer's mansion is now likened to Dublin's alleyways and Norwalk's wilderness passages. All three produce in Clithero emotional-psychological complexities, anxiety, and disorientation.

slept within. The bed which she occupied was concealed by curtains. Whether she were there, I did not stop to examine. I cannot recollect that any tokens were given of wakefulness or alarm. It was not till I reached the door of her own apartment that my heart began to falter.

It was now that the momentousness of the question I was about to decide, rushed with its genuine force, upon my apprehension. Appaled and aghast, I had scarcely power to move the bolt. If the imagination of her death was not to be supported, how should I bear the spectacle of wounds and blood? Yet this was reserved for me. A few paces would set me in the midst of a scene, of which I was the abhorred contriver. Was it right to proceed? There were still the remnants of doubt. My forebodings might possibly be groundless. All within might be safety and serenity. A respite might be gained from the execution of an irrevocable sentence. What could I do? Was not any thing easy to endure in comparison with the agonies of suspense? If I could not obviate the evil I must bear it, but the torments of suspense were susceptible of remedy.

I drew back the bolt, and entered with the reluctance of fear, rather than the cautiousness of guilt. I could not lift my eyes from the ground. I advanced to the middle of the room. Not a sound like that of the dying saluted my ear. At length, shaking off the fetters of hopelesness, I looked up. . . .

I saw nothing calculated to confirm my fears. Every where there reigned quiet and order. My heart leaped with exultation. Can it be, said I, that I have been betrayed with shadows? . . . But this is not sufficient. . . .

Within an alcove was the bed that belonged to her. If her safety were inviolate, it was here that she reposed. What remained to convert tormenting doubt into ravishing certainty? I was insensible to the perils of my present situation. If she, indeed, were there, would not my intrusion awaken her? She would start and perceive me, at this hour, standing at her bed-side. How should I account for an intrusion so unexampled and audacious? I could not communicate my fears. I could not tell her that the blood with which my hands were stained had flowed from the wounds of her brother.

My mind was inaccessible to such considerations. They did not even modify my predominant idea. Obstacles like these, had they existed, would have been trampled under foot.

Leaving the lamp, that I bore, on the table, I approached the bed. I slowly drew aside the curtain and beheld her tranquilly slumbering. I listened, but so profound was her sleep that not even her breathings could be overheard. I dropped the curtain and retired.

How blissful and mild were the illuminations of my bosom at this discovery. A joy that surpassed all utterance succeeded the fierceness of desperation. I stood, for some moments, wrapt in delightful contemplation. Alas! It was a luminous but transient interval. The madness, to whose black suggestions it bore so strong a contrast, began now to make sensible approaches on my understanding.

True, said I, she lives. Her slumber is serene and happy. She is blind to her approaching destiny. Some hours will at least be rescued from anguish and death.

When she wakes the phantom that soothed her will vanish. The tidings cannot be withheld from her. The murderer of thy brother cannot hope to enjoy thy smiles. Those ravishing accents, with which thou hast used to greet me, will be changed. Scouling and reproaches, the invectives of thy anger and the maledictions of thy justice will rest upon my head.

What is the blessing which I made the theme of my boastful arrogance? This interval of being and repose is momentary. She will awake but only to perish at the spectacle of my ingratitude. She will awake only to the consciousness of instantly impending death. When she again sleeps she will wake no more. I her son, I, whom the law of my birth doomed to poverty and hardship, but whom her unsolicited beneficence snatched from those evils, and endowed with the highest good known to intelligent beings, the consolations of science and the blandishments of affluence; to whom the darling of her life, the offspring in whom are faithfully preserved the lineaments of its angelic mother, she has not denied! . . . What is the recompense that I have made? How have I discharged the measureless debt of gratitude to which she is entitled? Thus! . . .

Cannot my guilt be extenuated? Is there not a good that I can do thee? Must I perpetrate unmingled evil? Is the province assigned me that of an infernal emissary, whose efforts are concentred in a single purpose and that purpose a malignant one? I am the author of thy calamities. Whatever misery is reserved for thee, I am the source whence it flows. Can I not set bounds to the stream? Cannot I prevent thee from returning to a consciousness which, till it ceases to exist, will not cease to be rent and mangled?

Yes. It is in my power to screen thee from the coming storm: to accelerate thy journey to rest. I will do it. . . .

The impulse was not to be resisted. I moved with the suddenness of lightning. Armed with a pointed implement that lay. . . . it was a dagger. As I set down the lamp, I struck the edge. Yet I saw it not, or noticed it not till I needed its assistance. By what accident it came hither, to what deed of darkness it had already been subservient, I had no power to inquire. I stepped to the table and seized it.[6]

The time which this action required was insufficient to save me. My doom was ratified by powers which no human energies can counterwork. . . . Need I go farther? Did you entertain any imagination of so frightful a catastrophe? I am overwhelmed by turns with dismay and with wonder. I am prompted by turns to tear my heart from my breast, and deny faith to the verdict of my senses.

---

[6] The dreamlike "coincidence" of a dagger appearing at this moment and in this setting, as an iconic prop for unconscious, automatized, vengeful action, is echoed in Chapter 16 when Edgar discovers "an Indian Tom-hawk" in a similar way (see note 16.5). This is one of many ways in which Brown has Edgar progressively double Clithero throughout the narrative (see the discussion of this motif in the Introduction). George Lippard's 1845 novel *The Quaker City* is dedicated to Brown and pays homage to this scene by repeating many of its details in a similar situation (Book I, Chapter 14).

Was it I that hurried to the deed? No. It was the dæmon that possessed me. My limbs were guided to the bloody office by a power foreign and superior to mine. I had been defrauded, for a moment, of the empire of my muscles. A little moment for that sufficed.

If my destruction had not been decreed why was the image of Clarice so long excluded? Yet why do I say long? The fatal resolution was conceived, and I hastened to the execution, in a period too brief for more than itself to be viewed by the intellect.

What then? Were my hands embrued in this precious blood? Was it to this extremity of horror that my evil genius was determined to urge me? Too surely this was his purpose; too surely I was qualified to be its minister.

I lifted the weapon. Its point was aimed at the bosom of the sleeper. The impulse was given. . . .

At the instant a piercing shriek was uttered behind me, and a stretched-out hand, grasping the blade, made it swerve widely from its aim. It descended, but without inflicting a wound. Its force was spent upon the bed.

O! for words to paint that stormy transition! I loosed my hold of the dagger. I started back, and fixed eyes of frantic curiosity on the author of my rescue. He that interposed to arrest my deed, that started into being and activity at a moment so pregnant with fate, without tokens of his purpose or his coming being previously imparted, could not, methought, be less than divinity.

The first glance that I darted on this being corroborated my conjecture. It was the figure and the lineaments of Mrs. Lorimer. Negligently habited in flowing and brilliant white, with features bursting with terror and wonder, the likeness of that being who was stretched upon the bed, now stood before me.

All that I am able to conceive of angel was comprised in the moral constitution of this woman. That her genius had overleaped all bounds, and interposed to save her, was no audacious imagination. In the state in which my mind then was no other belief than this could occupy the first place.

My tongue was tied. I gazed by turns upon her who stood before me, and her who lay upon the bed, and who, awakened by the shriek that had been uttered, now opened her eyes. She started from her pillow, and, by assuming a new and more distinct attitude, permitted me to recognize *Clarice herself!*

Three days before, I had left her, beside the bed of a dying friend, at a solitary mansion in the mountains of Donnegal.[7] Here it had been her resolution to remain till her friend should breathe her last. Fraught with this persuasion; knowing this to be the place and hour of repose of my lady, hurried forward by the impetuosity of my own conceptions, deceived by the faint gleam which penetrated through the curtain and imperfectly irradiated features which bore, at all times, a powerful resemblance to those of Mrs. Lorimer, I had rushed to the brink of this terrible precipice!

---

[7] "In the mountains of Donnegal": that is, in County Donegal, northwest Ireland, a considerable distance from Dublin (about 200 kilometers by land).

Why did I linger on the verge? Why, thus perilously situated, did I not throw myself headlong? The steel was yet in my hand. A single blow would have pierced my heart, and shut out from my remembrance and foresight the past and the future.

The moment of insanity had gone by, and I was once more myself. Instead of regarding the act which I had meditated as the dictate of compassion or of justice, it only added to the sum of my ingratitude, and gave wings to the whirlwind that was sent to bear me to perdition.

Perhaps I was influenced by a sentiment which I had not leisure to distribute into parts. My understanding was, no doubt, bewildered in the maze of consequences which would spring from my act. How should I explain my coming hither in this murderous guise, my arm lifted to destroy the idol of my soul, and the darling child of my patroness? In what words should I unfold the tale of Wiatte, and enumerate the motives that terminated in the present scene? What penalty had not my infatuation and cruelty deserved? What could I less than turn the dagger's point against my own bosom?

A second time, the blow was thwarted and diverted. Once more this beneficent interposer held my arm from the perpetration of a new iniquity. Once more frustrated the instigations of that dæmon, of whose malice a mysterious destiny had consigned me to be the sport and the prey.

Every new moment added to the sum of my inexpiable guilt. Murder was succeeded, in an instant, by the more detestable enormity of suicide. She, to whom my ingratitude was flagrant in proportion to the benefits of which she was the author, had now added to her former acts, that of rescuing me from the last of mischiefs.

I threw the weapon on the floor. The zeal which prompted her to seize my arm, this action occasioned to subside, and to yield place to those emotions which this spectacle was calculated to excite. She watched me in silence, and with an air of ineffable solicitude. Clarice, governed by the instinct of modesty, wrapt her bosom and face in the bed-clothes, and testified her horror by vehement, but scarcely articulate exclamations.

I moved forward, but my steps were random and tottering. My thoughts were fettered by reverie, and my gesticulations destitute of meaning. My tongue faltered without speaking, and I felt as if life and death were struggling within me for the mastery.

My will, indeed, was far from being neutral in this contest. To such as I, annihilation is the supreme good. To shake off the ills that fasten on us by shaking off existence, is a lot which the system of nature has denied to man. By escaping from life, I should be delivered from this scene, but should only rush into a world of retribution, and be immersed in new agonies.

I was yet to live. No instrument of my deliverance was within reach. I was powerless. To rush from the presence of these women, to hide me forever from their scrutiny, and their upbraiding, to snatch from their minds all traces of the existence of Clithero, was the scope of unutterable longings.

Urged to flight by every motive of which my nature was susceptible, I was yet rooted to the spot. Had the pause been only to be interrupted by me, it would have lasted forever.

At length, the lady, clasping her hands and lifting them, exclaimed, in a tone melting into pity and grief:

Clithero! what is this? How came you hither and why?

I struggled for utterance: I came to murder you. Your brother has perished by my hands. Fresh from the commission of this deed, I have hastened hither, to perpetrate the same crime upon you.

My brother! replied the lady, with new vehemence, O! say not so! I have just heard of his return from Sarsefield and that he lives.

He is dead, repeated I, with fierceness: I know it. It was I that killed him.

Dead! she faintly articulated, And by thee Clithero? O! cursed chance that hindered thee from killing me also! Dead! Then is the omen fulfilled! Then am I undone! Lost forever!

Her eyes now wandered from me, and her countenance sunk into a wild and rueful expression. Hope was utterly extinguished in her heart, and life forsook her at the same moment. She sunk upon the floor pallid and breathless. . . .

How she came into possession of this knowledge I know not. It is possible that Sarsefield had repented of concealment, and, in the interval that passed between our separation and my encounter with Wiatte, had returned, and informed her of the reappearance of this miscreant.

Thus then was my fate consummated. I was rescued from destroying her by a dagger, only to behold her perish by the tidings which I brought. Thus was every omen of mischief and misery fulfilled. Thus was the enmity of Wiatte, rendered efficacious, and the instrument of his destruction, changed into the executioner of his revenge.

Such is the tale of my crimes. It is not for me to hope that the curtain of oblivion will ever shut out the dismal spectacle. It will haunt me forever. The torments that grow out of it, can terminate only with the thread of my existence, but that I know full well will never end. Death is but a shifting of the scene, and the endless progress of eternity, which, to the good, is merely the perfection of felicity, is, to the wicked, an accumulation of woe. The self-destroyer is his own enemy; this has ever been my opinion. Hitherto it has influenced my action. Now, though the belief continues, its influence on my conduct is annihilated. I am no stranger to the depth of that abyss, into which I shall plunge. No matter. Change is precious for its own sake.

Well: I was still to live. My abode must be somewhere fixed. My conduct was henceforth the result of a perverse and rebellious principle. I banished myself forever from my native soil. I vowed never more to behold the face of my Clarice, to abandon my friends, my books, all my wonted labours, and accustomed recreations.

I was neither ashamed nor afraid. I considered not in what way the justice of the country would affect me. It merely made no part of my contemplations. I was not embarrassed by the choice of expedients, for trammeling up the visible consequences and for eluding suspicion. The idea of abjuring my country, and flying forever from the hateful scene, partook, to my apprehension, of the vast, the boundless, and strange: of plunging from the height of fortune to obscurity and indigence, corresponded with my present state of mind. It was of a piece with the tremendous and wonderful events that had just happened.

These were the images that haunted me, while I stood speechlessly gazing at the ruin before me. I heard a noise from without, or imagined that I heard it. My reverie was broken, and my muscular power restored. I descended into the street, through doors of which I possessed one set of keys, and hurried by the shortest way beyond the precincts of the city. I had laid no plan. My conceptions, with regard to the future, were shapeless and confused. Successive incidents supplied me with a clue, and suggested, as they rose, the next step to be taken.

I threw off the garb of affluence, and assumed a beggar's attire. That I had money about me for the accomplishment of my purposes was wholly accidental. I travelled along the coast, and when I arrived at one town, knew not why I should go further; but my restlessness was unabated, and change was some relief. I at length arrived at Belfast. A vessel was preparing for America. I embraced eagerly the opportunity of passing into a new world. I arrived at Philadelphia. As soon as I landed I wandered hither, and was content to wear out my few remaining days in the service of Inglefield.

I have no friends. Why should I trust my story to another? I have no solicitude about concealment; but who is there who will derive pleasure or benefit from my rehearsal? And why should I expatiate on so hateful a theme? Yet now have I consented to this. I have confided in you the history of my disasters. I am not fearful of the use that you may be disposed to make of it. I shall quickly set myself beyond the reach of human tribunals. I shall relieve the ministers of law from the trouble of punishing. The recent events which induced you to summon me to this conference, have likewise determined me to make this disclosure.

I was not aware, for some time, of my perturbed sleep. No wonder that sleep cannot soothe miseries like mine: that I am alike infested by memory in wakefulness and slumber. Yet I was anew distressed at the discovery that my thoughts found their way to my lips, without my being conscious of it, and that my steps wandered forth unknowingly and without the guidance of my will.

The story you have told is not incredible. The disaster to which you allude did not fail to excite my regret. I can still weep over the untimely fall of youth and worth. I can no otherwise account for my frequenting this shade than by the distant resemblance which the death of this man bore to that of which I was the perpetrator. This resemblance occurred to me at first. If time were able to weaken the impression which was produced by my crime, this similitude was adapted to revive and inforce them.

The wilderness, and the cave to which you followed me, were familiar to my sunday rambles. Often have I indulged in audible griefs on the cliffs of that valley. Often have I brooded over my sorrows in the recesses of that cavern. This scene is adapted to my temper. Its mountainous asperities supply me with images of desolation and seclusion, and its headlong streams lull me into temporary forgetfulness of mankind.

I comprehend you. You suspect me of concern in the death of Waldegrave. You could not do otherwise. The conduct that you have witnessed was that of a murderer. I will not upbraid you for your suspicions, though I have bought exemption from them at an high price.

Chapter IX

THERE ended his narrative. He started from the spot where he stood, and, without affording me any opportunity of replying or commenting, disappeared amidst the thickest of the wood. I had no time to exert myself for his detention. I could have used no arguments for this end, to which it is probable he would have listened. The story I had heard was too extraordinary, too completely the reverse of all my expectations, to allow me to attend to the intimations of self-murder which he dropped.

The secret, which I imagined was about to be disclosed, was as inscrutable as ever. Not a circumstance, from the moment when Clithero's character became the subject of my meditations, till the conclusion of his tale, but served to confirm my suspicion. Was this error to be imputed to credulity? Would not any one, from similar appearances, have drawn similar conclusions? Or is there a criterion by which truth can always be distinguished? Was it owing to my imperfect education that the inquietudes of this man were not traced to a deed performed at the distance of a thousand leagues, to the murder of his patroness and friend?

I had heard a tale which apparently related to scenes and persons far distant, but though my suspicions have appeared to have been misplaced, what should hinder but that the death of my friend was, in like manner, an act of momentary insanity and originated in a like spirit of mistaken benevolence?

But I did not consider this tale merely in relation to myself. My life had been limited and uniform. I had communed with romancers and historians,[1] but the impression made upon me by this incident was unexampled in my experience. My reading had furnished me with no instance, in any degree, parallel to this, and I found that to be a distant and second-hand spectator of events was widely different from witnessing them myself and partaking in their consequences. My judgement was, for a time, sunk into imbecility and confusion. My mind was full of the images unavoidably suggested by this tale, but they existed in a kind of chaos, and not otherwise, than gradually, was I able to reduce them to distinct particulars, and subject them to a deliberate and methodical inspection.

How was I to consider this act of Clithero? What a deplorable infatuation! Yet it was the necessary result of a series of ideas mutually linked and connected. His conduct was dictated by a motive allied to virtue. It was the fruit of an ardent and grateful spirit.

The death of Wiatte could not be censured. The life of Clithero was unspeakably more valuable than that of his antagonist. It was the instinct of self-preservation that

---

[1] "I had communed with romancers and historians": this phrasing echoes an important relation Brown establishes between history as the documentation of events and romance or the novel as the explanation of causes and conditions of events. Brown explains his understanding of these generic terms in his essay "The Difference Between History and Romance" (April 1800), published shortly after the appearance of *Edgar Huntly* (August 1799). For more on this topic, see this essay in the Related Texts and the discussion of Brown's novelistic method in the Introduction.

swayed him. He knew not his adversary in time enough, to govern himself by that knowledge. Had the assailant been an unknown ruffian, his death would have been followed by no remorse. The spectacle of his dying agonies would have dwelt upon the memory of his assassin like any other mournful sight, in the production of which he bore no part.

It must at least be said that his will was not concerned in this transaction. He acted in obedience to an impulse which he could not controul, nor resist. Shall we impute guilt where there is no design? Shall a man extract food for self-reproach from an action to which it is not enough to say that he was actuated by no culpable intention, but that he was swayed by no intention whatever? If consequences arise that cannot be foreseen, shall we find no refuge in the persuasion of our rectitude and of human frailty? Shall we deem ourselves criminal because we do not enjoy the attributes of deity? Because our power and our knowledge are confined by impassable boundaries?

But whence arose the subsequent intention? It was the fruit of a dreadful mistake. His intents were noble and compassionate. But this is of no avail to free him from the imputation of guilt. No remembrance of past beneficence can compensate for this crime. The scale, loaded with the recriminations of his conscience, is immovable by any counter-weight.

But what are the conclusions to be drawn by dispassionate observers? Is it possible to regard this person with disdain or with enmity? The crime originated in those limitations which nature has imposed upon human faculties. Proofs of a just intention are all that are requisite to exempt us from blame. He is thus in consequence of a double mistake. The light in which he views this event is erroneous. He judges wrong and is therefore miserable.

How imperfect are the grounds of all our decisions![2] Was it of no use to superintend his childhood, to select his instructors and examples, to mark the operations of his principles, to see him emerging into youth, to follow him through various scenes and trying vicissitudes, and mark the uniformity of his integrity? Who would have predicted his future conduct? Who would not have affirmed the impossibility of an action like this?

How mysterious was the connection between the fate of Wiatte and his sister! By such circuitous, and yet infallible means, were the prediction of the lady and the vengeance of the brother accomplished! In how many cases may it be said, as in this, that the prediction was the cause of its own fulfilment? That the very act, which considerate observers, and even himself, for a time, imagined to have utterly precluded

---

[2] "How imperfect are the grounds of all our decisions!": this is the first of several exclamations Edgar makes about the difficulties of understanding complex situations and making decisions about them. More dramatic formulations will appear late in the narrative, in Chapter 27. This difficulty underlines the novel's environmentalist argument by pointing out the pressures and limits on individual action. And given how often Edgar and the novel's other characters are mistaken, how often they make hasty judgments and jump to mistaken conclusions, the statement may also imply that enlightened action requires a rational grasp of the larger context of action rather than automatized responses based on the passions or backward-looking codes of behavior.

the execution of Wiatte's menaces, should be that inevitably leading to it. That the execution should be assigned to him, who, abounding in abhorrence, and in the act of self-defence, was the slayer of the menacer.

As the obstructor of his designs, Wiatte way-laid and assaulted Clithero. He perished in the attempt. Were his designs frustrated? . . . No, It was thus that he secured the gratification of his vengeance. His sister was cut off in the bloom of life and prosperity. By a refinement of good fortune, the voluntary minister of his malice had entailed upon himself exile without reprieve and misery without end.

But what chiefly excited my wonder was the connection of this tale with the destiny of Sarsefield. This was he whom I have frequently mentioned to you as my preceptor. About four years previous to this era,[3] he appeared in this district without fortune or friend. He desired, one evening, to be accomodated at my uncle's house. The conversation turning on the objects of his journey, and his present situation, he professed himself in search of lucrative employment. My uncle proposed to him to become a teacher, there being a sufficient number of young people in this neighbourhood to afford him occupation and subsistence. He found it his interest to embrace this proposal.

I, of course, became his pupil, and demeaned myself in such a manner as speedily to grow into a favourite. He communicated to us no part of his early history, but informed us sufficiently of his adventures in Asia and Italy, to make it plain that this was the same person alluded to by Clithero. During his abode among us his conduct was irreproachable. When he left us, he manifested the most poignant regret, but this originated chiefly in his regard to me. He promised to maintain with me an epistolary intercourse. Since his departure, however, I had heard nothing respecting him. It was with unspeakable regret that I now heard of the disappointment of his hopes, and was inquisitive respecting the measures which he would adopt in his new situation. Perhaps he would once more return to America, and I should again be admitted to the enjoyment of his society. This event I anticipated with the highest satisfaction.

At present, the fate of the unhappy Clithero was the subject of abundant anxiety. On his suddenly leaving me, at the conclusion of his tale, I supposed that he had gone upon one of his usual rambles, and that it would terminate only with the day. Next morning a message was received from Inglefield inquiring if any one knew what had become of his servant. I could not listen to this message with tranquility. I recollected the hints that he had given of some design upon his life, and admitted the most dreary forebodings. I speeded to Inglefield's. Clithero had not returned, they told me, the preceding evening. He had not apprized them of any intention to change his abode. His boxes, and all that composed his slender property, were found in their ordinary state. He had expressed no dissatisfaction with his present condition.

Several days passed, and no tidings could be procured of him. His absence was a topic of general speculation, but was a source of particular anxiety to no one but myself. My apprehensions were surely built upon sufficient grounds. From the moment

---

[3] "About four years previous to this era": since the narrative takes place in 1787, Sarsefield arrived in Pennsylvania in 1783.

that we parted, no one had seen or heard of him. What mode of suicide he had selected, he had disabled us from discovering, by the impenetrable secrecy in which he had involved it.

In the midst of my reflections upon this subject, the idea of the wilderness occurred. Could he have executed his design in the deepest of its recesses? These were unvisited by human footsteps, and his bones might lie for ages in this solitude without attracting observation. To seek them where they lay, to gather them together and provide for them a grave, was a duty which appeared incumbent on me, and of which the performance was connected with a thousand habitual sentiments and mixed pleasures.

Thou knowest my devotion to the spirit that breathes its inspiration in the gloom of forests and on the verge of streams. I love to immerse myself in shades and dells, and hold converse with the solemnities and secrecies of nature in the rude retreats of Norwalk.[4] The disappearance of Clithero had furnished new incitements to ascend its cliffs and pervade its thickets, as I cherished the hope of meeting in my rambles, with some traces of this man. But might he not still live? His words had imparted the belief that he intended to destroy himself. This catastrophe, however, was far from certain. Was it not in my power to avert it? Could I not restore a mind thus vigorous, to tranquil and wholesome existence? Could I not subdue his perverse disdain and immeasurable abhorrence of himself? His upbraiding and his scorn were unmerited and misplaced. Perhaps they argued phrensy rather than prejudice; but phrensy, like prejudice, was curable. Reason was no less an antidote to the illusions of insanity like his, than to the illusions of error.[5]

I did not immediately recollect that to subsist in this desert was impossible. Nuts were the only fruits it produced, and these were inadequate to sustain human life. If it were haunted by Clithero, he must occasionally pass its limits and beg or purloin victuals. This deportment was too humiliating and flagitious to be imputed to him. There was reason to suppose him smitten with the charms of solitude, of a lonely abode in the midst of mountainous and rugged nature; but this could not be uninterruptedly enjoyed. Life could be supported only by occasionally visiting the haunts of men, in the guise of a thief or a mendicant. Hence, since Clithero was not known to have reappeared, at any farm-house in the neighbourhood, I was compelled to conclude, either that he had retired far from this district, or that he was dead.

Though I designed that my leisure should chiefly be consumed in the bosom of Norwalk, I almost dismissed the hope of meeting with the fugitive. There were indeed two sources of my hopelessness on this occasion. Not only it was probable that Clithero had fled far away, but, should he have concealed himself in some nook or

---

[4] "The rude retreats of Norwalk": here, applied to a landscape, "rude" means "rugged, rough; uncultivated, wild" (OED).

[5] "But phrensy, like prejudice, was curable. Reason was no less an antidote to the illusions of insanity like his, than to the illusions of error": Edgar believes that insanity can be cured through rational conversation that clears away and resolves confusion. This notion belongs to the prehistory of psychoanalysis's faith in the talking cure of the therapist's couch.

cavern, within these precincts, his concealment was not to be traced. This arose from the nature of that sterile region.

It would not be easy to describe the face of this district, in a few words. Half of Solebury, thou knowest, admits neither of plough nor spade. The cultivable space lies along the river, and the desert, lying on the north, has gained, by some means, the apellation of Norwalk. Canst thou imagine a space, somewhat circular, about six miles in diameter, and exhibiting a perpetual and intricate variety of craggy eminences and deep dells?

The hollows are single, and walled around by cliffs, ever varying in shape and height, and have seldom any perceptible communication with each other. These hollows are of all dimensions, from the narrowness and depth of a well, to the amplitude of one hundred yards. Winter's snow is frequently found in these cavities at midsummer. The streams that burst forth from every crevice, are thrown, by the irregularities of the surface, into numberless cascades, often disappear in mists or in chasms, and emerge from subterranean channels, and, finally, either subside into lakes, or quietly meander through the lower and more level grounds.

Wherever nature left a flat it is made rugged and scarcely passable by enormous and fallen trunks, accumulated by the storms of ages, and forming, by their slow decay, a moss-covered soil, the haunt of rabbets and lizards. These spots are obscured by the melancholy umbrage of pines, whose eternal murmurs are in unison with vacancy and solitude, with the reverberations of the torrents and the whistling of the blasts. Hiccory and poplar, which abound in the low-lands, find here no fostering elements.

A sort of continued vale, winding and abrupt, leads into the midst of this region and through it. This vale serves the purpose of a road. It is a tedious maze, and perpetual declivity, and requires, from the passenger, a cautious and sure foot. Openings and ascents occasionally present themselves on each side, which seem to promise you access to the interior region, but always terminate, sooner or later, in insuperable difficulties, at the verge of a precipice, or the bottom of a steep.

Perhaps no one was more acquainted with this wilderness than I, but my knowledge was extremely imperfect. I had traversed parts of it, at an early age, in pursuit of berries and nuts, or led by a roaming disposition. Afterwards the sphere of my rambles was enlarged and their purpose changed. When Sarsefield came among us, I became his favourite scholar and the companion of all his pedestrian excursions. He was fond of penetrating into these recesses, partly from the love of picturesque scenes, partly to investigate its botanical and mineral productions, and, partly to carry on more effectually that species of instruction which he had adopted with regard to me, and which chiefly consisted in moralizing narratives or synthetical reasonings.[6] These excursions had familiarized me with its outlines and most accessible

---

[6] "The love of picturesque scenes . . . moralizing narratives or synthetical reasonings": like the "romantic structure" of the landscape in Chapter 3, the landscape here is experienced in terms of eighteenth-century aesthetic and rationalist categories; the picturesque is a category of painting that emphasizes the most charming or pleasing aspects of the landscape. Because Edgar explored Norwalk with Sarsefield when Sarsefield was his teacher, he associates it with the enlightened intellectual

parts; but there was much which, perhaps, could never be reached without wings, and much the only paths to which I might forever overlook.

Every new excursion indeed added somewhat to my knowledge. New tracks were pursued, new prospects detected, and new summits were gained. My rambles were productive of incessant novelty, though they always terminated in the prospect of limits that could not be overleaped. But none of these had led me wider from my customary paths than that which had taken place when in pursuit of Clithero. I had faint remembrance of the valley, into which I had descended after him, but till then I had viewed it at a distance, and supposed it impossible to reach the bottom but by leaping from a precipice some hundred feet in height. The opposite steep seemed no less inaccessible, and the cavern at the bottom was impervious to any views which my former positions had enabled me to take of it.

My intention to re-examine this cave and ascertain whither it led, had, for a time, been suspended by different considerations. It was now revived with more energy than ever. I reflected that this had formerly been haunted by Clithero, and might possibly have been the scene of the desperate act which he had meditated. It might at least conceal some token of his past existence. It might lead into spaces hitherto un-visited, and to summits from which wider landscapes might be seen.

One morning I set out to explore this scene. The road which Clithero had taken was laboriously circuitous. On my return from the first pursuit of him, I ascended the cliff in my former footsteps, but soon lighted on the beaten track which I had al-ready described. This enabled me to shun a thousand obstacles, which had lately risen before me, and opened an easy passage to the cavern.

I once more traversed this way. The brow of the hill was gained. The ledges of which it consisted, afforded sufficient footing, when the attempt was made, though viewed at a distance they seemed to be too narrow for that purpose. As I descended the rugged stair, I could not but wonder at the temerity and precipitation with which this descent had formerly been made. It seemed if the noon-day-light and the tardi-est circumspection would scarcely enable me to accomplish it, yet then it had been done with headlong speed, and with no guidance but the moon's uncertain rays.

I reached the mouth of the cave. Till now I had forgotten that a lamp or a torch might be necessary to direct my subterranean foot-steps. I was unwilling to defer the attempt. Light might possibly be requisite, if the cave had no other outlet. Somewhat might present itself within to the eyes, which might forever elude the hands, but I was more inclined to consider it merely as an avenue, terminating in an opening on the summit of the steep, or on the opposite side of the ridge. Caution might supply the place of light, or, having explored the cave as far as possible at present, I might hereafter return, better furnished for the scrutiny.

---

systems and principles, the "moralizing narratives" and "synthetical reasonings" he learned there. These associations seem somewhat ironic, given the savagery and irrationality soon to be associated with Norwalk's wilderness.

Chapter X

WITH these determinations, I proceeded. The entrance was low, and compelled me to resort to hands as well as feet. At a few yards from the mouth the light disappeared, and I found myself immersed in the dunnest obscurity. Had I not been persuaded that another had gone before me, I should have relinquished the attempt. I proceeded with the utmost caution, always ascertaining, by out-stretched arms, the height and breadth of the cavity before me. In a short time the dimensions expanded on all sides, and permitted me to resume my feet.

I walked upon a smooth and gentle declivity. Presently the wall, on one side, and the ceiling receded beyond my reach. I began to fear that I should be involved in a maze, and should be disabled from returning. To obviate this danger it was requisite to adhere to the nearest wall, and conform to the direction which it should take, without straying through the palpable obscurity. Whether the ceiling was lofty or low, whether the opposite wall of the passage was distant or near, this, I deemed no proper opportunity to investigate.

In a short time, my progress was stopped by an abrupt descent. I set down the advancing foot with caution, being aware that I might at the next step encounter a bottomless pit. To the brink of such an one I seemed now to have arrived. I stooped, and stretched my hand forward and downward, but all was vacuity.

Here it was needful to pause. I had reached the brink of a cavity whose depth it was impossible to ascertain. It might be a few inches beyond my reach, or hundreds of feet. By leaping down I might incur no injury, or might plunge into a lake or dash myself to pieces on the points of rocks.

I now saw with new force the propriety of being furnished with a light. The first suggestion was to return upon my foot-steps, and resume my undertaking on the morrow. Yet, having advanced thus far, I felt reluctance to recede without accomplishing my purposes. I reflected likewise that Clithero had boldly entered this recess, and had certainly came forth at a different avenue from that at which he entered.

At length it occurred to me, that though I could not go forward, yet I might proceed along the edge of this cavity. This edge would be as safe a guidance, and would serve as well for a clue by which I might return, as the wall which it was now necessary to forsake.

Intense dark is always the parent of fears. Impending injuries cannot in this state be descried, nor shunned, nor repelled. I began to feel some faltering of my courage and seated myself, for a few minutes, on a stoney mass which arose before me. My situation was new. The caverns I had hitherto met with, in this desert, were chiefly formed of low-browed rocks. They were chambers, more or less spacious, into which twi-light was at least admitted; but here it seemed as if I was surrounded by barriers that would forever cut off my return to air and to light.

Presently I resumed my courage and proceeded. My road appeared now to ascend. On one side I seemed still upon the verge of a precipice, and, on the other, all was empty and waste. I had gone no inconsiderable distance, and persuaded myself that my career would speedily terminate. In a short time, the space on the left hand, was again occupied, and I cautiously proceeded between the edge of the gulf and a rugged wall. As the space between them widened I adhered to the wall.

I was not insensible that my path became more intricate and more difficult to re-tread in proportion as I advanced. I endeavoured to preserve a vivid conception of the way which I had already passed, and to keep the images of the left, and right-hand wall, and the gulf, in due succession in my memory.

The path which had hitherto been considerably smooth, now became rugged and steep. Chilling damps, the secret trepidation which attended me, the length and dif-ficulties of my way, enhanced by the ceaseless caution and the numerous expedients which the utter darkness obliged me to employ, began to overpower my strength. I was frequently compelled to stop and recruit myself by rest. These respites from toil were of use, but they could not enable me to prosecute an endless journey, and to re-turn was scarcely a less arduous task than to proceed.

I looked anxiously forward in the hope of being comforted by some dim ray, which might assure me that my labours were approaching an end. At last this propitious token appeared, and I issued forth into a kind of chamber, one side of which was open to the air and allowed me to catch a portion of the checquered sky. This spec-tacle never before excited such exquisite sensations in my bosom. The air, likewise, breathed into the cavern, was unspeakably delicious.

I now found myself on the projecture of a rock. Above and below the hill-side was nearly perpendicular. Opposite, and at the distance of fifteen or twenty yards, was a similar ascent. At the bottom was a glen, cold, narrow and obscure. The projecture, which served as a kind of vestibule to the cave, was connected with a ledge, by which, though not without peril and toil, I was conducted to the summit.

This summit was higher than any of those which were interposed between itself and the river. A large part of this chaos of rocks and precipices was subjected, at one view, to the eye. The fertile lawns and vales which lay beyond this, the winding course of the river, and the slopes which rose on its farther side, were parts of this extensive scene. These objects were at any time fitted to inspire rapture. Now my delight was enhanced by the contrast which this lightsome and serene element bore to the glooms from which I had lately emerged. My station, also, was higher, and the limits of my view, consequently more ample than any which I had hitherto enjoyed.[1]

I advanced to the outer verge of the hill, which I found to overlook a steep, no less inaccessible, and a glen equally profound. I changed frequently my station in order to diversify the scenery. At length it became necessary to inquire by what means I

---

[1] The strange and gothic mountain scene into which Edgar has emerged is the center of the novel's wilderness topography and the most extreme development of Norwalk's dreamlike features. The "desolate and solitary grandeur" and "phantastic shapes" Edgar describes in the following para-graphs center on the circular mountain-within-a-mountain where he will encounter Clithero and the savage panther. Edgar emerges into this scene three times, discovering the scene here in Chapter 10, then returning with food for a sleeping Clithero in Chapter 11, and finally encountering the savage panther here in Chapter 12.

should return. I traversed the edge of the hill, but on every side it was equally steep and always too lofty to permit me to leap from it. As I kept along the verge, I perceived that it tended in a circular direction, and brought me back, at last, to the spot from which I had set out. From this inspection, it seemed as if return was impossible by any other way than that through the cavern.

I now turned my attention to the interior space. If you imagine a cylindrical mass, with a cavity dug in the centre, whose edge conforms to the exterior edge; and, if you place in this cavity another cylinder, higher than that which surrounds it, but so small as to leave between its sides and those of the cavity, an hollow space, you will gain as distinct an image of this hill as words can convey. The summit of the inner rock was rugged and covered with trees of unequal growth. To reach this summit would not render my return easier; but its greater elevation would extend my view, and perhaps furnish a spot from which the whole horizon was conspicuous.

As I had traversed the outer, I now explored the inner edge of this hill. At length I reached a spot where the chasm, separating the two rocks, was narrower than at any other part. At first view, it seemed as if it were possible to leap over it, but a nearer examination shewed me that the passage was impracticable. So far as my eye could estimate it, the breadth was thirty or forty feet. I could scarcely venture to look beneath. The height was dizzy, and the walls, which approached each other at top, receded at the bottom, so as to form the resemblance of an immense hall, lighted from a rift, which some convulsion of nature had made in the roof. Where I stood there ascended a perpetual mist, occasioned by a torrent that dashed along the rugged pavement below.

From these objects I willingly turned my eye upon those before and above me, on the opposite ascent. A stream, rushing from above, fell into a cavity, which its own force seemed gradually to have made. The noise and the motion equally attracted my attention. There was a desolate and solitary grandeur in the scene, enhanced by the circumstances in which it was beheld, and by the perils through which I had recently passed, that had never before been witnessed by me.

A sort of sanctity and awe environed it, owing to the consciousness of absolute and utter loneliness. It was probable that human feet had never before gained this recess, that human eyes had never been fixed upon these gushing waters. The aboriginal inhabitants had no motives to lead them into caves like this, and ponder on the verge of such a precipice. Their successors were still less likely to have wandered hither. Since the birth of this continent, I was probably the first who had deviated thus remotely from the customary paths of men.

While musing upon these ideas, my eye was fixed upon the foaming current. At length, I looked upon the rocks which confined and embarrassed its course. I admired their phantastic shapes, and endless irregularities. Passing from one to the other of these, my attention lighted, at length, as if by some magical transition, on . . . an human countenance!

My surprise was so abrupt, and my sensations so tumultuous that I forgot for a moment the perilous nature of my situation. I loosened my hold of a pine branch, which had been hitherto one of my supports, and almost started from my seat. Had my station been, in a slight degree nearer the brink than it was, I should have fallen headlong into the abyss.

To meet an human creature, even on that side of the chasm which I occupied, would have been wholly adverse to my expectation. My station was accessible by no other road than that through which I had passed, and no motives were imaginable by which others could be prompted to explore this road. But he whom I now beheld, was seated where it seemed impossible for human efforts to have placed him. . . .

But this affected me but little in comparison with other incidents. Not only the countenance was human, but in spite of shaggy and tangled locks, and an air of melancholy wildness, I speedily recognized the features of the fugitive Clithero!

One glance was not sufficient to make me acquainted with this scene. I had come hither partly in pursuit of this man, but some casual appendage of his person, something which should indicate his past rather than his present existence, was all that I hoped to find. That he should be found alive in this desert; that he should have gained this summit, access to which was apparently impossible, were scarcely within the boundaries of belief.

His scanty and coarse garb, had been nearly rent away by brambles and thorns, his arms, bosom and cheek were overgrown and half-concealed by hair.[2] There was somewhat in his attitude and looks denoting more than anarchy of thoughts and passions. His rueful, ghastly, and immoveable eyes, testified not only that his mind was ravaged by despair, but that he was pinched with famine.

These proofs of his misery thrilled to my inmost heart. Horror and shuddering invaded me as I stood gazing upon him, and, for a time, I was without the power of deliberating on the measures which it was my duty to adopt for his relief. The first suggestion was, by calling, to inform him of my presence. I knew not what counsel or comfort to offer. By what words to bespeak his attention, or by what topics to molify his direful passions I knew not. Though so near, the gulf by which we were separated was impassable. All that I could do was to speak.

My surprise and my horror were still strong enough to give a shrill and piercing tone to my voice. The chasm and the rocks loudened and reverberated my accents while I exclaimed . . . *Man! Clithero!*

My summons was effectual. He shook off his trance in a moment. He had been stretched upon his back, with his eyes fixed upon a craggy projecture above, as if he were in momentary expectation of its fall, and crushing him to atoms. Now he started on his feet. He was conscious of the voice, but not of the quarter whence it came. He was looking anxiously around when I again spoke . . . Look hither: It is I who called.

---

[2] "Overgrown and half-concealed by hair": the passage describes a sudden, dramatic transformation of Clithero's bearing and appearance. He appears to be in a "trance" (three paragraphs later) and suddenly hairy. Edgar notes his "shaggy and tangled locks" and remarks that "his arms, bosom and cheek were overgrown and half-concealed by hair." For more on possible implications of this transformation, see the Introduction's discussion of Brown's use of folk and gothic legends concerning werewolves as personifications of Irish rebellion.

He looked. Astonishment was now mingled with every other dreadful meaning in his visage. He clasped his hands together and bent forward, as if to satisfy himself that his summoner was real. At the next moment he drew back, placed his hands upon his breast, and fixed his eyes on the ground.

This pause was not likely to be broken but by me. I was preparing again to speak. To be more distinctly heard, I advanced closer to the brink. During this action, my eye was necessarily withdrawn from him. Having gained a somewhat nearer station, I looked again, but . . . he was gone!

The seat which he so lately occupied was empty. I was not forewarned of his disappearance, or directed to the course of his flight by any rustling among leaves. These indeed would have been overpowered by the noise of the cataract. The place where he sat was the bottom of a cavity, one side of which terminated in the verge of the abyss, but the other sides were perpendicular or overhanging. Surely he had not leaped into this gulf, and yet that he had so speedily scaled the steep was impossible.

I looked into the gulf, but the depth and the gloom allowed me to see nothing with distinctness. His cries or groans could not be overhead amidst the uproar of the waters. His fall must have instantly destroyed him, and that he had fallen was the only conclusion I could draw.

My sensations on this incident cannot be easily described. The image of this man's despair, and of the sudden catastrophe to which my inauspicious interference had led, filled me with compunction and terror. Some of my fears were relieved by the new conjecture, that, behind the rock on which he had lain, there might be some aperture or pit into which he had descended, or in which he might be concealed.

I derived consolation from this conjecture. Not only the evil which I dreaded might not have happened, but some alleviation of his misery was possible. Could I arrest his foot-steps and win his attention, I might be able to insinuate the lessons of fortitude; but if words were impotent, and arguments were nugatory, yet to set by him in silence, to moisten his hand with tears, to sigh in unison, to offer him the spectacle of sympathy, the solace of believing that his demerits were not estimated by so rigid a standard by others as by himself, that one at least among his fellow men regarded him with love and pity, could not fail to be of benign influence.

These thoughts inspired me with new zeal. To effect my purpose it was requisite to reach the opposite steep. I was now convinced that this was not an impracticable undertaking, since Clithero had already performed it. I once more made the circuit of the hill. Every side was steep and of enormous height, and the gulf was no where so narrow as at this spot. I therefore returned hither, and once more pondered on the means of passing this tremendous chasm in safety.

Casting my eyes upward, I noted the tree at the root of which I was standing. I compared the breadth of the gulf with the length of the trunk of this tree, and it appeared very suitable for a bridge. Happily it grew obliquely, and, if felled by an axe, would probably fall of itself, in such a manner as to be suspended across the chasm. The stock was thick enough to afford me footing, and would enable me to reach the opposite declivity without danger or delay.

A more careful examination of the spot, the scite of the tree, its dimensions and the direction of its growth convinced me fully of the practicability of this expedient, and I determined to carry it into immediate execution. For this end I must hasten home, procure an axe, and return with all expedition hither. I took my former way, once more entered the subterranean avenue, and slowly re-emerged into day. Before I reached home, the evening was at hand, and my tired limbs and jaded spirits obliged me to defer my undertaking till the morrow.

Though my limbs were at rest, my thoughts were active through the night. I carefully reviewed the situation of this hill, and was unable to conjecture by what means Clithero could place himself upon it. Unless he occasionally returned to the habitable grounds, it was impossible for him to escape perishing by famine. He might intend to destroy himself by this means, and my first efforts were to be employed to overcome this fatal resolution. To persuade him to leave his desolate haunts might be a laborious and tedious task, meanwhile all my benevolent intentions would be frustrated by his want of sustenance. It was proper, therefore, to carry bread with me, and to place it before him. The sight of food, the urgencies of hunger, and my vehement intreaties might prevail on him to eat, though no expostulation might suffice to make him seek food at a distance.

Chapter XI

NEXT morning I stored a small bag with meat and bread, and throwing an axe on my shoulder, set out, without informing any one of my intentions, for the hill. My passage was rendered more difficult by these incumbrances, but my perseverance surmounted every impediment, and I gained, in a few hours, the foot of the tree, whose trunk was to serve me for a bridge. In this journey I saw no traces of the fugitive.

A new survey of the tree confirmed my former conclusions, and I began my work with diligence. My strokes were repeated by a thousand echoes, and I paused at first somewhat startled by reverberations, which made it appear as if not one, but a score of axes, were employed at the same time on both sides of the gulf.

Quickly the tree fell, and exactly in the manner which I expected and desired. The wide-spread limbs occupied and choked up the channel of the torrent, and compelled it to seek a new outlet and multiplied its murmurs. I dared not trust myself to cross it in an upright posture, but clung, with hands and feet, to its rugged bark. Having reached the opposite cliff I proceeded to examine the spot where Clithero had disappeared. My fondest hopes were realised, for a considerable cavity appeared, which, on a former day, had been concealed from my distant view by the rock.

It was obvious to conclude that this was his present habitation, or that an avenue, conducting hither and terminating in the unexplored sides of this pit, was that by which he had come hither, and by which he had retired. I could not hesitate long to slide into the pit. I found an entrance through which I fearlessly penetrated. I was prepared to encounter obstacles and perils similar to those which I have already described, but was rescued from them by ascending, in a few minutes, into a kind of passage, open above, but walled by a continued rock on both sides. The sides of this passage conformed with the utmost exactness to each other. Nature, at some former period, had occasioned the solid mass to dispart at this place, and had thus afforded access to the summit of the hill. Loose stones and ragged points formed the flooring of this passage, which rapidly and circuitously ascended.

I was now within a few yards of the surface of the rock. The passage opened into a kind of chamber or pit, the sides of which were not difficult to climb. I rejoiced at the prospect of this termination of my journey. Here I paused, and throwing my weary limbs on the ground, began to examine the objects around me, and to meditate on the steps that were next to be taken.

My first glance lighted on the very being of whom I was in search. Stretched upon a bed of moss, at the distance of a few feet from my station, I beheld Clithero. He had not been roused by my approach, though my foot-steps were perpetually stumbling and sliding. This reflection gave birth to the fear that he was dead. A nearer inspection dispelled my apprehensions, and shewed me that he was merely buried in profound slumber. Those vigils must indeed have been long which were at last succeeded by a sleep so oblivious.

This meeting was, in the highest degree, propitious. It not only assured me of his existence, but proved that his miseries were capable to be suspended. His slumber enabled me to pause, to ruminate on the manner by which his understanding might be most successfully addressed; to collect and arrange the topics fitted to rectify his gloomy and disastrous perceptions.

Thou knowest that I am qualified for such tasks neither by my education nor my genius. The headlong and ferocious energies of this man could not be repelled or diverted into better paths by efforts so undisciplined as mine. A despair so stormy and impetuous would drown my feeble accents. How should I attempt to reason with him? How should I outroot prepossessions so inveterate; the fruits of his earliest education, fostered and matured by the observation and experience of his whole life? How should I convince him that since the death of Wiatte was not intended, the deed was without crime; that, if it had been deliberately concerted, it was still a virtue, since his own life could, by no other means, be preserved; that when he pointed a dagger at the bosom of his mistress he was actuated, not by avarice, or ambition, or revenge, or malice. He desired to confer on her the highest and the only benefit of which he believed her capable. He sought to rescue her from tormenting regrets and lingering agonies.

These positions were sufficiently just to my own view, but I was not called upon to reduce them to practice. I had not to struggle with the consciousness of having been rescued by some miraculous contingency, from embruing my hands in the blood of her whom I adored; of having drawn upon myself suspicions of ingratitude and murder too deep to be ever effaced; of having bereft myself of love, and honour, and friends, and spotless reputation; of having doomed myself to infamy and detestation, to hopeless exile, penury, and servile toil. These were the evils which his malignant destiny had made the unalterable portion of Clithero, and how should my imperfect eloquence annihilate these evils? Every man, not himself the victim of irretreivable disasters, perceives the folly of ruminating on the past, and of fostering a grief which cannot reverse or recall the decrees of an immutable necessity; but every man who suffers is unavoidably shackled by the errors which he censures in his neighbour, and his efforts to relieve himself are as fruitless as those with which he attempted the relief of others.

No topic, therefore, could be properly employed by me on the present occasion. All that I could do was to offer him food, and, by pathetic supplications, to prevail on him to eat. Famine, however obstinate, would scarcely refrain when bread was placed within sight and reach. When made to swerve from his resolution in one instance, it would be less difficult to conquer it a second time. The magic of sympathy, the perseverance of benevolence, though silent, might work a gradual and secret revolution, and better thoughts might insensibly displace those desperate suggestions which now governed him.

Having revolved these ideas, I placed the food which I had brought at his right hand, and, seating myself at his feet, attentively surveyed his countenance. The emotions, which were visible during wakefulness, had vanished during this cessation of remembrance and remorse, or were faintly discernible. They served to dignify and solemnize his features, and to embellish those immutable lines which betokened the spirit of his better days. Lineaments were now observed which could never co-exist with folly, or associate with obdurate guilt.

I had no inclination to awaken him. This respite was too sweet to be needlessly abridged. I determined to await the operation of nature, and to prolong, by silence and by keeping interruption at a distance, this salutary period of forgetfulness. This interval permitted new ideas to succeed in my mind.

Clithero believed his solitude to be unapproachable. What new expedients to escape inquiry and intrusion might not my presence suggest! Might he not vanish, as he had done on the former day, and afford me no time to assail his constancy and tempt his hunger? If, however, I withdrew during his sleep, he would awake without disturbance, and be, unconscious for a time, that his secrecy had been violated. He would quickly perceive the victuals and would need no foreign inducements to eat. A provision, so unexpected and extraordinary, might suggest new thoughts, and be construed into a kind of heavenly condemnation of his purpose. He would not readily suspect the motives or person of his visitant, would take no precaution against the repetition of my visit, and, at the same time, our interview would not be attended with so much surprise. The more I revolved these reflections, the greater force they acquired. At length, I determined to withdraw, and, leaving the food where it could scarcely fail of attracting his notice, I returned by the way that I had come. I had scarcely reached home, when a messenger from Inglefield arrived, requesting me to spend the succeeding night at his house, as some engagement had occurred to draw him to the city.

I readily complied with this request. It was not necessary, however, to be early in my visit. I deferred going till the evening was far advanced. My way led under the branches of the elm which recent events had rendered so memorable. Hence my reflections reverted to the circumstances which had lately occurred in connection with this tree.

I paused, for some time, under its shade. I marked the spot where Clithero had been discovered digging. It shewed marks of being unsettled, but the sod which had formerly covered it and which had lately been removed, was now carefully replaced. This had not been done by him on that occasion in which I was a witness of his behaviour. The earth was then hastily removed and as hastily thrown again into the hole from which it had been taken.

Some curiosity was naturally excited by this appearance. Either some other person, or Clithero, on a subsequent occasion, had been here. I was now likewise led to reflect on the possible motives that prompted the maniac to turn up this earth. There is always some significance in the actions of a sleeper. Somewhat was, perhaps, buried in this spot, connected with the history of Mrs. Lorimer or of Clarice. Was it not possible to ascertain the truth in this respect?

There was but one method. By carefully uncovering this hole, and digging as deep as Clithero had already dug, it would quickly appear whether any thing was hidden. To do this publickly by day-light was evidently indiscreet. Besides, a moment's delay was superfluous. The night had now fallen, and before it was past this new undertaking might be finished. An interview was, if possible, to be gained with Clithero on the morrow, and for this interview the discoveries made on this spot might eminently qualify me. Influenced by these considerations, I resolved to dig. I was first, however, to converse an hour with the house-keeper, and then to withdraw to my chamber. When the family were all retired, and there was no fear of observation or interruption, I proposed to rise and hasten, with a proper implement, hither.

One chamber, in Inglefield's house, was usually reserved for visitants. In this chamber thy unfortunate brother died, and here it was that I was to sleep. The image of its last inhabitant could not fail of being called up, and of banishing repose; but the scheme which I had meditated was an additional incitement to watchfulness. Hither I repaired, at the due season, having previously furnished myself with candles, since I knew not what might occur to make a light necessary.

I did not go to bed, but either sat musing by a table or walked across the room. The bed before me was that on which my friend breathed his last. To rest my head upon the same pillow, to lie on that pallet which sustained his cold and motionless limbs, were provocations to remembrance and grief that I desired to shun. I endeavoured to fill my mind with more recent incidents, with the disasters of Clithero, my subterranean adventures, and the probable issue of the schemes which I now contemplated.

I recalled the conversation which had just ended with the house-keeper. Clithero had been our theme, but she had dealt chiefly in repetitions of what had formerly been related by her or by Inglefield. I inquired what this man had left behind, and found that it consisted of a square box, put together by himself with uncommon strength, but of rugged workmanship. She proceeded to mention that she had advised her brother, Mr. Inglefield, to break open this box and ascertain its contents, but this he did not think himself justified in doing. Clithero was guilty of no known crime, was responsible to no one for his actions, and might sometime return to claim his property. This box contained nothing with which others had a right to meddle. Somewhat might be found in it, throwing light upon his past or present situation, but curiosity was not to be gratified by these means. What Clithero thought proper to conceal, it was criminal for us to extort from him.

The house-keeper was by no means convinced by these arguments, and at length, obtained her brother's permission to try whether any of her own keys would unlock this chest. The keys were produced, but no lock nor key-hole were discoverable. The lid was fast, but by what means it was fastened, the most accurate inspection could not detect. Hence she was compelled to lay aside her project. This chest had always stood in the chamber which I now occupied.

These incidents were now remembered, and I felt disposed to profit by this opportunity of examining this box.[1] It stood in a corner, and was easily distinguished by its

---

[1] "This opportunity of examining this box": the plot device of a locked box or trunk containing precious information is frequent in gothic fiction of the Enlightenment. It features centrally in Godwin's *Caleb Williams* (1794), an important source for Brown, and Brown himself played on the motif one year earlier in "The Man at Home," an essay series in thirteen installments in *The Weekly Magazine* (February–April 1798). See this series in Brown, *The Rhapsodist and Other Uncollected Writings*. For more on the locked-trunk motif, see Verhoeven, "Opening the Text."

form. I lifted it and found its weight by no means extraordinary. Its structure was remarkable. It consisted of six sides, square and of similar dimensions. These were joined, not by mortice and tennon; not by nails, not by hinges, but the junction was accurate. The means by which they were made to cohere were invisible.

Appearances on every side were uniform, nor were there any marks by which the lid was distinguishable from its other surfaces.

During his residence with Inglefield, many specimens of mechanical ingenuity were given by his servant. This was the workmanship of his own hands. I looked at it, for some time, till the desire insensibly arose of opening and examining its contents.

I had no more right to do this than the Inglefields; perhaps indeed this curiosity was more absurd, and the gratification more culpable in me than in them. I was acquainted with the history of Clithero's past life, and with his present condition. Respecting these, I had no new intelligence to gain, and no doubts to solve. What excuse could I make to the proprietor, should he ever reappear to claim his own, or to Inglefield for breaking open a receptacle which all the maxims of society combine to render sacred?

But could not my end be gained without violence? The means of opening might present themselves on a patient scrutiny. The lid might be raised and shut down again without any tokens of my act; its contents might be examined, and all things restored to their former condition in a few minutes.

I intended not a theft. I intended to benefit myself without inflicting injury on others. Nay, might not the discoveries I should make, throw light upon the conduct of this extraordinary man, which his own narrative had withheld? Was there reason to confide implicitly on the tale which I had heard?

In spite of the testimony of my own feelings, the miseries of Clithero appeared in some degree, phantastic and ground-less. A thousand conceivable motives might induce him to pervert or conceal the truth. If he were thoroughly known, his character might assume a new appearance, and what is now so difficult to reconcile to common maxims, might prove perfectly consistent with them. I desire to restore him to peace, but a thorough knowledge of his actions is necessary, both to shew that he is worthy of compassion, and to suggest the best means of extirpating his errors. It was possible that this box contained the means of this knowledge.

There were likewise other motives which, as they possessed some influence, however small, deserve to be mentioned. Thou knowest that I also am a mechanist. I had constructed a writing desk and cabinet, in which I had endeavoured to combine the properties of secrecy, security, and strength, in the highest possible degree. I looked upon this therefore with the eye of an artist, and was solicitous to know the principles on which it was formed. I determined to examine, and if possible to open it.

Chapter XII

I SURVEYED it with the utmost attention. All its parts appeared equally solid and smooth. It could not be doubted that one of its sides served the purpose of a lid, and was possible to be raised. Mere strength could not be applied to raise it, because there was no projecture which might be firmly held by the hand, and by which force could be exerted. Some spring, therefore, secretly existed which might forever elude the senses, but on which the hand, by being moved over it, in all directions, might accidentally light.

This process was effectual. A touch, casually applied at an angle, drove back a bolt, and a spring, at the same time, was set in action, by which the lid was raised above half an inch. No event could be supposed more fortuitous than this. An hundred hands might have sought in vain for this spring. The spot in which a certain degree of pressure was sufficient to produce this effect, was of all, the last likely to attract notice or awaken suspicion.

I opened the trunk with eagerness. The space within was divided into numerous compartments, none of which contained any thing of moment. Tools of different and curious constructions, and remnants of minute machinery, were all that offered themselves to my notice.

My expectations being thus frustrated, I proceeded to restore things to their former state. I attempted to close the lid; but the spring which had raised it refused to bend. No measure that I could adopt, enabled me to place the lid in the same situation in which I had found it. In my efforts to press down the lid, which were augmented in proportion to the resistance that I met with, the spring was broken. This obstacle being removed, the lid resumed its proper place; but no means, within the reach of my ingenuity to discover, enabled me to push forward the bolt, and thus to restore the fastening.

I now perceived that Clithero had provided not only against the opening of his cabinet, but likewise against the possibility of concealing that it had been opened. This discovery threw me into some confusion. I had been tempted thus far, by the belief that my action was without witnesses, and might be forever concealed. This opinion was now confuted. If Clithero should ever reclaim his property, he would not fail to detect the violence of which I had been guilty. Inglefield would disapprove in another what he had not permitted to himself, and the unauthorized and clandestine manner in which I had behaved, would aggravate, in his eyes, the heinousness of my offence.

But now there was no remedy. All that remained was to hinder suspicion from lighting on the innocent, and to confess, to my friend, the offence which I had committed. Meanwhile my first project was resumed, and, the family being now wrapt in profound sleep, I left my chamber, and proceeded to the elm. The moon was extremely brilliant, but I hoped that this unfrequented road and unseasonable hour would hinder me from being observed. My chamber was above the kitchen, with which it communicated by a small stair-case, and the building to which it belonged was connected with the dwelling by a gallery. I extinguished the light, and left it in the kitchen, intending to relight it, by the embers that still glowed on the hearth, on my return.

I began to remove the sod, and cast out the earth, with little confidence in the success of my project. The issue of my examination of the box humbled and disheartened me. For some time I found nothing that tended to invigorate my hopes. I determined, however, to descend, as long as the unsettled condition of the earth shewed me that some one had preceded me. Small masses of stone were occasionally met with, which served only to perplex me with groundless expectations. At length my spade struck upon something which emitted a very different sound. I quickly drew it forth, and found it to be wood. Its regular form, and the crevices which were faintly discernible, persuaded me that it was human workmanship, and that there was a cavity within. The place in which it was found, easily suggested some connection between this and the destiny of Clithero. Covering up the hole with speed, I hastened with my prize to the house. The door, by which the kitchen was entered, was not to be seen from the road. It opened on a field, the farther limit of which was a ledge of rocks, which formed, on this side, the boundary of Inglefield's estate and the westernmost barrier of Norwalk.

As I turned the angle of the house, and came in view of this door, methought I saw a figure issue from it. I was startled at this incident, and, stopping, crouched close to the wall, that I might not be discovered. As soon as the figure passed beyond the verge of the shade, it was easily distinguished to be that of Clithero! He crossed the field with a rapid pace, and quickly passed beyond the reach of my eye.

This appearance was mysterious. For what end he should visit this habitation, could not be guessed. Was the contingency to be lamented, in consequence of which an interview had been avoided? Would it have compelled me to explain the broken condition of his trunk? I knew not whether to rejoice at having avoided this interview, or to deplore it.

These thoughts did not divert me from examining the nature of the prize which I had gained. I relighted my candle and hied once more to the chamber. The first object, which, on entering it, attracted my attention, was the cabinet broken into twenty fragments, on the hearth. I had left it on a low table, at a distant corner of the room.

No conclusion could be formed, but that Clithero had been here, had discovered the violence which had been committed on his property, and, in the first transport of his indignation, had shattered it to pieces. I shuddered on reflecting how near I had been to being detected by him in the very act, and by how small an interval I had escaped that resentment, which, in that case, would have probably been wreaked upon me.

My attention was withdrawn, at length, from this object, and fixed upon the contents of the box which I had dug up. This was equally inaccessible with the other. I had not the same motives for caution and forbearance. I was somewhat desperate, as the consequences of my indiscretion could not be aggravated, and my curiosity was more impetuous, with regard to the smaller than to the larger cabinet. I placed it on the ground and crushed it to pieces with my heel.

Something was within. I brought it to the light, and, after loosing numerous folds, at length drew forth a volume. No object, in the circle of nature, was more adapted than this, to rouse up all my faculties. My feelings were anew excited on observing that it was a manuscript. I bolted the door, and, drawing near the light, opened and began to read.

A few pages was sufficient to explain the nature of the work. Clithero had mentioned that his lady had composed a vindication of her conduct towards her brother, when her intercession in his favour was solicited and refused. This performance had never been published, but had been read by many, and was preserved by her friends as a precious monument of her genius and her virtue. This manuscript was now before me.

That Clithero should preserve this manuscript, amidst the wreck of his hopes and fortunes, was apparently conformable to his temper. That, having formed the resolution to die, he should seek to hide this volume from the profane curiosity of survivors, was a natural proceeding. To bury it rather than to burn, or disperse it into fragments, would be suggested by the wish to conceal, without committing what his heated fancy would regard as sacrilege. To bury it beneath the elm, was dictated by no fortuitous or inexplicable caprice. This event could scarcely fail of exercising some influence on the perturbations of his sleep, and thus, in addition to other causes, might his hovering near this trunk, and throwing up this earth, in the intervals of slumber, be accounted for. Clithero, indeed, had not mentioned this proceeding in the course of his narrative; but that would have contravened the end for which he had provided a grave for this book.

I read this copious tale with unspeakable eagerness. It essentially agreed with that which had been told by Clithero. By drawing forth events into all their circumstances, more distinct impressions were produced on the mind, and proofs of fortitude and equanimity were here given, to which I had hitherto known no parallel. No wonder that a soul like Clithero's, pervaded by these proofs of inimitable excellence, and thrillingly alive to the passion of virtuous fame, and the value of that existence which he had destroyed, should be overborne by horror at the view of the past.

The instability of life and happiness was forcibly illustrated, as well as the perniciousness of error. Exempt as this lady was from almost every defect, she was indebted for her ruin to absurd opinions of the sacredness of consanguinity, to her anxiety for the preservation of a ruffian, because that ruffian was her brother. The spirit of Clithero was enlightened and erect, but he weakly suffered the dictates of eternal justice to be swallowed up by gratitude. The dread of unjust upbraiding hurried him to murder and to suicide, and the imputation of imaginary guilt, impelled him to the perpetration of genuine and enormous crimes.

The perusal of this volume ended not but with the night. Contrary to my hopes, the next day was stormy and wet. This did not deter me from visiting the mountain. Slippery paths and muddy torrents were no obstacles to the purposes which I had adopted. I wrapt myself, and a bag of provisions, in a cloak of painted canvass and speeded to the dwelling of Clithero.

I passed through the cave and reached the bridge which my own ingenuity had formed. At that moment, torrents of rain poured from above, and stronger blasts thundered amidst these desolate recesses and profound chasms. Instead of lamenting the prevalence of this tempest, I now began to regard it with pleasure. It conferred new forms of sublimity and grandeur on this scene.

As I crept with hands and feet, along my imperfect bridge, a sudden gust had nearly whirled me into the frightful abyss below. To preserve myself, I was obliged to loose my hold of my burthen and it fell into the gulf. This incident disconcerted and distressed me. As soon as I had effected my dangerous passage, I screened myself behind a cliff, and gave myself up to reflection.

The purpose of this arduous journey was defeated, by the loss of the provisions I had brought. I despaired of winning the attention of the fugitive to supplications, or arguments tending to smother remorse, or revive his fortitude. The scope of my efforts was to consist in vanquishing his aversion to food; but these efforts would now be useless, since I had no power to supply his cravings.

This deficiency, however, was easily supplied. I had only to return home and supply myself anew. No time was to be lost in doing this; but I was willing to remain under this shelter, till the fury of the tempest had subsided. Besides, I was not certain that Clithero had again retreated hither. It was requisite to explore the summit of this hill, and ascertain whether it had any inhabitant. I might likewise discover what had been the success of my former experiment, and whether the food, which had been left here on the former day, was consumed or neglected.

While occupied with these reflections, my eyes were fixed upon the opposite steeps. The tops of the trees, waving to and fro, in the wildest commotion, and their trunks, occasionally bending to the blast, which, in these lofty regions, blew with a violence unknown in the tracts below, exhibited an awful spectacle. At length, my attention was attracted by the trunk which lay across the gulf, and which I had converted into a bridge. I perceived that it had already somewhat swerved from its original position, that every blast broke or loosened some of the fibres by which its root was connected with the opposite bank, and that, if the storm did not speedily abate, there was imminent danger of its being torn from the rock and precipitated into the chasm. Thus my retreat would be cut off, and the evils, from which I was endeavouring to rescue another, would be experienced by myself.

I did not just then reflect that Clithero had found access to this hill by other means, and that the avenue by which he came, would be equally commodious to me. I believed my destiny to hang upon the expedition with which I should re-cross this gulf. The moments that were spent in these deliberations were critical, and I shuddered to observe that the trunk was held in its place by one or two fibres which were already stretched almost to breaking.

To pass along the trunk, rendered slippery by the wet, and unsteadfast by the wind, was eminently dangerous. To maintain my hold, in passing, in defiance of the whirlwind, required the most vigorous exertions. For this end it was necessary to discommode myself of my cloak, and of the volume, which I carried in the pocket of my cloak. I believed there was no reason to dread their being destroyed or purloined, if left, for a few hours or a day, in this recess. If laid beside a stone, under shelter of this cliff, they would, no doubt, remain unmolested till the disappearance of the storm should permit me to revisit this spot in the after-noon or on the morrow.

Just as I had disposed of these incumbrances, and had risen from my seat, my attention was again called to the opposite steep, by the most unwelcome object that, at this time, could possibly occur. Something was perceived moving among the bushes and rocks, which, for a time, I hoped was no more than a racoon or oppossum; but which presently appeared to be a panther. His grey coat, extended claws, fiery eyes, and a cry which he at that moment uttered, and which, by its resemblance to the human voice, is peculiarly terrific, denoted him to be the most ferocious and untamable of that detested race.*

The industry of our hunters has nearly banished animals of prey from these precincts.[1] The fastnesses of Norwalk, however, could not but afford refuge to some of them. Of late I had met them so rarely, that my fears were seldom alive, and I trod, without caution, the ruggedest and most solitary haunts. Still, however, I had seldom been unfurnished in my rambles with the means of defence.

My temper never delighted in carnage and blood. I found no pleasure in plunging into bogs, wading through rivulets, and penetrating thickets, for the sake of dispatching wood-cocks and squirrels. To watch their gambols and flittings, and invite them to my hand, was my darling amusement when loitering among the woods and the rocks. It was much otherwise, however, with regard to rattlesnakes and panthers. These I thought it no breach of duty to exterminate wherever they could be found. These judicious and sanguinary spoilers were equally the enemies of man and of the harmless race that sported in the trees, and many of their skins are still preserved by me as trophies of my juvenile prowess.

As hunting was never my trade or my sport, I never loaded myself with fowling-piece or rifle. Assiduous exercise had made me master of a weapon of much easier carriage, and, within a moderate distance, more destructive and unerring. This was the Tom-hawk. With this I have often severed an oak branch and cut the sinews of a cat-o'mountain, at the distance of sixty feet.

The unfrequency with which I had lately encountered this foe, and the incumbrance of provision, made me neglect, on this occasion, to bring with me my usual arms.

---

* The grey Cougar. This animal has all the essential characteristics of a tyger. Though somewhat inferior in size and strength, these are such as to make him equally formidable to man [Brown's note].

[1] "The industry of our hunters has nearly banished . . .": here "banished" means both removed and made extinct. This is the second appearance of the novel's panthers (see notes 2.11 and 16.7). In this chapter Edgar calls the panther a "savage" and a member of "that detested race," and thus begins to link the panthers with the "savage" Delaware warriors who will appear in Chapter 17. Given the parallels between the panthers and the Delawares, the word "banished" also underscores the violent removal of the Indians from the region. For more on the novel's animalistic images and the way they may link the novel's Indian and Irish figures, see the Introduction.

The beast that was now before me, when stimulated by hunger, was accustomed to assail whatever could provide him with a banquet of blood. He would set upon the man and the deer with equal and irresistible ferocity. His sagacity was equal to his strength, and he seemed able to discover when his antagonist was armed and prepared for defence.

My past experience enabled me to estimate the full extent of my danger. He sat on the brow of the steep, eyeing the bridge, and apparently deliberating whether he should cross it. It was probable that he had scented my foot-steps thus far, and should he pass over, his vigilance could scarcely fail of detecting my assylum. The pit into which Clithero had sunk from my view was at some distance. To reach it was the first impulse of my fear, but this could not be done without exciting the observation and pursuit of this enemy. I deeply regretted the untoward chance that had led me, when I first came over, to a different shelter.

Should he retain his present station, my danger was scarcely lessened. To pass over in the face of a famished tyger was only to rush upon my fate. The falling of the trunk, which had lately been so anxiously deprecated, was now, with no less solicitude, desired. Every new gust, I hoped, would tear asunder its remaining bands, and, by cutting off all communication between the opposite steeps, place me in security.

My hopes, however, were destined to be frustrated. The fibres of the prostrate tree, were obstinately tenacious of their hold, and presently the animal scrambled down the rock and proceeded to cross it.

Of all kinds of death, that which now menaced me was the most abhorred. To die by disease, or by the hand of a fellow-creature, was propitious and lenient in comparison with being rent to pieces by the fangs of this savage. To perish, in this obscure retreat, by means so impervious to the anxious curiosity of my friends, to lose my portion of existence by so untoward and ignoble a destiny, was insupportable. I bitterly deplored my rashness in coming hither unprovided for an encounter like this.

The evil of my present circumstances consisted chiefly in suspense. My death was unavoidable, but my imagination had leisure to torment itself by anticipations. One foot of the savage was slowly and cautiously moved after the other. He struck his claws so deeply into the bark that they were with difficulty withdrawn. At length he leaped upon the ground. We were now separated by an interval of scarcely eight feet. To leave the spot where I crouched, was impossible. Behind and beside me, the cliff rose perpendicularly, and before me was this grim and terrific visage. I shrunk still closer to the ground and closed my eyes.

From this pause of horror I was roused by the noise occasioned by a second spring of the animal. He leaped into the pit, in which I had so deeply regretted that I had not taken refuge, and disappeared. My rescue was so sudden, and so much beyond my belief or my hope, that I doubted, for a moment, whether my senses did not deceive me. This opportunity of escape was not to be neglected. I left my place, and scrambled over the trunk with a precipitation which had liked to have proved fatal. The tree groaned and shook under me, the wind blew with unexampled violence, and I had scarcely reached the opposite steep when the roots were severed from the rock and the whole fell thundering to the bottom of the chasm.

My trepidations were not speedily quieted. I looked back with wonder on my hair-breadth escape, and on that singular concurrence of events, which had placed me, in so short a period, in absolute security. Had the trunk fallen a moment earlier, I should have been imprisoned on the hill or thrown headlong. Had its fall been delayed another moment I should have been pursued; for the beast now issued from his den, and testified his surprise and disappointment by tokens the sight of which made my blood run cold.

He saw me, and hastened to the verge of the chasm. He squatted on his hind-legs and assumed the attitude of one preparing to leap. My consternation was excited afresh by these appearances. It seemed at first as if the rift was too wide for any power of muscles to carry him in safety over; but I knew the unparalleled agility of this animal, and that his experience had made him a better judge of the practicability of this exploit than I was.

Still there was hope that he would relinquish this design as desperate. This hope was quickly at an end. He sprung, and his fore-legs touched the verge of the rock on which I stood. In spite of vehement exertions, however, the surface was too smooth and too hard to allow him to make good his hold. He fell, and a piercing cry, uttered below, shewed that nothing had obstructed his descent to the bottom.

Thus was I again rescued from death. Nothing but the pressure of famine could have prompted this savage to so audacious and hazardous an effort; but, by yielding to this impulse, he had made my future visits to this spot exempt from peril. Clithero was, likewise, relieved from a danger that was imminent and unforeseen. Prowling over these grounds the panther could scarcely have failed to meet with this solitary fugitive.

Had the animal lived, my first duty would have been to have sought him out, and assailed him with my Tom-hawk; but no undertaking would have been more hazardous. Lurking in the grass, or in the branches of a tree, his eye might have descried my approach, he might leap upon me unperceived, and my weapon would be useless.

With an heart beating with unwonted rapidity, I once more descended the cliff, entered the cavern, and arrived at Huntly farm, drenched with rain, and exhausted by fatigue.

By night the storm was dispelled; but my exhausted strength would not allow me to return to the mountain. At the customary hour I retired to my chamber. I incessantly ruminated on the adventures of the last day, and inquired into the conduct which I was next to pursue.

The bridge being destroyed, my customary access was cut off. There was no possibility of restoring this bridge. My strength would not suffice to drag a fallen tree from a distance, and there was none whose position would abridge or supersede that labour. Some other expedient must, therefore, be discovered to pass this chasm.

I reviewed the circumstances of my subterranean journey. The cavern was imperfectly explored. Its branches might be numerous. That which I had hitherto pursued, terminated in an opening at a considerable distance from the bottom. Other branches might exist, some of which might lead to the foot of the precipice, and thence a communication might be found with the summit of the interior hill.

The danger of wandering into dark and untried paths, and the commodiousness of that road which had at first been taken, were sufficient reasons for having hitherto suspended my examination of the different branches of this labyrinth. Now my customary road was no longer practicable, and another was to be carefully explored. For this end, on my next journey to the mountain, I determined to take with me a lamp, and unravel this darksome maze: This project I resolved to execute the next day.

I now recollected what, if it had more seasonably occurred, would have taught me caution. Some months before this a farmer, living in the skirts of Norwalk, discovered two marauders in his field, whom he imagined to be a male and female panther. They had destroyed some sheep, and had been hunted by the farmer, with long and fruitless diligence. Sheep had likewise been destroyed in different quarters; but the owners had fixed the imputation of the crime upon dogs, many of whom had atoned for their supposed offences by their death. He who had mentioned his discovery of panthers, received little credit from his neighbours; because a long time had elapsed since these animals were supposed to have been exiled from this district, and because no other person had seen them. The truth of this seemed now to be confirmed by the testimony of my own senses; but, if the rumour were true, there still existed another of these animals, who might harbour in the obscurities of this desert, and against whom it was necessary to employ some precaution. Henceforth I resolved never to traverse the wilderness unfurnished with my tom-hawk.

These images, mingled with those which the contemplation of futurity suggested, floated, for a time, in my brain; but at length gave place to sleep.[2]

---

[2] "But at length gave place to sleep": beginning with this final sentence of Chapter 12, Edgar moves toward an episode of sleeping that will dramatically change the narrative and the reader's understanding of him. His sleepiness is first mentioned here; after waking at the beginning of Chapter 13 because of his nightmares about Waldegrave, he again prepares to sleep but is interrupted by the arrival of Weymouth, who tells his story in Chapters 14 and 15. It is only in Chapter 16 that Edgar awakes from his sleep in new circumstances that determine the second half of the novel. Structurally, Chapters 13–15 may be seen as a hinge between the book's first half (twelve chapters), where action centers on Clithero, and its second half (also twelve chapters), where action centers on the Delawares.

Chapter XIII

SINCE my return home, my mind had been fully occupied by schemes and reflections relative to Clithero. The project suggested by thee, and to which I had determined to devote my leisure, was forgotten, or remembered for a moment and at wide intervals. What, however, was nearly banished from my waking thoughts, occurred, in an incongruous and half-seen form, to my dreams. During my sleep, the image of Waldegrave flitted before me. Methought the sentiment that impelled him to visit me, was not affection or complacency, but inquietude and anger. Some service or duty remained to be performed by me, which I had culpably neglected: to inspirit my zeal, to awaken my remembrance, and incite me to the performance of this duty, did this glimmering messenger, this half indignant apparition, come.

I commonly awake soon enough to mark the youngest dawn of the morning. Now, in consequence perhaps of my perturbed sleep, I opened my eyes before the stars had lost any of their lustre. This circumstance produced some surprise, until the images that lately hovered in my fancy, were recalled, and furnished somewhat like a solution of the problem. Connected with the image of my dead friend, was that of his sister. The discourse that took place at our last interview; the scheme of transcribing, for thy use, all the letters which, during his short but busy life, I received from him; the nature of this correspondence, and the opportunity which this employment would afford me of contemplating these ample and precious monuments of the intellectual existence and moral pre-eminence of my friend, occurred to my thoughts.

The resolution to prosecute the task was revived. The obligation of benevolence, with regard to Clithero, was not discharged. This, neither duty nor curiosity would permit to be overlooked or delayed; but why should my whole attention and activity be devoted to this man? The hours which were spent at home and in my chamber, could not be more usefully employed than in making my intended copy.

In a few hours after sun-rise I purposed to resume my way to the mountain. Could this interval be appropriated to a better purpose than in counting over my friend's letters, setting them apart from my own, and preparing them for that transcription from which I expected so high and yet so mournful a gratification?

This purpose, by no violent union, was blended with the recollection of my dream. This recollection infused some degree of wavering and dejection into my mind. In transcribing these letters I should violate pathetic and solemn injunctions frequently repeated by the writer. Was there some connection between this purpose and the incidents of my vision? Was the latter sent to enforce the interdictions which had been formerly imposed?

Thou art not fully acquainted with the intellectual history of thy brother. Some information on that head will be necessary to explain the nature of that reluctance which I now feel to comply with thy request, and which had formerly so much excited thy surprise.

Waldegrave, like other men, early devoted to meditation and books, had adopted, at different periods, different systems of opinion, on topics connected with religion and morals. His earliest creeds, tended to efface the impressions of his education; to deify necessity and universalize matter; to destroy the popular distinctions between soul and body, and to dissolve the supposed connection between the moral condition of man, anterior and subsequent to death.[1]

This creed he adopted with all the fulness of conviction, and propagated with the utmost zeal. Soon after our friendship commenced, fortune placed us at a distance from each other, and no intercourse was allowed but by the pen. Our letters, however, were punctual and copious. Those of Waldegrave were too frequently devoted to the defence of his favourite tenets.

Thou art acquainted with the revolution that afterwards took place in his mind. Placed within the sphere of religious influence, and listening daily to the reasonings and exhortations of Mr. S—, whose benign temper and blameless deportment was a visible and constant lesson, he insensibly resumed the faith which he had relinquished, and became the vehement opponent of all that he had formerly defended. The chief object of his labours, in this new state of his mind, was to counteract the effect of his former reasonings on my opinions.

At this time, other changes took place in his situation, in consequence of which we were once more permitted to reside under the same roof. The intercourse now ceased to be by letter, and the subtle and laborious argumentations which he had formerly produced against religion, and which were contained in a permanent form, were combatted in transient conversation. He was not only eager to subvert those opinions, which he had contributed to instil into me, but was anxious that the letters and manuscripts, which had been employed in their support, should be destroyed. He did not fear wholly or chiefly on my own account. He believed that the influence of former reasonings on my faith would be sufficiently eradicated by the new; but he dreaded lest these manuscripts might fall into other hands, and thus produce mischiefs which it would not be in his power to repair. With regard to me, the poison had been followed by its antidote; but with respect to others, these letters would communicate the poison when the antidote could not be administered.

I would not consent to this sacrifice. I did not entirely abjure the creed which had, with great copiousness and eloquence, been defended in these letters. Beside, mixed up with abstract reasonings, were numberless passages which elucidated the character and history of my friend. These were too precious to be consigned to oblivion, and to take them out of their present connection and arrangement, would be to mutilate and deform them.

---

[1] "Anterior and subsequent to death": in other words, Waldegrave was a materialist and deist, and in his letters he developed late Enlightenment arguments against religion and superstition. As he notes in the paragraphs that follow, Edgar still adheres to the "creed which had . . . been defended in these letters." Brown's close friend and roommate Elihu Hubbard Smith left behind deist writings that scandalized his family when he died in 1798. See the discussion of Brown's relation to Smith and his New York circle in the Introduction.

His intreaties and remonstrances were earnest and frequent, but always ineffectual. He had too much purity of motives to be angry at my stubbornness, but his sense of the mischievous tendency of these letters, was so great, that my intractability cost him many a pang.

He was now gone, and I had not only determined to preserve these monuments, but had consented to copy them for the use of another: for the use of one whose present and eternal welfare had been the chief object of his cares and efforts. Thou, like others of thy sex, art unaccustomed to metaphysical refinements.[2] Thy religion is the growth of sensibility and not of argument. Thou art not fortified and prepossessed against the subtleties, with which the being and attributes of the deity have been assailed. Would it be just to expose thee to pollution and depravity from this source? To make thy brother the instrument of thy apostacy, the author of thy fall? That brother, whose latter days were so ardently devoted to cherishing the spirit of devotion in thy heart?

These ideas now occurred with more force than formerly. I had promised, not without reluctance, to give thee the entire copy of his letters; but I now receded from this promise. I resolved merely to select for thy perusal such as were narrative or descriptive. This could not be done with too much expedition. It was still dark, but my sleep was at an end, and, by a common apparatus, that lay beside my bed, I could instantly produce a light.

The light was produced, and I proceeded to the cabinet where all my papers and books are deposited. This was my own contrivance and workmanship, undertaken by the advice of Sarsefield, who took infinite pains to foster that mechanical genius,[3] which displayed itself so early and so forcibly in thy friend. The key belonging to this, was, like the cabinet itself, of singular structure. For greater safety, it was constantly placed in a closet, which was likewise locked.

The key was found as usual, and the cabinet opened. The letters were bound together in a compact form, lodged in a parchment case, and placed in a secret drawer. This drawer would not have been detected by common eyes, and it opened by the motion of a spring, of whose existence none but the maker was conscious. This drawer I had opened before I went to sleep and the letters were then safe.

Thou canst not imagine my confusion and astonishment, when, on opening the drawer, I perceived that the pacquet was gone. I looked with more attention, and put my hand within it, but the space was empty. Whither had it gone, and by whom was it purloined? I was not conscious of having taken it away, yet no hands but mine could have done it. On the last evening I had doubtless removed it to some other

---

[2] "Unaccustomed to metaphysical refinements": Edgar patronizes Mary in assuming that, as a woman, she is incapable of the intellectual effort and discernment necessary to properly understand Waldegrave's letters.

[3] "Sarsefield, who took infinite pains to foster that mechanical genius . . .": like Clithero, Edgar has learned from Sarsefield how to make secretive boxes and other containers in which he hides valuable writings. This box-making skill is one of many parallels between Edgar and Clithero.

corner, but had forgotten it. I tasked my understanding and my memory. I could not conceive the possibility of any motives inducing me to alter my arrangements in this respect, and was unable to recollect that I had made this change.

What remained? This invaluable relique had disappeared. Every thought and every effort must be devoted to the single purpose of regaining it. As yet I did not despair. Until I had opened and ransacked every part of the cabinet in vain, I did not admit the belief that I had lost it. Even then this persuasion was tumultuous and fluctuating. It had vanished to my senses, but these senses were abused and depraved. To have passed, of its own accord, through the pores of this wood, was impossible; but if it were gone, thus did it escape.

I was lost in horror and amazement. I explored every nook a second and a third time, but still it eluded my eye and my touch. I opened my closets and cases. I pryed every where, unfolded every article of cloathing, turned and scrutinized every instrument and tool, but nothing availed.

My thoughts were not speedily collected or calmed. I threw myself on the bed and resigned myself to musing. That my loss was irretreivable, was a supposition not to be endured. Yet ominous terrors haunted me. A whispering intimation that a relique which I valued more than life was torn forever away by some malignant and inscrutable destiny. The same power that had taken it from this receptacle, was able to waft it over the ocean or the mountains, and condemn me to a fruitless and eternal search.

But what was he that committed the theft? Thou only, of the beings who live, wast acquainted with the existence of these manuscripts. Thou art many miles distant, and art utterly a stranger to the mode or place of their concealment. Not only access to the cabinet, but access to the room, without my knowledge and permission, was impossible. Both were locked during this night. Not five hours had elapsed since the cabinet and drawer had been opened, and since the letters had been seen and touched, being in their ordinary position. During this interval, the thief had entered, and despoiled me of my treasure.

This event, so inexplicable and so dreadful, threw my soul into a kind of stupor or distraction, from which I was suddenly roused by a foot-step, softly moving in the entry near my door. I started from my bed, as if I had gained a glimpse of the robber. Before I could run to the door, some one knocked. I did not think upon the propriety of answering the signal, but hastened with tremulous fingers and throbbing heart to open the door. My uncle, in his night-dress, and apparently just risen from his bed, stood before me!

He marked the eagerness and perturbation of my looks, and inquired into the cause. I did not answer his inquiries. His appearance in my chamber and in this guise, added to my surprise. My mind was full of the late discovery, and instantly conceived some connection between this unseasonable visit and my lost manuscript. I interrogated him in my turn as to the cause of his coming.

Why, said he, I came to ascertain whether it was you or not who amused himself so strangely at this time of night. What is the matter with you? Why are you up so early?

I told him that I had been roused by my dreams, and finding no inclination to court my slumber back again, I had risen, though earlier by some hours than the usual period of my rising.

But why did you go up stairs? You might easily imagine that the sound of your steps would alarm those below, who would be puzzled to guess who it was that had thought proper to amuse himself in this manner.

Up stairs? I have not left my room this night. It is not ten minutes since I awoke, and my door has not since been opened.

Indeed! That is strange. Nay, it is impossible. It was your feet surely that I heard pacing so solemnly and indefatigably across the *long-room* for near an hour. I could not for my life conjecture, for a time, who it was, but finally concluded that it was you. There was still, however, some doubt, and I came hither to satisfy myself.

These tidings were adapted to raise all my emotions to a still higher pitch. I questioned him with eagerness as to the circumstances he had noticed. He said he had been roused by a sound, whose power of disturbing him arose, not from its loudness, but from its uncommonness. He distinctly heard some one pacing to and fro with bare feet, in the long room: This sound continued, with little intermission, for an hour. He then noticed a cessation of the walking, and a sound as if some one were lifting the lid of the large cedar chest, that stood in the corner of this room. The walking was not resumed, and all was silent. He listened for a quarter of an hour, and busied himself in conjecturing the cause of this disturbance. The most probable conclusion was, that the walker was his nephew, and his curiosity had led him to my chamber to ascertain the truth.

This dwelling has three stories. The two lower stories are divided into numerous apartments. The upper story constitutes a single room whose sides are the four walls of the house, and whose ceiling is the roof. This room is unoccupied, except by lumber, and imperfectly lighted by a small casement at one end. In this room, were footsteps heard by my uncle.

The stair-case leading to it terminated in a passage near my door. I snatched the candle, and desiring him to follow me, added, that I would ascertain the truth in a moment. He followed, but observed that the walking had ceased long enough for the person to escape.

I ascended to the room, and looked behind and among the tables, and chairs, and casks, which, were confusedly scattered through it, but found nothing in the shape of man. The cedar chest, spoken of by Mr. Huntly, contained old books, and remnants of maps and charts, whose worthlessness unfitted them for accommodation elsewhere. The lid was without hinges or lock. I examined this repository, but there was nothing which attracted my attention.

The way between the kitchen door, and the door of the long-room, had no impediments. Both were usually unfastened but the motives by which any stranger to the dwelling, or indeed any one within it, could be prompted to chuse this place and hour, for an employment of this kind, were wholly incomprehensible.

When the family rose, inquiries were made but no satisfaction was obtained. The family consisted only of four persons, my uncle, my two sisters, and myself. I mentioned to them the loss I had sustained, but their conjectures were no less unsatisfactory on this than on the former incident.

There was no end to my restless meditations. Waldegrave was the only being, beside myself, acquainted with the secrets of my cabinet. During his life these manuscripts had been the objects of perpetual solicitude; to gain possession, to destroy, or secrete them, was the strongest of his wishes. Had he retained his sensibility on the approach of death, no doubt he would have renewed, with irresistable solemnity, his injunctions to destroy them.

Now, however, they had vanished. There were no materials of conjecture; no probabilities to be weighed, or suspicions to revolve. Human artifice or power was unequal to this exploit. Means less than preternatural would not furnish a conveyance for this treasure.

It was otherwise with regard to this unseasonable walker. His inducements indeed were beyond my power to conceive, but to enter these doors and ascend these stairs, demanded not the faculties of any being more than human.

This intrusion, and the pillage of my cabinet were contemporary events. Was there no more connection between them than that which results from time? Was not the purloiner of my treasure and the wanderer the same person? I could not reconcile the former incident with the attributes of man, and yet a secret faith, not to be outrooted or suspended, swayed me, and compelled me to imagine that the detection of this visitant, would unveil the thief.

These thoughts were pregnant with dejection and reverie. Clithero, during the day, was forgotten. On the succeeding night, my intentions, with regard to this man, returned. I derived some slender consolation from reflecting, that time, in its long lapse and ceaseless revolutions, might dissipate the gloom that environed me. Meanwhile I struggled to dismiss the images connected with my loss and to think only of Clithero.

My impatience was as strong as ever to obtain another interview with this man. I longed with vehemence for the return of day. I believed that every moment added to his sufferings, intellectual and physical, and confided in the efficacy of my presence to alleviate or suspend them. The provisions I had left would be speedily consumed, and the abstinence of three days was sufficient to undermine the vital energies. I, some times, hesitated whether I ought not instantly to depart. It was night indeed, but the late storm had purified the air, and the radiance of a full moon was universal and dazling.

From this attempt I was deterred by reflecting that my own frame needed the repairs of sleep. Toil and watchfulness, if prolonged another day, would deeply injure a constitution by no means distinguished for its force. I must, therefore, compel, if it were possible, some hours of repose. I prepared to retire to bed, when a new incident occurred to divert my attention for a time from these designs.

Chapter XIV

WHILE sitting alone by the parlour fire, marking the effects of moon-light, I noted one on horseback coming towards the gate. At first sight, methought his shape and guise were not wholly new to me; but all that I could discern was merely a resemblance to some one whom I had before seen. Presently he stopped, and, looking towards the house, made inquiries of a passenger who chanced to be near. Being apparently satisfied with the answers he received, he rode with a quick pace, into the court and alighted at the door. I started from my seat, and, going forth, waited with some impatience to hear his purpose explained.

He accosted me with the formality of a stranger, and asked if a young man, by name Edgar Huntly, resided here. Being answered in the affirmative, and being requested to come in, he entered, and seated himself, without hesitation, by the fire. Some doubt and anxiety were visible in his looks. He seemed desirous of information upon some topic, and yet betrayed terror lest the answers he might receive should subvert some hope, or confirm some foreboding.

Meanwhile I scrutinized his features with much solicitude. A nearer and more deliberate view convinced me that the first impression was just; but still I was unable to call up his name or the circumstances of our former meeting. The pause was at length ended by his saying, in a faltering voice:

My name is Weymouth. I came hither to obtain information on a subject in which my happiness is deeply concerned.

At the mention of his name, I started. It was a name too closely connected with the image of thy brother, not to call up affecting and vivid recollections. Weymouth thou knowest, was thy brother's friend. It is three years since this man left America,[1] during which time no tidings had been heard of him, at least, by thy brother. He had now returned, and was probably unacquainted with the fate of his friend.

After an anxious pause, he continued. . . . Since my arrival I have heard of an event which has, on many accounts, given me the deepest sorrow. I loved Waldegrave, and know not any person in the world whose life was dearer to me than his. There were considerations, however, which made it more precious to me than the life of one whose merits might be greater. With his life, my own existence and property were, I have reason to think, inseparably united.

On my return to my country, after a long absence, I made immediate inquiries after him. I was informed of his untimely death. I had questions, of infinite moment to my happiness, to decide with regard to the state and disposition of his property. I sought out those of his friends who had maintained with him the most frequent and confidential intercourse, but they could not afford me any satisfaction. At length, I was informed that a young man of your name, and living in this district, had enjoyed

---

[1] "Three years since this man left America": this passage, combined with the information that Waldegrave left North America in August 1784, in Chapter 15 (note 15.1), allows the narrative's action to be dated to the year 1787.

more of his affection and society than any other, had regulated the property which he left behind, and was best qualified to afford the intelligence which I sought. You, it seems, are this person, and of you I must make inquiries to which I conjure you to return sincere and explicit answers.

That, said I, I shall find no difficulty in doing. Whatever questions you shall think proper to ask, I will answer with readiness and truth.

What kind of property and to what amount was your friend possessed of at his death?

It was money, and consisted of deposits at the bank of North America. The amount was little short of eight thousand dollars.[2]

On whom has this property devolved?

His sister was his only kindred, and she is now in possession of it.

Did he leave any will by which he directed the disposition of his property? While thus speaking, Weymouth fixed his eyes upon my countenance, and seemed anxious to pierce into my inmost soul. I was somewhat surprised at his questions, but much more at the manner in which they were put. I answered him, however, without delay. . . . He left no will, nor was any paper discovered, by which we could guess at his intentions. No doubt, indeed, had he made a will his sister would have been placed precisely in the same condition in which she now is. He was not only bound to her by the strongest ties of kindred, but by affection and gratitude.

Weymouth now withdrew his eyes from my face, and sunk into a mournful reverie. He sighed often and deeply. This deportment and the strain of his inquiries excited much surprise. His interest in the fate of Waldegrave ought to have made the information he had received, a source of satisfaction rather than of regret. The property which Waldegrave left was much greater than his mode of life, and his own professions had given us reason to except, but it was no more than sufficient to insure to thee an adequate subsistence. It ascertained the happiness of those who were dearest to Waldegrave, and placed them forever beyond the reach of that poverty which had hitherto beset them. I made no attempt to interrupt the silence, but prepared to answer any new interrogatory. At length, Weymouth resumed:

Waldegrave was a fortunate man, to amass so considerable a sum in so short a time. I remember, when we parted, he was poor. He used to lament that his scrupulous integrity precluded him from all the common roads to wealth. He did not contemn riches, but he set the highest value upon competence; and imagined that he was doomed forever to poverty. His religious duty compelled him to seek his livelihood

---

[2] "Eight thousand dollars": this is an enormous sum in the 1780s, enough to allow Edgar and Mary to live independently (i.e., solely on the interest it would provide) if they were to keep the money Weymouth left with Waldegrave. Calculated relative to average unskilled wage compensation then and now, $8,000 in 1790 equals $3.399 million in 2005. Calculated relative to a gross domestic product per capita index then and now, $8,000 in 1790 equals $6.961 million in 2005. Explanations and supporting statistics for these different models for historical conversions of dollar value and a do-it-yourself calculator are available at Samuel H. Williamson, "What is Its Relative Value in U.S. Dollars?" Economic History Services, June 2006, http://eh.net/hmit/compare/.

by teaching a school of blacks.[3] The labour was disproportioned to his feeble constitution, and the profit was greatly disproportioned to the labour. It scarcely supplied
the necessities of nature, and was reduced sometimes even below that standard by his
frequent indisposition. I rejoice to find that his scruples had somewhat relaxed their
force, and that he had betaken himself to some more profitable occupation. Pray,
what was his new way of business?

Nay, said I, his scruples continued as rigid, in this respect, as ever. He was teacher of
the Negro free-school when he died.

Indeed! How then came he to amass so much money? Could he blend any more lucrative pursuit with his duty as a school-master?

So it seems.

What was his pursuit?

That question, I believe, none of his friends are qualified to answer. I thought myself acquainted with the most secret transactions of his life, but this had been carefully concealed from me. I was not only unapprised of any other employment of his
time, but had not the slightest suspicion of his possessing any property beside his
clothes and books. Ransacking his papers, with a different view, I lighted on his
bank-book, in which was a regular receipt for seven thousand five hundred dollars.
By what means he acquired this money, and even the acquisition of it, till his death
put us in possession of his papers, was wholly unknown to us.

Possibly he might have held it in trust for another. In this case some memorandums
or letters would be found explaining this affair.

True. This supposition could not fail to occur, in consequence of which the most
diligent search was made among his papers, but no shred or scrap was to be found
which countenanced our conjecture.

You may reasonably be surprised, and perhaps offended, said Weymouth, at these
inquiries; but it is time to explain my motives for making them. Three years ago I
was, like Waldegrave, indigent, and earned my bread by daily labour. During seven
years service in a public office, I saved, from the expences of subsistence, a few hundred dollars. I determined to strike into a new path, and, with this sum, to lay the
foundation of better fortune. I turned it into a bulky commodity, freighted and
loaded a small vessel, and went with it to Barcelona in Spain. I was not unsuccessful
in my projects, and, changing my abode to England, France and Germany, according
as my interest required, I became finally possessed of sufficient for the supply of all
my wants. I then resolved to return to my native country, and, laying out my money

---

[3] "Teaching a school of blacks": Waldegrave's teaching at a school for free African Americans indicates that he has strong abolitionist beliefs. Both this detail and Waldegrave's fear that his deist
sensibilities will be discovered after his death suggest that Brown is using details from the life of
his closest friend, Elihu Hubbard Smith (who was involved in support for a similar school). See
note 13.1 on the deism of Waldegrave and Smith, and Waterman, "'He Must, Indeed, Be
Wretched, Who Fears Inquiry': The Forms and Limits of Friendship in the Diary of Elihu Hubbard
Smith," in *The Friendly Club of New York City.*

in land, to spend the rest of my days in the luxury and quiet of an opulent farmer. For this end I invested the greatest part of my property in a cargo of wine from Madeira. The remainder I turned into a bill of exchange for seven thousand five hundred dollars. I had maintained a friendly correspondence with Waldegrave during my absence. There was no one with whom I had lived on terms of so much intimacy, and had boundless confidence in his integrity. To him therefore I determined to transmit this bill, requesting him to take the money into safe keeping until my return. In this manner I endeavoured to provide against the accidents that might befall my person or my cargo in crossing the ocean.

It was my fate to encounter the worst of these disasters. We were overtaken by a storm, my vessel was driven ashore on the coast of Portugal,[4] my cargo was utterly lost, and the greater part of the crew and passengers were drowned. I was rescued from the same fate by some fishermen. In consequence of the hardships to which I had been exposed, having laboured for several days at the pumps, and spent the greater part of a winter night, hanging from the rigging of the ship, and perpetually beaten by the waves, I contracted a severe disease, which bereaved me of the use of my limbs. The fishermen who rescued me, carried me to their huts, and there I remained three weeks helpless and miserable.

That part of the coast on which I was thrown, was, in the highest degree, sterile and rude. Its few inhabitants subsisted precariously on the produce of the ocean. Their dwellings were of mud, low, filthy, dark, and comfortless. Their fuel was the stalks of shrubs, sparingly scattered over a sandy desert. Their poverty scarcely allowed them salt and black bread with their fish, which was obtained in unequal and sometimes insufficient quantities, and which they ate with all its impurities and half cooked.

My former habits as well as my present indisposition required very different treatment from what the ignorance and penury of these people obliged them to bestow. I lay upon the moist earth, imperfectly sheltered from the sky, and with neither raiment or fire to keep me warm. My hosts had little attention or compassion to spare to the wants of others. They could not remove me to a more hospitable district, and here, without doubt, I should have perished had not a monk chanced to visit their hovels. He belonged to a convent of St. Jago,[5] some leagues farther from the shore,

---

[4] "My vessel was driven ashore on the coast of Portugal": by having Weymouth shipwreck in Portugal, Brown alludes to a country that was experiencing well-known cultural conflicts between gothic superstition and Enlightenment. Throughout the eighteenth century, Portugal was a byword for Jesuit-organized ignorance. Under the rule of Sebastião de Melo, Marquis of Pombal, the Jesuits were suppressed, and Portugal was modernized with England as its model. Brown discusses Pombal as a hero of enlightened modernity in his essay "Walstein's School of History" (August–September 1799), written at the same moment as *Edgar Huntly* (August 1799). This essay is in the Related Texts.

[5] "St. Jago": St. Jago is Saint James, patron of Spain, and the name of a port city there. As mentioned in the previous note, Weymouth's gothic mini-tale, like many gothic narratives, plays on stereotypical divisions between a "bigotted and sordid" Catholic-Mediterranean Europe (the "bigotted and sordid" monks of St. Jago) and an enlightened and more progressive Protestant northwest Europe (exemplified by the "Scottish surgeon" who restores Weymouth's health eight paragraphs later).

who used to send one of its members annually to inspect the religious concerns of those outcasts. Happily this was the period of their visitations.

My abode in Spain had made me somewhat conversant with its language. The dialect of this monk did not so much differ from Castilian, but that, with the assistance of Latin, we were able to converse. The jargon of the fishermen was unintelligible, and they had vainly endeavoured to keep up my spirits by informing me of this expected visit.

This monk was touched with compassion at my calamity, and speedily provided the means of my removal to his convent. Here I was charitably entertained, and the aid of a physician was procured for me. He was but poorly skilled in his profession, and rather confirmed than alleviated my disease. The Portuguese of his trade, especially in remoter districts, are little more than dealers in talismans and nostrums. For a long time I was unable to leave my pallet, and had no prospect before me but that of consuming my days in the gloom of this cloister.

All the members of this convent, but he who had been my first benefactor, and whose name was Chaledro, were bigotted and sordid. Their chief motive for treating me with kindness, was the hope of obtaining a convert from heresy. They spared no pains to subdue my errors, and were willing to prolong my imprisonment, in the hope of finally gaining their end. Had my fate been governed by those, I should have been immured in this convent, and compelled, either to adopt their fanatical creed or to put an end to my own life, in order to escape their well meant persecutions. Chaledro, however, though no less sincere in his faith and urgent in his intreaties, yet finding me invincible, exerted his influence to obtain my liberty.

After many delays, and strenuous exertions of my friend, they consented to remove me to Oporto. The journey was to be performed in an open cart over a mountainous country, in the heats of summer. The monks endeavoured to dissuade me from the enterprize, for my own sake, it being scarcely possible that one in my feeble state, should survive a journey like this; but I despaired of improving my condition by other means. I preferred death to the imprisonment of a Portuguese monastery, and knew that I could hope for no alleviation of my disease, but from the skill of Scottish or French physicians, whom I expected to meet with in that city. I adhered to my purpose with so much vehemence and obstinacy, that they finally yielded to my wishes.

My road lay through the wildest and most rugged districts. It did not exceed ninety miles, but seven days were consumed on the way. The motion of the vehicle racked me with the keenest pangs, and my attendants concluded that every stage would be my last. They had been selected without due regard to their characters. They were knavish and inhuman, and omitted nothing, but actual violence, to hasten my death. They purposely retarded the journey, and protracted to seven, what might have been readily performed in four days. They neglected to execute the orders which they had received, respecting my lodging and provisions, and from them, as well as from the peasants, who were sure to be informed that I was an heretic, I suffered every species of insult and injury. My constitution, as well as my frame, possessed a fund of strength of which I had no previous conception. In spite of hardship and exposure and abstinence, I, at last, arrived at Oporto.[6]

Instead of being carried, agreeably to Chaledro's direction, to a convent of St. Jago, I was left, late in the evening, in the porch of a common hospital. My attendants, having laid me on the pavement and loaded me with imprecations, left me to obtain admission by my own efforts. I passed the live-long night in this spot, and in the morning was received into the house, in a state which left it uncertain whether I was alive or dead.

After recovering my sensibility, I made various efforts to procure a visit from some English merchant. This was no easy undertaking for one in my deplorable condition. I was too weak to articulate my words distinctly, and these words were rendered by my foreign accent, scarcely intelligible. The likelihood of my speedy death made the people about me more indifferent to my wants and petitions.

I will not dwell upon my repeated disappointments, but content myself with mentioning that I gained the attention of a French gentleman, whose curiosity brought him to view the hospital. Through him, I obtained a visit from an English merchant, and finally gained the notice of a person, who formerly resided in America, and of whom I had imperfect knowledge. By their kindness I was removed from the hospital to a private house. A Scottish surgeon was summoned to my assistance, and in seven months, I was restored to my present state of health.

At Oporto, I embarked, in an American ship, for New-York. I was destitute of all property, and relied, for the pay-ment of the debts which I was obliged to contract, as well as for my future subsistence, on my remittance, to Waldegrave. I hastened to Philadelphia, and was soon informed that my friend was dead. His death had taken place a long time since my remittance to him, hence this disaster was a subject of regret chiefly on his own account. I entertained no doubt but that my property had been secured, and that either some testamentary directions, or some papers had been left behind respecting this affair.

I sought out those who were formerly our mutual acquaintance, I found that they were wholly strangers to his affairs. They could merely relate some particulars of his singular death, and point out the lodgings which he formerly occupied. Hither I forthwith repaired, and discovered that he lived in this house with his sister, disconnected with its other inhabitants. They described his mode of life in terms that shewed them to be very imperfectly acquainted with it. It was easy indeed to infer, from their aspect and manners, that little sympathy or union could have subsisted between them and their co-tenants, and this inference was confirmed by their insinuations, the growth of prejudice and envy. They told me that Waldegrave's sister had gone to live in the country, but whither or for how long, she had not condescended to inform them, and they did not care to ask. She was a topping dame whose notions were much too high for her station. Who was more nice than wise, and yet was one who could stoop, when it most became her to stand upright. It was no business of theirs, but they could not but mention their suspicions that she had good reasons for

---

[6] "Oporto": a port city in northern Portugal.

leaving the city, and for concealing the place of her retreat. Some things were hard to be disguised. They spoke for themselves, and the only way to hinder disagreeable discoveries, was to keep out of sight.[7]

I was wholly a stranger to Waldegrave's sister. I knew merely that he had such a relation. There was nothing therefore to outbalance this unfavourable report, but the apparent malignity and grossness of those who gave it. It was not, however, her character about which I was solicitous, but merely the place where she might be found, and the suitable inquiries respecting her deceased brother, be answered. On this head, these people professed utter ignorance and were either unable or unwilling to direct me to any person in the city who knew more than themselves. After much discourse they, at length, let fall an intimation that if any one knew her place of retreat, it was probably a country lad, by name Huntly, who lived near the *Forks* of Delaware. After Waldegrave's death, this lad had paid his sister a visit, and seemed to be admitted on a very confidential footing. She left the house, for the last time, in his company, and he, therefore, was most likely to know what had become of her.

The name of Huntly was not totally unknown to me. I myself was born and brought up in the neighbouring township of Chetasco.[8] I had some knowledge of your family, and your name used often to be mentioned by Waldegrave, as that of one who, at a maturer age, would prove himself useful to his country. I determined therefore to apply to you for what information you could give. I designed to visit my father who lives in Chetasco and relieve him from that disquiet which his ignorance of my fate could not fail to have inspired, and both these ends could be thus, at the same time, accomplished.

Before I left the city, I thought it proper to apply to the merchant on whom my bill had been drawn. If this bill had been presented and paid, he had doubtless preserved some record of it, and hence a clue might be afforded, though every other expedient should fail. My usual ill fortune pursued me upon this occasion, for the merchant had lately become insolvent, and, to avoid the rage of his creditors, had fled, without leaving any vestige of this or similar transactions behind him. He had, some years since, been an adventurer from Holland, and was suspected to have returned thither.[9]

---

[7] "To keep out of sight": in other words, Weymouth's informants are suggesting that Mary Waldegrave, Edgar's fiancée, is pregnant and has left the area to hide her condition.

[8] This is the first mention of Chetasco, another white settlement near Solebury that will become important in the story of the Indian raids in the second half of the novel. While the place name is invented for this novel, it suggests an abbreviation or anagram-like version of Chester County, just west of Philadelphia and southwest of the novel's action in the Forks of the Delaware. Brown's father Elijah came to Philadelphia from Chester County, and his novelistic character Arthur Mervyn grows up there.

[9] "Suspected to have returned thither": after Weymouth's tale has emphasized the riskiness and instability of the world of commerce, this basic theme is repeated in this final paragraph, which recounts the bankruptcy and flight of the merchant who carried out Weymouth's transfer of funds to Waldegrave. Bankruptcy and economic instability were a common feature of Brown's world and a constant emphasis in his fiction. For more on Brown's family business background, see the discussion of Brown's early life in the Introduction.

Chapter XV

I CAME hither with an heart desponding of success. Adversity had weakened my faith in the promises of the future, and I was prepared to receive just such tidings as you have communicated. Unacquainted with the secret motives of Waldegrave and his sister, it is impossible for me to weigh the probabilities of their rectitude. I have only my own assertion to produce in support of my claim. All other evidence, all vouchers and papers, which might attest my veracity, or sanction my claim in a court of law, are buried in the ocean. The bill was transmitted just before my departure from Madeira, and the letters by which it was accompanied, informed Waldegrave of my design to follow it immediately. Hence he did not, it is probable, acknowledge the receipt of my letters. The vessels in which they were sent, arrived in due season. I was assured that all letters were duly deposited in the post-office, where, at present, mine are not to be found.

You assure me that nothing has been found among his papers, hinting at any pecuniary transaction between him and me. Some correspondence passed between us previous to that event. Have no letters, with my signature, been found? Are you qualified, by your knowledge of his papers, to answer me explicitly? Is it not possible for some letters to have been mislaid?

I am qualified, said I, to answer your inquiries beyond any other person in the world. Waldegrave maintained only general intercourse with the rest of mankind. With me his correspondence was copious, and his confidence, as I imagined, without bounds. His books and papers were contained in a single chest, at his lodgings, the keys of which he had about him when he died. These keys I carried to his sister, and was authorized by her to open and examine the contents of this chest. This was done with the utmost care. These papers are now in my possession. Among them no paper, of the tenor you mention, was found, and no letter with your signature. Neither Mary Waldegrave nor I are capable of disguising the truth or committing an injustice. The moment she receives conviction of your right she will restore this money to you. The moment I imbibe this conviction, I will exert all my influence, and it is not small, to induce her to restore it. Permit me, however, to question you in your turn. Who was the merchant on whom your bill was drawn, what was the date of it, and when did the bill and its counterparts arrive?

I do not exactly remember the date of the bills. They were made out, however, six days before I myself embarked which happened on the tenth of August 1784.[1] They were sent by three vessels, one of which was bound to Charleston and the others to New-York. The last arrived within two days of each other, and about the middle of November in the same year. The name of the payer was Monteith.

---

[1] "The tenth of August 1784": this date, combined with the timeline Weymouth presents in Chapter 14 (see note 14.1), sets the novel's action in the year 1787. Mid-1784 is also the moment when Brown's father Elijah was jailed for debt. See Kafer, *Charles Brockden Brown's Revolution*, 43–44.

After a pause of recollection, I answered, I will not hesitate to apprise you of every thing which may throw light upon this transaction, and whether favourable or otherwise to your claim. I have told you among my friends' papers your name is not to be found. I must likewise repeat that the possession of this money by Waldegrave was wholly unknown to us till his death. We are likewise unacquainted with any means by which he could get possession of so large a sum in his own right. He spent no more than his scanty stipend as a teacher, though this stipend was insufficient to supply his wants. This Bank-receipt is dated in December 1784, a fortnight, perhaps, after the date that you have mentioned. You will perceive how much this coincidence, which could scarcely have taken place by chance, is favourable to your claim.

Mary Waldegrave resides, at present, at Abingdon.[2] She will rejoice, as I do, to see one who, as her brother's friend, is entitled to her affection. Doubt not but that she will listen with impartiality and candour to all that you can urge in defence of your title to this money. Her decision will not be precipitate, but it will be generous and just, and founded on such reasons that, even if it be adverse to your wishes, you will be compelled to approve it.

I can entertain no doubt, he answered, as to the equity of my claim. The coincidences you mention are sufficient to convince me, that this sum was received upon my bill, but this conviction must necessarily be confined to myself. No one but I can be conscious to the truth of my own story. The evidence on which I build my faith, in this case, is that of my own memory and senses; but this evidence cannot make itself conspicuous to you. You have nothing but my bare assertion, in addition to some probabilities flowing from the conduct of Waldegrave. What facts may exist to corroborate my claim, which you have forgotten, or which you may think proper to conceal, I cannot judge. I know not what is passing in the secret of your hearts; I am unacquainted with the character of this lady and with yours. I have nothing on which to build surmises and suspicions of your integrity, and nothing to generate unusual confidence. The frailty of your virtue and the strength of your temptations I know not. However she decides in this case, and whatever opinion I shall form as to the reasonableness of her decision, it will not become me either to upbraid her, or to nourish discontentment and repinings.

I know that my claim has no legal support: that, if this money be resigned to me, it will be the impulse of spontaneous justice, and not the coercion of law to which I am indebted for it. Since, therefore, the justice of my claim is to be, measured not by law, but by simple equity, I will candidly acknowledge, that as yet it is uncertain whether I ought to receive, even should Miss Waldegrave be willing to give it. I know my own necessities and schemes, and in what degree this money would be subservient to these; but I know not the views and wants of others, and cannot estimate the usefulness of this money to them. However I decide upon your conduct in withholding or

---

[2] "Mary Waldegrave resides, at present, at Abingdon": Abington is a township in Montgomery County, Pennsylvania, about sixteen miles north of Philadelphia and about twenty miles southwest of Solebury, Pennsylvania. Abington was a village at this time; the population in 1790 was 881. It was the site of one of the earliest Quaker meetinghouses in the region, established in 1683.

retaining it, I shall make suitable allowance for my imperfect knowledge of your motives and wants, as well as for your unavoidable ignorance of mine.

I have related my sufferings from shipwreck and poverty, not to bias your judgment or engage your pity, but merely because the impulse to relate them chanced to awake; because my heart is softened by the remembrance of Waldegrave, who has been my only friend, and by the sight of one whom he loved.

I told you that my father lived in Chetasco. He is now aged, and I am his only child. I should have rejoiced in being able to relieve his grey hairs from labour to which his failing strength cannot be equal. This was one of my inducements in coming to America. Another was, to prepare the way for a woman whom I married in Europe, and who is now awaiting intelligence from me in London. Her poverty is not less than my own, and by marrying against the wishes of her kindred, she has bereaved herself of all support but that of her husband. Whether I shall be able to rescue her from indigence, whether I shall alleviate the poverty of my father or increase it by burthening his scanty funds by my own maintenance as well as his, the future alone can determine.

I confess that my stock of patience and hope has never been large, and that my misfortunes have nearly exhausted it. The flower of my years has been consumed in struggling with adversity, and my constitution has received a shock from sickness and mistreatment in Portugal, which I cannot expect long to survive. . . . But I make you sad (he continued.) I have said all that I meant to say in this interview. I am impatient to see my father, and night has already come. I have some miles yet to ride to his cottage and over a rough road. I will shortly visit you again, and talk to you at greater leisure on these and other topics. At present I leave you.

I was unwilling to part so abruptly with this guest, and intreated him to prolong his visit, but he would not be prevailed upon. Repeating his promise of shortly seeing me again, he mounted his horse and disappeared. I looked after him with affecting and complex emotions. I reviewed the incidents of this unexpected and extraordinary interview, as if it had existed in a dream. An hour had passed, and this stranger had alighted among us as from the clouds, to draw the veil from those obscurities which had bewildered us so long, to make visible a new train of disastrous consequence flowing from the untimely death of thy brother, and to blast that scheme of happiness on which thou and I had so fondly meditated.

But what wilt thou think of this new born claim?[3] The story, hadst thou observed the features and guize of the relater, would have won thy implicit credit. His countenance exhibited deep traces of the afflictions he had endured and the fortitude which he had exercised. He was sallow and emaciated, but his countenance was full of seriousness and dignity. A sort of ruggedness of brow, the token of great mental exertion and varied experience, argued a premature old age.

---

[3] "But what wilt thou think of this new born claim?": in the remainder of the chapter, Edgar reviews the consequences, for himself and fiancée Mary, of returning Weymouth's money.

What a mournful tale! Is such the lot of those who wander from their rustic homes in search of fortune? Our countrymen are prone to enterprize, and are scattered over every sea and every land in pursuit of that wealth which will not screen them from disease and infirmity, which is missed much oftener than found, and which, when gained, by no means compensates them for the hardships and vicissitudes endured in the pursuit.

But what if the truth of these pretentions be admitted? The money must be restored to its right owner. I know that whatever inconveniences may follow the deed, thou wilt not hesitate to act justly. Affluence and dignity, however valuable, may be purchased too dear. Honesty will not take away its keenness from the winter blast, its ignominy and unwholesomeness from servile labour, or strip of its charms the life of elegance and leisure; but these, unaccompanied with self-reproach, are less deplorable than wealth and honour, the possession of which is marred by our own disapprobation.

I know the bitterness of this sacrifice. I know the impatience with which your poverty has formerly been borne, how much your early education is at war with that degradation and obscurity to which your youth has been condemned. How earnestly your wishes panted after a state, which might exempt you from dependence upon daily labour and on the caprices of others, and might secure to you leisure to cultivate and indulge your love of knowledge and your social and beneficent affections.

Your motive for desiring a change of fortune has been greatly enforced since we have become known to each other. Thou hast honoured me with thy affection, but that a union, on which we rely for happiness, could not take place while both of us were poor. My habits, indeed, have made labour and rustic obscurity less painful than they would prove to my friend, but my present condition is wholly inconsistent with marriage. As long as my exertions are insufficient to maintain as both, it would be unjustifiable to burthen you with new cares and duties. Of this you are more thoroughly convinced than I am. The love of independence and ease, and impatience of drudgery, are woven into your constitution. Perhaps they are carried to an erroneous extreme, and derogate from that uncommon excellence by which your character is, in other respects, distinguished, but they cannot be removed.

This obstacle was unexpectedly removed by the death of your brother. However, justly to be deplored was this catastrophe, yet like every other event, some of its consequences were good. By giving you possession of the means of independence and leisure, by enabling us to complete a contract which poverty alone had thus long delayed, this event has been, at the same time, the most disastrous and propitious which could have happened.

Why thy brother should have concealed from us the possession of this money; why, with such copious means of indulgence and leisure, he should still pursue his irksome trade, and live in so penurious a manner, has been a topic of endless and unsatisfactory conjecture between us. It was not difficult to suppose that this money was held in trust for another, but in that case it was unavoidable that some document or memorandum, or at least some claimant would appear. Much time has since elapsed, and you have thought yourself at length justified in appropriating this money to your own use.

Our flattering prospects are now shut in. You must return to your original poverty, and once more depend for precarious subsistence on your needle. You cannot restore the whole, for unavoidable expenses, and the change of your mode of living, has consumed some part of it. For so much you must consider yourself as Weymouth's debtor.

Repine not my friend, at this unlooked-for reverse. Think upon the merits and misfortunes of your brother's friend, think upon his aged father whom we shall enable him to rescue from poverty; think upon his desolate wife, whose merits are, probably, at least equal to your own, and whose helplessness is likely to be greater. I am not insensible to the evils which have returned upon us with augmented force, after having, for a moment, taken their flight. I know the precariousness of my condition, and that of my sisters, that our subsistence hangs upon the life of an old man. My uncle's death will transfer this property to his son, who is a stranger and an enemy to us, and the first act of whose authority will unquestionably be to turn us forth from these doors. Marriage with thee was anticipated with joyous emotions, not merely on my own account, or on thine, but likewise for the sake of those beloved girls, to whom that event would enable me to furnish an asylum.

But wedlock is now more distant than ever. My heart bleeds to think of the sufferings which my beloved Mary is again fated to endure, but regrets are only aggravations of calamity. They are pernicious, and it is our duty to shake them off.

I can entertain no doubts as to the equity of Weymouth's claim. So many coincidences could not have happened by chance. The non-appearance of any letters or papers connected with it is indeed a mysterious circumstance, but why should Waldegrave be studious of preserving these? They were useless paper, and might, without impropriety, be cast away, or made to serve any temporary purpose. Perhaps, indeed, they still lurk in some unsuspected corner. To wish that time may explain this mystery in a different manner, and so as to permit our retention of this money is, perhaps, the dictate of selfishness. The transfer to Weymouth will not be productive of less benefit to him and to his family, than we should derive from the use of it.

These considerations, however, will be weighed when we meet. Meanwhile I will return to my narrative.

Chapter XVI

HERE, my friend, thou must permit me to pause. The following incidents are of a kind to which the most ardent invention has never conceived a parallel. Fortune, in her most wayward mood, could scarcely be suspected of an influence like this. The scene was pregnant with astonishment and horror. I cannot, even now, recall it without reviving the dismay and confusion which I then experienced.[1]

Possibly, the period will arrive when I shall look back without agony on the perils I have undergone. That period is still distant. Solitude and sleep are now no more than the signals to summon up a tribe of ugly phantoms. Famine, and blindness, and death, and savage enemies, never fail to be conjured up by the silence and darkness of the night. I cannot dissipate them by any efforts of reason. My cowardice requires the perpetual consolation of light. My heart droops when I mark the decline of the sun, and I never sleep but with a candle burning at my pillow. If, by any chance, I should awake and find myself immersed in darkness, I know not what act of desperation I might be suddenly impelled to commit.

I have delayed this narrative, longer than my duty to my friend enjoined. Now that I am able to hold a pen, I will hasten to terminate that uncertainty with regard to my fate, in which my silence has involved thee. I will recall that series of unheard of and disastrous vicissitudes which has constituted the latest portion of my life.

I am not certain, however, that I shall relate them in an intelligible manner. One image runs into another, sensations succeed in so rapid a train, that I fear, I shall be unable to distribute and express them with sufficient perspicuity. As I look back, my heart is sore and aches within my bosom. I am conscious to a kind of complex sentiment of distress and forlornness that cannot be perfectly pourtrayed by words; but I must do as well as I can. In the utmost vigour of my faculties, no eloquence that I possess would do justice to the tale. Now in my languishing and feeble state, I shall furnish thee with little more than a glimpse of the truth. With these glimpses, transient and faint as they are, thou must be satisfied.

I have said that I slept. My memory assures me of this: It informs of the previous circumstances of my laying aside my clothes, of placing the light upon a chair within reach of my pillow, of throwing myself upon the bed, and of gazing on the rays of the moon reflected on the wall, and almost obscured by those of the candle. I remember my occasional relapses into fits of incoherent fancies, the harbingers of sleep: I

---

[1] "The dismay and confusion which I then experienced": Chapter 16 represents a dramatic break in the narrative and the beginning of the second half of the novel. Edgar's statements in the first two paragraphs, about the anxiety he feels in recounting the dramatic events he is about to unfold, recall the similar statements about overcoming anxiety in order to write at the beginning of the novel, in the opening paragraphs of Chapter 1.

remember, as it were, the instant when my thoughts ceased to flow, and my senses were arrested by the leaden wand of forgetfulness.[2]

My return to sensation and to consciousness took place in no such tranquil scene. I emerged from oblivion by degrees so slow and so faint, that their succession cannot be marked. When enabled at length to attend to the information which my senses afforded, I was conscious, for a time, of nothing but existence. It was unaccompanied with lassitude or pain, but I felt disinclined to stretch my limbs, or raise my eye-lids. My thoughts were wildering and mazy, and though consciousness were present, it was disconnected with the loco-motive or voluntary power.[3]

From this state a transition was speedily effected. I perceived that my posture was supine, and that I lay upon my back. I attempted to open my eyes. The weight that oppressed them was too great for a slight exertion to remove. The exertion which I made cost me a pang more acute than any which I ever experienced. My eyes, however, were opened; but the darkness that environed me was as intense as before.

I attempted to rise, but my limbs were cold, and my joints had almost lost their flexibility. My efforts were repeated, and at length I attained a sitting posture. I was now sensible of pain in my shoulders and back. I was universally in that state to which the frame is reduced by blows of a club, mercilessly and endlessly repeated; my temples throbbed and my face was covered with clamy and cold drops, but that which threw me into deepest consternation was, my inability to see. I turned my head to different quarters, I stretched my eye-lids, and exerted every visual energy, but in vain. I was wrapt in the murkiest and most impenetrable gloom.

The first effort of reflection was to suggest the belief that I was blind; that disease is known to assail us in a moment and without previous warning. This surely was the misfortune that had now befallen me. Some ray, however fleeting and uncertain, could not fail to be discerned, if the power of vision were not utterly extinguished. In what circumstances could I possibly be placed, from which every particle of light should, by other means, be excluded?

This led my thoughts into a new train. I endeavoured to recall the past, but the past was too much in contradiction to the present, and my intellect was too much shattered by external violence, to allow me accurately to review it.

Since my sight availed nothing to the knowledge of my condition, I betook myself to other instruments. The element which I breathed was stagnant and cold. The spot where I lay was rugged and hard. I was neither naked nor clothed—a shirt and trossers[4] composed my dress, and the shoes and stockings, which always

---

[2] "By the leaden wand of forgetfulness": Edgar's recollections of sleep now complete the movement toward sleep he began at the end of Chapter 12. The sleep disturbances he has experienced are a sign of Edgar's sleep-walking and provide more parallels with Clithero.

[3] "Loco-motive or voluntary power": power over one's own motion or movement. Again, the novel uses language that recalls Erasmus Darwin's medical discussion of somnambulism. See the excerpts from Darwin's *Zoönomia* in Related Texts.

[4] "Trossers": trousers, pants. See Chapter 24, note 24.4, when this garment is noted again.

accompanied these, were now wanting, What could I infer from this scanty garb, this chilling atmosphere, this stony bed?

I had awakened as from sleep, What was my condition when I fell asleep? Surely it was different from the present. Then I inhabited a lightsome chamber, and was stretched upon a down bed. Now I was supine upon a rugged surface and immersed in palpable obscurity. Then I was in perfect health; now my frame was covered with bruises and every joint was racked with pain. What dungeon or den had received me, and by whose command was I transported hither?

After various efforts I stood upon my feet. At first I tottered and staggered. I stretched out my hands on all sides but met only with vacuity. I advanced forward. At the third step my foot moved something which lay upon the ground, I stooped and took it up, and found, on examination, that it was an Indian Tom-hawk.[5] This incident afforded me no hint from which I might conjecture my state.

Proceeding irresolutely and slowly forward, my hands at length touched a wall. This, like the flooring, was of stone, and was rugged and impenetrable. I followed this wall. An advancing angle occurred at a short distance, which was followed by similar angles. I continued to explore this clue, till the suspicion occurred that I was merely going round the walls of a vast and irregular apartment.

The utter darkness disabled me from comparing directions and distances. This discovery, therefore, was not made on a sudden and was still entangled with some doubt. My blood recovered some warmth, and my muscles some elasticity, but in proportion as my sensibility returned my pains augmented. Overpowered by my fears and my agonies I desisted from my fruitless search, and sat down, supporting my back against the wall.

My excruciating sensations for a time occupied my attention. These, in combination with other causes, gradually produced a species of delirium. I existed as it were in a wakeful dream. With nothing to correct my erroneous perceptions, the images of the past occurred in capricious combinations, and vivid hues. Methought I was the victim of some tyrant who had thrust me into a dungeon of his fortress,[6] and left me no power to determine whether he intended I should perish with famine, or linger out a long life in hopeless imprisonment: Whether the day was shut out by

---

[5] "An Indian Tom-hawk": the unexpected discovery of this "Tom-hawk" echoes the scene in Chapter 8 where Clithero discovers a dagger on Lorimer's bedside table (see note 8.6). In both cases the iconic weapon condenses the character's "unconscious" lapse into automatized revenge violence, and the repetition of the motif underlines the way in which Edgar progressively doubles Clithero throughout the novel.

[6] "Methought I was the victim of some tyrant who had thrust me into a dungeon of his fortress": Edgar initially believes he has fallen into a gothic castle's dungeon. As explained in the novel's "To the Public" preface, pages 3–4, Brown rejects irrational and superstitious gothic themes in favor of rationalized modern ones. Edgar's ravings and fantasies about captivity will recall Sarsefield's captivity as an imperialist functionary in India at the end of this chapter (see note 16.8) and will link up with other stories and fears about captivity throughout the novel.

insuperable walls, or the darkness that surrounded me, was owing to the night and to the smallness of those cranies through which day-light was to be admitted, I conjectured in vain.

Sometimes I imagined myself buried alive. Methought I had fallen into seeming death and my friends had consigned me to the tomb, from which a resurrection was impossible. That in such a case, my limbs would have been confined to a coffin, and my coffin to a grave, and that I should instantly have been suffocated, did not occur to destroy my supposition: Neither did this supposition overwhelm me with terror or prompt my efforts at deliverance. My state was full of tumult and confusion, and my attention was incessantly divided between my painful sensations and my feverish dreams.

There is no standard by which time can be measured, but the succession of our thoughts, and the changes that take place in the external world. From the latter I was totally excluded. The former made the lapse of some hours appear like the tediousness of weeks and months. At length, a new sensation, recalled my rambling meditations, and gave substance to my fears. I now felt the cravings of hunger, and perceived that unless my deliverance were speedily effected, I must suffer a tedious and lingering death.

I once more tasked my understanding and my senses, to discover the nature of my present situation and the means of escape. I listened to catch some sound. I heard an unequal and varying echo, sometimes near and sometimes distant, sometimes dying away and sometimes swelling into loudness. It was unlike any thing I had before heard, but it was evident that it arose from wind sweeping through spacious halls and winding passages. These tokens were incompatible with the result of the examination I had made. If my hands were true I was immured between walls, through which there was no avenue.

I now exerted my voice, and cried as loud as my wasted strength would admit. Its echoes were sent back to me in broken and confused sounds and from above. This effort was casual, but some part of that uncertainty in which I was involved, was instantly dispelled by it. In passing through the cavern on the former day, I have mentioned the verge of the pit at which I arrived. To acquaint me as far as was possible, with the dimensions of the place, I had hallooed with all my force, knowing that sound is reflected according to the distance and relative positions of the substances from which it is repelled.

The effect produced by my voice on this occasion resembled, with remarkable exactness, the effect which was then produced. Was I then shut up in the same cavern? Had I reached the brink of the same precipice and been thrown headlong into that vacuity? Whence else could arise the bruises which I had received, but from my fall? Yet all remembrance of my journey hither was lost. I had determined to explore this cave on the ensuing day, but my memory informed me not that this intention had been carried into effect. Still it was only possible to conclude that I had come hither on my intended expedition and had been thrown by another, or had, by some ill chance, fallen into the pit.

This opinion was conformable to what I had already observed. The pavement and walls were rugged like those of the footing and sides of the cave through which I had formerly passed.

But if this were true, what was the abhorred catastrophe to which I was now reserved? The sides of this pit were inaccessible: human foot-steps would never wander into these recesses. My friends were unapprised of my forlorn state. Here I should continue till wasted by famine. In this grave should I linger out a few days, in unspeakable agonies and then perish forever.

The inroads of hunger were already experienced, and this knowledge of the desperateness of my calamity, urged me to phrenzy. I had none but capricious and unseen fate to condemn. The author of my distress and the means he had taken to decoy me hither, were incomprehensible. Surely my senses were fettered or depraved by some spell. I was still asleep, and this was merely a tormenting vision, or madness had seized me, and the darkness that environed and the hunger that afflicted me, existed only in my own distempered imagination.

The consolation of these doubts could not last long. Every hour added to the proofs that my perceptions were real. My hunger speedily became ferocious. I tore the linen of my shirt between my teeth and swallowed the fragments. I felt a strong propensity to bite the flesh from my arm. My heart overflowed with cruelty, and I pondered on the delight I should experience in rending some living animal to pieces, and drinking its blood and grinding its quivering fibres between my teeth.

This agony had already passed beyond the limits of endurance. I saw that time, instead of bringing respite or relief, would only aggravate my wants, and that my only remaining hope was to die before I should be assaulted by the last extremes of famine. I now recollected that a Tom-hawk was at hand, and rejoiced in the possession of an instrument by which I could so effectually terminate my sufferings.

I took it in my hand, moved its edge over my fingers, and reflected on the force that was required to make it reach my heart. I investigated the spot where it should enter, and strove to fortify myself with resolution to repeat the stroke a second or third time, if the first should prove insufficient. I was sensible that I might fail to inflict a mortal wound, but delighted to consider that the blood which would be made to flow, would finally release me, and that meanwhile my pains would be alleviated by swallowing this blood.

You will not wonder that I felt some reluctance to employ so fatal though indispensable a remedy. I once more ruminated on the possibility of rescuing myself by other means. I now reflected that the upper termination of the wall could not be at an immeasurable distance from the pavement. I had fallen from an height, but if that height had been considerable, instead of being merely bruised, should I not have been dashed into pieces?

Gleams of hope burst anew upon my soul. Was it not possible, I asked, to reach the top of this pit? The sides were rugged and uneven. Would not their projectures and abruptnesses serve me as steps by which I might ascend in safety? This expedient was to be tried without delay. Shortly my strength would fail and my doom would be irrevocably sealed.

I will not enumerate my laborious efforts, my alternations of despondency and confidence, the eager and unwearied scrutiny with which I examined the surface, the attempts which I made, and the failures which, for a time, succeeded each other. An hundred times, when I had ascended some feet from the bottom, I was compelled to relinquish my undertaking by the untenable smoothness of the spaces which remained to be gone over. An hundred times I threw myself, exhausted by fatigue and my pains, on the ground. The consciousness was gradually restored that till I had attempted every part of the wall, it was absurd to despair, and I again drew my tottering limbs and aching joints to that part of the wall which had not been surveyed.

At length, as I stretched my hand upward, I found somewhat that seemed like a recession in the wall. It was possible that this was the top of the cavity, and this might be the avenue to liberty. My heart leaped with joy, and I proceeded to climb the wall. No undertaking could be conceived more arduous than this. The space between this verge and the floor was nearly smooth. The verge was higher from the bottom than my head. The only means of ascending that were offered me were by my hands, with which I could draw myself upward so as, at length, to maintain my hold with my feet.

My efforts were indefatigable, and at length I placed myself on the verge. When this was accomplished my strength was nearly gone. Had I not found space enough beyond this brink to stretch myself at length, I should unavoidably have fallen backward into the pit, and all my pains had served no other end than to deepen my despair and hasten my destruction.

What impediments and perils remained to be encountered I could not judge. I was now inclined to forbode the worst. The interval of repose which was necessary to be taken, in order to recruit my strength, would accelerate the ravages of famine, and leave me without the power to proceed.

In this state, I once more consoled myself that an instrument of death was at hand. I had drawn up with me the Tom-hawk, being sensible that should this impediment be overcome others might remain that would prove insuperable. Before I employed it, however, I cast my eyes wildly and languidly around. The darkness was no less intense than in the pit below, and yet two objects were distinctly seen.

They resembled a fixed and obscure flame. They were motionless. Though lustrous themselves they created no illumination around them. This circumstance, added to others, which reminded me of similar objects, noted on former occasions, immediately explained the nature of what I beheld. These were the eyes of a panther.

Thus had I struggled to obtain a post where a savage was lurking, and waited only till my efforts should place me within reach of his fangs.[7] The first impulse was to

---

[7] In the last of his three encounters with a panther (see notes 2.11 and 12.1), Edgar again refers to the animal as a "savage," prefiguring his encounter with the "savage" Delaware warriors in the following chapters. Edgar's brutal struggle with the animal and his own increasingly animal-like capacity for violence contribute to the novel's larger pattern of relations between Edgar, Clithero, and the Delaware leader Deb as all three undergo the larger pressures of British empire and expansionism.

arm myself against this enemy. The desperateness of my condition was, for a moment, forgotten. The weapon which was so lately lifted against my own bosom, was now raised to defend my life against the assault of another.

There was no time for deliberation and delay. In a moment he might spring from his station and tear me to pieces. My utmost speed might not enable me to reach him where he sat, but merely to encounter his assault. I did not reflect how far my strength was adequate to save me. All the force that remained was mustered up and exerted in a throw.

No one knows the powers that are latent in his constitution. Called forth by imminent dangers, our efforts frequently exceed our most sanguine belief. Though tottering on the verge of dissolution, and apparently unable to crawl from this spot, a force was exerted in this throw, probably greater than I had ever before exerted. It was resistless and unerring. I aimed at the middle space between these glowing orbs. It penetrated the scull and the animal fell, struggling and shrieking, on the ground.

My ears quickly informed me when his pangs were at an end. His cries and his convulsions lasted for a moment and then ceased. The effect of his voice, in these subterranean abodes, was unspeakably rueful.

The abruptness of this incident, and the preternatural exertion of my strength, left me in a state of languor and sinking from which slowly and with difficulty I recovered. The first suggestion that occurred was to feed upon the carcass of this animal. My hunger had arrived at that pitch where all fastidiousness and scruples are at an end. I crept to the spot. . . . I will not shock you by relating the extremes to which dire necessity had driven me. I review this scene with loathing and horror. Now that it is past I look back upon it as on some hideous dream. The whole appears to be some freak of insanity. No alternative was offered, and hunger was capable to be appeased, even by a banquet so detestable.

If this appetite has sometimes subdued the sentiments of nature, and compelled the mother to feed upon the flesh of her offspring, it will not excite amazement that I did not turn from the yet warm blood and reeking fibres of a brute.

One evil was now removed, only to give place to another. The first sensations of fullness had scarcely been felt when my stomach was seized by pangs whose acuteness exceeded all that I ever before experienced. I bitterly lamented my inordinate avidity. The excruciations of famine were better than the agonies which this abhorred meal had produced. Death was now impending with no less proximity and certainty, though in a different form. Death was a sweet relief for my present miseries, and I vehemently longed for its arrival. I stretched myself on the ground. I threw myself into every posture that promised some alleviation of this evil. I rolled along the pavement of the cavern, wholly inattentive to the dangers that environed me. That I did not fall into the pit, whence I had just emerged, must be ascribed to some miraculous chance.

How long my miseries endured, it is not possible to tell. I cannot even form a plausible conjecture. Judging by the lingering train of my sensations, I should conjecture that some days elapsed in this deplorable condition, but nature could not have so long sustained a conflict like this.

Gradually my pains subsided and I fell into a deep sleep. I was visited by dreams of a thousand hues. They led me to flowing streams and plenteous banquets, which, though placed within my view, some power forbade me to approach. From this sleep I recovered to the fruition of solitude and darkness, but my frame was in a state less feeble than before. That which I had eaten had produced temporary distress, but on the whole had been of use. If this food had not been provided for me I should scarcely have avoided death. I had reason therefore to congratulate myself on the danger that had lately occurred.

I had acted without foresight, and yet no wisdom could have prescribed more salutary measures. The panther was slain, not from a view to the relief of my hunger, but from the self-preserving and involuntary impulse. Had I fore-known the pangs to which my ravenous and bloody meal would give birth, I should have carefully abstained, and yet these pangs were a useful effort of nature to subdue and convert to nourishment the matter I had swallowed.

I was now assailed by the torments of thirst. My invention and my courage were anew bent to obviate this pressing evil. I reflected that there was some recess from this cavern, even from the spot where I now stood. Before, I was doubtful whether in this direction from this pit any avenue could be found, but since the panther had come hither there was reason to suppose the existence of some such avenue.

I now likewise attended to a sound, which, from its invariable tenour, denoted somewhat different from the whistling of a gale. It seemed like the murmur of a running stream. I now prepared to go forward, and endeavoured to move along in that direction in which this sound apparently came.

On either side and above my head, there was nothing but vacuity. My steps were to be guided by the pavement, which, though unequal and rugged, appeared, on the whole, to ascend. My safety required that I should employ both hands and feet in exploring my way.

I went on thus for a considerable period. The murmur, instead of becoming more distinct, gradually died away. My progress was arrested by fatigue, and I began once more to despond. My exertions, produced a perspiration, which, while it augmented my thirst, happily supplied me with imperfect means of appeasing it.

This expedient would, perhaps, have been accidentally suggested, but my ingenuity was assisted by remembering the history of certain English prisoners in Bengal, whom their merciless enemy imprisoned in a small room, and some of whom preserved themselves alive merely by swallowing the moisture that flowed from their bodies.[8] This experiment I now performed with no less success.

---

[8] "English prisoners in Bengal . . . swallowing the moisture that flowed from their bodies": now Edgar likens his experience in the cave to captivity experiences of British imperialists like Sarsefield in India. Edgar is recalling the tale of the "black hole of Calcutta," a widely known story of British imperialism in India. In 1756, Sirajud Daulah, the Nawab of Bengal, overcame the British and occupied Calcutta, at that time the most important possession of the East India Company. According to the sole survivor, John Holwell, 146 English prisoners were imprisoned in a tiny, airless dungeon, and, by the time the doors were opened, 123 of the prisoners had died. Holwell's story, which

This was slender and transitory consolation. I knew that, wandering at random, I might never reach the outlet of this cavern, or might be disabled, by hunger and fatigue, from going farther than the outlet. The cravings which had lately been satiated, would speedily return, and my negligence had cut me off from the resource which had recently been furnished. I thought not till now that a second meal might be indispensable.

To return upon my foot-steps to the spot where the dead animal lay was an heartless project. I might thus be placing myself at an hopeless distance from liberty. Besides my track could not be retraced. I had frequently deviated from a straight direction for the sake of avoiding impediments. All of which I was sensible was, that I was travelling up an irregular acclivity. I hoped sometime to reach the summit, but had no reason for adhering to one line of ascent in preference to another.

To remain where I was, was manifestly absurd. Whether I mounted or descended, a change of place was most likely to benefit me. I resolved to vary my direction, and, instead of ascending, keep along the side of what I accounted an hill. I had gone some hundred feet when the murmur, before described, once more saluted my ear.

This sound, being imagined to proceed from a running stream, could not but light up joy in the heart of one nearly perishing with thirst. I proceeded with new courage. The sound approached no nearer nor became more distinct, but as long as it died not away, I was satisfied to listen and to hope.

I was eagerly observant if any the least glimmering of light, should visit this recess. At length, on the right hand a gleam, infinitely faint, caught my attention. It was wavering and unequal. I directed my steps towards it. It became more vivid, and permanent. It was of that kind, however, which proceeded from a fire, kindled with dry sticks, and not from the sun. I now heard the crackling of flames.

This sound made me pause, or at least to proceed with circumspection. At length the scene opened, and I found myself at the entrance of a cave. I quickly reached a station when I saw a fire burning. At first no other object was noted, but it was easy to infer that the fire was kindled by men, and that they who kindled it could be at no great distance.

---

scholars now regard as exaggerated, rapidly became the basis for racist representations and hatred of Indians and their resistance to British colonialism. Edgar's recollection of this story thus relates to Sarsefield's East India Company years and the novel's wider allusions to British colonialism and imperialism in India. The original story is given in John Zephaniah Holwell, *A genuine narrative of the deplorable deaths of the English gentlemen and others who were suffocated in the Black-Hole, etc.* (London: A. Millar, 1758).

Chapter XVII

THUS was I delivered from my prison and restored to the enjoyment of the air and the light. Perhaps the chance was almost miraculous that led me to this opening. In any other direction, I might have involved myself in an inextricable maze, and rendered my destruction sure: but what now remained to place me in absolute security? Beyond the fire I could see nothing; but since the smoke rolled rapidly away, it was plain that on the opposite side the cavern was open to the air.

I went forward, but my eyes were fixed upon the fire; presently, in consequence of changing my station, I perceived several feet, and the skirts of blankets. I was somewhat startled at these appearances. The legs were naked, and scored into uncouth figures. The *mocassins* which lay beside them, and which were adorned in a grotesque manner, in addition to other incidents, immediately suggested the suspicion that they were Indians. No spectacle was more adapted than this to excite wonder and alarm. Had some mysterious power snatched me from the earth, and cast me, in a moment, into the heart of the wilderness? Was I still in the vicinity of my paternal habitation, or was I thousands of miles distant?

Were these the permanent inhabitants of this region, or were they wanderers and robbers? While in the heart of the mountain I had entertained a vague belief that I was still within the precincts of Norwalk. This opinion was shaken for a moment by the objects which I now beheld, but it insensibly returned; yet, how was this opinion to be reconciled to appearances so strange and uncouth, and what measure did a due regard to my safety enjoin me to take?

I now gained a view of four brawny and terrific figures, stretched upon the ground. They lay parallel to each other, on their left sides; in consequence of which their faces were turned from me. Between each was an interval where lay a musket. Their right hands seemed placed upon the stocks of their guns, as if to seize them on the first moment of alarm.

The aperture through which these objects were seen, was at the back of the cave, and some feet from the ground. It was merely large enough to suffer an human body to pass. It was involved in profound darkness, and there was no danger of being suspected or discovered as long as I maintained silence, and kept out of view.

It was easily imagined that these guests would make but a short sojourn in this spot. There was reason to suppose that it was now night, and that after a short repose, they would start up and resume their journey. It was my first design to remain shrouded in this covert till their departure, and I prepared to endure imprisonment and thirst somewhat longer.

Meanwhile my thoughts were busy in accounting for this spectacle. I need not tell thee that Norwalk is the termination of a sterile and narrow tract, which begins in the Indian country. It forms a sort of rugged and rocky vein, and continues upwards of fifty miles. It is crossed in a few places by narrow and intricate paths, by which a communication is maintained between the farms and settlements on the opposite sides of the ridge.

During former Indian wars,[1] this rude surface was sometimes traversed by the Red-men, and they made, by means of it, frequent and destructive inroads into the heart of the English settlements. During the last war, notwithstanding the progress of population, and the multiplied perils of such an expedition, a band of them had once penetrated into Norwalk, and lingered long enough to pillage and murder some of the neighbouring inhabitants.

I have reason to remember that event. My father's house was placed on the verge of this solitude. Eight of these assassins assailed it at the dead of night. My parents and an infant child were murdered in their beds; the house was pillaged, and then burnt to the ground. Happily, myself and my two sisters were abroad upon a visit. The preceding day had been fixed for our return to our father's house, but a storm occurred, which made it dangerous to cross the river, and by obliging us to defer our journey, rescued us from captivity or death.

Most men are haunted by some species of terror or antipathy, which they are, for the most part, able to trace to some incident which befel them in their early years. You will not be surprized that the fate of my parents, and the sight of the body of one of this savage band, who, in the pursuit that was made after them, was overtaken and killed, should produce lasting and terrific images in my fancy. I never looked upon, or called up the image of a savage without shuddering.

I knew that, at this time, some hostilities had been committed on the frontier; that a long course of injuries and encroachments had lately exasperated the Indian tribes; that an implacable and exterminating war was generally expected. We imagined ourselves at an inaccessible distance from the danger, but I could not but remember that this persuasion was formerly as strong as at present, and that an expedition, which had once succeeded, might possibly be attempted again. Here was every token of enmity and bloodshed. Each prostrate figure was furnished with a rifled musquet, and a leathern bag tied round his waist, which was, probably, stored with powder and ball.

From these reflections, the sense of my own danger was revived and enforced, but I likewise ruminated on the evils which might impend over others. I should, no doubt, be safe by remaining in this nook; but might not some means be pursued to warn others of their danger? Should they leave this spot, without notice of their approach being given to the fearless and pacific tenants of the neighbouring district, they might commit, in a few hours, the most horrid and irreparable devastation.

The alarm could only be diffused in one way. Could I not escape, unperceived, and without alarming the sleepers, from this cavern? The slumber of an Indian is broken by the slightest noise; but if all noise be precluded, it is commonly profound. It was

---

[1] "During former Indian wars . . .": Edgar refers generally to the settler-Indian fighting that followed the French and Indian War, the North American theater of the Seven Years War between England, France, and Spain (1756–1763). Like the references to Anglo-Indian wars in Chapter 6, these allusions situate the novel's settler-Indian violence in relation to global struggles between England and its principal rivals.

possible, I conceived, to leave my present post, to descend into the cave, and issue forth without the smallest signal. Their supine posture assured me that they were asleep. Sleep usually comes at their bidding, and if, perchance, they should be wakeful at an unseasonable moment, they always sit upon their haunches, and, leaning their elbows on their knees, consume the tedious hours in smoking. My peril would be great. Accidents which I could not foresee, and over which I had no command, might occur to awaken some one at the moment I was passing the fire. Should I pass in safety, I might issue forth into a wilderness, of which I had no knowledge, where I might wander till I perished with famine, or where my foot-steps might be noted and pursued, and overtaken by these implacable foes. These perils were enormous and imminent; but I likewise considered that I might be at no great distance from the habitations of men, and, that my escape might rescue them from the most dreadful calamities, I determined to make this dangerous experiment without delay.

I came nearer to the aperture, and had, consequently, a larger view of this recess. To my unspeakable dismay, I now caught a glimpse of one, seated at the fire. His back was turned towards me so that I could distinctly survey his gigantic form and fantastic ornaments.

My project was frustrated. This one was probably commissioned to watch and to awaken his companions when a due portion of sleep had been taken. That he would not be unfaithful or remiss in the performance of the part assigned to him was easily predicted. To pass him without exciting his notice, and the entrance could not otherwise be reached, was impossible. Once more I shrunk back and revolved with hopelessness and anguish, the necessity to which I was reduced.

This interval of dreary foreboding did not last long. Some motion in him that was seated by the fire attracted my notice. I looked, and beheld him rise from his place and go forth from the cavern. This unexpected incident led my thoughts into a new channel. Could not some advantage be taken of his absence? Could not this opportunity be seized for making my escape? He had left his gun and hatchet on the ground. It was likely, therefore, that he had not gone far, and would speedily return. Might not these weapons be seized, and some provision be thus made against the danger of meeting him without, or of being pursued?

Before a resolution could be formed, a new sound saluted my ear. It was a deep groan, succeeded by sobs that seemed struggling for utterance, but were vehemently counteracted by the sufferer. This low and bitter lamentation apparently proceeded from some one within the cave. It could not be from one of this swarthy band. It must then proceed from a captive, whom they had reserved for torment or servitude, and who had seized the opportunity afforded by the absence of him that watched, to give vent to his despair.

I again thrust my head forward, and beheld, lying on the ground, apart from the rest, and bound hand and foot, a young girl. Her dress was the coarse russet garb of the country, and bespoke her to be some farmer's daughter. Her features denoted the last degree of fear and anguish, and she moved her limbs in such a manner as shewed that the ligatures by which she was confined, produced, by their tightness, the utmost degree of pain.

My wishes were now bent not only to preserve myself, and to frustrate the future attempts of these savages, but likewise to relieve this miserable victim. This could only be done by escaping from the cavern and returning with seasonable aid. The sobs of the girl were likely to rouse the sleepers. My appearance before her would prompt her to testify her surprise by some exclamation or shriek. What could hence be predicted but that the band would start on their feet, and level their unerring pieces at my head!

I know not why I was insensible to these dangers. My thirst was rendered by these delays intolerable. It took from me, in some degree, the power of deliberation. The murmurs which had drawn me hither continued still to be heard. Some torrent or cascade could not be far distant from the entrance of the cavern, and it seemed as if one draught of clear water was a luxury cheaply purchased by death itself. This, in addition to considerations more disinterested, and which I have already mentioned, impelled me forward.

The girl's cheek rested on the hard rock, and her eyes were dim with tears. As they were turned towards me, however, I hoped that my movements would be noticed by her gradually and without abruptness. This expectation was fulfilled. I had not advanced many steps before she discovered me. This moment was critical beyond all others in the course of my existence. My life was suspended, as it were, by a spider's thread. All rested on the effect which this discovery should make upon this feeble victim.

I was watchful of the first movement of her eye, which should indicate a consciousness of my presence. I laboured, by gestures and looks, to deter her from betraying her emotion. My attention was, at the same time, fixed upon the sleepers, and an anxious glance was cast towards the quarter whence the watchful savage might appear.

I stooped and seized the musquet and hatchet. The space beyond the fire was, as I expected, open to the air. I issued forth with trembling steps. The sensations inspired by the dangers which environed me, added to my recent horrors, and the influence of the moon, which had now gained the zenith, and whose lustre dazzled my long benighted senses, cannot be adequately described.

For a minute I was unable to distinguish objects. This confusion was speedily corrected, and I found myself on the verge of a steep. Craggy eminences arose on all sides. On the left hand was a space that offered some footing, and hither I turned. A torrent was below me, and this path appeared to lead to it. It quickly appeared in sight, and all foreign cares were, for a time, suspended.

This water fell from the upper regions of the hill, upon a flat projecture which was continued on either side, and on part of which I was now standing. The path was bounded on the left by an inaccessible wall, and on the right terminated at the distance of two or three feet from the wall, in a precipice. The water was eight or ten paces distant, and no impediment seemed likely to rise between us. I rushed forward with speed.

My progress was quickly checked. Close to the falling water, seated on the edge, his back supported by the rock, and his legs hanging over the precipice, I now beheld the savage who left the cave before me. The noise of the cascade and the improbability of interruption, at least from this quarter, had made him inattentive to my motions.

I paused. Along this verge lay the only road by which I could reach the water, and by which I could escape. The passage was completely occupied by this antagonist. To advance towards him, or to remain where I was, would produce the same effect. I should, in either case, be detected. He was unarmed; but his outcries would instantly summon his companions to his aid. I could not hope to overpower him, and pass him in defiance of his opposition. But if this were effected, pursuit would be instantly commenced. I was unacquainted with the way. The way was unquestionably difficult. My strength was nearly annihilated: I should be overtaken in a moment, or their deficiency in speed would be supplied by the accuracy of their aim. Their bullets, at least, would reach me.

There was one method of removing this impediment. The piece which I held in my hand was cocked. There could be no doubt that it was loaded. A precaution of this kind would never be omitted by a warrior of this hue. At a greater distance than this, I should not fear to reach the mark. Should I not discharge it, and, at the same moment, rush forward to secure the road which my adversary's death would open to me?

Perhaps you will conceive a purpose like this to have argued a sanguinary and murderous disposition. Let it be remembered, however, that I entertained no doubts about the hostile designs of these men. This was sufficiently indicated by their arms, their guise, and the captive who attended them. Let the fate of my parents be, likewise, remembered. I was not certain but that these very men were the assassins of my family, and were those who had reduced me and my sisters to the condition of orphans and dependants. No words can describe the torments of my thirst. Relief to these torments, and safety to my life, were within view. How could I hesitate?

Yet I did hesitate. My aversion to bloodshed was not to be subdued but by the direst necessity. I knew, indeed, that the discharge of a musquet would only alarm the enemies which remained behind; but I had another and a better weapon in my grasp. I could rive the head of my adversary, and cast him headlong, without any noise which should be heard, into the cavern.

Still I was willing to withdraw, to re-enter the cave, and take shelter in the darksome recesses from which I had emerged. Here I might remain, unsuspected, till these detested guests should depart. The hazards attending my re-entrance were to be boldly encountered, and the torments of unsatisfied thirst were to be patiently endured, rather than imbrue my hands in the blood of my fellow men. But this expedient would be ineffectual if my retreat should be observed by this savage. Of that I was bound to be incontestibly assured. I retreated, therefore, but kept my eye fixed at the same time upon the enemy.

Some ill fate decreed that I should not retreat unobserved. Scarcely had I withdrawn three paces when he started from his seat, and, turning towards me, walked with a quick pace. The shadow of the rock, and the improbability of meeting an enemy here, concealed me for a moment from his observation. I stood still. The slightest motion would have attracted his notice. At present, the narrow space engaged all his vigilance. Cautious foot-steps, and attention to the path, were indispensable to his safety. The respite was momentary, and I employed it in my own defence.

How otherwise could I act? The danger that impended aimed at nothing less than my life. To take the life of another was the only method of averting it. The means were in my hand, and they were used. In an extremity like this, my muscles would have acted almost in defiance of my will.

The stroke was quick as lightning, and the wound mortal and deep. He had not time to descry the author of his fate; but, sinking on the path, expired without a groan. The hatchet buried itself in his breast, and rolled with him to the bottom of the precipice.

Never before had I taken the life of an human creature. On this head, I had, indeed, entertained somewhat of religious scruples.[2] These scruples did not forbid me to defend myself, but they made me cautious and reluctant to decide. Though they could not withhold my hand, when urged by a necessity like this, they were sufficient to make me look back upon the deed with remorse and dismay.

I did not escape all compunction in the present instance, but the tumult of my feelings was quickly allayed. To quench my thirst was a consideration by which all others were supplanted. I approached the torrent, and not only drank copiously, but laved my head, neck, and arms, in this delicious element.

---

[2] "Somewhat of religious scruples": because Edgar is Quaker, he is presumably committed to nonviolence. In this situation, Quaker nonviolence obviously provides an ironic contrast to Edgar's Indian-killing. For more on this topic, see the excerpts from Franklin and Barton on Quaker pacifism and Indian-fighting in the Related Texts.

Chapter XVIII

NEVER was any delight worthy of comparison with the raptures which I then experienced. Life, that was rapidly ebbing, appeared to return upon me with redoubled violence. My languors, my excruciating heat, vanished in a moment, and I felt prepared to undergo the labours of Hercules. Having fully supplied the demands of nature in this respect, I returned to reflection on the circumstances of my situation. The path winding round the hill was now free from all impediments. What remained but to precipitate my flight? I might speedily place myself beyond all danger. I might gain some hospitable shelter, where my fatigues might be repaired by repose, and my wounds be cured. I might likewise impart to my protectors seasonable information of the enemies who meditated their destruction.

I thought upon the condition of the hapless girl whom I had left in the power of the savages. Was it impossible to rescue her? Might I not relieve her from her bonds, and make her the companion of my flight? The exploit was perilous but not impracticable. There was something dastardly and ignominious in withdrawing from the danger, and leaving an helpless being exposed to it. A single minute might suffice to snatch her from death or captivity. The parents might deserve that I should hazard or even sacrifice my life, in the cause of their child.

After some fluctuation, I determined to return to the cavern, and attempt the rescue of the girl. The success of this project depended on the continuance of their sleep. It was proper to approach with wariness, and to heed the smallest token which might bespeak their condition. I crept along the path, bending my ear forward to catch any sound that might arise. I heard nothing but the half-stifled sobs of the girl.

I entered with the slowest and most anxious circumspection. Every thing was found in its pristine state. The girl noticed my entrance with a mixture of terror and joy. My gestures and looks enjoined upon her silence. I stooped down, and taking another hatchet, cut assunder the deer-skin thongs by which her wrists and ancles were tied. I then made signs for her to rise and follow me. She willingly complied with my directions; but her benumbed joints and lacerated sinews, refused to support her. There was no time to be lost; I therefore, lifted her in my arms, and, feeble and tottering as I was, proceeded with this burthen, along the perilous steep, and over a most rugged path.

I hoped that some exertion would enable her to retrieve the use of her limbs. I set her, therefore, on her feet, exhorting her to walk as well as she was able, and promising her my occasional assistance. The poor girl was not deficient in zeal, and presently moved along with light and quick steps. We speedily reached the bottom of the hill.

No fancy can conceive a scene more wild and desolate than that which now presented itself. The soil was nearly covered with sharp fragments of stone. Between these sprung brambles and creeping vines, whose twigs, crossing and intertwining with each other, added to the roughness below, made the passage infinitely toilsome. Scattered over this space were single cedars with their ragged spines and wreaths of moss, and copses of dwarf oaks, which were only new emblems of sterility.

I was wholly unacquainted with the scene before me. No marks of habitation or culture, no traces of the foot-steps of men, were discernible. I scarcely knew in what region of the globe I was placed. I had come hither by means so inexplicable, as to leave it equally in doubt, whether I was separated from my paternal abode by a river or an ocean.

I made inquiries of my companion, but she was unable to talk coherently. She answered my questions with weeping, and sobs, and intreaties, to fly from the scene of her distress. I collected from her, at length, that her father's house had been attacked on the preceding evening, and all the family but herself destroyed. Since this disaster she had walked very fast and a great way, but knew not how far or in what direction.

In a wilderness like this, my only hope was to light upon obscure paths, made by cattle. Meanwhile I endeavoured to adhere to one line, and to burst through the vexatious obstacles which encumbered our way. The ground was concealed by the bushes, and we were perplexed and fatigued by a continual succession of hollows and prominences. At one moment we were nearly thrown headlong into a pit. At another we struck our feet against the angles of stones. The branches of the oak rebounded in our faces or entangled our legs, and the unseen thorns inflicted on us a thousand wounds.

I was obliged, in these arduous circumstances, to support not only myself but my companion. Her strength was overpowered by her evening journey, and the terror of being overtaken, incessantly harrassed her.

Sometimes we lighted upon tracks which afforded us an easier footing, and inspired us with courage to proceed. These, for a time, terminated at a brook or in a bog, and we were once more compelled to go forward at random. One of these tracks insensibly became more beaten, and, at length, exhibited the traces of wheels. To this I adhered, confident that it would finally conduct us to a dwelling.

On either side, the undergrowth of shrubs and brambles continued as before. Sometimes small spaces were observed, which had lately been cleared by fire. At length a vacant space of larger dimensions than had hitherto occurred, presented itself to my view. It was a field of some acres, that had, apparently, been upturned by the hoe. At the corner of this field was a small house.

My heart leaped with joy at this sight. I hastened toward it, in the hope that my uncertainties, and toils, and dangers, were now drawing to a close. This dwelling was suited to the poverty and desolation which surrounded it. It consisted of a few unhewn logs laid upon each other, to the height of eight or ten feet, including a quadrangular space of similar dimensions, and covered by thatch. There was no window, light being sufficiently admitted into the crevices between the logs. These had formerly been loosely plastered with clay, but air and rain had crumbled and washed the greater part of this rude cement away. Somewhat like a chimney, built of half-burnt bricks, was perceived at one corner. The door was fastened by a leathern thong, tied to a peg.

All within was silence and darkness. I knocked at the door and called, but no one moved or answered. The tenant, whoever he was, was absent. His leave could not be obtained, and I, therefore, entered without it. The autumn had made some progress, and the air was frosty and sharp. My mind and muscles had been, of late, so strenuously occupied, that the cold had not been felt. The cessation of exercise, however, quickly restored my sensibility in this respect, but the unhappy girl complained of being half frozen.

Fire, therefore, was the first object of my search. Happily, some embers were found upon the hearth, together with potatoe stalks and dry chips. Of these, with much difficulty, I kindled a fire, by which some warmth was imparted to our shivering limbs. The light enabled me, as I sat upon the ground, to survey the interior of this mansion.

Three saplins, stripped of their branches, and bound together at their ends by twigs, formed a kind of bedstead, which was raised from the ground by four stones. Ropes stretched across these, and covered by a blanket, constituted the bed. A board, of which one end rested on the bedstead, and the other was thrust between the logs that composed the wall, sustained the stale fragments of a rye-loaf, and a cedar bucket kept entire by withs instead of hoops. In the bucket was a little water, full of droppings from the roof, drowned insects and sand, a basket or two neatly made, and an hoe, with a stake thrust into it by way of handle, made up all the furniture that was visible.

Next to cold, hunger was the most urgent necessity by which we were now pressed. This was no time to give ear to scruples. We, therefore, uncerimoniously divided the bread and the water between us. I had now leisure to bestow some regards upon the future.

These remnants of fire and food convinced me that this dwelling was usually inhabited, and that it had lately been deserted. Some engagement had probably carried the tenant abroad. His absence might be terminated in a few minutes, or might endure through the night. On his return, I questioned not my power to appease any indignation he might feel at the liberties which I had taken. I was willing to suppose him one who would readily afford us all the information and succour that we needed.

If he should not return till sunrise, I meant to resume my journey. By the comfortable meal we had made, and the repose of a few hours, we should be considerably invigorated and refreshed, and the road would lead us to some more hospitable tenement.

My thoughts were too tumultuous, and my situation too precarious, to allow me to sleep. The girl, on the contrary, soon sunk into a sweet oblivion of all her cares. She laid herself, by my advice, upon the bed, and left me to ruminate without interruption.

I was not wholly free from the apprehension of danger. What influence his boisterous and solitary life might have upon the temper of the being who inhabited this hut, I could not predict. How soon the Indians might awake, and what path they would pursue, I was equally unable to guess. It was by no means impossible that they might tread upon my foot-steps, and knock, in a few minutes, at the door of this cottage. It behoved me to make all the preparation in my power against untoward incidents.

I had not parted with the gun which I had first seized in the cavern, nor with the hatchet which I had afterwards used to cut the bands of the girl. These were, at once, my trophies and my means of defence, which it had been rash and absurd to have relinquished. My present reliance was placed upon these.

I now, for the first time, examined the prize that I had made. Other considerations had prevented me till now, from examining the structure of the piece, but I could not but observe that it had two barrels, and was lighter and smaller than an ordinary musquet. The light of the fire now enabled me to inspect it with more accuracy.

Scarcely had I fixed my eyes upon the stock, when I perceived marks that were familiar to my apprehension. Shape, ornaments, and cyphers, were evidently the same with those of a piece which I had frequently handled. The marks were of a kind which could not be mistaken. This piece was mine; and when I left my uncle's house, it was deposited, as I believed, in the closet of my chamber.[1]

Thou wilt easily conceive the inference which this circumstance suggested. My hairs rose and my teeth chattered with horror. My whole frame was petrified, and I paced to and fro, hurried from the chimney to the door, and from the door to the chimney, with the misguided fury of a maniac.

I needed no proof of my calamity more incontestible than this. My uncle and my sisters had been murdered; the dwelling had been pillaged, and this had been a part of the plunder. Defenceless and asleep, they were assailed by these inexorable enemies, and I, who ought to have been their protector and champion, was removed to an immeasurable distance, and was disabled, by some accursed chance, from affording them the succour which they needed.

For a time, I doubted whether I had not witnessed and shared this catastrophe. I had no memory of the circumstances that preceded my awaking in the pit. Had not the cause of my being cast into this abyss some connection with the ruin of my family? Had I not been dragged hither by these savages, and reduced, by their malice, to that breathless and insensible condition? Was I born to a malignant destiny never tired of persecuting? Thus had my parents and their infant offspring perished, and thus completed was the fate of all those to whom my affections cleaved, and whom the first disaster had spared.

Hitherto the death of the savage, whom I had dispatched with my hatchet, had not been remembered without some remorse. Now my emotions were totally changed: I

---

[1] This double-barreled musket, as the reader learns shortly (eight paragraphs later), was a gift to Edgar from Sarsefield and a souvenir of Sarsefield's experiences in India. More precisely, "it was the legacy of an English officer, who died in Bengal, to Sarsefield" and thus passes the legacy of imperialist conflict against native peoples on to Edgar. That this musket is double-barreled and associated with Sarsefield and Edgar's uncle, two veterans of British imperial campaigns and defeats on two sides of the world, provides more links that situate Edgar's Indian-killing in its global context.

was somewhat comforted in thinking that thus much of necessary vengeance had been executed. New and more vehement regrets were excited by reflecting on the forbearance I had practised when so much was in my power. All the miscreants had been at my mercy, and a bloody retribution might, with safety and ease, have been inflicted on their prostrate bodies.

It was now too late. What of consolation or of hope remained to me? To return to my ancient dwelling, now polluted with blood, or perhaps, nothing but a smoking ruin, was abhorred. Life, connected with remembrance of my misfortunes was detestable. I was no longer anxious for flight. No change of the scene but that which terminated all consciousness, could I endure to think of.

Amidst these gloomy meditations the idea was suddenly suggested of returning, with the utmost expedition, to the cavern. It was possible that the assassins were still asleep. He who was appointed to watch and to make, in due season, the signal for resuming their march, was forever silent. Without this signal it was not unlikely that they would sleep till dawn of day. But if they should be roused, they might be overtaken or met, and, by choosing a proper station, two victims might at least fall. The ultimate event to myself would surely be fatal; but my own death was an object of desire rather than of dread. To die thus speedily, and after some atonement was made for those who had already been slain, was sweet.

The way to the mountain was difficult and tedious, but the ridge was distinctly seen from the door of the cottage, and I trusted that auspicious chance would lead me to that part of it where my prey was to be found. I snatched up the gun and tom-hawk in a transport of eagerness. On examining the former, I found that both barrels were deeply loaded.

This piece was of extraordinary workmanship. It was the legacy of an English officer, who died in Bengal, to Sarsefield. It was constructed for the purposes not of sport but of war. The artist had made it a congeries of tubes and springs, by which every purpose of protection and offence was effectually served. A dagger's blade was attached to it, capable of being fixed at the end, and of answering the destructive purpose of a bayonet. On his departure from Solebury, my friend left it, as a pledge of his affection, in my possession. Hitherto I had chiefly employed it in shooting at a mark, in order to improve my sight; now was I to profit by the gift in a different way.

Thus armed, I prepared to sally forth on my adventurous expedition. Sober views might have speedily succeeded to the present tempest of my passions. I might have gradually discovered the romantic and criminal temerity of my project, the folly of revenge, and the duty of preserving my life for the benefit of mankind. I might have suspected the propriety of my conclusion, and have admitted some doubts as to the catastrophe which I imagined to have befallen my uncle and sisters. I might, at least, have consented to ascertain their condition with my own eyes; and for this end have returned to the cottage, and have patiently waited till the morning light should permit me to resume my journey.

This conduct was precluded by a new incident. Before I opened the door I looked through a crevice of the wall, and perceived three human figures at the farther end of the field. They approached the house. Though indistinctly seen, something in their port persuaded me that these were the Indians from whom I had lately parted. I was startled but not dismayed. My thirst of vengeance was still powerful, and I believed that the moment of its gratification was hastening. In a short time they would arrive and enter the house. In what manner should they be received?

I studied not my own security. It was the scope of my wishes to kill the whole number of my foes; but that being done, I was indifferent to the consequences. I desired not to live to relate or to exult in the deed.

To go forth was perilous and useless. All that remained was to sit upon the ground opposite the door, and fire at each as he entered. In the hasty survey I had taken of this apartment, one object had been overlooked, or imperfectly noticed. Close to the chimney was an aperture, formed by a cavity partly in the wall and in the ground. It was the entrance of an oven, which resembled, on the outside, a mound of earth, and which was filled with dry stalks of potatoes and other rubbish.

Into this it was possible to thrust my body. A sort of screen might be formed of the brush-wood, and more deliberate and effectual execution be done upon the enemy. I weighed not the disadvantages of this scheme, but precipitately threw myself into this cavity. I discovered, in an instant, that it was totally unfit for my purpose, but it was too late to repair my miscarriage.

This wall of the hovel was placed near the verge of a sand-bank. The oven was erected on the very brink. This bank being of a loose and mutable soil, could not sustain my weight. It sunk, and I sunk along with it. The height of the bank was three or four feet, so that, though disconcerted and embarrassed, I received no injury. I still grasped my gun, and resumed my feet in a moment.

What was now to be done? The bank screened me from the view of the savages. The thicket was hard by, and if I were eager to escape, the way was obvious and sure. But though single, though enfeebled by toil, by abstinence and by disease, and though so much exceeded in number and strength, by my foes, I was determined to await and provoke the contest.

In addition to the desperate impulse of passion, I was swayed by thoughts of the danger which beset the sleeping girl, and from which my flight would leave her without protection. How strange is the destiny that governs mankind! The consequence of shrouding myself in this cavity had not been foreseen. It was an expedient which courage, and not cowardice suggested, and yet it was the only expedient by which flight had been rendered practicable. To have issued from the door would only have been to confront, and not to elude the danger.

The first impulse prompted me to re-enter the cottage by this avenue, but this could not be done with certainty and expedition. What then remained? While I deliberated, the men approached, and, after a moment's hesitation, entered the house, the door being partly open.

The fire on the hearth enabled them to survey the room. One of them uttered a sudden exclamation of surprize. This was easily interpreted. They had noticed the girl who had lately been their captive lying asleep on the blanket. Their astonishment at finding her here, and in this condition, may be easily conceived.

I now reflected that I might place myself, without being observed, near the entrance, at an angle of the building, and shoot at each as he successively came forth. I perceived that the bank conformed to two sides of the house, and that I might gain a view of the front and of the entrance, without exposing myself to observation.

I lost no time in gaining this station The bank was as high as my breast. It was easy, therefore, to crouch beneath it, to bring my eye close to the verge, and, laying my gun upon the top of it among the grass, with its muzzles pointed to the door, patiently to wait their forth-coming.

My eye and my ear were equally attentive to what was passing. A low and muttering conversation was maintained in the house. Presently I heard an heavy stroke descend. I shuddered, and my blood ran cold at the sound. I entertained no doubt but that it was the stroke of an hatchet on the head or breast of the helpless sleeper.

It was followed by a loud shriek. The continuance of these shrieks proved that the stroke had not been instantly fatal. I waited to hear it repeated, but the sounds that now arose were like those produced by dragging somewhat along the ground. The shrieks, meanwhile, were incessant and piteous. My heart faltered, and I saw that mighty efforts must be made to preserve my joints and my nerves stedfast. All depended on the strenuous exertions and the fortunate dexterity of a moment.

One now approached the door, and came forth, dragging the girl, whom he held by the hair, after him. What hindered me from shooting at his first appearance, I know not. This had been my previous resolution. My hand touched the trigger, and as he moved, the piece was levelled at his right ear. Perhaps the momentous consequences of my failure, made me wait till his ceasing to move might render my aim more sure.

Having dragged the girl, still piteously shrieking, to the distance of ten feet from the house, he threw her from him with violence. She fell upon the ground, and observing him level his piece at her breast, renewed her supplications in a still more piercing tone. Little did the forlorn wretch think that her deliverance was certain and near. I rebuked myself for having thus long delayed. I fired, and my enemy sunk upon the ground without a struggle.

Thus far had success attended me in this unequal contest. The next shot would leave me nearly powerless. If that, however, proved as unerring as the first, the chances of defeat were lessened. The savages within, knowing the intentions of their associate with regard to the captive girl, would probably mistake the report which they heard for that of his piece. Their mistake, however, would speedily give place to doubts, and they would rush forth to ascertain the truth. It behoved me to provide a similar reception for him that next appeared.

It was as I expected. Scarcely was my eye again fixed upon the entrance, when a tawny and terrific visage was stretched fearfully forth. It was the signal of his fate. His glances cast wildly and swiftly round, lighted upon me, and on the fatal instrument which was pointed at his forehead. His muscles were at once exerted to withdraw his head, and to vociferate a warning to his fellow, but his movement was too slow. The ball entered above his ear: He tumbled headlong to the ground, bereaved of sensation, though not of life, and had power only to struggle and mutter.

Chapter XIX

THINK not that I relate these things with exultation or tranquility. All my education and the habits of my life tended to unfit me for a contest and a scene like this. But I was not governed by the soul which usually regulates my conduct. I had imbibed from the unparalleled events which had lately happened a spirit vengeful, unrelenting, and ferocious.[1]

There was now an interval for flight. Throwing my weapons away, I might gain the thicket in a moment. I had no ammunition, nor would time be afforded me to reload my piece. My antagonist would render my poniard and my speed of no use to me. Should he miss me as I fled, the girl would remain to expiate, by her agonies and death, the fate of his companions.

These thoughts passed through my mind in a shorter time than is demanded to express them. They yielded to an expedient suggested by the sight of the gun that had been raised to destroy the girl, and which now lay upon the ground. I am not large of bone, but am not deficient in agility and strength. All that remained to me of these qualities was now exerted; and dropping my own piece, I leaped upon the bank, and flew to seize my prize.

It was not till I snatched it from the ground, that the propriety of regaining my former post, rushed upon my apprehension. He that was still posted in the hovel would mark me through the seams of the wall, and render my destruction sure. I once more ran towards the bank, with the intention to throw myself below it. All this was performed in an instant; but my vigilant foe was aware of his advantage, and fired through an opening between the logs. The bullet grazed my cheek, and produced a benumbing sensation that made me instantly fall to the earth. Though bereaved of strength, and fraught with the belief that I had received a mortal wound, my caution was not remitted. I loosened not my grasp of the gun, and the posture into which I accidentally fell enabled me to keep an eye upon the house and an hand upon the trigger. Perceiving my condition, the savage rushed from his covert in order to complete his work; but at three steps from the threshold, he received my bullet in his breast. The uplifted tom-hawk fell from his hand, and, uttering a loud shriek, he fell upon the body of his companion. His cries struck upon my heart, and I wished that his better fortune had cast this evil from him upon me.

Thus I have told thee a bloody and disastrous tale. When thou reflectest on the mildness of my habits, my antipathy to scenes of violence and bloodshed, my unacquaintance with the use of fire-arms, and the motives of a soldier, thou wilt

---

[1] "A spirit vengeful, unrelenting, and ferocious": after killing four Indians, Edgar's transformation from a peaceful, intellectualized Quaker farmer to a surprisingly effective Indian fighter astonishes even himself. Edgar cannot understand the relation between the two sides of his experience. This chapter presents Edgar at the height of his newfound capacity for violence, before he begins his return to Solebury in Chapter 20.

scarcely allow credit to my story. That one rushing into these dangers, unfurnished with stratagems or weapons, disheartened and enfeebled by hardships and pain, should subdue four antagonists, trained from their infancy to the artifices and exertions of Indian warfare, will seem the vision of fancy, rather than the lesson of truth.

I lifted my head from the ground and pondered upon this scene. The magnitude of this exploit made me question its reality. By attending to my own sensations, I discovered that I had received no wound, or at least, none of which there was reason to complain. The blood flowed plentifully from my cheek, but the injury was superficial. It was otherwise with my antagonists. The last that had fallen now ceased to groan. Their huge limbs, inured to combat and *war-worn,* were useless to their own defence, and to the injury of others.

The destruction that I witnessed was vast. Three beings, full of energy and heroism, endowed with minds strenuous and lofty, poured out their lives before me. I was the instrument of their destruction. This scene of carnage and blood was laid by me. To this havock and horror was I led by such rapid foot-steps!

My anguish was mingled with astonishment. In spite of the force and uniformity with which my senses were impressed by external objects, the transition I had undergone was so wild and inexplicable; all that I had performed; all that I had witnessed since my egress from the pit, were so contradictory to precedent events, that I still clung to the belief that my thoughts were confused by delirium. From these reveries I was at length recalled by the groans of the girl, who lay near me on the ground.

I went to her and endeavoured to console her. I found that while lying in the bed, she had received a blow upon the side, which was still productive of acute pain. She was unable to rise or to walk, and it was plain that one or more of her ribs had been fractured by the blow.

I knew not what means to devise for our mutual relief. It was possible that the nearest dwelling was many leagues distant. I knew not in what direction to go in order to find it, and my strength would not suffice to carry my wounded companion thither in my arms. There was no expedient but to remain in this field of blood till the morning.

I had scarcely formed this resolution before the report of a musquet was heard at a small distance. At the same moment, I distinctly heard the whistling of a bullet near me. I now remembered that of the five Indians whom I saw in the cavern, I was acquainted with the destiny only of four. The fifth might be still alive, and fortune might reserve for him the task of avenging his companions. His steps might now be tending hither in search of them.

The musquet belonging to him who was shot upon the threshold, was still charged. It was discreet to make all the provision in my power against danger. I possessed myself of this gun, and seating myself on the ground, looked carefully on all sides, to descry the approach of the enemy. I listened with breathless eagerness.

Presently voices were heard. They ascended from that part of the thicket from which my view was intercepted by the cottage. These voices had something in them that bespoke them to belong to friends and countrymen. As yet I was unable to distinguish words.

Presently my eye was attracted to one quarter, by a sound as of feet trampling down bushes. Several heads were seen moving in succession, and at length, the whole person was conspicuous. One after another leaped over a kind of mound which bordered the field, and made towards the spot where I sat. This band was composed of ten or twelve persons, with each a gun upon his shoulder. Their guise, the moment it was perceived, dissipated all my apprehensions.

They came within the distance of a few paces before they discovered me. One stopped, and bespeaking the attention of his followers, called to know who was there? I answered that I was a friend, who intreated their assistance. I shall not paint their astonishment when, on coming nearer, they beheld me surrounded by the arms and dead bodies of my enemies.

I sat upon the ground, supporting my head with my left hand, and resting on my knee the stock of an heavy musquet. My countenance was wan and haggard, my neck and bosom were died in blood, and my limbs, almost stripped by the brambles of their slender covering, were lacerated by a thousand wounds. Three savages, two of whom were steeped in gore, lay at a small distance, with the traces of recent life on their visages. Hard by was the girl, venting her anguish in the deepest groans, and intreating relief from the new comers.

One of the company, on approaching the girl, betrayed the utmost perturbation. "Good God!" he cried, "is this a dream? Can it be you? Speak!"

"Ah, my father! my father!" answered she, "it is I indeed."

The company, attracted by this dialogue, crowded round the girl, whom her father, clasping in his arms, lifted from the ground, and pressed, in a transport of joy to his breast. This delight was succeeded by solicitude respecting her condition. She could only answer his inquiries by complaining that her side was bruised to pieces. How came you here? . . . Who hurt you? . . . Where did the Indians carry you? were questions to which she could make no reply but by sobs and plaints.

My own calamities were forgotten in contemplating the fondness and compassion of the man for his child. I derived new joy from reflecting that I had not abandoned her, and that she owed her preservation to my efforts. The inquiries which the girl was unable to answer, were now put to me. Every one interrogated who I was, whence I had come, and what had given rise to this bloody contest.

I was not willing to expatiate on my story. The spirit which had hitherto sustained me, began now to subside. My strength ebbed away with my blood. Tremors, lassitude, and deadly cold, invaded me, and I fainted on the ground.

Such is the capricious constitution of the human mind. While dangers were at hand, while my life was to be preserved only by zeal and vigilance, and courage, I was not wanting to myself. Had my perils continued or even multiplied, no doubt my energies would have kept equal pace with them, but the moment that I was encompassed by protectors, and placed in security, I grew powerless and faint. My weakness was proportioned to the duration and intensity of my previous efforts, and the swoon into which I now sunk, was no doubt, mistaken by the spectators, for death.

On recovering from this swoon, my sensations were not unlike those which I had experienced on awaking in the pit. For a moment a mistiness involved every object, and I was able to distinguish nothing. My sight, by rapid degrees, was restored, my painful dizziness was banished, and I surveyed the scene before me with anxiety and wonder.

I found myself stretched upon the ground. I perceived the cottage and the neighbouring thicket, illuminated by a declining moon. My head rested upon something, which, on turning to examine, I found to be one of the slain Indians. The other two remained upon the earth at a small distance, and in the attitudes in which they had fallen. Their arms, the wounded girl, and the troop who were near me when I fainted, were gone.

My head had reposed upon the breast of him whom I had shot in this part of his body. The blood had ceased to ooze from the wound, but my dishevelled locks were matted and steeped in that gore which had overflowed and choaked up the orifice. I started from this detestable pillow, and regained my feet.

I did not suddenly recall what had lately passed, or comprehend the nature of my situation. At length, however, late events were recollected.

That I should be abandoned in this forlorn state by these men, seemed to argue a degree of cowardice or cruelty, of which I should have thought them incapable. Presently, however, I reflected that appearances might have easily misled them into a belief of my death: on this supposition, to have carried me away, or to have stayed beside me, would be useless. Other enemies might be abroad, or their families, now that their fears were somewhat tranquilized, might require their presence and protection.

I went into the cottage. The fire still burned, and afforded me a genial warmth. I sat before it and began to ruminate on the state to which I was reduced, and on the measures I should next pursue. Day-light could not be very distant. Should I remain in this hovel till the morning, or immediately resume my journey? I was feeble, indeed, but by remaining here should I not increase my feebleness? The sooner I should gain some human habitation the better; whereas watchfulness and hunger would render me, at each minute, less able to proceed than on the former.

This spot might be visited on the next day; but this was involved in uncertainty. The visitants, should any come, would come merely to examine and bury the dead, and bring with them neither the clothing nor the food which my necessities demanded. The road was sufficiently discernible, and would, unavoidably, conduct me to some dwelling. I determined, therefore, to set out without delay. Even in this state I was not unmindful that my safety might require the precaution of being armed. Besides the fusil,[2] which had been given me by Sarsefield, and which I had so unexpectedly recovered, had lost none of its value in my eyes. I hoped that it had escaped the search of the troop who had been here, and still lay below the bank, in the spot where I had dropped it.

In this hope I was not deceived. It was found. I possessed myself of the powder and shot belonging to one of the savages, and loaded it. Thus equipped for defence, I

---

[2] "Fusil": a flintlock musket.

regained the road, and proceeded, with alacrity, on my way. For the wound in my cheek, nature had provided a styptic,[3] but the soreness was extreme, and I thought of no remedy but water, with which I might wash away the blood. My thirst likewise incommoded me, and I looked with eagerness for the traces of a spring. In a soil like that of the wilderness around me, nothing was less to be expected than to light upon water. In this respect, however, my destiny was propitious. I quickly perceived water in the ruts. It trickled hither from the thicket on one side, and, pursuing it among the bushes, I reached the bubbling source. Though scanty and brackish, it afforded me unspeakable refreshment.

Thou wilt think, perhaps, that my perils were now at an end; that the blood I had already shed was sufficient for my safety. I fervently hoped that no new exigence would occur, compelling me to use the arms that I bore in my own defence. I formed a sort of resolution to shun the contest with a new enemy, almost at the expense of my own life. I was satiated and gorged with slaughter, and thought upon a new act of destruction with abhorrence and loathing.

But though I dreaded to encounter a new enemy, I was sensible that an enemy might possibly be at hand. I had moved forward with caution, and my sight and hearing were attentive to the slightest tokens. Other troops, besides that which I encountered, might be hovering near, and of that troop, I remembered that one at least had survived.

The gratification which the spring had afforded me was so great, that I was in no haste to depart. I lay upon a rock, which chanced to be shaded by a tree behind me. From this post I could overlook the road to some distance, and, at the same time, be shaded from the observation of others.

My eye was now caught by movements which appeared like those of a beast. In different circumstances, I should have instantly supposed it to be a wolf, or panther, or bear. Now my suspicions were alive on a different account, and my startled fancy figured to itself nothing but an human adversary.

A thicket was on either side of the road. That opposite to my station was discontinued at a small distance by the cultivated field. The road continued along this field, bounded by the thicket on the one side, and the open space on the other. To this space the being who was now descried was cautiously approaching.

He moved upon all fours, and presently came near enough to be distinguished. His disfigured limbs, pendants from his ears and nose, and his shorn locks, were indubitable indications of a savage. Occasionally he reared himself above the bushes, and scanned, with suspicious vigilance, the cottage and the space surrounding it. Then he stooped, and crept along as before.

I was at no loss to interpret these appearances. This was my surviving enemy. He was unacquainted with the fate of his associates, and was now approaching the theatre of carnage, to ascertain their fate.

---

[3] "Styptic": an astringent, a substance that stops bleeding.

Once more was the advantage afforded me. From this spot might unerring aim be taken, and the last of this hostile troop be made to share the fate of the rest. Should I fire or suffer him to pass in safety?

My abhorrence of bloodshed was not abated. But I had not foreseen this occurrence. My success hitherto had seemed to depend upon a combination of fortunate incidents, which could not be expected again to take place; but now was I invested with the same power. The mark was near; nothing obstructed or delayed; I incurred no danger, and the event was certain.

Why should he be suffered to live? He came hither to murder and despoil my friends; this work he has, no doubt, performed. Nay, has he not borne his part in the destruction of my uncle and my sisters? He will live only to pursue the same sanguinary trade; to drink the blood and exult in the laments of his unhappy foes, and of my own brethren. Fate has reserved him for a bloody and violent death. For how long a time soever it may be deferred, it is thus that his career will inevitably terminate.

Should he be spared, he will still roam in the wilderness, and I may again be fated to encounter him. Then our mutual situation may be widely different, and the advantage I now possess may be his.

While hastily revolving these thoughts I was thoroughly aware that one event might take place which would render all deliberation useless. Should he spy me where I lay, my fluctuations must end. My safety would indispensably require me to shoot. This persuasion made me keep a stedfast eye upon his motions, and be prepared to anticipate his assault.

It now most seasonably occurred to me that one essential duty remained to be performed. One operation, without which fire arms are useless, had been unaccountably omitted. My piece was uncocked. I did not reflect that in moving the spring, a sound would necessarily be produced, sufficient to alarm him. But I knew that the chances of escaping his notice, should I be perfectly mute and still, were extremely slender, and that, in such a case, his movements would be quicker than the light; it behoved me, therefore, to repair my omission.

The sound struck him with alarm. He turned and darted at me an inquiring glance. I saw that forbearance was no longer in my power; but my heart sunk while I complied with what may surely be deemed an indispensable necessity. This faltering, perhaps it was, that made me swerve somewhat from the fatal line. He was disabled by the wound, but not killed.

He lost all power of resistance, and was, therefore, no longer to be dreaded. He rolled upon the ground, uttering doleful shrieks, and throwing his limbs into those contorsions which bespeak the keenest agonies to which ill-fated man is subject. Horror, and compassion, and remorse, were mingled into one sentiment, and took possession of my heart. To shut out this spectacle, I withdrew from the spot, but I stopped before I had moved beyond hearing of his cries.

The impulse that drove me from the scene was pusillanimous and cowardly. The past, however deplorable, could not be recalled; but could not I afford some relief to this wretch? Could not I, at least, bring his pangs to a speedy close? Thus he might continue, writhing and calling upon death for hours. Why should his miseries be uselessly prolonged?

There was but one way to end them. To kill him outright, was the dictate of compassion and of duty. I hastily returned, and once more levelled my piece at his head. It was a loathsome obligation, and was performed with unconquerable reluctance. Thus to assault and to mangle the body of an enemy, already prostrate and powerless, was an act worthy of abhorrence; yet it was, in this case, prescribed by pity.

My faltering hand rendered this second bullet ineffectual. One expedient, still more detestable, remained. Having gone thus far, it would have been inhuman to stop short. His heart might easily be pierced by the bayonet, and his struggles would cease.

This task of cruel lenity was at length finished. I dropped the weapon and threw myself on the ground, over-powered by the horrors of this scene. Such are the deeds which perverse nature compels thousands of rational beings to perform and to witness! Such is the spectacle, endlessly prolonged and diversified, which is exhibited in every field of battle; of which, habit and example, the temptations of gain, and the illusions of honour, will make us, not reluctant or indifferent, but zealous and delighted actors and beholders!

Thus, by a series of events impossible to be computed or foreseen, was the destruction of a band, selected from their fellows for an arduous enterprise, distinguished by prowess and skill, and equally armed against surprize and force, completed by the hand of a boy, uninured to hostility, unprovided with arms, precipitate and timerous! I have noted men who seemed born for no end but by their achievements to belie experience, and baffle foresight, and outstrip belief. Would to God that I had not deserved to be numbered among these! But what power was it that called me from the sleep of death, just in time to escape the merciless knife of this enemy? Had my swoon continued till he had reached the spot, he would have effectuated my death by new wounds and torn away the skin from my brows. Such are the subtile threads on which hangs the fate of man and of the universe!

While engaged in these reflections, I perceived that the moon-light had began to fade before that of the sun. A dusky and reddish hue spread itself over the east. Cheered by this appearance, I once more resumed my feet and the road. I left the savage where he lay, but made prize of his tom-hawk. I had left my own in the cavern; and this weapon added little to my burden. Prompted by some freak of fancy, I stuck his musquet in the ground, and left it standing upright in the middle of the road.

Chapter XX

I MOVED forward with as quick a pace as my feeble limbs would permit. I did not allow myself to meditate. The great object of my wishes was a dwelling where food and repose might be procured. I looked earnestly forward, and on each side, in search of some token of human residence; but the spots of cultivation, the *well-pole,* the *worm-fence,*[1] and the hay-rick, were no where to be seen. I did not even meet with a wild hog, or a bewildered cow. The path was narrow, and on either side was a trackless wilderness. On the right and left were the waving lines of mountainous ridges which had no peculiarity enabling me to ascertain whether I had ever before seen them.

At length I noticed that the tracks of wheels had disappeared from the path that I was treading; that it became more narrow, and exhibited fewer marks of being frequented. These appearances were discouraging. I now suspected that I had taken a wrong direction, and instead of approaching, was receding from the habitation of men.

It was wisest, however, to proceed. The road could not but have some origin as well as end. Some hours passed away in this uncertainty. The sun rose, and by noon-day I seemed to be farther than ever from the end of my toils. The path was more obscure, and the wilderness more rugged. Thirst more incommoded me than hunger, but relief was seasonally afforded by the brooks that flowed across the path.

Coming to one of these, and having slaked my thirst, I sat down upon the bank, to reflect on my situation. The circuity of the path had frequently been noticed, and I began to suspect that though I had travelled long, I had not moved far from the spot where I had commenced my pilgrimage.

Turning my eyes on all sides, I noticed a sort of pool, formed by the rivulet, at a few paces distant from the road. In approaching and inspecting it, I observed the footsteps of cattle, who had retired by a path that seemed much beaten; I likewise noticed a cedar bucket, broken and old, lying on the margin. These tokens revived my drooping spirits, and I betook myself to this new track. It was intricate; but, at length, led up a steep, the summit of which was of better soil than that of which the flats consisted. A clover field, and several apple-trees, sure attendants of man, were now discovered. From this space I entered a corn-field, and at length, to my inexpressible joy, caught a glimpse of an house.

This dwelling was far different from that I had lately left. It was as small and as low, but its walls consisted of boards. A window of four panes admitted the light, and a chimney of brick, well burnt, and neatly arranged, peeped over the roof. As I approached I heard the voice of children, and the hum of a spinning-wheel.

I cannot make thee conceive the delight which was afforded me by all these tokens. I now found myself, indeed, among beings like myself, and from whom hospitable entertainment might be confidently expected. I compassed the house, and made my appearance at the door.

---

[1] "Worm-fence": a split-rail fence.

A good woman, busy at her wheel, with two children playing on the ground before her, were the objects that now presented themselves. The uncouthness of my garb, my wild and weather-worn appearance, my fusil and tom-hawk, could not but startle them. The woman stopt her wheel, and gazed as if a spectre had started into view.

I was somewhat aware of these consequences, and endeavoured to elude them, by assuming an air of supplication and humility. I told her that I was a traveller, who had unfortunately lost his way, and had rambled in this wild till nearly famished for want. I intreated her to give me some food; any thing however scanty or coarse, would be acceptable.

After some pause she desired me, though not without some marks of fear, to walk in. She placed before me some brown bread and milk. She eyed me while I eagerly devoured this morsel. It was, indeed, more delicious than any I had ever tasted. At length she broke silence, and expressed her astonishment and commiseration at my seemingly forlorn state, adding, that perhaps I was the man whom the men were looking after who had been there some hours before.

My curiosity was roused by this intimation. In answer to my interrogations, she said, that three persons had lately stopped, to inquire if her husband had not met, within the last three days, a person of whom their description seemed pretty much to suit my person and dress. He was tall, slender, wore nothing but shirt and trowsers,[2] and was wounded on the cheek.

What, I asked, did they state the rank or condition of the person to be?

He lived in Solebury. He was supposed to have rambled in the mountains, and to have lost his way, or to have met with some mischance. It was three days since he had disappeared, but had been seen, by some one, the last night, at Deb's hut.

What and where was Deb's hut?

It was a hut in the wilderness, occupied by an old Indian woman, known among her neighbours by the name of Old Deb. Some people called her Queen Mab. Her dwelling was eight *long* miles from this house.

A thousand questions were precluded, and a thousand doubts solved by this information. *Queen Mab* were sounds familiar to my ears; for they originated with myself.

This woman originally belonged to the tribe of Delawares or Lennilennapee. All these districts were once comprised within the dominions of that nation. About thirty years ago, in consequence of perpetual encroachments of the English colonists, they abandoned their ancient seats and retired to the banks of the Wabash and Muskingum.[3]

---

[2] "Trowsers": see the notes concerning these trousers in Chapters 16 (note 16.4) and 24 (note 24.4).

[3] "The banks of the Wabash and Muskingum": the Lenape or Delaware Indians originally occupied the Delaware Valley area in what is now eastern Pennsylvania and New Jersey. Edgar notes that white colonization has driven the tribe west to the Old Northwest—that is, the Great Lakes area around the Muskingum River in what is now Ohio, and the Wabash River in what is now Indiana. This area supported a multiethnic population of displaced Indians from many tribes, runaway slaves, and European settlers including Irish settlers and émigré radicals. Some of these radicals returned to Ireland and wrote about their experiences in the area's mixed settlements, which for a time

This emigration was concerted in a general council of the tribe, and obtained the concurrence of all but one female. Her birth, talents, and age, gave her much consideration and authority among her countrymen; and all her zeal and eloquence were exerted to induce them to lay aside their scheme. In this, however, she could not succeed. Finding them refractory, she declared her resolution to remain behind, and maintain possession of the land which her countrymen should impiously abandon.

The village inhabited by this clan was built upon ground which now constitutes my uncle's barn yard and orchard. On the departure of her countrymen, this female burnt the empty wigwams and retired into the fastnesses of Norwalk. She selected a spot suitable for an Indian dwelling and a small plantation of maize, and in which she was seldom liable to interruption and intrusion.

Her only companions were three dogs, of the Indian or wolf species. These animals differed in nothing from their kinsmen of the forest, but in their attachment and obedience to their mistress. She governed them with absolute sway: they were her servants and protectors, and attended her person or guarded her threshold, agreeable to her directions.[4] She fed them with corn and they supplied her and themselves with meat, by hunting squirrels, racoons, and rabbits.

To the rest of mankind they were aliens or enemies. They never left the desert but in company with their mistress, and when she entered a farm-house, waited her return at a distance. They would suffer none to approach them, but attacked no one who did not imprudently crave their acquaintance, or who kept at a respectful distance from their wigwam. That sacred asylum they would not suffer to be violated, and no stranger could enter it but at the imminent hazard of his life, unless accompanied and protected by their dame.

The chief employment of this woman, when at home, besides plucking the weeds from among her corn; bruising the grain between two stones, and setting her snares, for rabbits and apossums, was to talk. Though in solitude, her tongue was never at rest but when she was asleep; but her conversation was merely addressed to her dogs. Her voice was sharp and shrill, and her gesticulations were vehement and grotesque. An hearer would naturally imagine that she was scolding; but, in truth, she was merely giving them directions. Having no other object of contemplation or subject of discourse, she always found, in their postures and looks, occasion for praise, or blame, or command. The readiness with which they understood, and the docility with which they obeyed her movements and words, were truly wonderful.

---

lived in relative peace as "village republics," autonomous from European empires or the United States. See White, *The Middle Ground,* and Linebaugh, "The Red-Crested Bird and Black Duck." The frame narrative of Brown's novel *Memoirs of Stephen Calvert* is set in this area, where the novel's protagonist has fled for protection and relief.

[4] Deb's ferocious and obedient dogs "of the Indian or wolf species" seem an apt image for the Delaware warriors that Deb commands. Like earlier associations of "savage" panthers with the Irishman Clithero and Delaware warriors in Chapters 2, 12, and 16, these dogs develop the novel's web of associations concerning animalistic violence, revenge, and resistance to domination. For more on this topic, see the discussion of these animals in the last section of the Introduction.

If a stranger chanced to wander near her hut, and overhear her jargon, incessant as it was, and shrill, he might speculate in vain on the reason of these sounds. If he waited in expectation of hearing some reply, he waited in vain. The strain, always voluble and sharp, was never intermitted for a moment, and would continue for hours at a time.

She seldom left the hut but to visit the neighbouring inhabitants, and demand from them food and cloathing, or whatever her necessities required. These were exacted as her due: to have her wants supplied was her prerogative, and to withhold what she claimed was rebellion. She conceived that by remaining behind her countrymen she succeeded to the government, and retained the possession of all this region. The English were aliens and sojourners, who occupied the land merely by her connivance and permission, and whom she allowed to remain on no terms but those of supplying her wants.

Being a woman aged and harmless, her demands being limited to that of which she really stood in need, and which her own industry could not procure, her pretensions were a subject of mirth and good humour, and her injunctions obeyed with seeming deference and gravity. To me she early became an object of curiosity and speculation. I delighted to observe her habits and humour her prejudices. She frequently came to my uncle's house, and I sometimes visited her; insensibly she seemed to contract an affection for me, and regarded me with more complacency and condescension than any other received.

She always disdained to speak English, and custom had rendered her intelligible to most in her native language, with regard to a few simple questions. I had taken some pains to study her jargon, and could make out to discourse with her on the few ideas which she possessed. This circumstance, likewise, wonderfully prepossessed her in my favour.

The name by which she was formerly known was Deb; but her pretensions to royalty, the wildness of her aspect and garb, her shrivelled and diminutive form, a constitution that seemed to defy the ravages of time and the influence of the elements; her age, which some did not scruple to affirm exceeded an hundred years, her romantic solitude and mountainous haunts suggested to my fancy the appellation of *Queen Mab*. There appeared to me some rude analogy between this personage and her whom the poets of old-time have delighted to celebrate: thou perhaps wilt discover nothing but incongruities between them, but, be that as it may, Old Deb and Queen Mab soon came into indiscriminate and general use.[5]

---

[5] "Old Deb and Queen Mab soon came into indiscriminate and general use": clearly, Deb appears in the novel as a personification of the Delawares and their historical dispossession, and both of her Anglicized names have rich associations that are relevant to the story.

In *Judges* 4–5, Deborah, like Old Deb here, is a female warrior associated with revolt and prophetic language, a priestess and judge who organizes and predicts the victory of the Israelites over Sisera. Although some scholars have assumed that Deb cannot be her real name since it is European, Norman Grabo suggested that Deb is "a name indicating that she may have been a Christianized Indian" (Grabo, "Introduction," xiii). There is no indication that Deb is Christianized, however, and

She dwelt in Norwalk upwards of twenty years. She was not forgotten by her countrymen, and generally received from her brothers and sons an autumnal visit; but no solicitations or entreaties could prevail on her to return with them. Two years ago, some suspicion or disgust induced her to forsake her ancient habitation, and to seek a new one. Happily she found a more convenient habitation twenty miles to the westward, and in a spot abundantly sterile and rude.

This dwelling was of logs, and had been erected by a Scottish emigrant, who not being rich enough to purchase land, and entertaining a passion for solitude and independence, cleared a field in the unappropriated wilderness, and subsisted on its produce. After some time he disappeared. Various conjectures were formed as to the cause of his absence. None of them were satisfactory; but that which obtained most credit was, that he had been murdered by the Indians, who, about the same period, paid their annual visit to the *Queen*. This conjecture acquired some force, by observing that the old woman shortly after took possession of his hut, his implements of tillage, and his corn-field.

She was not molested in her new abode, and her life passed in the same quiet tenour as before. Her periodical rambles, her regal claims, her guardian wolves, and her uncouth volubility, were equally remarkable, but her circuits were new. Her distance made her visits to Solebury more rare, and had prevented me from ever extending my pedestrian excursions to her present abode.

These recollections were now suddenly called up by the information of my hostess. The hut where I had sought shelter and relief was, it seems, the residence of Queen Mab. Some fortunate occurrence had called her away during my visit. Had she and her dogs been at home, I should have been set upon by these ferocious centinels, and, before their dame could have interfered, have been, together with my helpless companion, mangled or killed. These animals never barked, I should have entered unaware of my danger, and my fate could scarcely have been averted by my fusil.

---

there are many reasons to look at her as a figure of resistance to colonizing impulses such as renaming.

Queen Mab is a warrior queen in Celtic legend (Medb of Connaught, also known as Queen Wolf) frequently evoked in English literature as a fairie queen by Herrick, Spencer, Shakespeare, Shelley, and many others. In the Ulster cycle of Irish mythology, Mab was queen of Connaught. Her name is cognate with the English word "mead," and she is associated with drunkenness and the mystical power of femininity. In the Ulster cycle, her tales involve a series of personal revenge and group battles resulting from rape and disrupted marriage, a desire to be an equal to men, and sexual license in taking male lovers. For more on the Mab legend, see the discussion in the Introduction.

The most familiar version of the figure appears in Mercutio's speech in Act I scene 4 of Shakespeare's *Romeo and Juliet*, where Mab brings dreams to sleepers and presides over childbirth. These functions may be relevant to this novel's dramatizations of sleep-walking, Mary's likely pregnancy, and Lorimer's miscarriage in the letters that end the novel. "Mab" is the name Edgar gives this figure, and this naming may suggest that Edgar has a romanticized or unrealistic view of Native Americans. Whichever name is used, Edgar's emphasis on Anglicized names and a patronizing interpretation of the Indian matriarch reflects the settlers' amnesia concerning the Indians' presence and claims on the land.

Her absence at this unseasonable hour was mysterious. It was now the time of year when her countrymen were accustomed to renew their visit. Was there a league between her and the plunderers whom I had encountered?

But who were they by whom my foot-steps were so industriously traced? Those whom I had seen at Deb's hut were strangers to me, but the wound upon my face was known only to them. To this circumstance was now added my place of residence and name. I supposed them impressed with the belief that I was dead; but this mistake must have speedily been rectified. Revisiting the spot, finding me gone, and obtaining some intelligence of my former condition, they had instituted a search after me.

But what tidings were these? I was supposed to have been bewildered in the mountains, and three days were said to have passed since my disappearance. Twelve hours had scarcely elapsed since I emerged from the cavern. Had two days and an half been consumed in my subterranean prison?

These reflections were quickly supplanted by others. I now gained a sufficient acquaintance with the region that was spread around me. I was in the midst of a vale, included between ridges that gradually approached each other, and when joined, were broken up into hollows and steeps, and spreading themselves over a circular space, assumed the appellation of Norwalk. This vale gradually widened as it tended to the westward, and was, in this place ten or twelve miles in breadth. My devious foot-steps[6] had brought me to the foot of the southern barrier. The outer basis of this was laved by the river, but, as it tended eastward, the mountain and river receded from each other, and one of the cultivable districts lying between them was Solebury, my natal *township*. Hither it was now my duty to return with the utmost expedition.

There were two ways before me. One lay along the interior base of the hill, over a sterile and trackless space, and exposed to the encounter of savages, some of whom might possibly be lurking here. The other was the well frequented road, on the outside and along the river, and which was to be gained by passing over this hill. The practicability of the passage was to be ascertained by inquiries made to my hostess. She pointed out a path that led to the rocky summit and down to the river's brink. The path was not easy to be kept in view or to be trodden, but it was undoubtedly to be preferred to any other.

A route, somewhat circuitous, would terminate in the river road. Thenceforward the way to Solebury was level and direct; but the whole space which I had to traverse was not less than thirty miles. In six hours it would be night, and, to perform the journey in that time would demand the agile boundings of a leopard and the indefatigable sinews of an elk.

My frame was in miserable plight. My strength had been assailed by anguish, and fear, and watchfulness; by toil, and abstinence, and wounds. Still, however, some remnant was left; would it not enable me to reach my home by night-fall? I had delighted, from my childhood, in feats of agility and perseverance. In roving through

---

[6] "Devious foot-steps": "devious" here means wandering, roundabout, errant; not sly or cunning.

the maze of thickets and precipices, I had put my energies both moral and physical, frequently to the test. Greater achievements than this had been performed, and I disdained to be out-done in perspicacity by the lynx, in his sure-footed instinct by the roe, or in patience under hardship, and contention with fatigue, by the Mohawk.[7] I have ever aspired to transcend the rest of animals in all that is common to the rational and brute, as well as in all by which they are distinguished from each other.

---

[7] "Mohawk": Edgar likens his skill to that of the Mohawks, a tribe who were bitter enemies of the groups descended from the Delawares.

Chapter XXI

I LIKEWISE burned with impatience to know the condition of my family, to dissipate at once their tormenting doubts and my own, with regard to our mutual safety. The evil that I feared had befallen them was too enormous to allow me to repose in suspense, and my restlessness and ominous forebodings would be more intolerable than any hardship or toils to which I could possibly be subjected during this journey.

I was much refreshed and invigorated by the food that I had taken, and by the rest of an hour. With this stock of recruited force I determined to scale the hill. After receiving minute directions, and returning many thanks for my hospitable entertainment, I set out.

The path was indeed intricate, and deliberate attention was obliged to be exerted in order to preserve it. Hence my progress was slower than I wished. The first impulse was to fix my eye upon the summit, and to leap from crag to crag till I reached it, but this my experience had taught me was impracticable. It was only by winding through gullies, and coasting precipices and bestriding chasms, that I could hope finally to gain the top, and I was assured that by one way only was it possible to accomplish even this.

An hour was spent in struggling with impediments, and I seemed to have gained no way. Hence a doubt was suggested whether I had not missed the true road. In this doubt I was confirmed by the difficulties which now grew up before me. The brooks, the angles and the hollows, which my hostess had described, were not to be seen. Instead of these, deeper dells, more headlong torrents and wider gaping rifts were incessantly encountered.

To return was as hopeless as to proceed. I consoled myself with thinking that the survey which my informant had made of the hill-side, might prove inaccurate, and that in spite of her predictions, the heights might be reached by other means than by those pointed out by her. I will not enumerate my toilsome expedients, my frequent disappointments and my desperate exertions. Suffice it to say that I gained the upper space, not till the sun had dipped beneath the horizon.

My satisfaction at accomplishing thus much was not small, and I hied, with renovated spirits, to the opposite brow. This proved to be a steep that could not be descended. The river flowed at its foot. The opposite bank was five hundred yards distant, and was equally towering and steep as that on which I stood. Appearances were adapted to persuade you that these rocks had formerly joined, but by some mighty effort of nature, had been severed, that the stream might find way through the chasm. The channel, however, was encumbered with asperities over which the river fretted and foamed with thundering impetuosity.

I pondered for a while on these stupendous scenes. They ravished my attention from considerations that related to myself; but this interval was short, and I began to measure the descent, in order to ascertain the practicability of treading it. My survey terminated in bitter disappointment. I turned my eye successively eastward and westward. Solebury lay in the former direction, and thither I desired to go. I kept along the verge in this direction, till I reached an impassable rift. Beyond this I saw that the steep grew lower, but it was impossible to proceed farther. Higher up the descent might be practicable, and though more distant from Solebury, it was better to reach the road, even at that distance, than never to reach it.

Changing my course, therefore, I explored the spaces above. The night was rapidly advancing, the grey clouds gathered in the south-east, and a chilling blast, the usual attendant of a night in October, began to whistle among the pigmy cedars that scantily grew upon these heights. My progress would quickly be arrested by darkness, and it behoved me to provide some place of shelter and repose. No recess, better than an hollow in the rock, presented itself to my anxious scrutiny.

Meanwhile I would not dismiss the hope of reaching the road, which I saw some hundred feet below, winding along the edge of the river, before daylight should utterly fail. Speedily these hopes derived new vigour from meeting a ledge that irregularly declined from the brow of the hill. It was wide enough to allow of cautious footing. On a similar stratum, or ledge, projecting still further from the body of the hill, and close to the surface of the river, was the road. This stratum ascended from the level of the stream, while that on which I trod rapidly descended. I hoped that they would speedily be blended, or at least approach so near as to allow me to leap from one to the other without enormous hazard.

This fond expectation was frustrated. Presently I perceived that the ledge below began to descend, while that above began to tend upward, and was quickly terminated by the uppermost surface of the cliff. Here it was needful to pause. I looked over the brink and considered whether I might not leap from my present station, without endangering my limbs. The road into which I should fall was a rocky pavement far from being smooth. The descent could not be less than forty or fifty feet. Such an attempt was, to the last degree, hazardous, but was it not better to risque my life by leaping from this eminence, than to remain and perish on the top of this inhospitable mountain? The toils which I had endured, in reaching this height appeared to my panic-struck fancy, less easy to be borne again than death.

I know not but that I should have finally resolved to leap, had not different views been suggested by observing that the outer edge of the road was, in like manner, the brow of a steep which terminated in the river. The surface of the road, was twelve or fifteen feet above the level of the stream, which, in this spot was still and smooth. Hence I inferred that the water was not of inconsiderable depth. To fall upon rocky points was, indeed, dangerous, but to plunge into water of sufficient depth, even from an height greater than that at which I now stood, especially to one to whom habit had rendered water almost as congenial an element as air, was scarcely attended with inconvenience. This expedient was easy and safe. Twenty yards from this spot, the channel was shallow, and to gain the road from the stream, was no difficult exploit.

Some disadvantages, however, attended this scheme. The water was smooth, but this might arise from some other cause than its depth. My gun, likewise, must be left behind me, and that was a loss to which I felt invincible repugnance. To let it fall upon the road, would put it in my power to retrieve the possession, but it was likely to be irreparably injured by the fall.

While musing upon this expedient, and weighing injuries with benefits, the night closed upon me. I now considered that should I emerge in safety from the stream, I should have many miles to travel before I could reach an house. My clothes mean-while would be loaded with wet. I should be heart-pierced by the icy blast that now blew, and my wounds and bruises would be chafed into insupportable pain.

I reasoned likewise on the folly of impatience and the necessity of repose. By thus long continuance in one posture, my sinews began to stiffen, and my reluctance to make new exertions to encrease. My brows were heavy, and I felt an irresistible propensity to sleep. I concluded to seek some shelter, and resign myself, my painful recollections, and my mournful presages to sweet forgetfulness. For this end, I once more ascended to the surface of the cliff. I dragged my weary feet forward, till I found somewhat that promised me the shelter that I sought.

A cluster of cedars appeared, whose branches over-arched a space that might be called a bower. It was a slight cavity, whose flooring was composed of loose stones and a few faded leaves blown from a distance, and finding a temporary lodgement here. On one side was a rock, forming a wall rugged and projecting above. At the bottom of the rock was a rift, some-what resembling a coffin in shape, and not much larger in dimensions. This rift terminated on the opposite side of the rock, in an opening that was too small for the body of a man to pass. The distance between each entrance was twice the length of a man.

This bower was open to the South-east whence the gale now blew. It therefore im-perfectly afforded the shelter of which I stood in need; but it was the best that the place and the time afforded. To stop the smaller entrance of the cavity with a stone, and to heap before the other, branches lopped from the trees with my hatchet, might somewhat contribute to my comfort.

This was done, and thrusting myself into this recess, as far as I was able, I prepared for repose. It might have been reasonably suspected to be the den of rattle-snakes or panthers; but my late contention with superior dangers and more formidable ene-mies made me reckless of these, but another inconvenience remained. In spite of my precautions, my motionless posture and slender covering exposed me so much to the cold that I could not sleep.

The air appeared to have suddenly assumed the temperature of mid-winter. In a short time, my extremities were benumbed, and my limbs shivered and ached as if I had been seized by an ague. My bed likewise was dank and uneven, and the posture I was obliged to assume, unnatural and painful. It was evident that my purpose could not be answered by remaining here.

I, therefore, crept forth, and began to reflect upon the possibility of continuing my journey. Motion was the only thing that could keep me from freezing, and my frame was in that state which allowed me to take no repose in the absence of warmth; since warmth were indispensable. It now occurred to me to ask whether it were not possi-ble to kindle a fire.

Sticks and leaves were at hand. My hatchet and a pebble would enable me to extract a spark. From this, by suitable care and perseverance, I might finally procure suffi-cient fire to give me comfort and ease, and even enable me to sleep. This boon was delicious and I felt as if I were unable to support a longer deprivation of it.

I proceeded to execute this scheme. I took the dryest leaves, and endeavoured to use them as tinder, but the driest leaves were moistened by the dews. They were only to be found in the hollows, in some of which were pools of water and others were dank. I was not speedily discouraged, but my repeated attempts failed, and I was finally compelled to relinquish this expedient.

All that now remained was to wander forth and keep myself in motion till the morning. The night was likely to prove tempestuous and long. The gale seemed freighted with ice, and acted upon my body like the points of a thousand needles. There was no remedy, and I mustered my patience to endure it.

I returned again, to the brow of the hill. I ranged along it till I reached a place where the descent was perpendicular, and, in consequence of affording no sustenance to trees or bushes, was nearly smooth and bare. There was no road to be seen, and this circumstance, added to the sounds which the ripling current produced, afforded me some knowledge of my situation.

The ledge, along which the road was conducted, disappeared near this spot. The opposite sides of the chasm through which flowed the river, approached nearer to each other, in the form of jutting promontories. I now stood upon the verge of that on the northern side. The water flowed at the foot, but, for the space of ten or twelve feet from the rock, was so shallow as to permit the traveller and his horse to wade through it, and thus to regain the road which the receding precipice had allowed to be continued on the farther side.

I knew the nature and dimensions of this ford. I knew that, at a few yards from the rock, the channel was of great depth. To leap into it, in this place, was a less danger-ous exploit, than at the spot where I had formerly been tempted to leap. There I was unacquainted with the depth, but here I knew it to be considerable. Still there was some ground of hesitation and fear. My present station was loftier, and how deeply I might sink into this gulf, how far the fall and the concussion would bereave me of my presence of mind, I could not determine. This hesitation vanished, and placing my tom-hawk and fusil upon the ground, I prepared to leap.

This purpose was suspended, in the moment of its execution, by a faint sound, heard from the quarter whence I had come. It was the warning of men, but had nothing in common with those which I had been accustomed to hear. It was not the howling of a wolf or the yelling of a panther. These had often been over-heard by night during my last year's excursion to the lakes. My fears whispered that this was the vociferation of a savage.

I was unacquainted with the number of the enemies who had adventured into this district. Whether those whom I had encountered at *Deb's hut* were of that band whom I had met with in the cavern, was merely a topic of conjecture. There might be an half-score of troops, equally numerous, spread over the wilderness, and the signal I had just heard might betoken the approach of one of these. Yet by what means they should gain this nook, and what prey they expected to discover, were not easily conceived.

The sounds, somewhat diversified, nearer and rising from different quarters, were again heard. My doubts and apprehensions were increased. What expedient to adopt for my own safety, was a subject of rapid meditation. Whether to remain stretched upon the ground or to rise and go forward. Was it likely the enemy would coast along the edge of the steep? Would they ramble hither to look upon the ample scene which spread on all sides around the base of this rocky pinnacle? In that case, how should I conduct myself! My arms were ready for use. Could I not elude the necessity of shedding more blood? Could I not anticipate their assault by casting myself without delay into the stream?

The sense of danger demanded more attention to be paid to external objects than to the motives by which my future conduct should be influenced. My post was on a circular projecture, in some degree, detached from the body of the hill, the brow of which continued in a streight line, uninterrupted by this projecture, which was somewhat higher than the continued summit of the ridge. This line ran at the distance of a few paces from my post. Objects moving along this line could merely be perceived to move, in the present obscurity.

My scrutiny was entirely directed to this quarter. Presently the treading of many feet was heard, and several figures were discovered, following each other in that streight and regular succession which is peculiar to the Indians. They kept along the brow of the hill joining the promontory. I distinctly marked seven figures in succession.

My resolution was formed. Should any one cast his eye hither, suspect, or discover an enemy, and rush towards me, I determined to start upon my feet, fire on my foe as he advanced, throw my piece on the ground, and then leap into the river.

Happily, they passed unobservant and in silence. I remained, in the same posture, for several minutes. At length, just as my alarms began to subside, the halloos, before heard, arose, and from the same quarter as before. This convinced me that my perils were not at an end. This now appeared to be merely the vanguard, and would speedily be followed by others, against whom the same caution was necessary to be taken.

My eye, anxiously bent the only way by which any one could approach, now discerned a figure, which was indubitably that of a man armed: none other appeared in company, but doubtless others were near. He approached, stood still, and appeared to gaze stedfastly at the spot where I lay.

The optics of a *Lennilennapee* I knew to be far keener than my own. A log or a couched fawn would never be mistaken for a man, nor a man for a couched fawn or a log. Not only a human being would be instantly detected, but a decision be unerringly made whether it were friend or foe. That my prostrate body was the object on which the attention of this vigilant and stedfast gazer was fixed, could not be doubted. Yet, since he continued an inactive gazer, there was ground for a possibility to stand upon, that I was not recognized. My fate, therefore, was still in suspense.

This interval was momentary. I marked a movement, which my fears instantly interpreted to be that of leveling a gun at my head. This action was sufficiently conformable to my prognostics. Supposing me to be detected, there was no need for him to change his post. Aim might too fatally be taken, and his prey be secured, from the distance at which he now stood.

These images glanced upon my thought, and put an end to my suspense. A single effort placed me on my feet. I fired with precipitation that precluded the certainty of hitting my mark, dropped my piece upon the ground, and leaped from this tremendous height into the river, I reached the surface, and sunk in a moment to the bottom.

Plunging endlong into the water, the impetus created by my fall from such an height, would be slowly resisted by this denser element. Had the depth been less, its resistance would not perhaps have hindered me from being mortally injured against the rocky bottom. Had the depth been greater, time enough would not have been allowed me to regain the surface. Had I fallen on my side, I should have been bereaved of life or sensibility by the shock which my frame would have received. As it was, my fate was suspended on a thread. To have lost my presence of mind, to have forborne to counteract my sinking, for an instant, after I had reached the water, would have made all exertions to regain the air, fruitless. To so fortunate a concurrence of events, was thy friend indebted for his safety!

Yet I only emerged from the gulf to encounter new perils. Scarcely had I raised my head above the surface, and inhaled the vital breath, when twenty shots were aimed at me from the precipice above. A shower of bullets fell upon the water. Some of them did not fall further than two inches from my head. I had not been aware of this new danger, and now that it assailed me continued gasping the air, and floundering at random. The means of eluding it did not readily occur. My case seemed desperate and all caution was dismissed.

This state of discomfiting surprise quickly disappeared. I made myself acquainted, at a glance, with the position of surrounding objects. I conceived that the opposite bank of the river would afford me most security, and thither I tended with all the expedition in my power.

Meanwhile, my safety depended on eluding the bullets that continued incessantly to strike the water at an arm's length from my body. For this end I plunged beneath the surface, and only rose to inhale fresh air. Presently the firing ceased, the flashes that lately illuminated the bank disappeared, and a certain bustle and murmur of confused voices gave place to solitude and silence.

Chapter XXII

I REACHED without difficulty the opposite bank, but the steep was inaccessible. I swam along the edge in hopes of meeting with some projection or recess where I might, at least, rest my weary limbs, and if it were necessary to recross the river, to lay in a stock of recruited spirits and strength for that purpose. I trusted that the water would speedily become shoal, or that the steep would afford rest to my feet. In both these hopes I was disappointed.

There is no one to whom I would yield the superiority in swimming, but my strength, like that of other human beings, had its limits. My previous fatigues had been enormous, and my clothes, heavy with moisture, greatly incumbered and retarded my movements. I had proposed to free myself from this imprisonment, but I foresaw the inconveniences of wandering over this scene in absolute nakedness, and was willing therefore, at whatever hazard, to retain them. I continued to struggle with the current and to search for the means of scaling the steeps. My search was fruitless, and I began to meditate the recrossing of the river.

Surely my fate has never been paralleled! Where was this series of hardships and perils to end? No sooner was one calamity eluded, than I was beset by another. I had emerged from abhorred darkness in the heart of the earth, only to endure the extremities of famine and encounter the fangs of a wild beast. From these I was delivered only to be thrown into the midst of savages, to wage an endless and hopeless war with adepts in killing; with appetites that longed to feast upon my bowels and to quaff my heart's-blood. From these likewise was I rescued, but merely to perish in the gulfs of the river, to welter on unvisited shores or to be washed far away from curiosity or pity.

Formerly water was not only my field of sport but my sofa and my bed. I could float for hours on the surface, enjoying its delicious cool, almost without the expense of the slightest motion. It was an element as fitted for repose as for exercise, but now the buoyant spirit seemed to have flown. My muscles were shrunk, the air and water were equally congealed, and my most vehement exertions were requisite to sustain me on the surface.

At first I had moved along with my wonted celerity and ease, but quickly my forces were exhausted. My pantings and efforts were augmented and I saw that to cross the river again was impracticable. I must continue, therefore, to search out some accessible spot in the bank along which I was swimming.

Each moment diminished my stock of strength, and it behoved me to make good my footing before another minute should escape. I continued to swim, to survey the bank, and to make ineffectual attempts to grasp the rock. The shrubs which grew upon it would not uphold me, and the fragments which, for a moment, inspired me with hope, crumbled away as soon as they were touched.

At length, I noticed a pine, which was rooted in a crevice near the water. The trunk, or any part of the root, was beyond my reach, but I trusted that I could catch hold of the branch which hung lowest, and that, when caught, it would assist me in gaining the trunk, and thus deliver me from the death which could not be otherwise averted.

The attempt was arduous. Had it been made when I first reached the bank, no difficulty had attended it, but now, to throw myself some feet above the surface could scarcely be expected from one whose utmost efforts seemed to be demanded to keep him from sinking. Yet this exploit, arduous as it was, was attempted and accomplished. Happily the twigs were strong enough to sustain my weight till I caught at other branches and finally placed myself upon the trunk.

This danger was now past, but I admitted the conviction that others, no less formidable remained to be encountered and that my ultimate destiny was death. I looked upward. New efforts might enable me to gain the summit of this steep, but, perhaps, I should thus be placed merely in the situation from which I had just been delivered. It was of little moment whether the scene of my imprisonment was a dungeon not to be broken, or a summit from which descent was impossible.

The river, indeed, severed me from a road which was level and safe, but my recent dangers were remembered only to make me shudder at the thought of incurring them a second time, by attempting to cross it. I blush at the recollection of this cowardice. It was little akin to the spirit which I had recently displayed. It was, indeed, an alien to my bosom, and was quickly supplanted by intrepidity and perseverance.

I proceeded to mount the hill. From root to root, and from branch to branch, lay my journey. It was finished, and I sat down upon the highest brow to meditate on future trials. No road lay along this side of the river. It was rugged and sterile, and farms were sparingly dispersed over it. To reach one of these was now the object of my wishes. I had not lost the desire of reaching Solebury before morning, but my wet clothes and the coldness of the night seemed to have bereaved me of the power.

I traversed this summit, keeping the river on my right hand. Happily, its declinations and ascents were by no means difficult, and I was cheered in the midst of my vexations, by observing that every mile brought me nearer to my uncle's dwelling. Meanwhile I anxiously looked for some tokens of an habitation. These at length presented themselves. A wild heath, whistled over by October blasts, meagerly adorned with the dry stalks of scented shrubs and the bald heads of the sapless mullen, was succeeded by a fenced field and a corn-stack. The dwelling to which these belonged was eagerly sought.

I was not surprised that all voices were still and all lights extinguished, for this was the hour of repose. Having reached a piazza before the house, I paused. Whether, at this drousy time, to knock for admission, to alarm the peaceful tenants and take from them the rest which their daily toils and their rural innocence had made so sweet, or to retire to what shelter an hay-stack or barn could afford, was the theme of my deliberations.

Meanwhile I looked up at the house. It was the model of cleanliness and comfort. It was built of wood; but the materials had undergone the plane, as well as the axe and the saw. It was painted white, and the windows not only had sashes, but these sashes were supplied, contrary to custom, with glass.[1] In most cases, the aperture where

---

[1] "The windows not only had sashes, but . . . glass": that the house has such windows and other embellishments suggests middle-class gentility and prosperity.

glass should be is stuffed with an old hat or a petticoat. The door had not only all its parts entire, but was embellished with mouldings and a pediment. I gathered from these tokens that this was the abode not only of rural competence and innocence, but of some beings, raised by education and fortune, above the intellectual medioc- rity of clowns.[2]

Methought I could claim consanguinity[3] with such beings. Not to share their char- ity and kindness would be inflicting as well as receiving injury. The trouble of af- fording shelter, and warmth, and wholesome diet to a wretch destitute as I was, would be eagerly sought by them.

Still I was unwilling to disturb them. I bethought myself that their kitchen might be entered, and all that my necessities required be obtained without interrupting their slumber. I needed nothing but the warmth which their kitchen hearth would afford. Stretched upon the bricks, I might dry my clothes, and perhaps enjoy some unmo- lested sleep. In spite of presages of ill and the horrid remembrances of what I had per- formed and endured, I believed that nature would afford a short respite to my cares.

I went to the door of what appeared to be a kitchen. The door was wide open. This circumstance portended evil. Though it be not customary to lock or to bolt, it is still less usual to have entrances unclosed. I entered with suspicious steps, and saw enough to confirm my apprehensions. Several pieces of wood half burned, lay in the midst of the floor. They appeared to have been removed hither from the chimney, doubtless with a view to set fire to the whole building.

The fire had made some progress on the floor, but had been seasonably extin- guished by pails-full of water, thrown upon it. The floor was still deluged with wet, the pail not emptied of all its contents stood upon the hearth. The earthen vessels and plates whose proper place was the dresser, were scattered in fragments in all parts of the room. I looked around me for some one to explain this scene, but no one appeared.

The last spark of fire was put out, so that had my curiosity been idle, my purpose could not be accomplished. To retire from this scene, neither curiosity nor benevo- lence would permit. That some mortal injury had been intended was apparent. What greater mischief had befallen, or whether greater might not, by my inter- position, be averted, could only be ascertained by penetrating further into the

---

[2] "Above the intellectual mediocrity of clowns": "clown," in this eighteenth-century usage, means uneducated farmer, peasant, field hand. Edgar takes in the house's genteel details and assumes that the inhabitants are educated, benevolent, and "civilized" that is, just like him. Given the grotesque scene that follows, Edgar's exaggeratedly idealistic assumptions about the "civilized" setting he dis- covers in this scene are grossly mistaken. Brown almost seems to mock Edgar here, and, once again, he shows Edgar jumping to conclusions based on appearances. Edgar's encounter with the Irish and very un-Quaker inhabitants of Chetasco may possibly refer to upper-class Quaker contempt for the Scots-Irish on the Pennsylvania frontier. Edgar will use the term again in this sense in Chapter 23, page 154.

[3] "Consanguinity": literally "blood relations," but here used more generally as ethno-racial or social proximity and "kinship" in that extended sense.

house. I opened a door on one side which led to the main body of the building and entered to a bed-chamber. I stood at the entrance and knocked, but no one answered my signals.

The sky was not totally clouded, so that some light pervaded the room. I saw that a bed stood in the corner, but whether occupied or not, its curtains hindered me from judging. I stood in suspense a few minutes, when a motion in the bed shewed me that some one was there. I knocked again but withdrew to the outside of the door. This roused the sleeper, who, half-groaning and puffing the air through his nostrils, grumbled out in the hoarsest voice that I ever heard, and in a tone of surly impatience . . . Who is there?

I hesitated for an answer, but the voice instantly continued in the manner of one half-asleep and enraged at being disturbed . . . Is't you Peg? Damn ye, stay away, now; I tell ye stay away, or, by God I will cut your throat . . . I will. . . . He continued to mutter and swear, but without coherence or distinctness.[4]

These were the accents of drunkenness, and denoted a wild and ruffian life. They were little in unison with the external appearances of the mansion, and blasted all the hopes I had formed of meeting under this roof with gentleness and hospitality. To talk with this being, to attempt to reason him into humanity and soberness, was useless. I was at a loss in what manner to address him, or whether it was proper to maintain any parley. Meanwhile, my silence was supplied by the suggestions of his own distempered fancy. Ay, said he, ye will, will ye? well come on, let's see who's the better at the oak-stick. If I part with ye, before I have bared your bones . . . I'll teach ye to be always dipping in my dish, ye devil's dam! ye!

So saying, he tumbled out of bed. At the first step, he struck his head against the bed-post, but setting himself upright, he staggered towards the spot where I stood. Some new obstacle occurred. He stumbled and fell at his length upon the floor.

To encounter or expostulate with a man in this state was plainly absurd. I turned and issued forth, with an aching heart, into the court before the house. The miseries which a debauched husband or father inflicts upon all whom their evil destiny allies to him were pictured by my fancy, and wrung from me tears of anguish. These images, however, quickly yielded to reflections on my own state. No expedient now remained, but to seek the barn, and find a covering and a bed of straw.

I had scarcely set foot within the barn-yard when I heard a sound as of the crying of an infant. It appeared to issue from the barn. I approached softly and listened at the door. The cries of the babe continued, but were accompanied by intreaties of a nurse

---

[4] "Without coherence or distinctness": because the speaker is drunk, abusive, using dialect (in the paragraphs that follow), and lashing out at a spouse or companion named Peg, the implication is that the sleeper and his family are Irish. If Clithero is associated with the subversive energies of the United Irishmen and other Irish revolutionaries of the 1790s, the Selbys here evoke familiar stereotypes and contemporary fears about the backcountry Irish and connect with the novel's larger concern with paternalism and patriarchy. In a letter to Joseph Bringhurst of July 29–August 1, 1793, Brown narrates a somewhat similar scene concerning an Irish immigrant named Jackey Cooke, an abusive, alcoholic father who is seen beating his wife to death and then whipping his eldest daughter.

or a mother to be quiet. These intreaties were mingled with heart-breaking sobs and exclamations of . . . Ah! me, my babe! Canst thou not sleep and afford thy unhappy mother some peace? Thou art cold, and I have not sufficient warmth to cherish thee! What will become of us? Thy deluded father cares not if we both perish.

A glimpse of the true nature of the scene seemed to be imparted by these words. I now likewise recollected incidents that afforded additional light. Somewhere on this bank of the river, there formerly resided one by name Selby. He was an aged person, who united science and taste to the simple and laborious habits of an husbandman. He had a son who resided several years in Europe, but on the death of his father, returned home, accompanied by a wife. He had succeeded to the occupation of the farm, but rumour had whispered many tales to the disadvantage of his morals. His wife was affirmed to be of delicate and polished manners, and much unlike her companion.

It now occurred to me that this was the dwelling of the Selbys, and I seemed to have gained some insight into the discord and domestic miseries by which the unhappy lady suffered. This was no time to waste my sympathy on others. I could benefit her nothing. Selby had probably returned from a carousal, with all his malignant passions raised into phrensy by intoxication. He had driven his desolate wife from her bed and house, and to shun outrage and violence she had fled, with her helpless infant, to the barn. To appease his fury, to console her, to suggest a remedy for this distress, was not in my power.[5] To have sought an interview would be merely to excite her terrors and alarm her delicacy, without contributing to alleviate her calamity. Here then was no asylum for me. A place of rest must be sought at some neighbouring habitation. It was probable that one would be found at no great distance, the path that led from the spot where I stood, through a gate into a meadow, might conduct me to the nearest dwelling, and this path I immediately resolved to explore.

I was anxious to open the gate without noise, but I could not succeed. Some creaking of its hinges, was unavoidably produced, which I feared would be overheard by the lady and multiply her apprehensions and perplexities. This inconvenience was irremediable. I therefore closed the gate and pursued the foot way before me with the utmost expedition. I had not gained the further end of the meadow when I lighted on something which lay across the path, and which, on being closely inspected, appeared to be an human body. It was the corse of a girl, mangled by an hatchet. Her head gory and deprived of its locks, easily explained the kind of enemies by whom she had been assailed. Here was proof that this quiet and remote habitation had been visited, in their destructive progress by the Indians. The girl had been slain by them,

---

[5] "To suggest a remedy for this distress, was not in my power": Edgar surprisingly makes no effort to help the abused woman. Like his patronizing relationship with his fiancée Mary Waldegrave, Edgar's willingness to leave this woman without help while going to extreme lengths to aid Clithero suggests that his standards of benevolence are gendered, related to his own concerns and self-interest (e.g., his desire to solve the murder of Waldegrave or figure out Clithero's relation to his former tutor Sarsefield), and thus, like much else in his behavior, significantly determined by wider structural causes.

and her scalp, according to their savage custom, had been torn away to be preserved as a trophy.

The fire which had been kindled on the kitchen floor was now remembered, and corroborated the inferences which were drawn from this spectacle. And yet that the mischief had been thus limited, that the besotted wretch who lay helpless on his bed, and careless of impending danger, and that the mother and her infant should escape, excited some degree of surprise. Could the savages have been interrupted in their work, and obliged to leave their vengeance unfinished?

Their visit had been recent. Many hours had not elapsed since they prowled about these grounds. Had they wholly disappeared and meant they not to return? To what new danger might I be exposed in remaining thus guideless and destitute of all defence?

In consequence of these reflections, I proceeded with more caution. I looked with suspicious glances, before and on either side of me. I now approached the fence which, on this side, bounded the meadow. Something was discerned or imagined, stretched close to the fence, on the ground, and filling up the path-way. My apprehensions of a lurking enemy, had been previously awakened, and my fancy instantly figured to itself an armed man, lying on the ground and waiting to assail the unsuspecting passenger.

At first I was prompted to fly, but a second thought shewed me that I had already approached near enough to be endangered. Notwithstanding my pause, the form was motionless. The possibility of being misled in my conjectures was easily supposed. What I saw might be a log or it might be another victim to savage ferocity. This tract was that which my safety required me to pursue. To turn aside or go back would be merely to bewilder myself anew.

Urged by these motives, I went nearer, and at least was close enough to perceive that the figure was human. He lay upon his face, near his right hand was a musquet, unclenched. This circumstance, his death-like attitude and the garb and ornaments of an Indian, made me readily suspect the nature and cause of this catastrophe. Here the invaders had been encountered and repulsed, and one at least of their number had been left upon the field.

I was weary of contemplating these rueful objects. Custom, likewise, even in so short a period, had inured me to spectacles of horror. I was grown callous and immoveable. I staid not to ponder on the scene, but snatching the musquet, which was now without an owner, and which might be indispensable to my defence, I hastened into the wood. On this side the meadow was skirted by a forest, but a beaten road lead into it, and might therefore be attempted without danger.

Chapter XXIII

THE road was intricate and long. It seemed designed to pervade the forest in every possible direction. I frequently noticed cut wood, piled in heaps upon either side, and rejoiced in these tokens that the residence of men was near. At length I reached a second fence, which proved to be the boundary of a road still more frequented. I pursued this, and presently beheld, before me, the river and its opposite barriers.

This object afforded me some knowledge of my situation. There was a ford over which travellers used to pass, and in which the road that I was now pursuing terminated. The stream was rapid and tumultuous, but in this place it did not rise higher than the shoulders. On the opposite side was an highway, passable by horses and men, though not carriages, and which led into the midst of Solebury. Should I not rush into the stream, and still aim at reaching my uncle's house before morning? Why should I delay?

Thirty hours of incessant watchfulness and toil, of enormous efforts and perils, preceded and accompanied by abstinence and wounds, were enough to annihilate the strength and courage of ordinary men. In the course of them, I had frequently believed myself to have reached the verge beyond which my force would not carry me, but experience as frequently demonstrated my error. Though many miles, were yet to be traversed, though my clothes were once more to be drenched and loaded with moisture, though every hour seemed to add somewhat to the keenness of the blast: yet how should I know, but by trial, whether my stock of energy was not sufficient for this last exploit?

My resolution to proceed was nearly formed, when the figure of a man moving slowly across the road, at some distance before me, was observed. Hard by this ford lived a man by name Bisset, of whom I had slight knowledge. He tended his two hundred acres with a plodding and money-doating spirit, while his son overlooked a Gristmill, on the river. He was a creature of gain, coarse and harmless. The man whom I saw before me might be he, or some one belonging to his family. Being armed for defence, I less scrupled a meeting with any thing in the shape of man. I therefore called. The figure stopped and answered me, without surliness or anger. The voice was unlike that of Bisset, but this person's information I believed would be of some service.

Coming up to him, he proved to be a clown, belonging to Bisset's habitation. His panic and surprise on seeing me made him aghast. In my present garb I should not have easily been recognized by my nearest kinsman, and much less easily by one who had seldom met me.

It may be easily conceived that my thoughts, when allowed to wander from the objects before me, were tormented with forebodings and inquietudes on account of the ills which I had so much reason to believe had befallen my family. I had no doubt that some evil had happened, but the full extent of it was still uncertain. I desired and dreaded to discover the truth, and was unable to interrogate this person in a direct manner. I could deal only in circuities and hints. I shuddered while I waited for an answer to my inquiries.

Had not Indians, I asked, been lately seen in this neighbourhood? Were they not suspected of hostile designs? Had they not already committed some mischief? Some passenger, perhaps, had been attacked; or fire had been set to some house? On which side of the river had their steps been observed, or any devastation been committed? Above the ford or below it? At what distance from the river?

When his attention could be withdrawn from my person and bestowed upon my questions, he answered that some alarm had indeed been spread about Indians, and that parties from Solebury and Chetasko were out in pursuit of them, that many persons had been killed by them, and that one house in Solebury had been rifled and burnt on the night before the last.

These tidings were a dreadful confirmation of my fears. There scarcely remained a doubt: but still my expiring hope prompted me to inquire to whom did the house belong?

He answered that he had not heard the name of the owner. He was a stranger to the people on the other side of the river.

Were any of the inhabitants murdered?

Yes. All that were at home except a girl whom they carried off. Some said that the girl had been retaken.

What was the name? Was it Huntly?

Huntly? Yes. No. He did not know. He had forgotten.

I fixed my eyes upon the ground. An interval of gloomy meditation succeeded. All was lost, all for whose sake I desired to live, had perished by the hands of these assassins. That dear home, the scene of my sportive childhood, of my studies, labours and recreations, was ravaged by fire and the sword: was reduced to a frightful ruin.

Not only all that embellished and endeared existence was destroyed, but the means of subsistence itself. Thou knowest that my sisters and I were dependants on the bounty of our uncle. His death would make way for the succession of his son, a man fraught with envy and malignity: who always testified a mortal hatred to us, merely because we enjoyed the protection of his father. The ground which furnished me with bread was now become the property of one, who, if he could have done it with security, would gladly have mingled poison with my food.

All that my imagination or my heart regarded as of value had likewise perished. Whatever my chamber, my closets, my cabinets contained, my furniture, my books, the records of my own skill, the monuments of their existence whom I loved, my very cloathing, were involved in indiscriminate and irretreivable destruction. Why should I survive this calamity?

But did not he say that one had escaped? The only females in the family were my sisters. One of these had been reserved for a fate worse than death; to gratify the innate and insatiable cruelty of savages by suffering all the torments their invention can suggest, or to linger out years of dreary bondage and unintermitted hardship in the bosom of the wilderness. To restore her to liberty; to cherish this last survivor of my unfortunate race was a sufficient motive to life and to activity.

But soft! Had not rumour whispered that the captive was retaken? Oh! who was her angel of deliverance? Where did she now abide? Weeping over the untimely fall of her protector and her friend. Lamenting and upbraiding the absence of her brother? Why should I not haste to find her? To mingle my tears with hers, to assure her of my safety and expiate the involuntary crime of my desertion, by devoting all futurity to the task of her consolation and improvement?

The path was open and direct. My new motives, would have trampled upon every impediment and made me reckless of all dangers and all toils. I broke from my reverie, and without taking leave or expressing gratitude to my informant, I ran with frantic expedition towards the river, and plunging into it gained the opposite side in a moment.

I was sufficiently acquainted with the road. Some twelve or fifteen miles remained to be traversed. I did not fear that my strength would fail in the performance of my journey. It was not my uncle's habitation to which I directed my steps. Inglefield was my friend. If my sister had existence, or was snatched from captivity, it was here that an asylum had been afforded to her, and here was I to seek the knowledge of my destiny. For this reason having reached a spot where the road divided into two branches, one of which led to Inglefield's and the other to Huntly's, I struck into the former.

Scarcely had I passed the angle when I noticed a building, on the right hand, at some distance from the road. In the present state of my thoughts, it would not have attracted my attention, had not a light gleamed from an upper window, and told me that all within were not at rest.

I was acquainted with the owner of this mansion. He merited esteem and confidence, and could not fail to be acquainted with recent events. From him I should obtain all the information that I needed, and I should be delivered from some part of the agonies of my suspense. I should reach his door in a few minutes, and the window-light was a proof that my entrance at this hour would not disturb the family, some of whom were stirring.

Through a gate, I entered an avenue of tall oaks, that led to the house. I could not but reflect on the effect which my appearance would produce upon the family. The sleek locks, neat apparel, pacific guise, sobriety and gentleness of aspect by which I was customarily distinguished, would in vain be sought in the apparition which would now present itself before them. My legs, neck and bosom were bare, and their native hue were exchanged for the livid marks of bruises and scarrifications. An horrid scar upon my cheek, and my uncombed locks; hollow eyes, made ghastly by abstinence and cold, and the ruthless passions of which my mind had been the theatre, added to the musquet which I carried in my hand, would prepossess them with the notion of a maniac or ruffian.

Some inconveniences might hence arise, which however could not be avoided. I must trust to the speed with which my voice and my words should disclose my true character and rectify their mistake.

I now reached the principal door of the house. It was open, and I unceremoniously entered. In the midst of the room stood a German stove, well heated. To thaw my half frozen limbs was my first care. Meanwhile, I gazed around me, and marked the appearances of things.

Two lighted candles stood upon the table. Beside them were cyder-bottles and pipes of tobacco. The furniture and room was in that state which denoted it to have been lately filled with drinkers and smokers, yet neither voice, nor visage, nor motion were any where observable. I listened but neither above nor below, within or without, could any tokens of an human being be perceived.

This vacancy and silence must have been lately preceded by noise and concourse and bustle. The contrast was mysterious and ambiguous. No adequate cause of so quick and absolute a transition occurred to me. Having gained some warmth and lingered some ten or twenty minutes in this uncertainty, I determined to explore the other apartments of the building. I knew not what might betide in my absence, or what I might encounter in my search to justify precaution, and, therefore, kept the gun in my hand. I snatched a candle from the table and proceeded into two other apartments on the first floor and the kitchen. Neither was inhabited, though chairs and tables were arranged in their usual order, and no traces of violence or hurry were apparent.

Having gained the foot of the stair-case, I knocked, but my knocking was wholly disregarded. A light had appeared in an upper chamber. It was not, indeed, in one of those apartments which the family permanently occupied, but in that which, according to rural custom, was reserved for guests; but it indubitably betokened the presence of some being by whom my doubts might be solved. These doubts were too tormenting to allow of scruples and delay.—I mounted the stairs.

At each chamber door I knocked, but I knocked in vain. I tried to open, but found them to be locked. I at length reached the entrance of that in which a light had been discovered. Here, it was certain, that some one would be found; but here, as well as elsewhere, my knocking was unnoticed.

To enter this chamber was audacious, but no other expedient was afforded me to determine whether the house had any inhabitants. I, therefore, entered, though with caution and reluctance. No one was within, but there were sufficient traces of some person who had lately been here. On the table stood a travelling escrutoire, open, with pens and ink-stand.[1] A chair was placed before it, and a candle on the right hand. This apparatus was rarely seen in this country. Some traveller it seemed occupied this room, though the rest of the mansion was deserted. The pilgrim, as these appearances testified, was of no vulgar order, and belonged not to the class of periodical and every-day guests.

It now occurred to me that the occupant of this appartment could not be far off, and that some danger and embarrassment could not fail to accrue from being found, thus accoutred and garbed, in a place sacred to the study and repose of another. It

---

[1] "A travelling escrutoire, open, with pens and ink-stand": an escritoire, a portable writing desk, or "secretary," in furniture parlance. These were made of wood, with folding panels that open up to provide a writing surface and drawers to hold stationery and writing supplies (ink bottles, quills, sharpeners, wax, seals, etc.). As Edgar observes, such an object suggests that its owner is a wealthy and well-heeled traveler.

was proper, therefore, to withdraw, and either to resume my journey, or wait for the stranger's return, whom perhaps some temporary engagement had called away, in the lower and public room. The former now appeared to be the best expedient, as the return of this unknown person was uncertain, as well as his power to communicate the information which I wanted.

Had paper, as well as the implements of writing, lain upon the desk, perhaps my lawless curiosity would not have scrupled to have pryed into it. On the first glance nothing of that kind appeared, but now, as I turned towards the door, somewhat, lying beside the desk, on the side opposite the candle, caught my attention. The impulse was instantaneous and mechanical, that made me leap to the spot, and lay my hand upon it. Till I felt it between my fingers, till I brought it near my eyes and read frequently the inscriptions that appeared upon it, I was doubtful whether my senses had deceived me.

Few, perhaps, among mankind have undergone vicissitudes of peril and wonder equal to mine. The miracles of poetry, the transitions of enchantment, are beggarly and mean compared with those which I had experienced: Passage into new forms, overleaping the bars of time and space, reversal of the laws of inanimate and intelligent existence had been mine to perform and to witness.

No event had been more fertile of sorrow and perplexity than the loss of thy brother's letters. They went by means invisible, and disappeared at a moment when foresight would have least predicted their disappearance. They now placed themselves before me, in a manner equally abrupt, in a place and by means, no less contrary to expectation. The papers which I now seized were those letters. The parchment cover, the string that tied, and the wax that sealed them, appeared not to have been opened or violated.

The power that removed them from my cabinet, and dropped them in this house, a house which I rarely visited, which I had not entered during the last year, with whose inhabitants I maintained no cordial intercourse, and to whom my occupations and amusements, my joys and my sorrows, were unknown, was no object even of conjecture. But they were not possessed by any of the family. Some stranger was here, by whom they had been stolen, or into whose possession, they had, by some incomprehensible chance, fallen.

That stranger was near. He had left this apartment for a moment. He would speedily return. To go hence, might possibly occasion me to miss him. Here then I would wait, till he should grant me an interview. The papers were mine, and were recovered. I would never part with them. But to know by whose force or by whose stratagems I had been bereaved of them thus long, was now the supreme passion of my soul, I seated myself near a table and anxiously awaited for an interview, on which I was irresistably persuaded to believe that much of my happiness depended.

Meanwhile, I could not but connect this incident with the destruction of my family. The loss of these papers had excited transports of grief, and yet, to have lost them thus, was perhaps the sole expedient, by which their final preservation could be rendered possible. Had they remained in my cabinet, they could not have escaped the destiny which overtook the house and its furniture. Savages are not accustomed to leave their exterminating work unfinished. The house which they have plundered, they are careful to level with the ground. This not only their revenge, but their caution prescribes. Fire may originate by accident as well as by design, and the traces of pillage and murder are totally obliterated by the flames.

These thoughts were interrupted by the shutting of a door below, and by foot-steps ascending the stairs. My heart throbbed at the sound. My seat became uneasy and I started on my feet. I even advanced half way to the entrance of the room. My eyes were intensely fixed upon the door. My impatience would have made me guess at the person of this visitant by measuring his shadow, if his shadow were first seen; but this was precluded by the position of the light. It was only when the figure entered, and the whole person was seen, that my curiosity was gratified. He who stood before me was the parent and fosterer of my mind,[2] the companion and instructor of my youth, from whom I had been parted for years; from whom I believed myself to be forever separated;—*Sarsefield* himself!

---

[2] "The parent and fosterer of my mind . . .": here and throughout the finale of the book in Chapters 24–27 and the concluding letters, Sarsefield assumes a paternal relation to Edgar. This is not mere emotion, for in eighteenth-century culture the legal power and symbolic authority of the father is immense. In this "patriarchal" scheme, as Edgar put it in Chapter 2, subordination to the father is social order itself. Thus Edgar's changing relations to Sarsefield in the concluding chapters concern the possibility of his reentry or participation in the paternal and normative order from which he is excluded because of the death of his own father and his now problematic plans to marry Mary Waldegrave. Since Lorimer and possibly Mary are pregnant at this time (see Chapter 14, note 14.7), prospects for paternity become increasingly tangled and dubious as the novel draws to a close.

Chapter XXIV

MY deportment, at an interview so much desired and so wholly unforeseen, was that of a maniac. The petrifying influence of surprise, yielded to the impetuosities of passion. I held him in my arms: I wept upon his bosom, I sobbed with emotion which, had it not found passage at my eyes, would have burst my heart-strings. Thus I who had escaped the deaths that had previously assailed me in so many forms, should have been reserved to solemnize a scene like this by . . . *dying for joy!*

The sterner passions and habitual austerities of my companion, exempted him from pouring out this testimony of his feelings. His feelings were indeed more allied to astonishment and incredulity than mine had been. My person was not instantly recognized. He shrunk from my embrace, as if I were an apparition or impostor. He quickly disengaged himself from my arms, and withdrawing a few paces, gazed upon me as on one whom he had never before seen.

These repulses were ascribed to the loss of his affection. I was not mindful of the hideous guise in which I stood before him, and by which he might justly be misled to imagine me a ruffian or a lunatic. My tears flowed now on a new account, and I articulated in a broken and faint voice—My master! my friend! Have you forgotten! have you ceased to love me?

The sound of my voice made him start and exclaim—Am I alive? am I awake? Speak again I beseech you, and convince me that I am not dreaming or delirious.

Can you need any proof, I answered, that it is Edgar Huntly, your pupil, your child that speaks to you?

He now withdrew his eyes from me and fixed them on the floor. After a pause he resumed, in emphatic accents. Well, I have lived to this age in unbelief.[1] To credit or trust in miraculous agency was foreign to my nature, but now I am no longer sceptical. Call me to any bar, and exact from me an oath that you have twice been dead and twice recalled to life; that you move about invisibly, and change your place by the force, not of muscles, but of thought, and I will give it.

How came you hither? Did you penetrate the wall? Did you rise through the floor?

Yet surely 'tis an error. You could not be he whom twenty witnesses affirmed to have beheld a lifeless and mangled corpse upon the ground, whom my own eyes saw in that condition.

In seeking the spot once more to provide you a grave, you had vanished. Again I met you. You plunged into a rapid stream, from an height from which it was impossible to fall and to live: yet, as if to set the limits of nature at defiance; to sport with human penetration, you rose upon the surface: You floated; you swam: Thirty bullets were aimed at your head, by marks-men celebrated for the exactness of their sight. I myself was of the number, and I never missed what I desired to hit.

---

[1] "I have lived to this age in unbelief": Sarsefield, like his former pupil Edgar, is a freethinking non-believer—that is, not a Christian. Like the novel's other principal characters, however, he is prone to leap to erroneous conclusions when searching for explanations.

My predictions were confirmed by the event. You ceased to struggle; you sunk to rise no more, and yet after these accumulated deaths, you light upon this floor: so far distant from the scene of your catastrophe; over spaces only to be passed, in so short a time as has since elapsed, by those who have wings.

My eyes, my ears bear testimony to your existence now, as they formerly convinced me of your death—What am I to think; What proofs am I to credit?—There he stopped.

Every accent of this speech added to the confusion of my thoughts. The allusions that my friend had made were not unintelligible. I gained a glimpse of the complicated errors by which we had been mutually deceived. I had fainted on the area before Deb's hut. I was found by Sarsefield in this condition, and imagined to be dead.

The man whom I had seen upon the promontory was not an Indian. He belonged to a numerous band of pursuers, whom my hostile and precipitate deportment caused to suspect me for an enemy. They that fired from the steep were friends. The interposition that screened me from so many bullets, was indeed miraculous. No wonder that my voluntary sinking, in order to elude their shots, was mistaken for death, and that, having accomplished the destruction of this foe, they resumed their pursuit of others. But how was Sarsefield apprized that it was I who plunged into the river? No subsequent event was possible to impart to him the incredible truth.

A pause of mutual silence ensued. At length, Sarsefield renewed his expressions of amazement at this interview, and besought me to explain why I had disappeared by night from my Uncle's house, and by what series of unheard of events this interview was brought about. Was it indeed Huntly whom he examined and mourned over at the threshold of Deb's hut? Whom he had sought in every thicket and cave in the ample circuit of Norwalk and Chetasco? Whom he had seen perish in the current of the Delaware?

Instead of noticing his questions, my soul was harrowed with anxiety respecting the fate of my uncle and sisters. Sarsefield could communicate the tidings which would decide on my future lot, and set my portion in happiness or misery. Yet I had not breath to speak my inquiries. Hope tottered, and I felt as if a single word would be sufficient for its utter subversion. At length, I articulated the name of my Uncle.

The single word sufficiently imparted my fears, and these fears needed no verbal confirmation. At that dear name, my companion's features were overspread by sorrow—Your Uncle, said he, is dead.

Dead? Merciful Heaven! And my sisters too! Both?

Your Sisters are alive and well.

Nay, resumed I, in faultering accents, jest not with my feelings. Be not cruel in your pity. Tell me the truth.

I have said the truth. They are well, at Mr. Inglefield's.

My wishes were eager to assent to the truth of these tidings. The better part of me was then safe: but how did they escape the fate that overtook my uncle? How did they evade the destroying hatchet and the midnight conflagration? These doubts were imparted in a tumultuous and obscure manner to my friend. He no sooner fully comprehended them, than he looked at me, with some inquietude and surprise.

Huntly, said he, are you mad—What has filled you with these hideous prepossessions? Much havoc has indeed been committed in Chetasco and the wilderness; and a log hut has been burnt by design or by accident in Solebury, but that is all. Your house has not been assailed by either fire-brand or tom-hawk. Every thing is safe and in its ancient order. The master indeed is gone, but the old man fell a victim to his own temerity and hardihood.[2] It is thirty years since he retired with three wounds, from the field of Braddock;[3] but time, in no degree, abated his adventurous and

---

[2] "Fell a victim to his own temerity and hardihood": "temerity" is unreasonable disregard for danger or opposition, "rashness, foolhardiness, recklessness" (OED). Recall that Edgar is an orphan (his parents were killed by Indians) and has been living under the protection of his uncle, protection that will be removed by a hostile cousin as soon as the uncle dies (as Edgar noted in Chapter 23). Especially after the disappearance of the money that Edgar and Mary had hoped to inherit from Waldegrave (now reclaimed by Weymouth in Chapters 14 and 15), the uncle's death leaves Edgar without any source of support and particularly vulnerable to the offer of support from Sarsefield that Sarsefield will first mention later in this chapter.

[3] "It is thirty years since he retired with three wounds, from the field of Braddock": Edgar's uncle served under the British general Edward Braddock in the French and Indian War, the North American theater of the Seven Years War. See the notes in Chapter 6 for information on the novel's other references to this conflict as it occurred in India. The novel links the war's Asian and North American theaters, whose imperial stakes include the fate of the British colonies in North America, the shape of global commerce, and relations between European whites and native peoples in both Asia and America. For discussions of the effects of the French and Indian War and Braddock's defeat on Quaker-Indian relations in frontier Pennsylvania, see Kafer, *Charles Brockden Brown's Revolution,* 27–28; Jennings, *Empire of Fortune;* and White, *The Middle Ground.*

In this passage, the reader learns that Edgar's uncle was wounded in Braddock's disastrous 1755 defeat in western Pennsylvania. On July 9, 1755, an inexperienced Braddock led his forces against the French frontier stronghold, Fort Duquesne, overlooking the Allegheny and the Monongahela rivers near what is today Pittsburgh. Braddock's men were almost accidentally ambushed in what is alternatively called the Battle of the Wilderness, the Battle of the Monongahela, or, more popularly, Braddock's Defeat. The battle was marked by great confusion and disorganization among the Anglo-American forces. The French captured the heavy guns the British had slogged through the wilderness, then turned them against the English-speakers. Seeing the British army pinned down by their static line of defense, many American colonials left the lines to engage in informal, guerilla-like skirmishes, with the result that they were often fired on by the British, who mistook them for Indians.

The battle ended with nearly all the British officers and two-thirds of their subordinates either killed or wounded by a French force half their size. During the confused retreat after the battle, the demoralized British forces destroyed their supplies and equipment as a defensive tactic even though they still outnumbered an opposing force that wasn't even pursuing them. Braddock himself died four days later, on July 13, 1755, of wounds received during the battle. The defeat allowed for a series of retaliatory raids by the Indians on white settlers in Virginia, Maryland, and Pennsylvania, where they affected Quaker frontier communities and almost reached Philadelphia itself. Braddock's defeat was thus a significant turning point in the loss of confidence by American colonials in the military superiority of the British Imperial Army, and thus an event that helped prepare conditions for the American Revolution. A twenty-three-year-old George Washington participated in the expedition as a volunteer officer, helped carry the fatally wounded Braddock off the field, and came out of the debacle with his reputation for bravery greatly enhanced.

military spirit. On the first alarm, he summoned his neighbours, and led them in pursuit of the invaders. Alas! he was the first to attack them, and the only one who fell in the contest.

These words were uttered in a manner that left me no room to doubt of their truth. My uncle had already been lamented, and the discovery of the nature of his death, so contrary to my forebodings, and of the safety of my girls, made the state of my mind partake more of exultation and joy, than of grief or regret.

But how was I deceived? Had not my fusil been found in the hands of an enemy? Whence could he have plundered it but from my own chamber? It hung against the wall of a closet; from which no stranger could have taken it except by violence. My perplexities and doubts were not at an end, but those which constituted my chief torment were removed. I listened to my friend's intreaties to tell him the cause of my elopement, and the incidents that terminated in the present interview.

I began with relating my return to consciousness in the bottom of the pit; my efforts to free myself from this abhorred prison; the acts of horror to which I was impelled by famine, and their excruciating consequences; my gaining the outlet of the cavern, the desperate expedient by which I removed the impediment to my escape, and the deliverance of the captive girl; the contest I maintained before Deb's hut; my subsequent wanderings; the banquet which hospitality afforded me; my journey to the river-bank; my meditations on the means of reaching the road; my motives for hazarding my life, by plunging into the stream; and my subsequent perils and fears till I reached the threshold of this habitation.

Thus, continued I, I have complied with your request. I have told all that I, myself, know. What were the incidents between my sinking to rest at my Uncle's, and my awaking in the chambers of the hill; by which means and by whose contrivance, preternatural or human, this transition was effected, I am unable to explain; I cannot even guess.

What has eluded my sagacity may not be beyond the reach of another. Your own reflections on my tale, or some facts that have fallen under your notice, may enable you to furnish a solution. But, meanwhile, how am I to account for your appearance on this spot? This meeting was unexpected and abrupt to you, but it has not been less so to me. Of all mankind, Sarsefield was the farthest from my thoughts, when I saw these tokens of a traveller and a stranger.

You were imperfectly acquainted with my wanderings. You saw me on the ground before Deb's hut. You saw me plunge into the river. You endeavoured to destroy me while swimming; and you knew, before my narrative was heard, that Huntly was the object of your enmity. What was the motive of your search in the desert, and how were you apprized of my condition? These things are not less wonderful than any of those which I have already related.

In the end, Edgar's uncle dies "a victim to his own temerity and hardihood," because he cannot free himself from the desire for revenge. Obsessively reenacting Braddock's self-defeating campaign, he leads the settlers to repeat many of the same errors Braddock made thirty years earlier, such as their mistaking Edgar for an Indian and firing on him.

During my tale the features of Sarsefield betokened the deepest attention. His eye strayed not a moment from my face. All my perils and forebodings, were fresh in my remembrance, they had scarcely gone by; their skirts, so to speak, were still visible. No wonder that my eloquence was vivid and pathetic, that I pourtrayed the past as if it were the present scene; and that not my tongue only, but every muscle and limb, spoke.

When I had finished my relation, Sarsefield sunk into thoughtfulness. From this, after a time, he recovered and said, Your tale, Huntly, is true, yet, did I not see you before me, were I not acquainted with the artlessness and rectitude of your character, and, above all, had not my own experience, during the last three days, confirmed every incident, I should question its truth. You have amply gratified my curiosity, and deserve that your own, should be gratified as fully. Listen to me.

Much has happened since we parted, which shall not be now mentioned. I promised to inform you of my welfare by letter, and did not fail to write, but whether my letters were received, or any were written by you in return, or if written were ever transmitted, I cannot tell; none were ever received.

Some days since, I arrived, in company with a lady who is my wife, in America. You have never been forgotten by me. I knew your situation to be little in agreement with your wishes, and one of the benefits which fortune has lately conferred upon me, is the power of snatching you from a life of labour and obscurity; whose goods, scanty as they are, were transient and precarious; and affording you the suitable leisure and means of intellectual gratification and improvement.

Your silence made me entertain some doubts concerning your welfare, and even your existence. To solve these doubts, I hastened to Solebury, some delays upon the road, hindered me from accomplishing my journey by day-light. It was night before I entered the Norwalk path, but my ancient rambles with you made me familiar with it, and I was not affraid of being obstructed or bewildered.

Just as I gained the southern outlet, I spied a passenger on foot, coming towards me with a quick pace. The incident was of no moment, and yet the time of night, the seeming expedition of the walker, recollection of the mazes and obstacles which he was going to encounter, and a vague conjecture that, perhaps, he was unacquainted with the difficulties that awaited him, made me eye him with attention as he passed.

He came near, and I thought I recognized a friend in this traveller. The form, the gesture, the stature bore a powerful resemblance to those of Edgar Huntly. This resemblance was so strong, that I stopped, and after he had gone by, called him by your name. That no notice was taken of my call proved that the person was mistaken, but even though it were another, that he should not even hesitate or turn at a summons which he could not but perceive to be addressed, though erroneously, to him, was the source of some surprize. I did not repeat my call, but proceeded on my way.

All had retired to repose in your uncle's dwelling. I did not scruple to rouse them, and was received with affectionate and joyous greetings. That you allowed your uncle to rise before you, was a new topic of reflection. To my inquiries concerning you, answers were made that accorded with my wishes. I was told that you were in good health and were then abed. That you had not heard and risen at my knocking, was mentioned with surprise, but your uncle accounted for your indolence by saying that during the last week you had fatigued yourself by rambling night and day, in search of some maniac, or visionary who was supposed to have retreated into Norwalk.

I insisted upon awakening you myself. I anticipated the effect of this sudden and unlooked for meeting, with some emotions of pride as well as of pleasure. To find, in opening your eyes, your old preceptor standing by your bedside and gazing in your face, would place you, I conceived, in an affecting situation.

Your chamber door was open, but your bed was empty. Your uncle and sisters were made acquainted with this circumstance. Their surprise gave way to conjectures that your restless and romantic spirit, had tempted you from your repose, that you had rambled abroad on some phantastic errand, and would probably return before the dawn. I willingly acquiesced in this opinion, and my feelings being too thoroughly aroused to allow me to sleep, I took possession of your chamber, and patiently awaited your return.

The morning returned but Huntly made not his appearance. Your uncle became somewhat uneasy at this unseasonable absence. Much speculation and inquiry, as to the possible reasons of your flight was made. In my survey of your chamber, I noted that only part of your cloathing remained beside your bed. Coat, hat, stockings and shoes lay upon the spot where they had probably been thrown when you had disrobed yourself, but the pantaloons,[4] which according to Mr. Huntly's report, completed your dress, were no where to be found. That you should go forth on so cold a night so slenderly appareled, was almost incredible. Your reason or your senses had deserted you, before so rash an action could be meditated.

I now remembered the person I had met in Norwalk. His resemblance to your figure, his garb, which wanted hat, coat, stockings and shoes, and your absence from your bed at that hour, were remarkable coincidences: but why did you disregard my call? Your name, uttered by a voice that could not be unknown, was surely sufficient to arrest your steps.

Each hour added to the impatience of your friends; to their recollections and conjectures, I listened with a view to extract from them some solution of this mystery. At length, a story was alluded to, of some one who, on the preceding night, had been heard walking in the long room; to this was added, the tale of your anxieties and wonders occasioned by the loss of certain manuscripts.

---

[4] "Pantaloons": trousers, long pants. Sarsefield is noting the trousers or "trossers" that Edgar mentioned on waking up in the cave in Chapter 16. Before the French Revolution, pantaloons or trousers were associated with lower-class attire worn by laborers and artisans, as opposed to the stockings and knee breeches of gentlemen. It was only after the revolutionary era that long trousers gradually, over the next generation (by the 1820s and 1830s), became standard attire for all males regardless of class. During the French Revolution, urban working-class insurgents and peasant rebels were referred to derisively as "sans-culottes" because they did not wear the "culottes" or breeches of the upper class, and throughout the 1790s the term "sans-culottes" was commonly used in English to mean dangerously radical or subversive. Given all this, it may be suggestive that Edgar dons pantaloons during his sleep-walking, and that it is Sarsefield who notes this detail.

While ruminating upon these incidents, and endeavouring to extract from this intelligence a clue, explanatory of your present situation, a single word, casually dropped by your uncle, instantly illuminated my darkness and dispelled my doubts.—After all, said the old man, ten to one, but Edgar himself was the man whom we heard walking, but the lad was asleep, and knew not what he was about.[5]

Surely said I, this inference is just. His manuscripts could not be removed by any hands but his own, since the rest of mankind were unacquainted not only with the place of their concealment, but with their existence. None but a man, insane or asleep, would wander forth so slightly dressed, and none but a sleeper would have disregarded my calls. This conclusion was generally adopted, but it gave birth in my mind, to infinite inquietudes. You had roved into Norwalk, a scene of inequalities, of prominences and pits, among which, thus destitute of the guidance of your senses, you could scarcely fail to be destroyed, or at least, irretreivably bewildered. I painted to myself the dangers to which you were subjected. Your careless feet would bear you into some whirlpool or to the edge of some precipice, some internal revolution or outward shock would recall you to consciousness at some perilous moment. Surprise and fear would disable you from taking seasonable or suitable precautions, and your destruction be made sure.

The lapse of every new hour, without bringing tidings of your state, enhanced these fears. At length, the propriety of searching for you occurred, Mr. Huntly and I determined to set out upon this pursuit, as well as to commission others. A plan was laid by which every accessible part of Norwalk, the wilderness beyond the flats of Solebury, and the valey of Chetasco, should be traversed and explored.

Scarcely had we equipped ourselves for this expedition, when a messenger arrived, who brought the disastrous news of Indians being seen within these precincts, and on the last night a farmer was shot in his fields, a dwelling in Chetasco was burnt to the ground, and its inhabitants murdered or made captives. Rumour and inquiry had been busy, and a plausible conjecture had been formed, as to the course and number of the enemies. They were said to be divided into bands, and to amount in the whole to thirty or forty warriors. This messenger had come to warn us of danger which might impend, and to summon us to join in the pursuit and extirpation of these detestable foes.

Your uncle, whose alacrity and vigour age had not abated, eagerly engaged in this scheme. I was not averse to contribute my efforts to an end like this. The road which we had previously designed to take, in search of my fugitive pupil, was the same by which we must trace or intercept the retreat of the savages. Thus two purposes, equally momentous, would be answered by the same means.

---

[5] "But the lad was asleep and knew not what he was about": while the narrative has already hinted that Edgar wound up in the cave in Chapter 16 by sleep-walking, this passage now confirms that sleep-walking is the immediate explanation for Edgar's astonishing situation.

Mr. Huntly armed himself with your fusil; Inglefield supplied me with a gun; during our absence the dwelling was closed and locked, and your sisters placed under the protection of Inglefield, whose age and pacific sentiments unfitted him for arduous and sanguinary enterprises. A troop of rustics[6] was collected, half of whom remained to traverse Solebury and the other, whom Mr. Huntly and I accompanied, hastened to Chetasco.

---

[6] "Rustics": country servants, workers, dependents.

Chapter XXV

IT was noon day before we reached the theatre of action. Fear and revenge combined to make the people of Chetasco diligent and zealous in their own defence. The havock already committed had been mournful. To prevent a repetition of the same calamities, they resolved to hunt out the hostile foot-steps and exact a merciless retribution.[1]

It was likely that the enemy, on the approach of day, had withdrawn from the valley and concealed themselves in the thickets, between the parrallel ridges of the mountain. This space, which, according to the object with which it is compared is either a vale or the top of an hill, was obscure and desolate. It was undoubtedly the avenue by which the robbers had issued forth, and by which they would escape to the Ohio. Here they might still remain, intending to emerge from their concealment on the next night, and perpetrate new horrors.

A certain distribution was made of our number, so as to move in all directions at the same time. I will not dwell upon particulars. It will suffice to say that keen eyes and indefatigable feet, brought us at last to the presence of the largest number of these marauders. Seven of them were slain by the edge of a brook, where they sat wholly unconscious of the danger which hung over them. Five escaped, and one of these secured his retreat by wresting your fusil from your uncle, and shooting him dead. Before our companion could be rescued or revenged, the assassin, with the remnant of the troop, disappeared, and bore away with him the fusil as a trophy of his victory.

This disaster was deplored not only on account of that life which had thus been sacrificed, but because a sagacious guide and intrepid leader was lost. His acquaintance with the habits of the Indians, and his experience in their wars made him trace their foot-steps with more certainty than any of his associates.

The pursuit was still continued, and parties were so stationed that the escape of the enemy was difficult, if not impossible. Our search was unremitted, but during twelve or fourteen hours, unsuccessful. Queen Mab did not elude all suspicion. Her hut was visited by different parties, but the old woman and her dogs had disappeared.

Meanwhile your situation was not forgotten. Every one was charged to explore your foot-steps as well as those of the savages, but this search was no less unsuccessful than the former. None had heard of you or seen you.

---

[1] "A merciless retribution": Sarsefield implies that the inhabitants of Chetasco bear significant responsibility for provoking the latest round of violence by retaliating for former wrongs, acting out of "fear and revenge" and exacting "merciless retribution." Most of the damage from the Indian raid occurs in Chetasco, and the white party from Solebury, led by Sarsefield and Edgar's uncle, went there to help repulse the raids. Along with Edgar's final explanation of the events leading to the war party in Chapter 27 (note 27.4), this passage shows Brown dramatizing Philadelphia Quaker efforts to shift responsibility for frontier violence onto Scots-Irish settlers in the backcountry. See the discussion of this context in the Introduction and the excerpts from Franklin and Barton in Related Texts.

This continued till midnight. Three of us, made a pause at a brook, and intended to repair our fatigues by a respite of a few hours, but scarcely had we stretched ourselves on the ground when we were alarmed by a shot which seemed to have been fired at a short distance. We started on our feet and consulted with each other on the measures to be taken. A second, a third and a fourth shot, from the same quarter, excited our attention anew. Mab's hut was known to stand at the distance and in the direction of this sound, and hither we resolved to repair.

This was done with speed but with the utmost circumspection. We shortly gained the road that leads near this hut and at length gained a view of the building. Many persons were discovered, in a sort of bustling inactivity, before the hut. They were easily distinguished to be friends, and were therefore approached without scruple.

The objects that presented themselves to a nearer view were five bodies stretched upon the ground. Three of them were savages. The fourth was a girl, who though alive seemed to have received a mortal wound. The fifth, breathless and mangled and his features almost concealed by the blood that overspread his face, was Edgar; the fugitive for whom I had made such anxious search.

About the same hour on the last night I had met you hastening into Norwalk. Now were you, lying in the midst of savages, at the distance of thirty miles from your home, and in a spot, which it was impossible for you to have reached unless by an immense circuit over rocks and thickets. That you had found a rift at the basis of the hill, and thus permeated its solidities, and thus precluded so tedious and circuitous a journey as must otherwise have been made, was not to be imagined.

But whence arose this scene? It was obvious to conclude that my associates had surprised their enemies in this house, and exacted from them the forfeit of their crimes, but how you should have been confounded with their foes, or whence came the wounded girl was a subject of astonishment.

You will judge how much this surprise was augmented when I was informed that the party whom we found had been attracted hither by the same signals, by which we had been alarmed. That on reaching this spot you had been discovered, alive, seated on the ground and still sustaining the gun with which you had apparently completed the destruction of so many adversaries. In a moment after their arrival you sunk down and expired.

This scene was attended with inexplicable circumstances. The musquet which lay beside you appeared to have belonged to one of the savages. The wound by which each had died was single. Of the four shots we had distinguished at a distance, three of them were therefore fatal to the Indians and the fourth was doubtless that by which you had fallen, yet three musquets only were discoverable.

The arms were collected, and the girl carried to the nearest house in the arms of her father. Her situation was deemed capable of remedy, and the sorrow and wonder which I felt at your untimely and extraordinary fate, did not hinder me from endeavouring to restore the health of this unfortunate victim. I reflected likewise that some light might be thrown upon transactions so mysterious, by the information which might be collected from her story. Numberless questions and hints were necessary to extract from her a consistent or intelligible tale. She had been dragged, it seems, for miles, at the heels of her conquerors, who at length, stopped in a cavern for the sake of some repose; all slept but one, who sat and watched. Something called him away, and, at the same moment, you appeared at the bottom of the cave half naked and without arms. You instantly supplied the last deficiency, by seizing the gun and tom-hawk of him who had gone forth, and who had negligently left his weapons behind. Then stepping over the bodies of the sleepers, you rushed out of the cavern.

She then mentioned your unexpected return, her deliverance and flight, and arrival at Deb's hut. You watched upon the hearth and she fell asleep upon the blanket. From this sleep she was aroused by violent and cruel blows. She looked up:—you were gone and the bed on which she lay was surrounded by the men from whom she had so lately escaped. One dragged her out of the hut and levelled his gun at her breast. At the moment when he touched the trigger, a shot came from an unknown quarter, and he fell at her feet. Of subsequent events she had an incoherent recollection. The Indians were successively slain, and you came to her, and interrogated and consoled her.

In your journey to the hut you were armed. This in some degree accounted for appearances, but where were your arms? Three musquets only were discovered and these undoubtedly belonged to your enemies.

I now had leisure to reflect upon your destiny. I had arrived soon enough on this shore merely to witness the catastrophe of two beings whom I most loved. Both were overtaken by the same fate, nearly at the same hour. The same hand had possibly accomplished the destruction of uncle and nephew.

Now, however, I began to entertain an hope that your state might not be irretrievable. You had walked and spoken after the firing had ceased, and your enemies had ceased to contend with you. A wound had, no doubt, been previously received. I had hastily inferred that the wound was mortal, and that life could not be recalled. Occupied with attention to the wailings of the girl, and full of sorrow and perplexity I had admitted an opinion which would have never been adopted in different circumstances. My acquaintance with wounds would have taught me to regard sunken muscles, lividness and cessation of the pulse as mere indications of a swoon, and not as tokens of death.

Perhaps my error was not irreparable. By hastening to the hut, I might ascertain your condition and at least transport your remains to some dwelling and finally secure to you the decencies of burial.

Of twelve savages, discovered on the preceding day, ten were now killed. Two, at least remained, after whom the pursuit was still zealously maintained. Attention to the wounded girl, had withdrawn me from the party, and I had now leisure to return to the scene of these disasters. The sun had risen, and, accompanied by two others, I repaired thither.

A sharp turn in the road, at the entrance of the field, set before us a starting spectacle. An Indian, mangled by repeated wounds of bayonet and bullet, was discovered. His musquet was stuck in the ground, by way of beacon attracting our attention to the spot. Over this space I had gone a few hours before, and nothing like this was then seen. The parties abroad, had hied away to a distant quarter. Some invisible power seemed to be enlisted in our defence and to preclude the necessity of our arms.

We proceeded to the hut. The savages were there, but Edgar had risen and flown! Nothing now seemed to be incredible. You had slain three foes, and the weapon with which the victory had been achieved, had vanished. You had risen from the dead, had assailed one of the surviving enemies, had employed bullet and dagger in his destruction, with both of which you could only be supplied by supernatural means, and had disappeared. If any inhabitant of Chetasco had done this, we should have heard of it.

But what remained? You were still alive. Your strength was sufficient to bear you from this spot. Why were you still invisible and to what dangers might you not be exposed, before you could disinvolve yourself from the mazes of this wilderness?

Once more I procured indefatigable search to be made after you. It was continued till the approach of evening and was fruitless. Inquiries were twice made at the house where you were supplied with food and intelligence. On the second call I was astonished and delighted by the tidings received from the good woman. Your person and demeanour and arms were described, and mention made of your resolution to cross the southern ridge, and traverse the Solebury road with the utmost expedition.

The greater part of my inquietudes were now removed. You were able to eat and to travel, and there was little doubt that a meeting would take place between us on the next morning. Meanwhile, I determined to concur with those who pursued the remainder of the enemy. I followed you, in the path that you were said to have taken, and quickly joined a numerous party who were searching for those who, on the last night, had attacked a plantation that lies near this, and destroyed the inhabitants.

I need not dwell upon our doublings and circuities. The enemy was traced to the house of Selby. They had entered, they had put fire on the floor, but were compelled to relinquish their prey. Of what number they consisted could not be ascertained, but one, lingering behind his fellows, was shot, at the entrance of the wood, and on the spot where you chanced to light upon him.

Selby's house was empty, and before the fire had made any progress we extinguished it. The drunken wretch whom you encountered, had probably returned from his nocturnal debauch, after we had left the spot.

The flying enemy was pursued with fresh diligence. They were found, by various tokens, to have crossed the river, and to have ascended the mountain. We trod closely on their heels. When we arrived at the promontory, described by you, the fatigues of the night and day rendered me unqualified to proceed, I determined that this should be the bound of my excursions. I was anxious to obtain an interview with you, and unless I paused here, should not be able to gain Inglefield's as early in the morning as I wished. Two others concurred with me in this resolution and prepared to return to this house which had been deserted by its tenants till the danger was past and which had been selected as the place of rendezvous.

At this moment, dejected and weary, I approached the ledge which severed the head-land from the mountain. I marked the appearance of some one stretched upon the ground where you lay. No domestic animal would wander hither and place himself upon this spot. There was something likewise in the appearance of the object that bespoke it to be man, but if it were man, it was, incontrovertibly, a savage and a foe. I determined therefore to rouse you by a bullet.

My decision was perhaps absurd. I ought to have gained more certainty before I hazarded your destruction. Be that as it will, a moment's lingering on your part would have probably been fatal. You started on your feet, and fired. See the hole which your random shot made through my sleeve! This surely was a day destined to be signalized by hair-breadth escapes.

Your action seemed incontestably to confirm my prognostics. Every one hurried to the spot and was eager to destroy an enemy. No one hesitated to believe that some of the shots aimed at you, had reached their mark, and that you had sunk to rise no more.

The gun which was fired and thrown down was taken and examined. It had been my companion in many a toilsome expedition. It had rescued me and my friends from a thousand deaths.[2] In order to recognize it, I needed only to touch and handle it. I instantly discovered that I held in my hand the fusil which I had left with you on parting, with which your uncle had equipped himself, and which had been ravished from him by a savage. What was I hence to infer respecting the person of the last possessor?

My inquiries respecting you of the woman whose milk and bread you had eaten, were minute. You entered, she said, with an hatchet and gun in your hand. While you ate, the gun was laid upon the table. She sat near, and the piece became the object of inquisitive attention. The stock and barrels were described by her in such terms as left no doubt that this was the *Fusil.*

A comparison of incidents enabled me to trace the manner in which you came into possession of this instrument. One of those whom you found in the cavern was the assassin of your uncle. According to the girl's report, on issuing from your hiding place, you seized a gun that was unoccupied, and this gun chanced to be your own.

Its two barrels was probably the cause of your success in that unequal contest at Mab's hut. On recovering from *deliquium,*[3] you found it where it had been dropped by you, out of sight and unsuspected by the party that had afterwards arrived. In your passage to the river had it once more fallen into hostile hands, or, had you missed the way, wandered to this promontory, and mistaken a troop of friends for a band of Indian marauders?

Either supposition was dreadful. The latter was the most plausible. No motives were conceivable by which one of the fugitives could be induced to post himself here, in this conspicuous station: whereas, the road which lead you to the summit of the hill, to that spot where descent to the river road was practicable, could not be found

---

[2] "The gun . . . from a thousand deaths": Sarsefield recognizes the musket that is his legacy from imperial struggles in India and that he has passed on to Edgar and Edgar's uncle. See Chapter 18, note 18.1 for the gun's first appearance. Here and two paragraphs later, he emphasizes this gun's efficacy in campaigns against native peoples on two ends of the empire.

[3] "*Deliquium*": Sarsefield is a surgeon and here uses Latin *deliquium* to describe an episode of fainting or loss of consciousness.

but by those who were accustomed to traverse it. The directions which you had exacted from your hostess, proved your previous unacquaintance with these tracts.

I acquiesced in this opinion with an heavy and desponding heart. Fate had led us into a maze, which could only terminate in the destruction of one or of the other. By the breadth of an hair, had I escaped death from your hand. The same fortune had not befriended you. After my tedious search, I had lighted on you, forlorn, bewildered, perishing with cold and hunger. Instead of recognizing and affording you relief, I compelled you to leap into the river, from a perilous height, and had desisted from my persecution only when I had bereaved you of life, and plunged you to the bottom of the gulf.

My motives in coming to America were numerous and mixed. Among these was the parental affection with which you had inspired me. I came with fortune and a better gift than fortune in my hand. I intended to bestow both upon you, not only to give you competence, but one who would endear to you that competence, who would enhance, by participating, every gratification.[4]

My schemes were now at an end. You were gone, beyond the reach of my benevolence and justice. I had robbed your two sisters of a friend and guardian. It was some consolation to think that it was in my power to stand, with regard to them, in your place, that I could snatch them from the poverty, dependence and humiliation, to which your death and that of your uncle had reduced them.

I was now doubly weary of the enterprise in which I was engaged, and returned, with speed, to this rendezvouz. My companions have gone to know the state of the family who resided under this roof and left me to beguile the tedious moments in whatever manner I pleased.

I have omitted mentioning one incident that happened between the detection of your flight and our expedition to Chetasco. Having formed a plausible conjecture as to him who walked in the Long-room, it was obvious to conclude that he who purloined your manuscripts and the walker were the same personage. It was likewise easily inferred that the letters were secreted in the Cedar Chest or in some other part of the room. Instances similar to this have heretofore occurred. Men have employed anxious months in search of that which, in a freak of Noctambulation,[5] was hidden by their own hands.

A search was immediately commenced, and your letters were found, carefully concealed between the rafters and shingles of the roof, in a spot, where, if suspicion had not been previously excited, they would have remained till the vernal rains and the summer heats, had insensibly destroyed them. This pacquet I carried with me, knowing the value which you set upon them, and there being no receptacle equally safe, but your own cabinet, which was locked.

---

[4] "Who would enhance, by participating, every gratification": this is Sarsefield's second suggestion that he intends to offer Edgar support. Now he begins to suggest what he will later state explicitly, that he intends to offer Edgar a marriage with Clarice, the same illegitimate daughter of Wiatte who was earlier betrothed to Clithero in Chapters 5, 7, and 8.

[5] "In a freak of Noctambulation": noctambulation or night-walking, another term for sleepwalking.

Having, as I said, reached this house, and being left alone, I bethought me of the treasure I possessed. I was unacquainted with the reasons for which these papers were so precious. They probably had some momentous and intimate connection with your own history. As such they could not be of little value to me, and this moment of inoccupation and regrets, was as suitable as any other to the task of perusing them. I drew them forth, therefore, and laid them on the table in this chamber.

The rest is known to you. During a momentary absence you entered. Surely no interview of ancient friends ever took place in so unexpected and abrupt a manner. You were dead. I mourned for you, as one whom I loved, and whom fate had snatched forever from my sight. Now, in a blissful hour, you had risen, and my happiness in thus embracing you, is tenfold greater than would have been experienced, if no uncertainties and perils had protracted our meeting.

Chapter XXVI

HERE ended the tale of Sarsefield. Humiliation and joy were mingled in my heart. The events that preceded my awakening in the cave were now luminous and plain. What explication was more obvious? What but this solution ought to have been suggested by the conduct I had witnessed in Clithero?

Clithero! Was not this the man whom Clithero had robbed of his friend? Was not this the lover of Mrs. Lorimer, the object of the persecutions of Wiatte? Was it not now given me to investigate the truth of that stupendous tale? To dissipate the doubts which obstinately clung to my imagination respecting it?

But soft! Had not Sarsefield said that he was married? Was Mrs. Lorimer so speedily forgotten by him, or was the narrative of Clithero the web of imposture or the raving of insanity?

These new ideas banished all personal considerations from my mind. I looked eagerly into the face of my friend, and exclaimed in a dubious accent—How say you? Married? When? To whom?

Yes, Huntly, I am wedded to the most excellent of women. To her am I indebted for happiness and wealth and dignity and honour. To her do I owe the power of being the benefactor and protector of you and your sisters. She longs to embrace you as a son. To become truly her son, will depend upon your own choice and that of one, who was the companion of our voyage.

Heavens! cried I, in a transport of exultation and astonishment. Of whom do you speak. Of the mother of Clarice? The sister of Wiatte? The sister of the ruffian who laid snares for her life? Who pursued you and the unhappy Clithero, with the bitterest animosity?

My friend started at these sounds as if the earth had yawned at his feet. His countenance was equally significant of terror and rage. As soon as he regained the power of utterance, he spoke—Clithero! Curses light upon thy lips for having uttered that detested name! Thousands of miles have I flown to shun the hearing of it. Is the madman here? Have you set eyes upon him? Does he yet crawl upon the face of the earth? Unhappy? Unparalleled, unheard of, thankless miscreant! Has he told his execrable falsehoods here? Has he dared to utter names so sacred as those of Euphemia Lorimer and Clarice?

He has: He has told a tale, that had all the appearances of truth—

Out upon the villain! The truth! Truth would prove him to be unnatural; develish; a thing for which no language has yet provided a name! He has called himself unhappy? No doubt, a victim to injustice! Overtaken by unmerited calamity. Say! Has he fooled thee with such tales?

No. His tale was a catalogue of crimes and miseries of which he was the author and sufferer. You know not his motives, his horrors:—

His deeds were monstrous and infernal. His motives were sordid and flagitious. To display all their ugliness and infamy was not his province. No: He did not tell you that he stole at midnight to the chamber of his mistress: a woman who astonished the world by her loftiness and magnanimity; by indefatigable beneficence and unswerving equity; who had lavished on this wretch, whom she snatched from the dirt, all the goods of fortune; all the benefits of education; all the treasures of love; every provocation to gratitude; every stimulant to justice.

He did not tell you that in recompense for every benefit, he stole upon her sleep and aimed a dagger at her breast. There was no room for flight or ambiguity or prevarication. She whom he meant to murder stood near, saw the lifted weapon, and heard him confess and glory in his purposes.

No wonder that the shock bereft her, for a time, of life. The interval was seized by the ruffian to effect his escape. The rebukes of justice, were shunned by a wretch conscious of his inexpiable guilt. These things he has hidden from you, and has supplied their place by a tale specious as false.

No. Among the number of his crimes, hypocrisy is not to be numbered. These things are already known to me: he spared himself too little in the narrative. The excellencies of his lady; her claims to gratitude and veneration, were urged beyond their true bounds. His attempts upon her life, were related. It is true that he desired and endeavoured to destroy her.

How? Has he told you this?

He has told me all. Alas! the criminal intention has been amply expiated—

What mean you? Whence and how came he hither? Where is he now? I will not occupy the same land, the same world with him. Have this woman and her daughter lighted on the shore haunted by this infernal and implacable enemy?

Alas! It is doubtful whether he exists. If he lives, he is no longer to be feared; but he lives not. Famine and remorse have utterly consumed him.

Famine? Remorse? You talk in riddles.

He has immured himself in the desert. He has abjured the intercourse of mankind. He has shut himself in caverns where famine must inevitably expedite that death for which he longs as the only solace of his woes. To no imagination are his offences blacker and more odious than to his own. I had hopes of rescuing him from this fate, but my own infirmities and errors have afforded me sufficient occupation.

Sarsefield renewed his imprecations on the memory of that unfortunate man: and his inquiries as to the circumstances that led him into this remote district. His inquiries were not to be answered by one in my present condition—My languors and fatigues had now gained a pitch that was insupportable. The wound in my face had been chafed, and inflamed by the cold water and the bleak air; and the pain attending it, would no longer suffer my attention to stray. I sunk upon the floor, and intreated him to afford me the respite of a few hours repose.

He was sensible of the deplorableness of my condition, and chid himself for the negligence of which he had already been guilty. He lifted me to the bed, and deliberated on the mode he should pursue for my relief. Some molifying application to my wound, was immediately necessary; but in our present lonely condition, it was not at hand. It could only be procured from a distance. It was proper therefore to hasten to the nearest inhabited dwelling, which belonged to one, by name Walton, and supply himself with such medicines as could be found.

Meanwhile there was no danger of molestation and intrusion. There was reason to expect the speedy return of those who had gone in pursuit of the savages. This was their place of rendezvous, and hither they appointed to re-assemble before the morrow's dawn. The distance of the neighbouring farm was small, and Sarsefield promised to be expeditious. He left me to myself and my own ruminations.

Harrassed by fatigue and pain, I had yet power to ruminate on that series of unparalleled events, that had lately happened. I wept, but my tears flowed from a double source; from sorrow, on account of the untimely fate of my uncle, and from joy, that my sisters were preserved, that Sarsefield had returned and was not unhappy.

I reflected on the untoward destiny of Clithero. Part of his calamity consisted in the consciousness of having killed his patronness; but it now appeared, though by some infatuation, I had not previously suspected, that the first impulse of sorrow in the lady, had been weakened by reflection and by time. That the prejudice persuading her that her life and that of her brother were to endure and to terminate together, was conquered by experience or by argument. She had come, in company with Sarsefield and Clarice to America. What influence might these events have upon the gloomy meditations of Clithero? Was it possible to bring them together; to win the maniac from his solitude, wrest from him his fatal purposes, and restore him to communion with the beings whose imagined indignation is the torment of his life?

These musings were interrupted by a sound from below which were easily interpreted into tokens of the return of those with whom Sarsefield had parted at the promontory, voices were confused and busy but not turbulent. They entered the lower room and the motion of chairs and tables shewed that they were preparing to rest themselves after their toils.

Few of them were unacquainted with me, since they probably were residents in this district. No inconvenience, therefore, would follow from an interview, though, on their part, wholly unexpected. Besides, Sarsefield would speedily return and none of the present visitants would be likely to withdraw to this apartment.

Meanwhile I lay upon the bed, with my face turned towards the door, and languidly gazing at the ceiling and walls. Just then a musquet was discharged in the room below. The shock affected me mechanically and the first impulse of surprise, made me almost start upon my feet.

The sound was followed by confusion and bustle. Some rushed forth and called on each other to run different ways, and the words "That is he"—"Stop him" were spoken in a tone of eagerness, and rage. My weakness and pain were for a moment forgotten, and my whole attention was bent to discover the meaning of this hubbub. The musquet which I had brought with me to this chamber, lay across the bed. Unknowing of the consequences of this affray, with regard to myself, I was prompted by a kind of self-preserving instinct, to lay hold of the gun, and prepare to repel any attack that might be made upon me.

A few moments elapsed when I thought I heard light footsteps in the entry leading to this room. I had no time to construe these signals, but watching fearfully the entrance, I grasped my weapon with new force, and raised it so as to be ready at the moment of my danger. I did not watch long. A figure cautiously thrust itself forward.

The first glance was sufficient to inform me that this intruder was an Indian, and, of consequence, an enemy. He was unarmed. Looking eagerly on all sides, he at last spied me as I lay. My appearance threw him into consternation, and after the fluctuation of an instant, he darted to the window, threw up the sash, and leaped out upon the ground.

His flight might have been easily arrested by my shot, but surprize, added to my habitual antipathy to bloodshed, unless in cases of absolute necessity, made me hesitate. He was gone, and I was left to mark the progress of the drama. The silence was presently broken by firing at a distance. Three shots, in quick succession, were followed by the deepest pause.

That the party, recently arrived, had brought with them one or more captives, and that by some sudden effort, the prisoners had attempted to escape, was the only supposition that I could form. By what motives either of them could be induced to seek concealment in my chamber, could not be imagined.

I now heard a single step on the threshold below. Some one entered the common room. He traversed the floor during a few minutes, and then, ascending the staircase, he entered my chamber. It was Sarsefield. Trouble and dismay were strongly written on his countenance. He seemed totally unconscious of my presence, his eyes were fixed upon the floor, and as he continued to move across the room, he heaved forth deep sighs.

This deportment was mournful and mysterious. It was little in unison with those appearances which he wore at our parting, and must have been suggested by some event that had since happened. My curiosity impelled me to recall him from his reverie. I rose and seizing him by the arm, looked at him with an air of inquisitive anxiety. It was needless to speak.

He noticed my movement, and turning towards me, spoke in a tone of some resentment—Why did you deceive me? Did you not say Clithero was dead?

I said so because it was my belief. Know you any thing to the contrary? Heaven grant that he is still alive, and that our mutual efforts may restore him to peace.

Heaven grant, replied my friend, with a vehemence that bordered upon fury. Heaven grant that he may live thousands of years, and know not, in their long course, a moment's respite from remorse and from anguish; but this prayer is fruitless. He is not dead, but death hovers over him. Should he live, he will live only to defy justice and perpetrate new horrors. My skill might perhaps save him, but a finger shall not be moved to avert his fate.

Little did I think, that the wretch whom my friends rescued from the power of the savages, and brought wounded and expiring hither was Clithero. They sent for me in haste to afford him surgical assistance. I found him stretched upon the floor below, deserted, helpless and bleeding. The moment I beheld him, he was recognized. The last of evils was to look upon the face of this assassin, but that evil is past, and shall never be endured again.

Rise and come with me. Accommodation is prepared for you at Walcot's. Let us leave this house, and the moment you are able to perform a journey, abandon forever this district.

I could not readily consent to this proposal. Clithero had been delivered from captivity but was dying for want of that aid which Sarsefield was able to afford. Was it not inhuman to desert him in this extremity? What offence had he committed that deserved such implacable vengeance? Nothing I had heard from Sarsefield was in contradiction to his own story. His deed, imperfectly observed, would appear to be atrocious and detestable, but the view of all its antecedent and accompanying events and motives, would surely place it in the list not of crimes, but of misfortunes.

But what is that guilt which no penitence can expiate? Had not Clithero's remorse been more than adequate to crimes far more deadly and enormous than this? This, however, was no time to argue with the passions of Sarsefield. Nothing but a repetition of Clithero's tale, could vanquish his prepossessions and mollify his rage, but this repetition was impossible to be given by me, till a moment of safety and composure.

These thoughts made me linger, but hindered me from attempting to change the determination of my friend. He renewed his importunities for me to fly with him. He dragged me by the arm, and wavering and reluctant I followed where he chose to lead. He crossed the common-room, with hurried steps and eyes averted from a figure, which instantly fastened my attention.

It was, indeed, Clithero, whom I now beheld, supine, polluted with blood, his eyes closed and apparently insensible. This object was gazed at with emotions that rooted me to the spot. Sarsefield, perceiving me determined to remain where I was, rushed out of the house, and disappeared.

Chapter XXVII

I HUNG over the unhappy wretch whose emaciated form and rueful features, sufficiently bespoke that savage hands had only completed that destruction which his miseries had begun. He was mangled by the tom-hawk in a shocking manner, and there was little hope that human skill could save his life.

I was sensible of nothing but compassion. I acted without design, when seating myself on the floor I raised his head and placed it on my knees. This movement awakened his attention, and opening his eyes he fixed them on my countenance. They testified neither insensibility, nor horror nor distraction. A faint emotion of surprise gave way to an appearance of tranquillity—Having perceived these tokens of a state less hopeless than I at first imagined, I spoke to him:—My friend! How do you feel? Can any thing be done for you?

He answered me, in a tone more firm and with more coherence of ideas than previous appearances had taught me to expect. No, said he, thy kindness good youth, can avail me nothing. The end of my existence here is at hand. May my guilt be expiated by the miseries that I have suffered, and my good deeds only attend me to the presence of my divine judge.

I am waiting, not with trembling or dismay, for this close of my sorrows. I breathed but one prayer, and that prayer has been answered. I asked for an interview with thee, young man, but feeling as I now feel, this interview, so much desired, was beyond my hope. Now thou art come, in due season, to hear the last words that I shall need to utter.

I wanted to assure thee that thy efforts for my benefit were not useless. They have saved me from murdering myself, a guilt more inexpiable than any which it was in my power to commit.

I retired to the innermost recess of Norwalk, and gained the summit of an hill, by subterranean paths. This hill I knew to be on all sides inaccessible to human footsteps, and the subterranean passages was closed up by stones. Here I believed my solitude exempt from interruption and my death, in consequence of famine, sure.

This persuasion was not taken away by your appearance on the opposite steep. The chasm which severed us I knew to be impassable. I withdrew from your sight.

Some time after, awakening from a long sleep, I found victuals beside me. He that brought it was invisible. For a time, I doubted whether some messenger of heaven had not interposed for my salvation. How other than by supernatural means, my retreat should be explored, I was unable to conceive. The summit was encompassed by dizzy and profound gulfs, and the subterranean passages was still closed.

This opinion, though corrected by subsequent reflection, tended to change the course of my desperate thoughts. My hunger, thus importunately urged, would not abstain, and I ate of the food that was provided. Henceforth I determined to live, to resume the path of obscurity and labour, which I had relinquished, and wait till my God should summon me to retribution. To anticipate his call, is only to redouble our guilt.

I designed not to return to Inglefield's service, but to chuse some other and remoter district. Meanwhile, I had left in his possession, a treasure, which my determination

180

to die, had rendered of no value, but which, my change of resolution, restored. In-closed in a box at Inglefield's, were the memoirs of Euphemia Lorimer, by which in all my vicissitudes, I had been hitherto accompanied, and from which I consented to part only because I had refused to live. My existence was now to be prolonged and this manuscript was once more to constitute the torment and the solace of my being.

I hastened to Inglefield's by night. There was no need to warn him of my purpose. I desired that my fate should be an eternal secret to my ancient master and his neigh-bours. The apartment, containing my box was well known, and easily accessible.

The box was found but broken and rifled of its treasure. My transports of astonish-ment, and indignation and grief yielded to the resumption of my fatal purpose. I has-tened back to the hill, and determined anew to perish.

This mood continued to the evening of the ensuing day. Wandering over rocks and pits, I discovered the manuscript, lying under a jutting precipice. The chance that brought it hither was not less propitious and miraculous than that by which I had been supplied with food. It produced a similar effect upon my feelings, and, while in possession of this manuscript I was reconciled to the means of life. I left the moun-tain, and traversing the wilderness, stopped in Chetasco. That kind of employment which I sought was instantly procured; but my new vocation was scarcely assumed when a band of savages invaded our security.

Rambling in the desert, by moonlight, I encountered these foes. They rushed upon me, and after numerous wounds which, for the present, neither killed nor disabled me, they compelled me to keep pace with them in their retreat. Some hours have passed since the troop was overtaken, and my liberty redeemed. Hardships, and repeated wounds, inflicted at the moment when the invaders were surprised and slain, have brought me to my present condition. I rejoice that my course is about to terminate.

Here the speaker was interrupted by the tumultuous entrance of the party, by whom he had been brought hither. Their astonishment at seeing me, sustaining the head of the dying man, may be easily conceived. Their surprise was more strongly ex-cited by the disappearance of the captive whom they had left in this apartment, bound hand and foot. It now appeared that of the savage troop who had adventured thus far in search of pillage and blood, all had been destroyed but two, who, had been led hither as prisoners. On their entrance into this house, one of the party had been sent to Walcot's to summon Sarsefield to the aid of the wounded man, while others had gone in search of chords to secure the arms and legs of the captives, who had hitherto been manacled imperfectly.

The chords were brought and one of them was bound, but the other, before the same operation was begun upon him, broke, by a sudden effort, the feeble ligatures by which he was at present constrained, and seizing a musquet that lay near him, fired on his enemies, and then rushed out of doors. All eagerly engaged in the pur-suit. The savage was fleet as a deer and finally eluded his pursuers.

While their attention was thus engaged abroad, he that remained found means to extricate his wrists and ancles from his bonds and betaking himself to the stairs, es-caped, as I before described, through the window of the room which I had occupied. They pestered me with their curiosity and wonder, for I was known to all of them;

but waving the discussion of my own concerns I intreated their assistance to carry Clithero to the chamber and the bed which I had just deserted.

I now in spite of pain, fatigue and watchfulness, set out to go to Walton's. Sarsefield was ready to receive me at the door, and the kindness and compassion of the family were active in my behalf. I was conducted to a chamber and provided with suitable attendance and remedies.

I was not unmindful of the more deplorable condition of Clithero. I incessantly meditated on the means for his relief. His case stood in need of all the vigilance and skill of a physician, and Sarsefield was the only one of that profession whose aid could be seasonably administered. Sarsefield therefore must be persuaded to bestow this aid.

There was but one mode of conquering his abhorrence of this man. To prepossess my friend with the belief of the innocence of Clithero, or to soothe him into pity by a picture of remorse and suffering. This could best be done, and in the manner most conformable to truth, by a simple recital of the incidents that had befallen, and by repeating the confession which had been extorted from Clithero.

I requested all but my friend to leave my chamber, and then, soliciting a patient hearing, began the narrative of Waldegrave's death! of the detection of Clithero beneath the shade of the elm! of the suspicions which were thence produced; and of the forest interview to which these suspicions gave birth; I then repeated, without variation or addition, the tale which was then told. I likewise mentioned my subsequent transactions in Norwalk so far as they illustrated the destiny of Clithero.

During this recital, I fixed my eyes upon the countenance of Sarsefield, and watched every emotion as it rose or declined. With the progress of my tale, his indignation and his fury grew less, and at length gave place to horror and compassion.

His seat became uneasy, his pulse throbbed with new vehemence. When I came to the motives which prompted the unhappy man to visit the chamber of his mistress, he started from his seat, and sometimes strode across the floor in a troubled mood, and sometimes stood before me, with his breath almost suspended in the eagerness of his attention. When I mentioned the lifted dagger, the shriek from behind, and the apparition that interposed, he shuddered and drew back as if a dagger had been aimed at his breast.

When the tale was done, some time elapsed in mutual and profound silence. My friend's thoughts were involved in a mournful and indefinable reverie. From this he at length recovered and spoke.

It is true. A tale like this could never be the fruit of invention or be invented to deceive. He has done himself injustice. His character was spotless and fair: All his moral properties seemed to have resolved themselves into gratitude, fidelity, and honour.

We parted at the door, late in the evening, as he mentioned, and he guessed truly that subsequent reflection had induced me to return and to disclose the truth to Mrs. Lorimer. Clarice relieved by the sudden death of her friend, and unexpectedly by all, arrived at the same hour.

These tidings, astonished, afflicted, and delighted the lady. Her brother's death had been long believed by all but herself. To find her doubts verified, and his existence ascertained was the dearest consolation that he ever could bestow. She was afflicted at the proofs that had been noted of the continuance of his depravity, but she dreaded no danger to herself from his malignity or vengeance.

The ignorance and prepossessions of this woman were remarkable. On this subject only she was perverse, headlong, obstinate. Her anxiety to benefit this arch-ruffian occupied her whole thoughts and allowed her no time to reflect upon the reasonings or remonstrances of others. She could not be prevailed on to deny herself to his visits, and I parted from her in the utmost perplexity.

A messenger came to me at mid-night intreating my immediate presence. Some disaster had happened, but of what kind the messenger was unable to tell. My fears easily conjured up the image of Wiatte. Terror scarcely allowed me to breathe. When I entered the house of Mrs. Lorimer, I was conducted to her chamber. She lay upon the bed in a state of stupefaction, that rose from some mental cause. Clarice sat by her, wringing her hands and pouring forth her tears without intermission. Neither could explain to me the nature of the scene. I made inquiries of the servants and attendants. They merely said that the family as usual had retired to rest, but their lady's bell rung with great violence, and called them in haste, to her chamber, where they found her in a swoon upon the floor and the young lady in the utmost affright and perturbation.

Suitable means being used Mrs. Lorimer had, at length, recovered, but was still nearly insensible. I went to Clithero's apartments but he was not to be found, and the domestics informed me that since he had gone with me, he had not returned. The doors between this chamber and the court were open; hence that some dreadful interview had taken place, perhaps with Wiatte, was an unavoidable conjecture. He had withdrawn, however, without committing any personal injury.

I need not mention my reflections upon this scene. All was tormenting doubt and suspence till the morning arrived, and tidings were received that Wiatte had been killed in the streets: This event was antecedent to that which had occasioned Mrs. Lorimer's distress and alarm. I now remembered that fatal prepossession by which the lady was governed, and her frantic belief that her death and that of her brother were to fall out at the same time. Could some witness of his death, have brought her tidings of it: Had he penetrated, unexpected and unlicensed to her chamber, and were these the effects produced by the intelligence?

Presently I knew that not only Wiatte was dead, but that Clithero had killed him. Clithero had not been known to return and was no where to be found. He then was the bearer of these tidings, for none but he could have found access or egress without disturbing the servants.

These doubts were at length at an end. In a broken and confused manner, and after the lapse of some days the monstrous and portentous truth was disclosed. After our interview, the lady and her daughter had retired to the same chamber; the former had withdrawn to her closet and the latter to bed. Some one's entrance alarmed the lady, and coming forth after a moment's pause, the spectacle which Clithero has too faithfully described, presented itself.

What could I think? A life of uniform hypocrisy or a sudden loss of reason were the only suppositions to be formed. Clithero was the parent of fury and abhorrence in my heart. In either case I started at the name. I shuddered at the image of the apostate or the maniac.

What? Kill the brother whose existence was interwoven with that of his benefactress and his friend? Then hasten to her chamber, and attempt her life? Lift a dagger to destroy her who had been the author of his being and his happiness?

He that could meditate a deed like this was no longer man. An agent from Hell had mastered his faculties. He was become the engine of infernal malice against whom it was the duty of all mankind to rise up in arms and never to desist till, by shattering it to atoms, its power to injure was taken away.

All inquiries to discover the place of his retreat were vain. No wonder methought that he wrapt himself in the folds of impenetrable secrecy. Curbed, checked, baffled in the midst of his career, no wonder that he shrunk into obscurity, that he fled from justice and revenge, that he dared not meet the rebukes of that eye which, dissolving in tenderness or flashing with disdain, had ever been irresistable.

But how shall I describe the lady's condition? Clithero she had cherished from his infancy. He was the stay, the consolation, the pride of her life. His projected alliance with her daughter,[1] made him still more dear. Her eloquence was never tired of expatiating on his purity and rectitude. No wonder that she delighted in this theme, for he was her own work. His virtues were the creatures of her bounty.

How hard to be endured was this sad reverse? She can be tranquil, but never more will she be happy. To promote her forgetfulness of him, I persuaded her to leave her country, which contained a thousand memorials of past calamity, and which was lapsing fast into civil broils.[2] Clarice has accompanied us, and time may effect the happiness of others, by her means, though she can never remove the melancholy of her mother.

I have listened to your tale, not without compassion. What would you have me to do? To prolong his life, would be merely to protract his misery.

He can never be regarded with complacency by my wife. He can never be thought of without shuddering by Clarice. Common ills are not without a cure less than death, but here, all remedies are vain. Consciousness itself is the malady; the pest; of which he only is cured who ceases to think.

I could not but assent to this mournful conclusion; yet, though death was better to Clithero than life, could not some of his mistakes be rectified? Euphemia Lorimer, contrary to his belief, was still alive. He dreamed that she was dead, and a thousand evils were imagined to flow from that death. This death and its progeny of ills, haunted his fancy, and added keenness to his remorse. Was it not our duty to rectify this error?

---

[1] "His projected alliance with her daughter": "daughter" is used loosely, since Clarice is Lorimer's niece, the illegitimate daughter of Wiatte.

[2] "Which was lapsing fast into civil broils": Sarsefield refers to ongoing insurrections and attempts at full-scale rebellion that convulsed Ireland in the 1780s and only intensified up to the time of this novel's publication in 1799. Many leaders of Irish revolutionary efforts in the 1790s (such as Wolfe Tone and members of the United Irishmen) took refuge in Philadelphia and were well known to Brown. Again, Clithero's strange story provides a dark allegory of the political situation in Ireland, where English colonialism was producing repeated waves of Irish insurrection and revolt.

Sarsefield reluctantly assented to the truth of my arguments on this head. He consented to return, and afford the dying man, the consolation of knowing that the being whom he adored as a benefactor and parent, had not been deprived of existence, though bereft of peace by his act.

During Sarsefield's absence my mind was busy in revolving the incidents that had just occurred. I ruminated the last words of Clithero. There was somewhat in his narrative that was obscure and contradictory. He had left the manuscript which he so much and so justly prized, in his cabinet. He entered the chamber in my absence, and found the cabinet unfastened and the manuscript gone. It was I by whom the cabinet was opened, but the manuscript supposed to be contained in it, was buried in the earth beneath the elm. How should Clithero be unacquainted with its situation, since none but Clithero could have dug for it this grave?

This mystery vanished when I reflected on the history of my own manuscript. Clithero had buried his treasure with his own hands as mine had been secreted by myself, but both acts had been performed during sleep. The deed was neither prompted by the will, nor noticed by the senses of him, by whom it was done. Disastrous and humiliating is the state of man! By his own hands, is constructed the mass of misery and error in which his steps are forever involved.

Thus it was with thy friend. Hurried on by phantoms too indistinct to be now recalled, I wandered from my chamber to the desart. I plunged into some unvisited cavern, and easily proceeded till I reached the edge of a pit. There my step was deceived, and I tumbled headlong from the precipice. The fall bereaved me of sense, and I continued breathless and motionless during the remainder of the night and the ensuing day.

How little cognizance have men over the actions and motives of each other? How total is our blindness with regard to our own performances! Who would have sought me in the bowels of this mountain? Ages might have passed away, before my bones would be discovered in this tomb, by some traveller whom curiosity had prompted to explore it.

I was roused from these reflections by Sarsefield's return. Inquiring into Clithero's condition; he answered that the unhappy man was insensible, but that notwithstanding numerous and dreadful gashes, in different parts of his body, it was possible that by submitting to the necessary treatment, he might recover.

Encouraged by this information, I endeavoured to awaken the zeal and compassion of my friend in Clithero's behalf. He recoiled with involuntary shuddering from any task which would confine him to the presence of this man. Time and reflection he said, might introduce different sentiments and feelings, but at present he could not but regard this person as a maniac, whose disease was irremediable, and whose existence could not be protracted, but to his own misery and the misery of others.

Finding him irreconcilably averse to any scheme, connected with the welfare of Clithero, I began to think that his assistance as a surgeon was by no means necessary. He had declared that the sufferer needed nothing more than common treatment, and to this the skill of a score of aged women in this district, furnished with simples culled from the forest, and pointed out, of old time, by Indian *Leeches*[3] was no less

---

[3] "Leeches": "leech" is an archaic term for physician or surgeon.

adequate than that of Sarsefield. These women were ready and officious in their charity, and none of them were prepossessed against the sufferer by a knowledge of his genuine story.

Sarsefield, meanwhile, was impatient for my removal to Inglefield's habitation, and that venerable friend was no less impatient to receive me. My hurts were superficial, and my strength sufficiently repaired by a night's repose. Next day, I went thither, leaving Clithero to the care of his immediate neighbours.

Sarsefield's engagements compelled him to prosecute his journey into Virginia, from which he had somewhat deviated, in order to visit Solebury. He proposed to return in less than a month and then to take me in his company to New-York. He has treated me with paternal tenderness, and insists upon the privilege of consulting for my interest, as if he were my real father. Meanwhile, these views have been disclosed to Inglefield, and it is with him that I am to remain, with my sisters, until his return.

My reflections have been various and tumultuous. They have been busy in relation to you, to Weymouth, and especially to Clithero. The latter polluted with gore and weakened by abstinence, fatigue and the loss of blood, appeared in my eyes, to be in a much more dangerous condition than the event proved him to be. I was punctually informed of the progress of his cure, and proposed in a few days to visit him. The duty of explaining the truth, respecting the present condition of Mrs. Lorimer, had devolved upon me. By imparting this intelligence, I hoped to work the most auspicious revolutions in his feelings, and prepared therefore, with alacrity, for an interview.

In this hope I was destined to be disappointed. On the morning on which I intended to visit him, a messenger arrived from the house in which he was entertained, and informed us that the family on entering the sick man's apartment, had found it deserted. It appeared that Clithero, had, during the night, risen from his bed, and gone secretly forth. No traces of his flight have since been discovered.

But, O! my friend? The death of Waldegrave, thy brother, is at length divested of uncertainty and mystery. Hitherto, I had been able to form no conjecture respecting it, but the solution was found shortly after this time.

Queen Mab, three days after my adventure, was seized in her hut on suspicion of having aided and counselled her countrymen, in their late depredations. She was not to be awed or intimidated by the treatment she received, but readily confessed and gloried in the mischief she had done; and accounted for it by enumerating the injuries which she had received from her neighbours.

These injuries consisted in contemptuous or neglectful treatment, and in the rejection of groundless and absurd claims. The people of Chetasco were less obsequious to her humours than those of Solebury,[4] her ancient neighbourhood, and her imagination

---

[4] "The people of Chetasco were less obsequious": in Edgar's final comments about the Delaware war party, he blames the settlers of Chetasco for provoking Deb and thereby causing the raids that killed Waldegrave and brought harm to Solebury. Although his uncle's farm now occupies the very site of the Delaware village that was Deb's home and "neighbourhood" (he recalls this in Chapter 20), Edgar nonetheless complains that the Chetasco settlers are less "obsequious" than those of Solebury and thus responsible for Deb's anger. Like Sarsefield's suggestions that the Chetasco settlers were

brooded for a long time, over nothing but schemes of revenge. She became sullen, irascible and spent more of her time in solitude than ever.

A troop of her countrymen at length visited her hut. Their intentions being hostile, they concealed from the inhabitants their presence in this quarter of the country. Some motives induced them to withdraw and postpone, for the present, the violence which they meditated. One of them, however, more sanguinary and audacious than the rest would not depart, without some gratification of his vengeance. He left his associates and penetrated by night into Solebury, resolving to attack the first human being whom he should meet. It was the fate of thy unhappy brother to encounter this ruffian, whose sagacity made him forbear to tear away the usual trophy from the dead, least he should afford grounds for suspicion as to the authors of the evil.

Satisfied with this exploit he rejoined his companions, and after an interval of three weeks returned with a more numerous party, to execute a more extensive project of destruction. They were councelled and guided, in all their movements, by Queen Mab, who now explained these particulars, and boldly defied her oppressors. Her usual obstinacy and infatuation induced her to remain in her ancient dwelling and prepare to meet the consequences.

This disclosure awakened anew all the regrets and anguish which flowed from that disaster. It has been productive, however, of some benefit. Suspicions and doubts, by which my soul was harrassed, and which were injurious to the innocent are now at an end. It is likewise some imperfect consolation to reflect that the assassin has himself been killed and probably by my own hand. The shedder of blood no longer lives to pursue his vocation, and justice is satisfied.

Thus have I fulfilled my promise to compose a minute relation of my sufferings. I remembered my duty to thee, and as soon as I was able to hold a pen, employed it to inform thee of my welfare. I could not at that time enter into particulars, but reserved a more copious narrative till a period of more health and leisure.

On looking back I am surprised at the length to which my story has run. I thought that a few days would suffice to complete it, but one page has insensibly been added to another till I have consumed weeks and filled volumes. Here I will draw to a close; I will send you what I have written, and discuss with you in conversation, my other immediate concerns, and my schemes for the future. As soon as I have seen Sarsefield, I will visit you.

FAREWELL.

E. H.

Solebury, November, 10.

---

overzealous in retaliating for earlier raids (see Chapter 25, note 25.1), this passage seems to dramatize real Quaker attempts to shift their part in responsibility for settler-Indian violence onto Scots-Irish settlers in the backcountry.

LETTER I

TO MR. SARSEFIELD.

Philadelphia.

I CAME hither but ten minutes ago, and write this letter in the bar of the Stage-house. I wish not to lose a moment in informing you of what has happened. I cannot do justice to my own feelings when I reflect upon the rashness of which I have been guilty.

I will give you the particulars tomorrow. At present, I shall only say that Clithero is alive, is apprised of your wife's arrival and abode in New-York, and has set out, with mysterious intentions to visit her.

May heaven avert the consequences of such a design. May you be enabled by some means to prevent their meeting. If you cannot prevent it—but I must not reason on such an event, nor lengthen out this letter.

E. H.

LETTER II

TO THE SAME.

I WILL now relate the particulars which I yesterday promised to send you. You heard through your niece of my arrival at Inglefield's in Solebury: My inquiries, you may readily suppose, would turn upon the fate of my friend's servant, Clithero, whose last disappearance was so strange and abrupt, and of whom since that time, I had heard nothing. You are indifferent to his fate and are anxious only that his existence and misfortunes may be speedily forgotten. I confess that it is somewhat otherwise with me. I pity him: I wish to relieve him, and cannot admit the belief that his misery is without a cure. I want to find him out; I want to know his condition, and if possible to afford him comfort, and inspire him with courage and hope.

Inglefield replied to my questions. O yes! He has appeared. The strange being is again upon the stage. Shortly after he left his sick bed, I heard from Philip Beddington, of Chetasco, that Deb's hut had found a new tenant. At first, I imagined that the Scotsman who built it had returned, but making closer inquiries, I found that the new tenant was my servant. I had no inclination to visit him myself, but frequently inquired respecting him of those, who lived or past that way, and find that he still lives there.

But how, said I. What is his mode of subsistance? The winter has been no time for cultivation, and he found, I presume, nothing in the ground.

Deb's hut, replied my friend, is his lodging and his place of retirement, but food and cloathing he procures by labouring on a neighbouring farm. This farm is next to that of Beddington, who consequently knows something of his present situation. I find little or no difference in his present deportment; and those appearances which he assumed, while living with me, except that he retires every night to his hut, and holds as little intercourse as possible with the rest of mankind. He dines at his employer's table, but his supper, which is nothing but rye-bread, he carries home with him, and at all those times when disengaged from employment, he secludes himself in his hut, or wanders nobody knows whither.

This was the substance of Inglefield's intelligence. I gleaned from it some satisfaction. It proved the condition of Clithero to be less deplorable and desperate than I had previously imagined. His fatal and gloomy thoughts seemed to have somewhat yielded to tranquility.

In the course of my reflections, however, I could not but perceive, that his condition, though eligible when compared with what it once was, was likewise disastrous and humiliating, compared with his youthful hopes and his actual merits. For such an one to mope away his life in this unsocial and savage state, was deeply to be deplored. It was my duty, if possible, to prevail on him to relinquish his scheme. And what would be requisite, for that end, but to inform him of the truth?

The source of his dejection was the groundless belief that he had occasioned the death of his benefactress. It was this alone that could justly produce remorse or grief. It was a distempered imagination both in him and in me, that had given birth to this opinion, since the terms of his narrative, impartially considered, were far from implying that catastrophe. To him, however, the evidence which he possessed was incontestable. No deductions from probability could overthrow his belief. This could only be effected by similar and counter evidence. To apprize him that she was now alive, in possession of some degree of happiness, the wife of Sarsefield, and an actual resident on this shore, would dissipate the sanguinary apparition that haunted him; cure his diseased intellects, and restore him to those vocations for which his talents, and that rank in society for which his education had qualified him. Influenced by these thoughts, I determined to visit his retreat. Being obliged to leave Solebury the next day, I resolved to set out the same afternoon, and stopping in Chetasco, for the night, seek his habitation at the hour when he had probably retired to it.

This was done. I arrived at Beddington's, at night-fall. My inquiries respecting Clithero obtained for me the same intelligence from him, which I had received from Inglefield. Deb's hut was three miles from this habitation, and thither, when the evening had somewhat advanced, I repaired. This was the spot which had witnessed so many perils during the last year, and my emotions, on approaching it, were awful. With palpitating heart and quick steps I traversed the road, skirted on each side by thickets, and the area before the house. The dwelling was by no means in so ruinous a state as when I last visited it. The crannies between the logs had been filled up, and the light within was perceivable only at a crevice in the door.

Looking through this crevice I perceived a fire in the chimney, but the object of my visit was no where to be seen. I knocked and requested admission, but no answer was made. At length I lifted the latch and entered. Nobody was there.

It was obvious to suppose that Clithero had gone abroad for a short time, and would speedily return, or perhaps some engagement had detained him at his labour, later than usual. I therefore seated myself on some straw near the fire, which, with a woollen rug, appeared to constitute his only bed. The rude bedstead which I formerly met with, was gone. The slender furniture, likewise, which had then engaged my attention, had disappeared. There was nothing capable of human use, but a heap of faggots in the corner, which seemed intended for fuel. How slender is the accommodation which nature has provided for man, and how scanty is the portion which our physical necessities require.

While ruminating upon this scene, and comparing past events with the objects before me, the dull whistling of the gale without gave place to the sound of foot-steps. Presently the door opened, and Clithero entered the apartment. His aspect and guise were not essentially different from those which he wore when an inhabitant of Solebury.

To find his hearth occupied by another, appeared to create the deepest surprise. He looked at me without any tokens of remembrance! His features assumed a more austere expression, and after scowling on my person for a moment, he withdrew his eyes, and placing in a corner, a bundle which he bore in his hand, he turned and seemed preparing to withdraw.

I was anxiously attentive to his demeanor, and as soon as I perceived his purpose to depart, leaped on my feet to prevent it. I took his hand, and affectionately pressing it, said, do you not know me? Have you so soon forgotten me who is truly your friend?

He looked at me with some attention, but again withdrew his eyes, and placed himself in silence on the seat which I had left. I seated myself near him, and a pause of mutual silence ensued.

My mind was full of the purpose that brought me hither, but I knew not in what manner to communicate my purpose. Several times I opened my lips to speak, but my perplexity continued, and suitable words refused to suggest themselves. At length, I said, in a confused tone—

I came hither with a view to benefit a man, with whose misfortunes his own lips have made me acquainted, and who has awakened in my breast the deepest sympathy. I know the cause and extent of his dejection. I know the event which has given birth to horror and remorse in his heart. He believes that, by his means, his patroness and benefactress has found an untimely death.

These words produced a visible shock in my companion, which evinced that I had at least engaged his attention. I proceeded:

This unhappy lady was cursed with a wicked and unnatural brother. She conceived a disproportionate affection for this brother, and erroneously imagined that her fate was blended with his; that their lives would necessarily terminate at the same period, and that therefore, whoever was the contriver of his death, was likewise, by a fatal and invincible necessity, the author of her own.

Clithero was her servant, but was raised by her bounty, to the station of her son and the rank of her friend. Clithero, in self-defence took away the life of that unnatural brother, and, in that deed, falsely but cogently believed, that he had perpetrated the destruction of his benefactress.

To ascertain the truth, he sought her presence. She was found, the tidings of her brother's death were communicated, and she sunk breathless at his feet.

At these words Clithero started from the ground, and cast upon me looks of furious indignation—And come you hither, he muttered, for this end; to recount my offences, and drive me again to despair?

No, answered I, with quickness, I come to out-root a fatal, but powerful illusion. I come to assure you that the woman, with whose destruction you charge yourself, is *not dead.*

These words, uttered with the most emphatical solemnity, merely produced looks in which contempt was mingled with anger. He continued silent.

I perceive, resumed I, that my words are disregarded. Would to Heaven I were able to conquer your incredulity, could shew you not only the truth, but the probability of my tale. Can you not confide in me that Euphemia Lorimer is now alive, is happy, is the wife of Sarsefield; that her brother is forgotten and his murderer regarded without enmity or vengeance?

He looked at me with a strange expression of contempt—Come, said he, at length, make out thy assertion to be true. Fall on thy knees and invoke the thunder of heaven to light on thy head if thy words be false. Swear that Euphemia Lorimer is alive; happy; forgetful of Wiatte and compassionate of me. Swear that thou hast seen her; talked with her; received from her own lips the confession of her pity for him who aimed a dagger at her bosom. Swear that she is Sarsefield's wife.

I put my hands together, and lifting my eyes to heaven, exclaimed: I comply with your conditions; I call the omniscient God to witness that Euphemia Lorimer is alive; that I have seen her with these eyes; have talked with her; have inhabited the same house for months.

These asseverations were listened to with shuddering. He laid not aside, however, an air of incredulity and contempt. Perhaps, said he, thou canst point out the place of her abode. Canst guide me to the city, the street, the very door of her habitation?

I can. She rises at this moment in the city of New-York; in Broadway; in an house contiguous to the——.

'Tis well, exclaimed my companion, in a tone, loud, abrupt, and in the utmost degree, vehement. 'Tis well. Rash and infatuated youth. Thou hast ratified, beyond appeal or forgiveness, thy own doom. Thou hast once more let loose my steps, and sent me on a fearful journey. Thou hast furnished the means of detecting thy imposture. I will fly to the spot which thou describest. I will ascertain thy falsehood with my own eyes. If she be alive then am I reserved for the performance of a new crime. My evil destiny will have it so. If she be dead, I shall make *thee* expiate.

So saying, he darted through the door, and was gone in a moment, beyond my sight and my reach. I ran to the road, looked on every side, and called; but my calls were repeated in vain. He had fled with the swiftness of a deer.

My own embarrassment, confusion and terror were inexpressible. His last words were incoherent. They denoted the tumult and vehemence of phrenzy. They intimated his resolution to seek the presence of your wife. I had furnished a clue, which could not fail to conduct him to her presence. What might not be dreaded from the interview? Clithero is a maniac. This truth cannot be concealed. Your wife can with difficulty preserve her tranquillity, when his image occurs to her remembrance. What must it be when he starts up before her in his neglected and ferocious guise, and armed with purposes, perhaps as terrible as those, which had formerly led him to her secret chamber, and her bed side?

His meaning was obscurely conveyed. He talked of a deed, for the performance of which, his malignant fate had reserved him; which was to ensue their meeting, and which was to afford disastrous testimony of the infatuation which had led me hither.

Heaven grant that some means may suggest themselves to you of intercepting his approach. Yet I know not what means can be conceived. Some miraculous chance may befriend you; yet this is scarcely to be hoped. It is a visionary and fantastic base on which to rest our security.

I cannot forget that my unfortunate temerity has created this evil. Yet who could foresee this consequence of my intelligence? I imagined, that Clithero was merely a victim of erroneous gratitude, a slave of the errors of his education, and the prejudices of his rank, that his understanding was deluded by phantoms in the mask of virtue and duty, and not as you have strenuously maintained, utterly subverted.

I shall not escape your censure, but I shall, likewise, gain your compassion. I have erred, not through sinister or malignant intentions, but from the impulse of misguided, indeed, but powerful benevolence.

E. H.

LETTER III

TO EDGAR HUNTLY.

New-York.

Edgar,

AFTER the fatigues of the day, I returned home. As I entered, my wife was breaking the seal of a letter, but, on seeing me, she forbore and presented the letter to me.

I saw, said she, by the superscription of this letter, who the writer was. So agreeably to your wishes, I proceeded to open it, but you have come just time enough to save me the trouble.

This letter was from you. It contained information relative to Clithero. See how imminent a chance it was that saved my wife from a knowledge of its contents. It required all my efforts to hide my perturbation from her, and excuse myself from shewing her the letter.

I know better than you the character of Clithero, and the consequences of a meeting between him and my wife. You may be sure that I would exert myself to prevent a meeting.

The method for me to pursue was extremely obvious. Clithero is a madman whose liberty is dangerous, and who requires to be fettered and imprisoned as the most atrocious criminal.

I hastened to the chief Magistrate, who is my friend, and by proper representations, obtained from him authority to seize Clithero wherever I should meet with him, and effectually debar him from the perpetration of new mischiefs.

New-York does not afford a place of confinement for lunatics, as suitable to his case, as Pennsylvania. I was desirous of placing him as far as possible from the place of my wife's residence. Fortunately there was a packet for Philadelphia, on the point of setting out on her voyage. This vessel I engaged to wait a day or two, for the purpose of conveying him to the Pennsylvania hospital.[1] Meanwhile, proper persons were stationed at Powles-hook,[2] and at the quays where the various stageboats from Jersey arrive.

These precautions were effectual. Not many hours after the receipt of your intelligence, this unfortunate man applied for a passage at Elizabeth-town,[3] was seized the moment he set his foot on shore, and was forthwith conveyed to the packet, which immediately set sail.

---

[1] "The Pennsylvania hospital": the Pennsylvania Hospital, on Pine Street in Philadelphia, was founded in 1751 by Benjamin Franklin and Thomas Bond and began admitting patients in 1756 as the first hospital in North America. In the 1780s and 1790s, it was the most advanced medical institution in the American colonies and early United States. It was the first North American hospital to set aside space for the care of the mentally ill. The hospital's west wing, completed in 1797, was built to care for an increasing number of mentally ill patients, who outnumbered the physically ill patients of the hospital at the time Brown was writing *Edgar Huntly.*

[2] "Powles-hook": the land on the west bank of the Hudson directly across from lower Manhattan, now the site of Jersey City, New Jersey.

[3] "Elizabeth-town": what is now Elizabeth, New Jersey.

I designed that all these proceedings should be concealed from the women, but unfortunately neglected to take suitable measures for hindering the letter which you gave me reason to expect on the ensuing day, from coming into their hands. It was delivered to my wife in my absence and opened immediately by her.

You know what is, at present, her personal condition. You know what strong reasons I had to prevent any danger or alarm from approaching her. Terror could not assume a shape, more ghastly than this. The effects have been what might have been easily predicted. Her own life has been imminently endangered and an untimely birth, has blasted my fondest hope. Her infant, with whose future existence so many pleasures were entwined, *is dead.*

I assure you Edgar, my philosophy has not found itself lightsome and active under this burden. I find it hard to forbear commenting on your rashness in no very mild terms. You acted in direct opposition to my council, and to the plainest dictates of propriety. Be more circumspect and more obsequious for the future.

You knew the liberty that would be taken of opening my letters; you knew of my absence from home, during the greatest part of the day, and the likelihood therefore that your letters would fall into my wife's hands before they came into mine. These considerations should have prompted you to send them under cover to Whitworth or Harvey, with directions to give them immediately to me.

Some of these events happened in my absence, for I determined to accompany the packet myself and see the madman safely delivered to the care of the hospital.

I will not torture your sensibility by recounting the incidents of his arrest and detention. You will imagine that his strong, but perverted reason exclaimed loudly against the injustice of his treatment. It was easy for him to outreason his antagonist, and nothing but force could subdue his opposition. On me devolved the province of his jailor and his tyrant; a province which required an heart more steeled by spectacles of suffering and the exercise of cruelty, than mine had been.

Scarcely had we passed *The Narrows,*[4] when the lunatic, being suffered to walk the deck, as no apprehensions were entertained of his escape in such circumstances, threw himself overboard, with a seeming intention to gain the shore. The boat was immediately manned, the fugitive was pursued, but at the moment, when his flight was overtaken, he forced himself beneath the surface, and was seen no more.

With the life of this wretch, let our regrets and our forebodings terminate. He has saved himself from evils, for which no time would have provided a remedy, from lingering for years in the noisome dungeon of an hospital. Having no reason to continue my voyage, I put myself on board a coasting sloop, and regained this city in a few hours. I persuade myself that my wife's indisposition will be temporary. It was impossible to hide from her the death of Clithero, and its circumstances. May this be the last arrow in the quiver of adversity! Farewell.

END

---

[4] "*The Narrows*": the mouth of New York Bay; what is now called the Verrazano Narrows, crossed by the Verrazano-Narrows Bridge.

RELATED TEXTS

A. William Godwin, excerpts from *Enquiry Concerning Political Justice* (1793).

Godwin's Political Justice *is a key work of the Woldwinite circle, the most complete artic-ulation of its social principles and program. Along with Thomas Paine's writings, God-win's were tremendously popular among the college-educated young men who formed the core of Brown's associates. Brown had access to the work in several editions; the text quoted here is the third edition (1798), which has few changes from the second edition (1796), which Brown probably used during his novelistic years. Godwin's political writings oper-ate as the common sense and moral compass for Brown's circle.*

These illustrative excerpts insist on the historical curse of coercive and absolutist regimes trapped in cycles of irrational violence motivated by revenge; the usurpation of social power by wealthy elites; the obligation for the virtuous to struggle for social reform through rational improvement; the power of benevolence as it acts through associative sen-timent; and the nightmarish tendency to reject progressive and cosmopolitan rationality in favor of irrational and servile loyalty to current modes of government.

*****

From Book I, Chapter I: "History of Political Society"

It is an old observation that the history of mankind is little else than a record of crimes. Society comes recommended to us by its tendency to supply our wants and promote our well being. If we consider the human species, as they were found previ-ously to the existence of political society, it is difficult not to be impressed with emo-tions of melancholy. But, though the chief purpose of society is to defend us from want and inconvenience, it effects this purpose in a very imperfect degree. We are still liable to casualties, disease, infirmity and death. Famine destroys its thousands, and pestilence its ten thousands. Anguish visits us under every variety of form, and day after day is spent in languor and dissatisfaction. Exquisite pleasure is a guest of very rare approach, and not less short continuance.

But, though the evils that arise to us from the structure of the material universe are neither trivial nor few, yet the history of political society sufficiently shows that man is of all other beings the most formidable enemy to man. Among the various schemes that he has formed to destroy and plague his kind, war is the most terrible. Satiated with petty mischief and retail of insulated crimes, he rises in this instance to a project that lays nations waste, and thins the population of the world. Man directs the mur-derous engine against the life of his brother; he invents with indefatigable care re-finements in destruction; he proceeds in the midst of gaiety and pomp to the execution of his horrid purpose; whole ranks of sensitive beings, endowed with the most admirable faculties, are mowed down in an instant; they perish by inches in the midst of agony and neglect, lacerated with every variety of method that can give torture to the frame.

This is indeed a tremendous scene! Are we permitted to console ourselves under the spectacle of its evils by the rareness with which it occurs, and the forcible reasons that compel men to have recourse to this last appeal of human society? Let us consider it under each of these heads.

War has hitherto been found the inseparable ally of political institution. The earliest records of time are the annals of conquerors and heroes, a Bacchus, a Sesostris, a Semiramis and a Cyrus. These princes led millions of men under their standard, and ravaged innumerable provinces. A small number only of their forces ever returned to their native homes, the rest having perished by diseases, hardship and misery. The evils they inflicted, and the mortality introduced in the countries against which their expeditions were directed, were certainly not less severe than those which their countrymen suffered.

No sooner does history become more precise than we are presented with the four great monarchies, that is, with four successful projects, by means of bloodshed, violence and murder, of enslaving mankind. The expeditions of Cambyses against Egypt, of Darius against the Scythians, and of Xerxes against the Greeks, seem almost to set credibility at defiance by the fatal consequences with which they were attended. The conquests of Alexander cost innumerable lives, and the immortality of Caesar is computed to have been purchased by the death of one million two hundred thousand men.

Indeed the Romans, by the long duration of their wars, and their inflexible adherence to their purpose, are to be ranked among the foremost destroyers of the human species. Their wars in Italy continued for more than four hundred years, and their contest for supremacy with the Carthaginians two hundred. The Mithridatic war began with a massacre of one hundred and fifty thousand Romans, and in three single actions five hundred thousand men were lost by the Eastern monarch. Sylla, his ferocious conqueror, next turned his arms against his country, and the struggle between him and Marius was attended with proscriptions, butcheries and murders that knew no restraint from humanity or shame. The Romans, at length, suffered the evils they had been so prompt to inflict upon others; and the world was vexed for three hundred years by the irruptions of Goths, Vandals, Ostrogoths, Huns and innumerable hordes of barbarians.

*****

From Book I, Chapter III: "Spirit of Political Institutions"

Two of the greatest abuses relative to the interior policy of nations, which at this time prevail in the world, consist in the irregular transfer of property, either first by violence, or secondly by fraud. . . . First then it is to be observed that, in the most refined states of Europe, the inequality of property has risen to an alarming height. . . . A second source of those destructive passions by which the peace of society is interrupted is to be found in the luxury, the pageantry and magnificence with which enormous wealth is usually accompanied. . . . A third disadvantage that is apt to connect poverty with discontent consists in the insolence and usurpation of the rich.

*****

From Book I, Chapter V: "The Voluntary Actions of Men Originate in their Opinions"

The corollaries respecting political truth, deducible from the simple proposition, which seems clearly established by the reasonings of the present chapter, that the voluntary actions of men are in all instances conformable to the deductions of their understanding, are of the highest importance. Hence we may infer what are the hopes and prospects of human improvement. The doctrine which may be founded upon these principles may perhaps best be expressed in the five following propositions: Sound reasoning and truth, when adequately communicated, must always be victorious over error: Sound reasoning and truth are capable of being so communicated: Truth is omnipotent: The vices and moral weakness of man are not invincible: Man is perfectible, or in other words susceptible of perpetual improvement.

*****

From Book II, Chapter IV: "Of Personal Virtue and Duty"

In the first sense I would define virtue to be any action or actions of an intelligent being proceeding from kind and benevolent intention, and having a tendency to contribute to general happiness. Thus defined, it distributes itself under two heads; and, in whatever instance either the tendency or the intention is wanting, the virtue is incomplete. An action, however pure may be the intention of the agent, the tendency of which is mischievous, or which shall merely be nugatory and useless in its character, is not a virtuous action. Were it otherwise, we should be obliged to concede the appellation of virtue to the most nefarious deeds of bigots, persecutors and religious assassins, and to the weakest observances of a deluded superstition. Still less does an action, the consequences of which shall be supposed to be in the highest degree beneficial, but which proceeds from a mean, corrupt and degrading motive, deserve the appellation of virtue. A virtuous action is that, of which both the motive and the tendency concur to excite our approbation.

*****

From Book IV, Chapter X: "Of Self-Love and Benevolence"

The system of disinterested benevolence proves to us that it is possible to be virtuous, and not merely to talk of virtue; that all which has been said by philosophers and moralists respecting impartial justice is not an unmeaning rant; and that, when we call upon mankind to divest themselves of selfish and personal considerations, we call upon them for something they are able to practice. An idea like this reconciles us to our species; teaches us to regard, with enlightened admiration, the men who have appeared to lose the feeling of their personal existence, in the pursuit of general advantage; and gives us reason to expect that, as men collectively advance in science and useful institution, they will proceed more and more to consolidate their private judgment, and their individual will, with abstract justice, and the unmixed approbation of general happiness.

*****

From Book IV, Chapter XI: "Of Good and Evil"

Taking these considerations along with us, the rashness of the optimist will appear particularly glaring, while we recollect the vast portion of the pain and calamity that is to be found in the world. Let us not amuse ourselves with a pompous and delusive survey of the whole, but let us examine parts severally and individually. All nature swarms with life. This may, in one view, afford an idea of an extensive theatre of pleasure. But unfortunately every animal preys upon his fellow. Every animal, however minute, has a curious and subtle structure, rendering him susceptible, as it should seem, of piercing anguish. We cannot move our foot, without becoming the means of destruction. The wounds inflicted are of a hundred kinds. These petty animals are capable of palpitating for days in the agonies of death. It may be said, with little license of phraseology, that all nature suffers. There is no day nor hour, in which, in some regions of the many-peopled globe, thousands of men, and millions of animals, are not tortured, to the utmost extent that organized life will afford. Let us turn our attention to our own species. Let us survey the poor; oppressed, hungry, naked, denied all the gratifications of life, and all that nourishes the mind. They are either tormented with the injustice, or chilled into lethargy. Let us view man, writing under the pangs of disease, or the fiercer tortures that are stored up for him by his brethren. Who is there that will look on and say, "All this is well; there is no evil in the world?" Let us recollect the pains of the mind; the loss of friends, the rankling tooth of ingratitude, the unrelenting rage of tyranny, the slow progress of justice, the brave and honest consigned to the fate of guilt. Let us plunge into the depth of dungeons. Let us observe youth languishing in hopeless despair, and talents and virtue shrouded in eternal oblivion. The evil does not consist merely in the pain endured. It is the injustice that inflicts it, that gives it its sharpest sting. Malignity, an unfeeling disposition, vengeance and cruelty, are inmates of every climate. As these are felt by the sufferer with peculiar acuteness, so they propagate themselves. Severity begets severity, and hatred engenders hate. The whole history of the human species, taken in one point of view, appears a vast abortion. Man seems adapted for wisdom and fortitude and benevolence. But he has always, through a vast majority of countries, been the victim of ignorance and superstition. Contemplate the physiognomy of the species. Observe the traces of stupidity, of low cunning, of rooted insolence, of withered hope, and narrow selfishness, where the characters of wisdom, independence and disinterestedness might have been inscribed. Recollect the horrors of war, that last invention of deliberate profligacy for the misery of man. Think of the variety of wounds, the multiplication of anguish, the desolation of countries, towns destroyed, harvests flaming, inhabitants perishing by thousands of hunger and cold.

*****

From Book V, Chapter XVI: "Of the Causes of War"

One of the most essential principles of political justice is diametrically the reverse of that which impostors, as well as patriots, have too frequently agreed to recommend. Their perpetual exhortation has been, "Love your country. Sink the personal existence of individuals in the existence of the community. Make little account of the particular men of whom the society consists, but aim at the general wealth, prosperity and glory. Purify your mind from the gross ideas of sense, and elevate it to the single contemplation of that abstract individual, of which particular men are so many detached members, valuable only for the place they fill."

The lessons of reason on this head are different from these. "Society is an ideal existence, and not, on its own account, entitled to the smallest regard. The wealth, prosperity and glory of the whole are unintelligible chimeras. Set no value on anything but in proportion as you are convinced of its tendency to make individual men happy and virtuous. Benefit, by every practicable mode, man wherever he exists; but be not deceived by the specious idea of affording services to a body of men, for which no individual man is the better. Society was instituted, not for the sake of glory, not to furnish splendid materials for the page of history, but for the benefit of its members. The love of our country, as the term has usually been understood, has too often been found to be one of those specious illusions which are employed by impostors for the purpose of rendering the multitude the blind instruments of their crooked designs."

In the meantime, the maxims which are here controverted have had by so much the more success in the world as they bear some resemblance to the purest sentiments of virtue. Virtue is nothing else but kind and sympathetic feelings reduced into principle. Undisciplined feeling would induce me, now to interest myself exclusively for one man, and now for another, to be eagerly solicitous for those who are present to me, and to forget the absent. Feeling ripened into virtue embraces the interests of the whole human race, and constantly proposes to itself the production of the greatest quantity of happiness. But, while it anxiously adjusts the balance of interests, and yields to no case, however urgent, to the prejudice of the whole, it keeps aloof from the unmeaning rant of romance, and uniformly recollects that happiness, in order to be real, must necessarily be individual.

The love of our country has often been found to be a deceitful principle, as its direct tendency is to set the interests of one division of mankind in opposition to another, and to establish a preference built upon accidental relations, and not upon reason. Much of what has been understood by the appellation is excellent, but perhaps nothing that can be brought within the strict interpretation of the phrase. A wise and well informed man will not fail to be the votary of liberty and justice. He will be ready to exert himself in their defense, wherever they exist. It cannot be a matter of indifference to him when his own liberty and that of other men with whose merits and capacities he has the best opportunity of being acquainted are involved in the event of the struggle to be made. But his attachment will be to the cause, as the cause of man, and not to the country. Wherever there are individuals who understand the value of political justice, and are prepared to assert it, that is his country. Wherever he can most contribute to the diffusion of these principles and the real happiness of mankind, that is his country. Nor does he desire, for any country, any other benefit than justice.

To apply these principles to the subject of war.—And, before that application can be adequately made, it is necessary to recollect, for a moment, the force of the term.

Because individuals were liable to error, and suffered their apprehensions of justice to be perverted by a bias in favor of themselves, government was instituted. Because nations were susceptible of a similar weakness, and could find no sufficient umpire to whom to appeal, war was introduced. Men were induced deliberately to seek each other's lives, and to adjudge the controversies between them, not according to the dictates of reason and justice, but as either should prove most successful in devastation and murder. This was no doubt in the first instance the extremity of exasperation and rage. But it has since been converted into a trade. One part of the nation pays another part, to murder and be murdered in their stead; and the most trivial causes, a supposed insult, or a sally of youthful ambition, have sufficed to deluge provinces with blood.

We can have no adequate idea of this evil unless we visit, at least in imagination, a field of battle. Here men deliberately destroy each other by thousands, without resentment against, or even knowledge of, each other. The plain is strewed with death in all its forms. Anguish and wounds display the diversified modes in which they can torment the human frame. Towns are burned; ships are blown up in the air, while the mangled limbs descend on every side; the fields are laid desolate; the wives of the inhabitants exposed to brutal insult; and their children driven forth to hunger and nakedness. It is an inferior circumstance, though by no means unattended with the widest and most deplorable effects, when we add, to these scenes of horror, and the subversion of all ideas of moral justice they must occasion in the auditors and spectators, the immense treasures which are wrung, in the form of taxes, from those inhabitants whose residence is removed from the seat of war.

After this enumeration, we may venture to enquire what are the justifiable causes and rules of war.

It is not a justifiable reason "that we imagine our own people would be rendered more cordial and orderly, if we could find a neighbor with whom to quarrel, and who might serve as a touchstone to try the characters and dispositions of individuals among ourselves." We are not at liberty to have recourse to the most complicated and atrocious of all mischiefs, in the way of an experiment.

It is not a justifiable reason, "that we have been exposed to certain insults, and that tyrants, perhaps, have delighted in treating with contempt, the citizens of our happy state who have visited their dominions." Government ought to protect the tranquility of those who reside within the sphere of its functions; but, if individuals think proper to visit other countries, they must be delivered over to the protection of general reason. Some proportion must be observed between the evil of which we complain and the evil which the nature of the proposed remedy inevitably includes.

It is not a justifiable reason "that our neighbor is preparing, or menacing, hostilities." If we be obliged to prepare in our turn, the inconvenience is only equal; and it is not to be believed that a despotic country is capable of more exertion than a free one, when the task incumbent on the latter is indispensable precaution.

It has sometimes been held to be sound reasoning upon this subject "that we ought not to yield little things, which may not, in themselves, be sufficiently valuable to authorize this tremendous appeal, because a disposition to yield only invites further experiments." Much otherwise; at least when the character of such a nation is sufficiently understood. A people that will not contend for nominal and trivial objects, that adheres to the precise line of unalterable justice, and that does not fail to be moved at the moment that it ought to be moved, is not the people that its neighbors will delight to urge to extremities.

"The vindication of national honour" is a very insufficient reason for hostilities. True honour is to be found only in integrity and justice. It has been doubted how far a view to reputation ought, in matters of inferior moment, to be permitted to influence the conduct of individuals; but, let the case of individuals be decided as it may, reputation, considered as a separate motive in the instance of nations, can perhaps never be justifiable. In individuals, it seems as if I might, consistently with the utmost real integrity, be so misconstrued and misrepresented by others as to render my efforts at usefulness almost necessarily abortive. But this reason does not apply to the case of nations. Their real story cannot easily be suppressed. Usefulness and public spirit, in relation to them, chiefly belong to the transactions of their members among themselves; and their influence in the transactions of neighboring nations is a consideration evidently subordinate. The question which respects the justifiable causes of war would be liable to few difficulties, if we were accustomed, along with the word, strongly to call up to our minds the thing which that word is intended to represent.

B. Erasmus Darwin, excerpts from *Zoönomia; or, The Laws of Organic Life* (1794).

Erasmus Darwin (1731–1802) was an influential physician, naturalist, and poet whose importance has often been overshadowed by the achievements of his intellectually vibrant descendants, including his grandsons, evolutionist Charles Darwin and eugenicist Francis Galton, as well as later descendants and their relations by marriage, including economist John Maynard Keynes.

Darwin is mainly known for Zoönomia; or, The Laws of Organic Life (1794–1796), his best-known work, and his earlier poetic work on biology, The Botanic Garden (1791). These were key sources, for Brown and his New York circle, of progressive ideas about medicine, the body, and the general relation of nature and society. Brown's close friend Elihu Hubbard Smith published the first U.S. edition of The Botanic Garden *in 1798, during the period when Brown was most closely associated with him, and wrote that* Zoönomia *was "the most masterly performance ever given the world on the subject of Medicine." For an interesting discussion of Darwin's significance for Brown's entire circle, see Teute, "The Loves of the Plants."*

These excerpts from Zoönomia *provide the medical-physiological understanding of somnambulism, reverie, and "sentimental love" that Brown utilizes in* Edgar Huntly *and in another novel that uses madness as a central theme,* Wieland; or, The Transformation. *In explaining these phenomena as symptoms of emotional and physical imbalance, Darwin provides Brown with a late eighteenth-century understanding of madness as the result of an imbalance of the senses. In* Zoönomia, *Darwin joins discussions of environmental causes for mental illness with a theory of biological generation that his grandson Charles Darwin viewed as the immediate source for naturalist Jean-Baptiste Lamarck's idea that acquired traits and skills are passed on to following generations.*

For Brown's circle, Darwin's ideas about the social conditions of physiology and illness connected with William Godwin's arguments that human behavior is preconditioned by society. When these sources are combined, they form the outlines of an entire intellectual orientation that Brown would use to calibrate his own literary compass. Darwin's significance for Brown also comes from his membership in an important group of scientists and thinkers in the English Midlands known as the Lunar Society. Another member was the dissident novelist Robert Bage, who wrote Hermsprong; or, Man As He is Not *(1796), which was an immediate influence on Brown at the moment when he began writing novels. Brown and his New York group planned, but did not complete, a stage version of* Hermsprong. Hermsprong's *influence on* Edgar Huntly *and its precursor* Sky-Walk *is captured both in* Hermsprong's *subtitle (a progressive "man and society" narrative) and in the central character Hermsprong, an American who grows up among Native Americans before arriving in England as the carrier of more natural, modern, and "virtuous" ethics.*

Overall, Darwin is crucial for Brown as a primary source of medical knowledge about the mind who has the added prestige of close association with literary figures that Brown himself looked to for inspiration.

The text used for these excerpts is that of the third edition (London: J. Johnson, 1801).

Diseases Class III.1.1.9.

Of Volition

9. Somnambulismus.

Sleep-walking is a part of reverie, or studium inane, described in Sect. XIX. In this malady the patients have only the general appearance of being asleep in respect to their inattention to the stimulus of external objects, but, like the epilepsies above described, it consists in voluntary exertions to relieve pain. The muscles are subservient to the will, as appears by the patient's walking about, and sometimes during the common offices of life. The ideas of the mind also are obedient to the will, because the patient's discourse is consistent, though he answers imaginary questions. The irritative ideas of external objects continue in this malady, because the patients do not run against the furniture of the room. And when they apply their volition to their organs of sense, they become sensible of the objects they attend to, but not otherwise, as general sensation is destroyed by the violence of their voluntary exertions. At the same time the sensations of pleasure in consequence of ideas excited by volition are vividly experienced, and other ideas, seem to be excited by these pleasurable sensations as appears in the case of Master A. Sect. XXXIV.3.1. where a history of a hunting scene was voluntarily recalled, with all the pleasurable ideas which attended it. In melancholy madness the patient is employed in voluntarily exciting one idea, with those which are connected to it, but not so violently as to exclude the stimuli of external objects. In reverie variety of ideas are occasionally excited by volition, and those which are connected with them either by sensitive or voluntary associations, and that so violently as to exclude the stimuli of external objects. These two situations of our sensual motions, or ideas, resemble convulsion and epilepsy; as in the former the stimulus of external objects is still perceived, but not in the latter. When this disease, so far from being connected with sleep, though it has by universal mistake acquired its name from it, arises from excess of volition, and not from a suspension of it; and though, like other kinds of epilepsy, it often attacks the patients in their sleep, yet those two, whom I saw, were more frequently seized with it while awake, the sleep-walking being a part of the reverie. See Sect. XIX. and XXXIV.3. and Class II.1.7.4. and III.1.2.18.

M.M. Opium in large doses before the expected paroxysm.

Class III.1.2.2.

2. Studium inane.

Reverie consists of violent voluntary exertions of ideas to relieve pain, with all the trains or tribes connected with them by sensations or associations. It frequently alternates with epileptic convulsions; with which it corresponds, in respect to the insensibility of the mind to the stimuli of external objects, in the same manner as madness corresponds with common convulsion, in the patient's possessing at the same time a sensibility of the stimuli of external objects.

Some have been reported to have been in reverie so perfectly, as not to have been disturbed by the discharge of a cannon; and others to have been insensible to torture, as the martyrs for religious opinions; but these seem more properly to belong to particular insanities than to reverie, like nostalgia and erotomania.

Reverie is distinguished from madness as described above; and from delirium, because the train of ideas are kept consistent by the power of volition, as the person reasons and deliberates in it. Somnambulismus is a part of reverie, somnambulism consisting in the exertions of the locomotive muscles, and reverie in the exertions of the organs of sense. See Class I.1.1.9. and Sect. XIX. Both of which are mixed, or alternate with each other, for the purpose of relieving pain.

When the patients in reverie exert their volition on their organs of sense, they can occasionally perceive the stimuli of external objects, as explained in Sect. XIX. And in this case it resembles sometimes an hallucination of the senses, as there is a mixture of fact and imagination in their discourse; but may be distinguished: hallucinations of the senses are allied to delirium, and are attended with quick pulse, and other symptoms of great debility; but reverie is without fever, and generally alternates with convulsions; and so much intuitive analogy (see Sect. XVII.3.7.) is retained in its paroxysms, as to preserve a consistency in the trains of ideas. . . .

Class III.1.2.4.

4. Erotomania.

Sentimental love. Described in its excess by romance writers and poets. As the object of love is beauty, and as our perception of beauty consists in a recognition by the sense of vision of those objects, which have before inspired our love, by the pleasure that have afforded to many of our senses (Sect. XVI.6.); and as brute animals have less accuracy of their sense of vision than mankind; we see the reason why this kind of love is not frequently observable in the brute creation, except perhaps in some married birds, or in the affection of the mother to her offspring. Men, who have not had leisure to cultivate their taste for visible objects, and who have not read the works of poets and romance writers, are less liable to sentimental love; and as ladies are educated rather with the idea of being chosen, than of choosing; there are many men, and more women, who have not much of this insanity; and are therefore more easily induced to marry for convenience or interest, or from the flattery of one sex to the other.

In its fortunate gratification sentimental love is supposed to supply the purest source of human felicity; and from the suddenness with which many of those patients, described in species I. of this genus, were seized with the maniacal hallucination, there is reason to believe, that the most violent sentimental love may be acquired in a moment of time, as represented by Shakspeare [*sic*] in the beginning of his Romeo and Juliet, as originally written.

This passion of love produces reverie in its first stage, which exertion alleviates the pain of it, and by the assistance of hope converts it into pleasure. Then the lover seeks solitude, lest this agreeable reverie should be interrupted by external stimuli, as described by Virgil.

> Tantum inter densas, umbrosa cacumina, fagos
> Assidue veniebat, ibi haec incondite folus
> Montibus et sylvis studio jactabat inani.[1]

When the pain of love is so great, as not to be relieved by the exertions of reverie, as above described; as when it is misplaced on an object, of which the lover cannot

---

[1] The lines describe the shepherd Corydon's love for Alexis, in *Eclogues* II, 3–5: "And so he went continually among the dense beech trees, canopied in shadows. Alone, with vain passion there, he flung these artless words to the woods and hills"; trans. A. S. Kline.

possess himself; it may still be counteracted or conquered by the stoic philosophy, which strips all things of their ornaments and inculcates "nil admirari." Of which lessons may be found in the meditations of Marcus Antoninus. The maniacal idea is said in some lovers to have been weakened by the action of other very energetic ideas; such as have been occasioned by the death of his favourite child, or by the burning of his house, or by his being shipwrecked. In those cases the violence of the new idea for a while expends so much sensorial power as to prevent the exertion of the maniacal one; and new catenations succeed. On this theory, the lover's leap, so celebrated by poets, might effect a cure, if the patient escaped with his life.

The third stage of this disease I suppose is irremediable; when a lover has previously been much encouraged, and at length meets with neglect or disdain; the maniacal idea is so painful as not to be for a moment relievable by the exertions of reverie, but is instantly followed by furious or melancholy insanity; and suicide, or revenge, have frequently been the consequence.

C. Benjamin Franklin, excerpts from "A Narrative of the Late Massacres, in Lancaster County, of a Number of Indians, Friends of this Province, by Persons Unknown. With Some Observations on the Same" (1764).

Franklin's well-known pamphlet on the aftermath of the Paxton Boys uprising is an example of the way upper-class and Quaker interests in Philadelphia blame the Irish— Franklin calls them the "Christian White Savages of Peckstang [Paxton] and Donegall"—for settler-Indian violence in the Pennsylvania backcountry. Forgetting the prior history of Quaker fraud and revenge violence against Indians and Irish immigrants, and invoking myths of Quaker benevolence and pastoral harmony between Penn and the Indians, Franklin acknowledges wrongful violence against native peoples and recognizes that the "barbarity" of dispossession sets off vicious cycles of revenge killings, but he shifts blame to the Irish immigrants, whom he regards as a savage and lesser people.

*****

These *Indians* were the Remains of a Tribe of the *Six Nations,* settled at *Conestogoe,* and thence called *Conestogoe Indians.* On the first Arrival of the *English* in *Pennsylvania,* Messengers from this Tribe came to welcome them, with Presents of Venison, Corn and Skins; and the whole Tribe entered into a Treaty of Friendship with the first Proprietor, WILLIAM PENN, which was to last "as long as the Sun should shine, or the Waters run in the Rivers."

This Treaty has been since frequently renewed, and the *Chain brightened,* as they express it, from time to time. It has never been violated, on their Part or ours, till now. As their Lands by Degrees were mostly purchased, and the Settlements of the White People began to surround them, the Proprietor assigned them Lands on the Manor of *Conestogoe,* which they might not part with; there they have lived many

Years in Friendship with their White Neighbours, who loved them for their peaceable inoffensive Behaviour. [3–4]

*****

These poor People have been always our Friends. Their Fathers received ours, when Strangers here, with Kindness and Hospitality. Behold the Return we have made them!—When we grew more numerous and powerful, they put themselves under our *Protection*. See, in the mangled Corpses of the last Remains of the Tribe, how effectually we have afforded it to them!—

  Unhappy People! to have lived in such Times, and by such Neighbours!—We have seen, that they would have been safer among the ancient *Heathens,* with whom the Rites of Hospitality were *sacred.*—They would have been considered as *Guests* of the Publick, and the Religion of the Country would have operated in their Favour. But our Frontier People call themselves *Christians*!—They would have been safer, if they had submitted to the *Turks;* for ever since *Mahomet's* Reproof to *Khaled,* even the *cruel Turks,* never kill Prisoners in cold Blood. These were not even Prisoners:—But what is the Example of *Turks* to Scripture *Christians?*—They would have been safer, though they had been taken in actual War against the *Saracens,* if they had once drank Water with them. These were not taken in War against us, and have drank with us, and we with them, for Fourscore Years.—But shall we compare *Saracens* to *Christians?*—They would have been safer among the *Moors* in *Spain,* though they had been *Murderers of Sons;* if Faith had once been pledged to them, and a Promise of Protection given. But these have had the Faith of the *English* given to them many Times by the Government, and, in Reliance on that Faith, they lived among us, and gave us the Opportunity of murdering them.—However, what was honourable in *Moors,* may not be a Rule to us; for we are *Christians*!—They would have been safer it seems among *Popish Spaniards,* even if Enemies, and delivered into their Hands by a Tempest. These were not Enemies; they were born among us, and yet we have killed them all.—But shall we imitate *idolatrous Papists,* we that are *enlightened Protestants?*—They would even have been safer among the *Negroes* of *Africa,* where at least one manly Soul would have been found, with Sense, Spirit and Humanity enough, to stand in their Defence:—But shall *Whitemen* and *Christians* act like a *Pagan Negroe?*—In short it appears, that they would have been safe in any Part of the known World,—except in the Neighbourhood of the CHRISTIAN WHITE SAVAGES of *Peckstang* and *Donegall.*—

  O ye unhappy Perpetrators of this horrid Wickedness! Reflect a Moment on the Mischief ye have done, the Disgrace ye have brought on your Country, on your Religion, and your Bible, on your Families and Children! Think on the Destruction of your captivated Country-folks (now among the wild *Indians*) which probably may follow, in Resentment of your Barbarity! Think on the Wrath of the United *Five Nations,* hitherto our Friends, but now provoked by your murdering one of their Tribes, in Danger of becoming our bitter Enemies.—Think of the mild and good Government you have so audaciously insulted; the Laws of your King, your Country, and your GOD, that you have broken; the infamous Death that hangs over your Heads:—For JUSTICE, though slow, will come at last.—All good People every where detest your Actions.—You have imbrued your Hands in innocent Blood; how will you make them clean?—The dying Shrieks and Groans of the Murdered, will often sound in your Ears: Their Spectres will sometimes attend you, and affright even your innocent Children!—Fly where you will, your Consciences will go with you:—Talking in your Sleep shall betray you, in the Delirium of a Fever you your-selves shall make your own Wickedness known. [26–28]

D. Thomas Barton, excerpts from "The conduct of the Paxton-men, impartially represented; the distresses of the frontiers, and the complaints and sufferings of the people fully stated . . . With some Remarks upon the Narrative of the Indian-massacre, lately publish'd. Interspers'd with several interesting anecdotes, relating to the military genius, and warlike principles of the people call'd Quakers: together with proper reflection and advice upon the whole. In a letter from a gentleman in one of the back counties, to a friend in Philadelphia" (1764).

As its detailed title suggests, Barton's pamphlet is a vigorous reply to Franklin's "A Narrative of the Late Massacres." It rejects the Anglo-Quaker strategy of displacing responsibility for frontier violence in the Paxton uprising onto the Irish and argues that the Quaker elite has hypocritically engaged in systematic violence and self-serving dishonesty not only against Indians but, even more outrageously, against Irish and lower-class settlers in general. Emphasizing the raw economic self-interest, and the class and ethno-racial animus of the Quaker leaders—and pointedly dated on St. Patrick's Day, "March 17, 1764, A Day dedicated to LIBERTY and SAINT PATRICK"—Barton's pamphlet articulates the grievances of backcountry Irish against the Philadelphia Quaker elite.

*****

The Names of RIOTERS, REBELS, MURDERERS, WHITE SAVAGES, etc. have been liberally and indiscriminately bestowed upon them: But all this they look upon only as the Effects of a disappointed Malice, and the Resentment of a destructive FACTION, who see their *darling Power* in Danger.—The *Merciful* and the *Good*, however, they trust, will rather pity than condemn them.—And they are pleased with the Thoughts that they have been able at last to lay bare the PHARASAICAL BOSOM OF QUAKERISM, by obliging the NON-RESISTING QUALITY to take up Arms, and to become Proselytes to *the first great Law of Nature*.

But this Triumph of theirs is founded on a false Supposition, that *Quakers* never us'd Arms before. —Whereas, it can prov'd that these People have *taken up Arms,* and *fought well too,* upon many other Occasions. —Whoever will take the Trouble to read the printed Trials of G. KEITH, will find, that when a *Quaker*-Sloop, belonging to *this* Province, was formerly taken by some PIRATES, and finding it impossible to save both the *Sloop,* and their so much-cried-up *Principle, against outward Force,* they at last resolved to give up the *Principle* rather than the *Sloop!* and so opposed Force to Force—retook their Vessel, and made some of the *Pirates* Prisoners!

It is plain that the first *Quakers* were never against Force of Arms, if *they* thought the Quarrel just. [9]

*****

In short, it is evident from the late Conduct of *Friends,* that the *Peaceable Testimony* which they have so long born to the World, at the Expence of the Lives and Proper- ties of Thousands of their Fellow Subjects, is now no more—and that they have no more Scruple against taking up Arms, and Fighting, than any others—Nay, that they can go into more violent Measures to *Resist Evil* than perhaps were ever hear'd of in the most *Warlike Nations.*—

Where do we find or read an Instance of *Trenches* being thrown up, and *Cannon* planted, to oppose an insignificant Mob? —And yet this was done by your *Philadelphia Quakers,* against a Handful of *Freemen* and the *King's Subjects,* who thought it their Duty to kill a Pack of villainous, faithless Savages, who they sus- pected, and had Reason to believe, were Murderers, Enemies to this *Majesty,* his Government, and Subjects—Were such violent Proceedings consistent with the Principles which *Quakers* have professed to the World? Were they consistent with the Lenity and Mercy of an *English* Constitution? Surely No. —Such severe *Meas- ures* will never do with a free People, who conceive themselves oppressed. —Even *France* and *Spain,* notwithstanding the arbitrary Government and severe Laws es- tablished in them, are not without their *Insurrections* and *Tumults*—I hope it will not be suspected that I am a Favourer or Encourager of Mobs and Riots—I solemnly declare I have as great an Aversion to Mobs, and all riotous Proceedings, as a Man can have, as any Man ought to have—But at the same Time, I must own, I shall never be for sacrificing the Lives and Liberties of a free People to the Caprice and Obstinacy of a destructive Faction. . . .

Now, Sir, had your Quakers, those *Children of Peace,* adopted these wise Senti- ments, and pursued these humane just and truly politic Measures, every Thing might have been easy. But instead of this, they neglected and despised the Com- plaints of an injured and oppressed People; refused to redress their Grievances; they promoted a *military Apparatus; fortified the Barracks; planted Cannon,* and strutted about in all the Parade of War, as if they chose rather to have the Province involv'd in a Civil War, and see the Blood of perhaps 5 or 600 of his Majesty's Subjects shed, than give up, or banish to their native Caves and Woods, a Parcel of treacherous, faithless, rascally Indians, some of which can be proved to be Murderers. But if they were all innocent, by what Law are we obliged to maintain 140 idle Vagabonds? Must *Pennsylvania* work for murdering Savages as their Lords and Masters? [12–14]

*****

O ungenerous, unfeeling Men! Was this the way to treat a ruined, despairing People? —Will not Religion, Reason, Humanity, Justice, Charity, answer No? —Who was it that reduc'd them to the most disagreeable Necessity of proceeding in the Manner they did? —From what Source are they to derive their Misery? and, Who was it that provok'd and moved them to Resentment? Who is it that has made them Rioters, and then Reproaches, and desires they may be *Shot* or *Hang'd* for being so? Who is it that has thrown so many Obstacles in the Way of their Protection and Security? Who is it that has screened and supported the Enemies of their Country, and pours out Vengeance and Destruction upon those that attempt to chastise and punish them? These are Questions which every Body, with a Moments Reflection, may answer.

A mighty Noise and Hubbub has been made about killing a few Indians in Lancaster-County; and even *Philosophers* and *Legislators* have been employed to raise the Holloo upon those that killed them; and to ransack *Tomes* and *Systems,* Writers ancient and modern, for Proofs of their Guilt and Condemnation! And what have they proved at last? Why, that the WHITE SAVAGES of *Paxton* and *Donnegall* have violated the Laws of Hospitality! I can sincerely assure the ingenious and worthy Author of the NARRATIVE, that a Shock of *Electricity* would have had a much more sensible Effect upon these People than all the Arguments and Quotations he has produced. [16–17]

*****

Is it any Wonder then if the unhappy Frontier People were really *mad with Rage* (as they express themselves) under such cruel Treatment? —Shall *Heathens,* shall *Traytors,* shall *Rebels* and *Murderers* be protected, cloathed, and fed? Shall they be invited from House to House, and riot at Feasts and Entertainments? Shall they be supported in Ease and Indolence, and provided with Physicians and Medicines whenever they complain? —And shall the *free born Subjects of Britain,* the brave and industrious Sons of *Pennsylvania,* be left naked and defenceless—abandoned to Misery and Want—to beg their Bread from the cold Hand of Charity—and for want of Medicine or Relief from a Surgeon or Physician, to linger out a miserable Life, and perish at last under the Wounds received perhaps from these very Villains? —My Soul rises with Indignation at the Thought! —This is a Consideration that must give Bitterness to every humane Spirit, though it should suffer no other Way than by Sympathy! What good Man is there, whose Heart does not bleed, when he sees a Set of Men amongst us embracing BARBARIANS, with more Tenderness and Hospitality than ever they shew'd to their distressed Countrymen and Fellow-subjects?— When he hears them express more Sorrow and Compassion, for the Death of a few *Savage Traytors,* than they ever expressed for the Calamities of their Country, and the

Murder of their Fellow-Christians?—When he sees them take up Arms to protect these cruel *Monsters,* which they would never do to protect their own Neighbours and the King's Subjects, from the most inhuman Butcheries?—When a Waggon-Load of the scalped and mangled Bodies of their Countrymen were brought to *Philadelphia* and laid at the *State-House Door,* and another Waggon-Load brought into the Town of *Lancaster,* did they rouse to Arms to avenge the Cause of their murder'd Friends?—Did we hear any of those Lamentations that are now so plentifully poured forth for the *Conestogoe Indians?*—O my dear Friends! Must I answer —No? The *Dutch* and *Irish* are murder'd without Pity. [29–30]

*****

Salus Populi suprema Lex esto [The safety of the populace is the supreme law]; is a Sentence that deserves to be written in Leaves of Gold—It is a Sentence that should be the Motto of every Government, where LIBERTY and FREEDOM have any Existence.

We are told that in the *wise,* the *free* Cities of ATHENS and ROME, "*The awful Authority of the* PEOPLE, *the sacred Privileges of the* PEOPLE, *the inviolable Majesty of the* PEOPLE, *the unappealable Judgment of the* PEOPLE" were common Phrases.

But it seems that there are Men in PENNSYLVANIA, who (to use the words of the great ALGERNON SIDNEY) look upon the People "like *Asses* and *Mastiff Dogs,* who ought to *work* and *fight,* to be *oppress'd* and *kill'd* for them."—And that they have neither *Privilege* or *Authority* to complain of their Sufferings, or remonstrate their Grievances. . . .

I shall now conclude, Sir, with this Request to you, that you will advise your visionary QUAKERS and DON QUIXOTES to consider these Things—And, that instead of yoking themselves to CANNON, and dragging them along to defend BARRACKS, and fight WIND-MILLS, they will suffer the Complaints of the People to be heard, their Grievances redress'd, and their Country rescued from total Ruin. —That they will immediately remove the INDIANS, or whatever else may create their Jealousy, and give them Cause to murmur. —And then we may expect to feel the happy Effects resulting from LIBERTY and LAW—to see the Quiet of the Province restor'd—and the Harmony and good Order of Government re-establish'd amongst us.

I am, etc.

Dated from my FARM-HOUSE, March 17th, 1764.*************
A Day dedicated to LIBERTY and ST. PATRICK.

FINIS.

[33–34]

210

E. The "Panther" Captivity Narrative (1787): Abraham Panther, "A Very Surprising Narrative of a Young Woman, Discovered in a Rocky-Cave. After Having Been Taken by the Savage Indians of the Wilderness, in the year 1777, and Seeing No Human Being for the Space of Nine Years. In a Letter from a Gentleman to his Friend (New York, 1790).

The "Panther" captivity narrative first appeared in 1787 (the year of Edgar Huntly's *action) and was reprinted over twenty times in editions that often differ slightly in their titles and other details. Scholars like Richard Slotkin have viewed it as a significant background text for* Edgar Huntly *(*Regeneration through Violence, *257–59, 384). Here we use the text of a 1790 New York printing, which is thus a version that may have been available to Brown. Although Brown rejects the fantastical elements of this kind of narrative and reverses the way captivity narratives typically shift blame for historical violence onto native peoples, several elements of this narrative seem to reappear in Brown's novel. The emphasis on patriarchal resistance to female empowerment, the dreamlike association of an empowered woman with threatening dogs, and the standard captivity narrative elements of the story are all relevant to* Edgar Huntly. *Since "Abraham Panther" is clearly a pseudonym and the text offers a parable of female empowerment and castrating revenge, Kathryn Derounian-Stodola points out that the writer of this narrative is as likely a woman as a man (*Women's Indian Captivity Narratives, *83–85).*

*****

Sir,

Having returned from the Westward—I now sit down, agreeable to your request, to give you an account of my journey—.

TWO days after you left my house Mr. *Camber* and myself, after providing ourselves with provisions, began our journey, determining to penetrate the Western Wilderness as far as prudence and safety would permit. We travelled for thirteen days in a westerly direction, without meeting anything uncommon or worthy description, except a very great variety of birds and wild beasts, which would frequently start before us and, as we had our muskets, contributed not a little to our amusement and support. The land we found exceedingly rich and fertile, every where well watered, and the variety of berries, nuts, ground-nuts, &c. afforded us very comfortable living.

On the 14th day of our travels, while we were observing a high hill, at the foot of which, ran a beautiful stream, which passing through a small plain, after a few windings, lost itself in a thicket—and observing the agreeable picturesque prospect, which presented itself on all sides, we were surprised at the sound of a voice, which seemed at no great distance.

At first we were uncertain whether the voice was a human one or that of some bird; as many extraordinary ones inhabited these wilds. After listening some time, the voice ceased, and we then determined to proceed up the hill, from whence, we judged, the sound to come; that we might, if possible, discover what voice it was that so much astonished us. Accordingly, crossing the brook, we proceeded up the hill; and having arrived near the summit, we again distinctly heard a voice singing in our own language a mournful song.—When the voice ceased, we observed a small foot path, we followed; and arriving at the top of the hill, passing round a large rock, then through a thicket of bushes, at the end of which, was a large opening: Upon our arrival here, to our inexpressible amazement, we beheld a most beautiful young Lady! sitting near the mouth of a cave!—She, not observing us, began again to sing. We now attempted to approach her; when a dog, which we had not before observed, sprung up and began to bark at us: at which she started up, and seeing us, gave a scream and swooned away.—We ran to her assistance, and having lifted her up, she soon recovered; and looking wildly at us, exclaimed—Heavens! Where am I?—And who, and from whence are you—We desired her to be under no uneasiness—told her were travellers—that we came only to view the country: but that in all our travels, we had not met with any thing that surprised us so much, as her extraordinary appearance, in a place we imagined totally unfrequented.

AFTER a little conversation, having convinced her of our peacable dispositions and that we intended her no injury, she invited us into the cave, when she refreshed us with some ground-nuts, a kind of apples, some Indian cake, and excellent water.—We found her to be an agreeable, sensible Lady; and after some conversation, we requested to know who she was, and how she came to this place.—She very readily complied with this request, and began her story as follows:—

"STRANGERS, your appearance and conversation, entitle you to my confidence; and, though my story cannot be very interesting or entertaining—yet it may possibly excite your pity, while it gratifies your curiosity.

"I was born near *Albany* in the year 1760.—My father was a man of some consequence, and considerable estate in the place where he lived.—I was his only child, and had I continued with him, possibly, I might have been happy. In the fifteenth year of my age, my father received into his family a young Gentleman of education, as his clerk. This young man, by his easy politeness—his good sense and agreeable manners, soon gained the esteem of all the family.—He had not been long with us, before he conceived an unfortunate passion for me; and, as, he had frequent opportunities, of conversing with me, his insinuating address, added to a sensible, engaging conversation, soon found way to my heart. He quickly perceived that I was not indifferent to him—and took occasion to declare his passion; which he did with so much ardour, and yet, with so much modesty, that I readily acknowledged a mutual attachment.

"After this we spent together many happy evenings, vowing unalterable love and fondly anticipating future happiness. We were however obliged to conceal our attachment from my father; who, as he was excessively eager in pursuit of riches, we had no reason to suppose he would countenance our loves, or consent to my marriage with a man destitute of fortune.

"It happened, one evening as we were discoursing by ourselves in a little garden, adjoining our house, that we were overheard by my father; who, either suspected our attachment to each other, or from some other motives, had purposely concealed himself in this place, where he knew we usually walked. Next morning, my father, with an angry countenance, upbraided my lover with treacherously engaging his daughter's affections—and calling him many hard names, dismissed him, with peremptory orders never again to enter his house. It was in vain to remonstrate; he insisted on being obeyed—and ordered me to my chamber where he confined me.— My lover then wrote to my father, stating to him our situation; requested leave to address me and informed him of our mutual engagements, with the reason for not sooner consulting him.—To this, my father ordered the young Gentleman to trouble him no further with his impertinence nor ever to think of any further connection with me. By means, however of an old servant, long attached to my lover, we found means to carry on a correspondence; and, in about a month after, we contrived matters, that I had an interview with my lover: I then agreed to quit my father's house, and retire into the country, to see whether my absence would not soften his heart, and induce him, to consent to my happiness: I therefore packed up some clothes, and other things, and left my father's house on the evening of the 10th of May, 1777, and retired several miles into the country, to a little hut, where my lover left me, and went in disguise, to see what effect my absence had upon my father. In five days he returned, and informed me, that, my father, enraged at my elopement, had hired several men to search the country in pursuit of us; and that he threatened vengeance to us both—and declared that he would be the death of the man who carried off his daughter.—Thunder-struck at this account, I knew not what to do. To attempt a reconciliation with my father was vain; or, if possible to be effected, my lover must be sacrificed to it, which would make me insupportably unhappy. In order to elude the search of those who were in pursuit of us, we proposed to move further into the country, and there to wait till time should calm my father's rage, or effectually cool his resentment.

"We accordingly left the hut, and traveled at an easy rate, for four days, determining to avoid being taken.—But, O! how shall I relate the horrid scene that followed?—Towards the evening of the 4th day, we were surrounded and made prisoners, by a party of Indians who led us about two miles, and then barbarously murdered my lover! cutting and mangling him in the most inhuman manner! then, after tying him to a stake, they kindled a fire round him! and, while he burnt, they ran round, singing and dancing, rejoicing in their brutal cruelty! I was at a few rods distance during this transaction! and this scene had well nigh deprived me of life.—I fainted away and lay some time motionless on the ground.—When I recovered my senses, I perceived that my guard had joined his companions, some of whom were seated round in rings, and others continued singing and dancing. Seeing them all engaged. I got up and stood for about an hour:—I then sat down by the side of a tree and, being overcome by fatigue, and the sight I had seen, I either fainted or fell asleep, and knew nothing till the next morning about 7 o'clock.—'Tis impossible for me to describe my feelings; or for you to conceive a situation more wretched than mine at this time. Surrounded, as I supposed, on all sides with danger, I knew not what to do, without a guide to direct, or friend to protect me. Often I was upon the point of returning, and endeavoring to find, and deliver myself a prisoner to those Indians, to whose cruelty I had so lately been a witness; and, had I then seen them, I certainly should have delivered myself into their power. At length I got up, and after walking some time, I resolved to seek some place of shelter, where I might be secure from storms by day, and from beasts at night; where I might dwell till a period should be put to my miserable existence.

"With this view I wandered about for fourteen days, without knowing whither I went. By day, the spontaneous produce of the earth supplied me with food; by night the ground was my couch, and the canopy of heaven my only covering.—In the afternoon of the fifteenth day I was surprised at seeing a man, of a gigantic figure walking towards me: to run I knew would be vain, and no less vain to attempt to hide. He soon came up with me, and accosted me in a language I did not understand, and after surveying me for some time, he took me by the hand, and led me to this cave; having entered, pointed to a stone seat on which I sat down; he then gave me to eat some nuts and some Indian cake, after which, he stretched himself out on a long stone, covered with skins which he used as a bed, and several times motioned to me to lay myself beside him. I declined his offer, and at length he rose in a passion, and went into another apartment of the cave and brought forth a sword and hatchet. He then motioned to me, that I must either accept of his bed, or expect death for my obstinacy. I still declined his offer, and was resolved to die rather than comply with his desire. He then brought a walnut bark, and having bound me, pointing to the east, intimating that he left me till morning to consider his proposal; he then returned to his bed and, happily for me, he soon fell asleep. Having the liberty of my teeth, I soon made out to bite the bark in two, with which he had bound me, by which I found means to liberate myself while he continued sleeping. I considered this as the only opportunity I should have of freeing myself from him—as I expected that he would use violence when he awoke, to make me partake of his bed, and, as I knew I could not escape him by flight, I did not long deliberate—but took up the hatchet he had brought, and, summoning resolution, I, with three blows, effectually put an end to his existence.

"I then cut off his head, and next-day, having cut him in quarters, drew him out of the cave, about half a mile distance; when, after covering him with leaves and bushes, returned to this place. I now found myself alone, in possession of this cave, in which are several apartments. I here found a kind of Indian corn, which I planted and have yearly raised a small quantity. I here contented myself as well as my wretched situation would permit—here have I existed for nine long years, in all which time this faithful Dog which I found in the cave, has been my only companion, and you are the only human beings, who ever heard me tell my tale."

HERE she finished her narration, and, after shedding a plentiful shower of tears, and a little conversation, she requested us to take rest, which request we willingly complied with.

Next morning she conducted us through the cave in which were four apartments, one of which appeared pretty deep in the earth, in which was a spring of excellent water.—in the other three were nothing very remarkable except four skulls, which we supposed were of persons murdered by the owner of the cave, or of his former companions. We found also three hatchets, four bows, and several arrows, one large tinder box, one sword, one old gun, and a number of skins of dead beasts, and a few clothes. The bows, some arrows, the sword, and one hatchet, we brought away, which are now in my possession.

After continuing in the cave five days, we proposed returning home, and requested the Lady to accompany us. At first she refused to quit her cave; but after some persuasion, she consented.

"Gentlemen, said she, I trust myself to your protection—I have no reason to question your good intentions, and willingly believe, from my small acquaintance with you, that you will not seek to heap affliction upon a weak woman, already borne down with misery and sorrow."

We together left the cave, on the morning of the sixth day after our arrival in it, and travelling the way we went, arrived at my house in seventeen days. After resting about a week, we accompanied the Lady, agreeable to her desire, to her father's house. The old man did not at first recognize his daughter, but being told who she was, he looked at her for some time, and then tenderly embraced her, crying, *"O! my child, my long lost child! do I once more hold thee in my arms!"* He then fainted away. We with difficulty brought him to life; but the scene had overcome him; he opened his eyes, and being a little recovered, requested to know where she had lived so long, and what had happened to her, since her leaving his house. We desired him to wait till he should be better recovered, but he begged to be satisfied immediately, observing that he had but a few moments to live. She then briefly related what had happened to her, and the tragical death of her lover.—He seemed much affected, and when she had finished, he took her by the hand, and affectionately squeezed it, and asked her forgiveness, and attempted to say something more—but immediately fainted; all our endeavors to recover him were in vain, he lay about seven hours, and then expired.

He left a handsome fortune to his daughter, who, notwithstanding his cruelty, was deeply affected at his sudden and unexpected death. This adventure, the most singular and extraordinary of my life, I have communicated, agreeable to your desire, as it really happened, without addition or diminition, and am Sir, your's, &c.

ABRAHAM PANTHER

F. Charles Brockden Brown, Elihu Hubbard Smith, William Dunlap; Dossier on *Sky-Walk* (March–April 1798).

Sky-Walk was the first novel Brown completed, but it was lost through a series of mishaps in 1798. It featured Brown's first use of somnambulism, references to the Delaware people, and other motifs and emphases that were revisited in Edgar Huntly *and other fictions, including the 1805 story "Somnambulism. A fragment." The excerpts here provide virtually all of the information that survives about this novel: an announcement of its planned publication from* The Weekly Magazine; *the one surviving passage from the novel, which was printed in that magazine to promote its upcoming publication; Brown's reply to a query about the meaning of the title* Sky-Walk; *and passages from the diaries of Elihu Hubbard Smith and William Dunlap, who read and responded to the novel in April 1798.*

Brown began the novel in late 1797 and appears to have finished it by the end of March 1798. After the manuscript circulated among friends in Brown's New York circle, it was at least partially set in book form in Philadelphia by printer James Watters, owner of The Weekly Magazine. *When Watters died in that year's yellow fever epidemic, however, his executors set the price of the finished sheets so high that Brown's friends could not repurchase them, and the manuscript and sheets were subsequently lost.*

*****

1. Speratus [C. B. Brown], "Letter I." *The Weekly Magazine* 1.7 (March 17 1798): 202.

To the Editor of the Weekly Magazine.

———

"Posthac paulo majora canamus"[2]

Virgil.

*****

You will be good enough to inform your readers that, in a short time, their patronage will be solicited to a work in which it is endeavoured to amuse the imagination and improve the heart. A tale that may rival the performances of this kind which have lately issued from the English press, will be unexampled in America. Whether the work alluded to deserve this praise the writer is, of all men, least qualified to judge.

Genius, like the joints and muscles of the frame, must have a progress. It is indeed a poor plea, by which to shield ourselves from the indignation of criticism, that our work, like ourselves, is juvenile, and that, aided and fostered by encouragement and lenity, the seed that is at present so inconsiderable may in time expand into the loveliness of the rose, and the deliciousness of the anana: yet this plea, however insufficient to procure us friends, may be true. This writer does not rest his hopes upon the indulgence due to the unripeness of his age, and limitedness of his experience. All

---

[2] "Paulo majora canamus" is a well-known epigram from Virgil, *Eclogues* IV, 1: "Let us sing of higher things." Brown adds the first word "Posthac," meaning "from now on." William Wordsworth used this phrase as the epigraph for his 1803–1805 "Ode: Intimations of Immortality."

that he can do to make his book a good one of the kind, he has done. Every new attempt will, of course, be more likely to succeed than the last.

To the story-telling moralist the United States is a new and untrodden field. He who shall examine objects with his own eyes, who shall employ the European models merely for the improvement of his taste, and adapt his fiction to all that is genuine and peculiar in the scene before him, will be entitled at least to the praise of originality.

Here, as elsewhere, every man is engaged in the gratification of some passion. Some pleasure, intellectual or corporeal, or the grand instrument of all kinds of pleasure, money, constitutes the scope of every one's pursuit: but our ecclesiastical and political system, our domestic and social maxims, are, in many respects, entirely our own. He, therefore, who paints, not from books, but from nature, who introduces those lines and hues in which we differ, rather than those in which we resemble our kindred nations beyond the ocean, may lay some claim to the patronage of his countrymen.

The value of such works lies without doubt in their moral tendency. The popular tales have their merit, but there is one thing in which they are deficient. They are generally adapted to one class of readers only. By a string of well connected incidents, they amuse the idle and thoughtless; but are spurned at by those who are satisfied with nothing but strains of lofty eloquence, by the exhibition of powerful motives, and a sort of audaciousness of character. The world is governed, not by the simpleton, but by the man of soaring passions and intellectual energy. By the display of such only can we hope to enchain the attention and ravish the souls of those who study and reflect. To gain their homage it is not needful to forego the approbation of those whose circumstances have hindered them from making the same progress. A contexture of facts capable of suspending the faculties of every soul in curiosity, may be joined with depth of views into human nature and all the subtleties of reasoning. Whether these properties be wedded in the present performance, the impartial reader must judge.

The writer is a native and resident of this city. Some part of his tale is a picture of truth. Facts have supplied the foundation of the whole. Its title is "SKY-WALK, or, THE MAN UNKNOWN TO HIMSELF.—*An American Tale.*"

SPERATUS.

*****

2. C. B. Brown, "Extract from the 'SKY-WALK.' *The Weekly Magazine,* 1.8 (March 24, 1798): 228–31.

[In our last number notice was given of a New Work of Invention and Reflection, which is ready to be offered to public patronage. The nature of its design, the singularity of its title, the circumstance of its being written by a native citizen of Philadelphia, and of its being on the point of soliciting the encouragement of the public, have induced us, for the satisfaction of our readers, to solicit, from the author, the privilege of making an extract from his manuscript. Although unable to fix on any *part* capable of conveying a perfect idea of the *whole,* we trust the following may serve as a specimen of the work.]

*****

I HAVE stated the amount of my obligations to my patroness, such as they continued to be for some time. I did not desire to increase them. I would much more willingly have consented to lessen the number, but her benevolence with regard to me, as well as others, was a principle that was never weary. She was eagle-eyed after occasions for bestowing a benefit. Her decision was judicious and prompt, and all obstacles must yield to the impetuosity with which she hastened to the execution of her purposes. My condition for some time, together with my disinclination to receive it, was such as disabled her from conferring any extraordinary or eccentric obligation. But events happened which put this in her power, and contributed to aggravate the remorse to which I was ultimately destined.

While on my travels, in company with *Ormond Courtney,* we took Bourdeaux in our route. We spent some time in this city. During our abode here, I formed an intimate acquaintance with a young Irish merchant, settled here. He had been a student in Dublin college, in which situation we first saw each other, and was afterwards apprenticed to a merchant in Bourdeaux. His apprenticeship having expired, he set up for himself, and his affairs were not unprosperous. He had married an amiable country-woman and had two lovely children. A guileless disposition was united in him with considerable talents. He loved literature, and enjoyed the uncommon felicity of possessing a wife equally enamoured of those pursuits, and exquisitely qualified to share with him in the advantages they promised. Notwithstanding this, he was sedulous, and unremitted in his attention to his profession, it being his aim to obtain, as soon as possible, a fund which would enable him to retire with his family to some pleasant spot in his native country, and spend the remainder of his life in his darling occupations, and in the education of his children.

His industry merited the success which it met with. In no long time he had accomplished his wishes; had disengaged himself from his profession, and converted his property into money. With this he embarked for Ireland, intending to purchase a small rural estate, and when every thing was prepared for their reception, to return to France, for his family who, meanwhile, remained at Bourdeaux.

I had heard, from time to time, of his motions and intentions, and had performed for him various little services for which my situation peculiarly qualified me. I had heard of his intention to return, and knew at what period, and in what ship he purposed to embark. I entertained a very sincere affection for this man. Those excellent qualities, which were hidden by his constitutional and invincible reserve from others, I had been able to discover, and appreciate at their just value. I looked for his arrival with considerable impatience. Day after day elapsed, and no tidings were received of him. On enquiry, I found that the vessel which was to waft him over had arrived, and that he had been one of the passengers. He had immediately landed his baggage, and disappeared. His proceeding was mysterious. I fully expected that he would come to me as soon as he landed, and could not conceive any ordinary cause that should prevent him from doing this. There was nothing, however, that could justify anxiety; and I was contented to believe that, sooner or later. I should be informed of his designs.

Sometime after I had occasion to visit one of the prisons of the city. One of Mrs. Courtney's tenants had been arrested for debt. There were strong symptoms of hardship and injustice in his case. She was desirous of doing something towards his relief; and, for this purpose, requested me to visit, and examine into the nature of the claim that was made upon him. I had performed my task, and was returning to the gate, when the figure of Annesley, my Bourdeaux friend, presented itself. He was pale with dejection, and disfigured with negligence. We easily recognised each other. After expressing my astonishment at the circumstances of this meeting, I desired him to account for his being found in his present situation.

This was done in a few words. He had been joint security with his father for a considerable debt. The debtor had absconded, and left the burthen of payment on his securities. His father was dead, and himself alone answerable. In the calculations he had made for the future, he had not omitted this incumbrance. Before he deemed himself in possession of a sufficiency, he was to obtain so much as would enable him both to discharge this debt, and to purchase an estate of a certain value. He had not concealed these views from his creditor, who by no means relished the delay which this plan rendered unavoidable. He conceived that if Annesley could be by any means prevailed upon to return, he might be compelled by the terrors of a law-suit, to discharge the debt immediately, though perhaps to the utter destruction of his fortune and his hopes. For this end expedients had been used to persuade Annesley, that the sum had been reimbursed by the original debtor, and that he might consequently return to his native country without fear of molestation.

Annesley now supposed, that the means by which this belief had been instilled into him, had been projected by the cunning of his creditor, who had acted with so much circumspection, that the validity of his claim was in no degree impaired by them. The artifice had been successful. Annesley had not been many minutes on his native shore when he was seized and conveyed to prison. This misfortune was aggravated by another. In the trepidation and dismay which was occasioned, by this unlooked-for event, he had neglected to pay a suitable attention to his baggage which had been rifled, and the whole amount of his fortune had become the prey of some rapacious hand. He was thus, in the course of a few hours, reduced from a state of comparative prosperity, to utter distress. So much had not been left as to exempt him from living upon charity, and he was unable even to hire a messenger who might inform his friends of his condition.

He was unable to bear up against disasters so terrible. He had resigned himself without a struggle to his destiny. The suddenness of this calamity had bereaved him of that force of mind by which he was usually distinguished. He looked forward to death and oblivion, as the only cure of his woes.

I found my friend in this situation. It was so completely the reverse of all that I had expected, that I could scarcely bring myself to believe it real. It became me to exert myself in behalf of my friend: I obviated his more urgent and immediate necessities: I went to his creditor: I made the strongest appeals to his justice and compassion: I stated the original of the debt: I dwelt upon the character of Annesley; the sincerity of his intention to pay this demand, as well as all others; his utter incapacity to do this, whatever his inclination should be; an incapacity produced merely by the creditor's own precipitation: I painted his distress, and those of his family; but all my eloquence was fruitless. The wretch with whom I had to deal was insensible to all considerations but those of interest and resentment. He perceived that he had put himself at a greater distance than ever from being paid. This reflection excited his rage. He ascribed his disappointment to Annesley's negligence, and was determined to punish him by all the rigours that the law would inflict.

The behaviour of this man exhibited a common, but instructive spectacle. He took up the theme of justice where I had dismissed it. The original debt had occurred in a way that indicated a grasping disposition in this man. Yet he alone, in his own eyes, was the injured person, and the sufferer. It was to him that reparation and vengeance were due. He must be just to himself, and to his family. The law must take its course. When paid what was indisputably his due, he should be satisfied. What more could be demanded? He was neither fool nor dotard to sacrifice his just claims for the sake of a whining tale. Annesley had none to accuse but himself. He must endure the consequences of his own act. Had he the impudence to require that another should suffer for his folly?

I quickly perceived that nothing was to be hoped from the flexibility of this man. Yet there was no other expedient. Search was instituted for the property stolen, but no traces of it could be discovered. All that I possessed in the world, was not sufficient to extricate him from the difficulty. It is not to be supposed, that these reflections did not impair my usual cheerfulness. The change was quickly discovered by the lady. She anxiously questioned me as to the cause. I believed no advantage would flow to any one from its disclosure. Nothing less than the whole sum would restore him to liberty; but this, though it would rescue him from gaol, would leave him and his family in indigence. I was besides unwilling to augment the burthen of obligation, which already exceeded my strength.

Her curiosity would not be baffled or eluded. Her interrogatories were too vehement and direct, to allow me to escape by silence or evasion. Having heard my tale, not without those tokens of sympathy which she was ever prone to shed, she reprimanded me gently for my unjustifiable reserve. Why should I suppose that if she were unable or unwilling to repair this evil to the utmost, she should not be disposed to go as far as her ability extended? It is true that the sum which was owing was large in itself, but was small when compared with her revenues, and those of her friends, on whose concurrence, in the relief of distress, she could depend. If I had justly represented the character of Annesley, to restore him to liberty, and raise him to security and independence, was conferring nothing less than a national benefit. She had noticed the first appearance of sadness in me. She had taken measures to ascertain the cause. She was already apprised of most of the facts that I had mentioned, and had formed her resolution. She concluded with directing me to pay this debt, and transfer to Annesley an estate, to be held by him on easy terms, by which he was placed in a situation little inferior to that which his fancy had sketched as the summit of his wishes.

*****

3. C. B. Brown, Untitled Reply to A. Z., *The Weekly Magazine* 1.10 (April 7, 1798): 318.

A. Z. requests to be informed of the meaning of the title of the work lately announced, for publication, in this Magazine. In answer to him, it may be said that *"Sky Walk,"* is nothing more than a popular corruption of "Ski Wakkee," or *Big Spring*, the name given by the Lenni Lennassee, or Delaware Indians, to the district where the principal scenes of this novel are transacted.

*****

4. E. H. Smith, excerpts from *The Diary of Elihu Hubbard Smith* (1973), 438–39.

Tuesday, 17 [April 1798] . . . Came home, & read the Introduction & first four Chapters of C.B. Brown's Novel—"Sky-Walk"—the Ms. of which Dunlap brought to me, as also the IIIrd and IVth parts of "Alcuin."[3] This "Sky-Walk" is an extraordinary thing. The basis of it is *Somnambulism*. . . .

Wednesday, 18 . . . The rest of the day has been devoted to the eager perusal of "Sky-Walk"—which I have not yet finished—tho I have read upon it this day, at least ten hours.

Thursday, 19 . . . In the morning I had finished "Sky-Walk." It had inexpressibly interested me. My whole spirit was affected by it. But my perusal had been too rapid, the interest too violent, too many other ideas had passed 'thro my mind, to allow me to judge properly of it.

On these occasions we must feel—examination follows—the last thing is to judge. Johnson[4] had two chapters. After Radclift's departure, he took up the book & read aloud the third and fourth. I followed him, and read to the tenth. The peculiar merits of the work were more obvious to me now, than before; for a double reason. My perusal was less passionate, & I had the opportunity to mark the effects it produced on my friend. He has retired to his bed in a throb & tumult of curiosity, interest, and admiration. I have also read the third and fourth parts of "Alcuin" to-day. . . .

---

[3] "Alcuin": Brown's feminist-Woldwinite dialogue, which Smith helped him publish in March–April 1798. On the same days Smith reads *Sky-Walk*, he is also proofreading *Alcuin*.

[4] William Johnson, a young attorney, Smith's roommate at 45 Pine Street, and another member of Brown's New York circle. Brown moved into the Pine Street apartment as a third roommate in July–August 1798. After Smith died of yellow fever on September 19, Brown and Johnson left New York together to recover at William Dunlap's home in Perth Amboy, New Jersey.

*****

5. William Dunlap, excerpts from *Diary of William Dunlap* (1943), 240, 248–49.

[April] 11th [1798; in Philadelphia] . . . Call on Brown who goes with me to the Booksellers Ormrod & Humphreys & gives me some account of his "Sky Walk" he says it is founded on Somnambulism. . . .

[April] 21st [in New York] . . . At Club in Smith's room Smith & Johnson (who drank tea with me) W W W[5] & Mr Radcliff. Smith reads in "Sky walk" which interests us all very much.

[April] 22nd . . . When I returned I found Smith who read in "Sky Walk" for us.

[April] 23rd . . . Read "Sky Walk" to my Wife. This is a very superior performance.

[April] 24th . . . Afternoon read "Sky Walk" Evening Theatre, "Siege of Belgrade & Modern Antiques" in the house 317$. W W W & [Dwight?] pass the evening with [us]: Smyth came in & staid after the others reading "Sky Walk" to us unto the end. I give high credit to Charles for this work, yet am I not satisfied; Is not Lorimer to much exalted—too fascinating? Why are we not satisfied as to the pistol of Avonedge? And how are we to account for the dagger, so opportunely ready in the Chamber of Mrs Courtney? perhaps these are trifles—the work is masterly.

G. Charles Brockden Brown, excerpt from "On the Effects of Theatric Exhibitions." *The Weekly Magazine of Original Essays, Fugitive Pieces, and Interesting Intelligence* 1.12 (April 1798).

This discussion of theater is a good example of Brown's ideas about the progressive social purpose of art, and of his desire to promote modern, forward-looking art forms. In this excerpt (the first third of the essay), Brown states his belief that the theater, and by extension all art forms, can be used to teach audiences and illustrate the ways in which virtue can occur. He is critical of current forms of American theater, however, and condemns the local staging of British plays, not because he wants a native or national art form, but because most British plays focus on premodern, aristocratic themes and behaviors that cannot provide appropriate models for the modern, bourgeois audience. A backward-looking theater, in fact, transmits counterproductive behaviors to its audience. In this passage, Brown argues on this basis that Shakespeare is particularly useless for contemporary audiences. Brown's criticism is not against viewer pleasure or popular forms of art, but against artistic pleasure that does not transmit progressive social ideas and behaviors.

*****

---

[5] William W. Woolsey, another member of the New York circle.

To ascertain the tendency of plays is by no means difficult. There is no more powerful mode of winning the attention, and swaying the passions of mankind. Mental power is quite a different consideration from the moral application of that power. Genius affords no security from error. The writers of plays have been generally necessitous and profligate. They have therefore written under the influence of wrong conceptions of duty and happiness; and, in order to effect their purpose, which was gain, have deemed themselves obliged to humor the caprices and pamper the vicious appetites, of those who frequent these spectacles.

This surely is no inequitable statement of the motives of dramatic writers. A very slight acquaintance with plays will convince us that this is the fact. It is equally easy to account for it: Nay, the circumstances of mankind have been such as to render this effect unavoidable. Our pieces are the productions of British writers. That this nation is luxurious and corrupt; that the progress of commerce and refinement have widely diffused the plagues of luxury and poverty; that those classes of the people who chiefly frequent the theatre are the opulent and voluptuous on the one hand, and, on the other, the ignorant and debauched, will surely be readily admitted. That dramatic writers have seldom been distinguished by purity of morals; that they have written to supply their pecuniary cravings, and have therefore studiously accommodated themselves to the circumstances of the times and the taste of their audience, is no less incontestable.

All the world have combined to idolize the genius of Shakespeare, but no one, that I know of, has applauded the rectitude of his morals. His pieces tend to shake the soul; to enchain the attention; and to captivate our sympathy. What then? If they furnish incitement to ill; obscure our moral discernment; and deprave our appetites and passions, their tendency may be safely pronounced to be injurious. Our judgment may applaud the fortunate invention and skilful contexture of characters and incidents, but these properties are perfectly consistent with the property of fostering our selfish passions and perverting our moral principles.

The tendency of a literary composition is variable. It may produce opposite effects in different persons or different circumstances. The dramas of this poet may be *read*, by some, with benefit. The worst book that ever was invented, may afford, to some minds, plentiful and valuable instruction; but the present question respects the influence of theatrical *exhibitions*. What benefit does an audience, as audiences are usually constituted, derive from the performance of Hamlet or Othello?

But Shakespeare is only one in a very extensive catalogue. The series of plays commonly exhibited, exclusive of those of Shakespeare, begins at the reign of Charles the Second. The enormous corruption of manners at that period, and the consequent corruptions of the drama are notorious. No one will be the champion of these. So far as the pieces of that age are now performed, it will be readily admitted that their tendency is hurtful.

It is commonly observed that the plays of a later period are less impure. It must be owned that manners have improved since that period, but the improvement is extremely slight. The tragedies are pompous, and, to the majority of theatrical spectators, totally unmeaning. Kings and nobles of some remote age, and acting upon maxims foreign to the experience of men of the present times and of middling classes, speaking a language as unintelligible as Greek, and raving about thrones and mistresses are not very edifying examples to the multitude. The comedies are strings of incidents occurring among persons of a polished rank in society, interlarded with the blunders of the ignorant, and the vices of the poor; and embellished with spurious or obscene wit. The farces are replete with broad mirth, low buffoonery, and pictures, which for their vulgarity and grossness, are well adapted to the taste of the majority of playgoers.

What is the tendency of these? Do they inculcate the virtues of temperance and fortitude? Do they contribute to exalt and purify the social affections, and make us sagacious to discern, and sedulous to pursue the general good? Do they rectify our mistaken notions of virtue and duty, and supply us with incitements to the practice of it? Or do they, on the contrary, generate the lust of power and riches, and diffuse the poison of dissipation and voluptuousness? These questions are easily answered. It is sufficiently manifest that the influence of these exhibitions, so far as that influence ought to be ascribed to the nature of the scene exhibited, is hurtful to morals and happiness. . . .

H. Charles Brockden Brown, "Walstein's School of History. From the German of Krants of Gotha." *The Monthly Magazine and American Review* 1:5 (August–September 1799).

Appearing in August–September 1799, at the height of Brown's novelistic phase and just as he was finishing Edgar Huntly, *"Walstein's School of History" is an important fictionalized essay in which Brown articulates his plan for novel writing, identifying both the rationale for his novels and the themes and techniques he will use to build them. Along with "The Difference Between History and Romance," which further analyzes the close relation of historical and fiction writing, this essay is a key document for understanding Brown's aims and methods in writing fiction. It also arguably establishes Brown as the first modern U.S. literary critic, in the sense of one who explores how texts construct meaning and function in society rather than simply asserting the relative merits of literary productions judged against an imaginary standard of excellence. In addition, as many scholars observe, the essay's final paragraphs provide an example of this method, which is, in fact, an accurate outline of the plot of Brown's novel* Arthur Mervyn.*

As noted in this volume's Introduction, the fictional framework of the piece concerns the literary productions of Walstein, a professor of history at Jena, and his leading student Engel. It is possible that Brown's choice of the name "Walstein" refers to influential German philosopher and writer Friedrich Schiller (1759–1805), a professor of history and philosophy at Jena, whose progressive dramas, fictions, and doctrines about art were well known to Brown and his friends.

In Brown's essay, Walstein provides a first model for the progressive novel by combining history and romance in such a way as to promote "moral and political" engagement while rejecting universal truths. Walstein's fictions concern classical or elite figures such as the

Roman orator Cicero (whose death marked the end of the Roman republic) and Portugal's Marquis de Pombal (an Enlightenment reformer and civic leader). Engel modernizes and develops Walstein's model by adding that a romance, to be effective in today's world, must be addressed to a wide popular audience and draw its characters not from the elite, but from the same lower-status group that will read and be moved by the work. Engel insists that history and romance alike should address issues and situations familiar to their modern audiences, most notably the common inequalities arising from sex and property. Thus Engel's modern literature will insert ordinary individuals like his character Olivo Ronsica, or Brown's Edgar Huntly, into situations of stress resulting from contemporary tensions related to money and other property relations, and erotic desire and other forms of personal relations. Finally, Engel adds that a thrilling style is also necessary if modern fictions are to hold readers' interest and move them toward progressive values and behaviors.

*****

WALSTEIN was professor of history at Jena, and, of course, had several pupils. Nine of them were more assiduous in their attention to their tutor than the others. This circumstance came at length to be noticed by each other, as well as by Walstein, and naturally produced good-will and fellowship among them. They gradually separated themselves from the negligent and heedless crowd, cleaved to each other, and frequently met to exchange and compare ideas. Walstein was prepossessed in their favor by their studious habits, and their veneration for him. He frequently admitted them to exclusive interviews, and, laying aside his professional dignity, conversed with them on the footing of a friend and equal.

Walstein's two books were read by them with great attention. These were justly to be considered as exemplifications of his rules, as specimens of the manner in which history was to be studied and written.

No wonder that they found few defects in the model; that they gradually adopted the style and spirit of his composition, and, from admiring and contemplating, should, at length, aspire to imitate. It could not but happen, however, that the criterion of excellence would be somewhat modified in passing through the mind of each; that each should have his peculiar modes of writing and thinking.

All observers, indeed, are, at the first and transient view, more affected by resemblances than differences. The works of Walstein and his disciples were hastily ascribed to the same hand. The same minute explication of motives, the same indissoluble and well-woven tissue of causes and effects, the same unity and coherence of design, the same power of engrossing the attention, and the same felicity, purity, and compactness of style, are conspicuous in all.

There is likewise evidence, that each had embraced the same scheme of accounting for events, and the same notions of moral and political duty. Still, however, there were marks of difference in the different nature of the themes that were adopted, and of the purpose which the productions of each writer seemed most directly to promote.

We may aim to exhibit the influence of some moral or physical cause, to enforce some useful maxim, or illustrate some momentous truth. This purpose may be more or less simple, capable of being diffused over the surface of an empire or a century, or of shrinking into the compass of a day, and the bounds of a single thought.

The elementary truths of morals and politics may merit the preference: our theory may adapt itself to, and derive confirmation from whatever is human. Newton and Xavier, Zengis and William Tell, may bear close and manifest relation to the system we adopt, and their fates be linked, indissolubly, in a common chain.

The physician may be attentive to the constitution and diseases of man in all ages and nations. Some opinions, on the influence of a certain diet, may make him eager to investigate the physical history of every human being. No fact, falling within his observation, is useless or anomalous. All sensibly contribute to the symmetry and firmness of some structure which he is anxious to erect. Distances of place and time, and diversities of moral conduct, may, by no means, obstruct their union into one homogeneous mass.

I am apt to think, that the moral reasoner may discover principles equally universal in their application, and giving birth to similar coincidence and harmony among characters and events. Has not this been effected by WALSTEIN?

Walstein composed two works. One exhibited, with great minuteness, the life of Cicero; the other, that of the Marquis of Pombal. What link did his reason discover, or his fancy create between times, places, situations, events, and characters so different? He reasoned thus:–

Human society is powerfully modified by individual members. The authority of individuals sometimes flows from physical incidents; birth, or marriage, for example. Sometimes it springs, independently of physical relation, and, in defiance of them, from intellectual vigor. The authority of kings and nobles exemplifies the first species of influence. Birth and marriage, physical, and not moral incidents, entitle them to rule.

The second kind of influence, that flowing from intellectual vigor, is remarkably exemplified in Cicero and Pombal. In this respect they are alike.

The mode in which they reached eminence, and in which they exercised power, was different, in consequence of different circumstances. One lived in a free, the other in a despotic state. One gained it from the prince, the other from the people. The end of both, for their degree of virtue was the same, was the general happiness. They promoted this end by the best means which human wisdom could suggest. One cherished, the other depressed the aristocracy. Both were right in their means as in their end; and each, had he exchanged conditions with the other, would have acted like that other.

Walstein was conscious of the uncertainty of history. Actions and motives cannot be truly described. We can only make approaches to the truth. The more attentively we observe mankind, and study ourselves, the greater will this uncertainty appear, and the farther shall we find ourselves from truth.

This uncertainty, however, has some bounds. Some circumstances of events, and some events, are more capable of evidence than others. The same may be said of motives. Our guesses as to the motives of some actions are more probable than the guesses that relate to other actions. Though no one can state the motives from which any action has flowed, he may enumerate motives from which it is quite certain, that the action did *not* flow.

The lives of Cicero and Pombal are imperfectly related by historians. An impartial view of that which history has preserved makes the belief of their wisdom and virtue more probable than the contrary belief.

Walstein desired the happiness of mankind. He imagined that the exhibition, of virtue and talents, forcing its way to sovereign power, and employing that power for the national good, was highly conducive to their happiness.

By exhibiting a virtuous being in opposite conditions, and pursuing his end by the means suited to his own condition, he believes himself displaying a model of right conduct, and furnishing incitements to imitate that conduct, supplying men not only with knowledge of just ends and just means, but with the love and the zeal of virtue.

How men might best promote the happiness of mankind in given situations, was the problem that he desired to solve. The more portraits of human excellence he was able to exhibit the better; but his power in this respect was limited. The longer his life and his powers endured the more numerous would his portraits become. Futurity, however, was precarious, and, therefore, it behoved him to select, in the first place, the most useful theme.

His purpose was not to be accomplished by a brief or meagre story. To illuminate the understanding, to charm curiosity, and sway the passions, required that events should be copiously displayed and artfully linked, that motives should be vividly depicted, and scenes made to pass before the eye. This has been performed. Cicero is made to compose the story of his political and private life from his early youth to his flight from Astura, at the coalition of Antony and Octavius. It is addressed to Atticus, and meant to be the attestor of his virtue, and his vindicator with posterity.

The style is energetic, and flows with that glowing impetuosity which was supposed to actuate the writer. Ardent passions, lofty indignation, sportive elegance, pathetic and beautiful simplicity, take their turns to controul his pen, according to the nature of the theme. New and striking portraits are introduced of the great actors on the stage. New lights are cast upon the principal occurrences. Everywhere are marks of profound learning, accurate judgment, and inexhaustible invention. Cicero here exhibits himself in all the forms of master, husband, father, friend, advocate, pro-consul, consul, and senator.

To assume the person of Cicero, as the narrator of his own transactions, was certainly an hazardous undertaking. Frequent errors and lapses, violations of probability, and incongruities in the style and conduct of this imaginary history with the genuine productions of Cicero, might be reasonably expected, but these are not found. The more conversant we are with the authentic monuments, the more is our admiration at the felicity of this imposture enhanced.

The conspiracy of Cataline is here related with abundance of circumstances not to be found in Sallust. The difference, however, is of that kind which result from a deeper insight into human nature, a more accurate acquaintance with the facts, more correctness of arrangement, and a deeper concern in the progress and issue of the story. What is false, is so admirable in itself, so conformable to Roman modes and sentiments, so self-consistent, that one is almost prompted to accept it as the gift of inspiration.

The whole system of Roman domestic manners, of civil and military government, is contained in this work. The facts are either collected from the best antiquarians, or artfully deduced from what is known, or invented with a boldness more easy to admire than to imitate. Pure fiction is never employed but when truth was unattainable.

The end designed by Walstein, is no less happily accomplished in the second, than in the first performance. The style and spirit of the narrative is similar; the same skill in the exhibition of characters and deduction of events, is apparent; but events and characters are wholly new. Portugal, its timorous populace, its besotted monks, its jealous and effeminate nobles, and its cowardly prince, are vividly depicted. The narrator of this tale is, as in the former instance, the subject of it. After his retreat from court, Pombal consecrates his leisure to the composition of his own memoirs.

Among the most curious portions of this work, are those relating to the constitution of the inquisition, the expulsion of the Jesuits, the earthquake, and the conspiracy of Daveiro.

The Romish religion, and the feudal institutions, are the causes that chiefly influence the modern state of Europe. Each of its kingdoms and provinces exhibits the operations of these causes, accompanied and modified by circumstances peculiar to each. Their genuine influence is thwarted, in different degrees, by learning and commerce. In Portugal, they have been suffered to produce the most extensive and unmingled mischiefs. Portugal, therefore, was properly selected as an example of moral and political degeneracy, and as a theatre in which virtue might be shewn with most advantage, contending with the evils of misgovernment and superstition.

In works of this kind, though the writer is actuated by a single purpose, many momentous and indirect inferences will flow from his story. Perhaps the highest and lowest degrees in the scale of political improvement have been respectively exemplified by the Romans and the Portuguese. The pictures that are here drawn, may be considered as portraits of the human species, in two of the most remarkable forms.

There are two ways in which genius and virtue may labor for the public good: first, by assailing popular errors and vices, argumentatively and through the medium of books; secondly, by employing legal or ministerial authority to this end.

The last was the province which Cicero and Pombal assumed. Their fate may evince the insufficiency of the instrument chosen by them, and teach us, that a change of national opinion is the necessary prerequisite of revolutions.

———

ENGEL, the eldest of Walstein's pupils, thought, like his master, that the narration of public events, with a certain licence of invention, was the most efficacious of moral instruments. Abstract systems, and theoretical reasonings, were not without their use, but they claimed more attention than many were willing to bestow. Their influence, therefore, was limited to a narrow sphere. A mode by which truth could be conveyed to a great number, was much to be preferred.

Systems, by being imperfectly attended to, are liable to beget error and depravity. Truth flows from the union and relation of many parts. These parts, fallaciously connected and viewed separately, constitute error. Prejudice, stupidity, and indolence, will seldom afford us a candid audience, are prone to stop short in their researches, to remit, or transfer to other objects their attention, and hence to derive new motives to injustice, and new confirmations in folly from that which, if impartially and accurately examined, would convey nothing but benefit.

Mere reasoning is cold and unattractive. Injury rather than benefit proceeds from convictions that are transient and faint; their tendency is not to reform and enlighten, but merely to produce disquiet and remorse. They are not strong enough to resist temptation and to change the conduct, but merely to pester the offender with dissatisfaction and regret.

The detail of actions is productive of different effects. The affections are engaged, the reason is won by incessant attacks; the benefits which our system has evinced to be possible, are invested with a seeming existence; and the evils which error was proved to generate, exchange the fleeting, misty, and dubious form of inference, for a sensible and present existence.

To exhibit, in an eloquent narration, a model of right conduct, is the highest province of benevolence. Our patterns, however, may be useful in different degrees. Duties are the growth of situations. The general and the statesman have arduous duties to perform; and to teach them their duty is of use: but the forms of human society allow few individuals to gain the station of generals and statesmen. The lesson, therefore, is reducible to practice by a small number; and, of these, the temptations to abuse their power are so numerous and powerful, that a very small part, and these, in a very small degree, can be expected to comprehend, admire, and copy the pattern that is set before them.

But though few may be expected to be monarchs and ministers, every man occupies a station in society in which he is necessarily active to evil or to good. There is a sphere of some dimensions, in which the influence of his actions and opinions is felt. The causes that fashion men into instruments of happiness or misery, are numerous, complex, and operate upon a wide surface. Virtuous activity may, in a thousand ways, be thwarted and diverted by foreign and superior influence. It may seem best to purify the fountain, rather than filter the stream; but the latter is, to a certain degree, within our power, whereas, the former is impracticable. Governments and general education, cannot be rectified, but individuals may be somewhat fortified against their influence. Right intentions may be instilled into them, and some good may be done by each within his social and domestic province.

The relations in which men, unendowed with political authority, stand to each other, are numerous. An extensive source of these relations, is property. No topic can engage the attention of man more momentous than this. Opinions, relative to property, are the immediate source of nearly all the happiness and misery that exist among mankind. If men were guided by justice in the acquisition and disbursement, the brood of private and public evils would be extinguished.

To ascertain the precepts of justice, and exhibit these precepts reduced to practice, was, therefore, the favourite task of Engel. This, however, did not constitute his whole scheme. Every man is encompassed by numerous claims, and is the subject of intricate relations. Many of these may be comprised in a copious narrative, without infraction of simplicity or detriment to unity.

Next to property the most extensive source of our relations is sex. On the circumstances which produce, and the principles which regulate the union between the sexes, happiness greatly depends. The conduct to be pursued by a virtuous man in those situations which arise from sex, it was thought useful to display.

Fictitious history has, hitherto, chiefly related to the topics of love and marriage. A monotony and sentimental softness have hence arisen that have frequently excited contempt and ridicule. The ridicule, in general, is merited; not because these topics are intrinsically worthless or vulgar, but because the historian was deficient in knowledge and skill.

Marriage is incident to all; its influence on our happiness and dignity, is more entire and lasting than any other incident can possess. None, therefore, is more entitled to discussion. To enable men to evade the evils and secure the benefits of this state, is to consult, in an eminent degree, their happiness.

A man, whose activity is neither aided by political authority nor by the *press,* may yet exercise considerable influence on the condition of his neighbours, by the exercise of intellectual powers. His courage may be useful to the timid or the feeble, and his knowledge to the ignorant, as well as his property to those who want. His benevolence and justice may not only protect his kindred and his wife, but rescue the victims of prejudice and passion from the yoke of those domestic tyrants, and shield the powerless from the oppression of power, the poor from the injustice of the rich, and the simple from the stratagems of cunning.

Almost all men are busy in acquiring subsistence or wealth by a fixed application of their time and attention. Manual or mental skill is obtained and exerted for this end. This application, within certain limits, is our duty. We are bound to chuse that species of industry which combines most profit to ourselves with the least injury to others; to select that instrument which, by most speedily supplying our necessities, leaves us at most leisure to act from the impulse of benevolence.

A profession, successfully pursued, confers power not merely by conferring property and leisure. The skill which is gained, and which, partly or for a time, may be exerted to procure subsistence, may, when this end is accomplished, continue to be exerted for the common good. The pursuits of law and medicine, enhance our power over the liberty, property, and health of mankind. They not only qualify us for imparting benefit, by supplying us with property and leisure, but by enabling us to obviate, by intellectual exertions, many of the evils that infest the world.

Engel endeavored to apply these principles to the choice of a profession, and to point out the mode in which professional skill, after it has supplied us with the means of subsistence, may be best exerted in the cause of general happiness.

Human affairs are infinitely complicated. The condition of no two beings is alike. No model can be conceived, to which our situation enables us to conform. No situation can be imagined perfectly similar to that of an actual being. This exact similitude is not required to render an imaginary portrait useful to those who survey it. The usefulness, undoubtedly, consists in suggesting a mode of reasoning and acting somewhat similar to that which is ascribed to a feigned person; and, for this end, some similitude is requisite between the real and imaginary situation; but that similitude is not hard to produce. Among the incidents which invention will set before us, those are to be culled out which afford most scope to wisdom and virtue, which are most analogous to facts, which most forcibly suggest to the reader the parallel between his state and that described, and most strongly excite his desire to act as the feigned personages act. These incidents must be so arranged as to inspire, at once, curiosity and belief, to fasten the attention, and thrill the heart. This scheme was executed in the life of "Olivo Ronsica."

Engel's principles inevitably led him to select, as the scene and period of his narrative, that in which those who should read it, should exist. Every day removed the reader farther from the period, but its immediate readers would perpetually recognize the objects, and persons, and events, with which they were familiar.

Olivo is a rustic youth, whom domestic equality, personal independence, agricultural occupations, and studious habits, had endowed with a strong mind, pure taste, and unaffected integrity. Domestic revolutions oblige him to leave his father's house in search of subsistence. He is destitute of property, of friends, and of knowledge of the world. These are to be acquired by his own exertions, and virtue and sagacity are to guide him in the choice and the use of suitable means.

Ignorance subjects us to temptation, and poverty shackles our beneficence. Olivo's conduct shows us how temptation may be baffled, in spite of ignorance, and benefits be conferred in spite of poverty.

He bends his way to Weimar. He is involved, by the artifices of others, and, in consequence of his ignorance of mankind, in many perils and perplexities. He forms a connection with a man of a great and mixed, but, on the whole, a vicious character. Semlits is introduced to furnish a contrast to the simplicity and rectitude of Olivo, to exemplify the misery of sensuality and fraud, and the influence which, in the present system of society, vice possesses over the reputation and external fortune of the good.

Men hold external goods, the pleasures of the senses, of health, liberty, reputation, competence, friendship, and life, partly by virtue of their own wisdom and activity. This, however, is not the only source of their possession. It is likewise dependent on physical accidents, which human foresight cannot anticipate, or human power prevent. It is also influenced by the conduct and opinions of others.

There is no external good, of which the errors and wickedness of others may not deprive us. So far as happiness depends upon the retention of these goods, it is held at the option of another. The perfection of our character is evinced by the transient or slight influence which privations and evils have upon our happiness, on the skillfulness of those exertions which we make to avoid or repair disasters, on the diligence and success with which we improve those instruments of pleasure to ourselves and to others which fortune has left in our possession.

Richardson has exhibited in Clarissa, a being of uncommon virtue, bereaved of many external benefits by the vices of others. Her parents and lover conspire to destroy her fortune, liberty, reputation, and personal sanctity. More talents and address cannot be easily conceived, than those which are displayed by her to preserve and to regain these goods. Her efforts are vain. The cunning and malignity with which she had to contend, triumphed in the contest.

Those evils and privations she was unable to endure. The loss of fame took away all activity and happiness, and she died a victim to errors, scarcely less opprobrious and pernicious, than those of her tyrants and oppressors. She misapprehended the value of parental approbation and a fair fame. She depreciated the means of usefulness and pleasure of which fortune was unable to deprive her.

Olivo is a different personage. His talents are exerted to reform the vices of others, to defeat their malice when exerted to his injury, to endure, without diminution of his usefulness or happiness, the injuries which he cannot shun.

Semlits is led, by successive accidents, to unfold his story to Olivo, after which, they separate. Semlits is supposed to destroy himself, and Olivo returns into the country.

A pestilential disease, prevalent throughout the north of Europe, at that time (1630), appears in the city. To ascertain the fate of one connected, by the ties of kindred and love, with the family in which Olivo resides, and whose life is endangered by residence in the city, he repairs thither, encounters the utmost perils, is seized with the reigning malady, meets, in extraordinary circumstances, with Semlits, and is finally received into the house of a physician, by whose skill he is restored to health, and to whom he relates his previous adventures.

He resolves to become a physician, but is prompted by benevolence to return, for a time, to the farm which he had lately left, The series of ensuing events, are long, intricate, and congruous, and exhibit the hero of the tale in circumstances that task his fortitude, his courage, and his disinterestedness,

Engel has certainly succeeded in producing a tale, in which are powerful displays of fortitude and magnanimity; a work whose influence must be endlessly varied by varieties of character and situation of the reader, but, from which, it is not possible for any one to rise without some degree of moral benefit, and much of that pleasure which always attends the emotions of curiosity and sympathy.

I. Charles Brockden Brown, "The Difference Between History and Romance." *The Monthly Magazine and American Review* 2:4 (April 1800).

This short essay is closely related to "Walstein's School of History" and an important piece in which Brown defines his literary project in relation to history writing. The close relation of history and fiction that Brown outlines here seems to inform not only Edgar Huntly and his other novels (or "romances," to use the language of this essay), but also the later histories and historical fictions that Brown wrote in the years after his last conventional novel appeared in 1801. Along with "Walstein's School of History," this essay clearly outlines the principles and methods that go into Brown's novels.

The essay rejects the common notion that history and fiction are different because one deals with factual and the other with fictional materials. Rather, Brown argues, history and fiction are intrinsically connected as two sides of one coin, because history describes and documents the results of actions, while fiction investigates the possible motives that cause these actions. Whereas the historian establishes facts about events and behaviors, a "romancer" is more concerned with asking why and how these events and behaviors took place. Thus the writing of romance (Brown's kind of novel) deals in conjecture about the causes, conditions, and consequences of events or social actions. This speculation is useful in that it helps illuminate the ways in which seemingly individual and personal acts or singular events are actually conditioned, although not narrowly determined, by larger social forces.

The difference between history as documentation and romance as interpretation also allows Brown to develop an implicit distinction between "romance" and "novel." Brown's definition here situates romance as the kind of narrative that educates readers about, and helps them recognize, the social processes in which they are embedded. Unlike the nineteenth century's contrast between realism and romance, where romance allows the imaginative flight of fancy from the mundane world (this is the way romance is understood in Nathaniel Hawthorne's prefaces of the 1850s, e.g.), Brown situates the novel as a fiction that seeks to amuse a passive reader, and romance as a fiction that seeks to train the reader as an active interpreter and interrogator of society. When Brown uses key words such as "curiosity" and "springs of action" in the preface to Edgar Huntly, *this indicates that he has designed his work as a romance, not a novel.*

Most basically, then, Brown's ideas about "the difference between history and romance" imply that Edgar Huntly's tale is intended to be read as an exploration into the causes of contemporary behaviors, events, and conflicts, rather than simply as a "terrific" tale of sensational wonder (see "Terrific Novels" for Brown's definition of that variety of narrative).

✳✳✳✳✳

HISTORY and romance are terms that have never been very clearly distinguished from each other. It should seem that one dealt in fiction, and the other in truth; that one is a picture of the *probable* and certain, and the other a tissue of untruths; that one describes what *might* have happened, and what has *actually* happened, and the other what never had existence.

These distinctions seem to be just; but we shall find ourselves somewhat perplexed, when we attempt to reduce them to practice, and to ascertain, by their assistance, to what class this or that performance belongs.

Narratives, whether fictitious or true, may relate to the processes of nature, or the actions of men. The former, if not impenetrable by human faculties, must be acknowledged to be, hitherto, very imperfectly known. Curiosity is not satisfied with viewing facts in their disconnected state and natural order, but is prone to arrange them anew, and to deviate from present and sensible objects, into speculations on the past or future; it is eager to infer from the present state of things, their former or future condition.

The observer or experimentalist, therefore, who carefully watches, and faithfully enumerates the appearances which occur, may claim the appellation of historian. He who adorns these appearances with cause and effect, and traces resemblances between the past, distant, and future, with the present, performs a different part. He is a dealer, not in certainties, but probabilities, and is therefore a romancer.

An historian will relate the noises, the sights, and the smells that attend an eruption of Vesuvius. A romancer will describe, in the first place, the *contemporary* ebullitions and inflations, the combustion and decomposition that take place in the bowels of the earth. Next he will go to the origin of things, and describe the centrical, primary, and secondary orbs composing the universe, as masses thrown out of an immense volcano called *chaos*. Thirdly, he will paint the universal dissolution that is hereafter to be produced by the influence of volcanic or internal fire.

An historian will form catalogues of stars, and mark their positions at given times. A romancer will arrange them in *clusters* and dispose them in *strata,* and inform you; what influences the orbs have been drawn into sociable knots and circles.

An electrical historian will describe appearances that happen when hollow cylinders of glass and metal are placed near each other, and the former is rubbed with a cloth. The romancer will replenish the space that exists between the sun and its train of planetary orbs, with a fluid called electrical; and describe the modes in which this fluid finds its way to the surface of these orbs through the intervenient atmosphere.

Historians can only differ in degrees of diligence and accuracy, but romancers may have more or less probability in their narrations. The same man is frequently both historian and romancer in the compass of the same work. Buffon, Linneus, and Herschel, are examples of this union. Their observations are as diligent as their theories are adventurous. Among the historians of nature, Haller was, perhaps, the most diligent: among romancers, he that came nearest to the truth was Newton.

It must not be denied that, though history be a term commonly applied to a catalogue of natural appearances, as well as to the recital of human actions, romance is chiefly limited to the latter. Some reluctance may be felt in calling Buffon and Herschel romancers, but that name will be readily conferred on Quintus Curtius and Sir Thomas More. There is a sufficient analogy, however, between objects and modes, in the physical and intellectual world, to justify the use of these distinctions in both cases.

Physical objects and appearances sometimes fall directly beneath our observation, and may be truly described. The duty of the *natural* historian is limited to this description. *Human* actions may likewise be observed, and be truly described. In this respect, the actions of *voluntary* and *involuntary* agents, are alike, but in other momentous respects they differ.

Curiosity is not content with noting and recording the *actions* of men. It likewise seeks to know the *motives* by which the agent is impelled to the performance of these actions; but motives are modifications of thought which cannot be subjected to the senses. They cannot be certainly known. They are merely topics of conjecture. Conjecture is the weighing of probabilities; the classification of probable events, according to the measure of probability possessed by each.

Actions of different men or performed at different times may be alike; but the motives leading to these actions must necessarily vary. In guessing at these motives, the knowing and sagacious will, of course, approach nearer to the truth than the ignorant and stupid; but the wise and the ignorant, the sagacious and stupid, when busy in assigning motives to actions, are not *historians* but *romancers.*

The motive is the cause, and therefore the antecedent of the action; but the action is likewise the cause of subsequent actions. Two contemporary and (so to speak) adjacent actions may both be faithfully described, because both may be witnessed; but the connection between them, that quality which constitutes one the effect of the other, is mere matter of conjecture, and comes with the province, not of *history,* but *romance.*

The description of human actions is of moment merely as they are connected with motives and tendencies. The delineation of tendencies and motives implies a description of the action; but the action is describable without the accompanyment of tendencies and motives.

An action may be simply described, but such descriptions, though they alone be historical, are of no use as they stand singly and disjoined from tendencies and motives, in the page of the historian or the mind of the reader. The writer, therefore, who does not blend the two characters, is essentially defective. It is true, that facts simply described, may be connected and explained by the reader; and that the describer may, at least, claim the merit of supplying the builder with materials. The merit of him who drags stones together, must not be depreciated; but must not be compared with him who hews these stones into just proportions, and piles them up into convenient and magnificent fabrics.

That which is done beneath my own inspection, it is possible for me certainly to know and exactly to record; but that which is performed at a distance, either in time or place, is the theme of foreign testimony. If it be related by me, I relate not what I have witnessed, but what I derived from others who were witnesses. The subject of my senses is merely the existence of the record, and not the deed itself which is recorded. The truth of the action can be weighed in no scales but those of probability.

A voluntary action is not only connected with cause and effect, but is itself a series of motives and incidents subordinate and successive to each other. Every action differs from every other in the number and complexity of its parts, but the most simple and brief is capable of being analyzed into a thousand subdivisions. If it be witnessed by others, probabilities are lessened in proportion as the narrative is circumstantial.

These principles may be employed to illustrate the distinction between history and romance. If history relate what is true, its relations must be limited to what is known by the testimony of our senses. Its sphere, therefore, is extremely narrow. The facts to which we are immediate witnesses, are, indeed, numerous; but time and place merely connect them. Useful narratives must comprise facts linked together by some other circumstance. They must, commonly, consist of events, for a knowledge of which the narrator is indebted to the evidence of others. This evidence, though accompanied with different degrees of probability, can never give birth to certainty. How wide, then, if romance be the narrative of mere probabilities, is the empire of romance? This empire is absolute and undivided over the motives and tendencies of human actions. Over actions themselves, its dominion, though not unlimited, is yet very extensive.

X.

J. Anonymous, excerpts from "The Traveler." *The Literary Magazine and American Register* (October 1803–January 1804).

Brown and his associates used the "Traveler" column, which appeared in Brown's Literary Magazine and American Register *in 1803–1804, to debate the nature of friendship. The seriousness of the topic, and uncertainty about its subject, seems to be manifested in the unusual nature of the column. Recurring columns like "The Traveler" are usually written by a single voice, either a lone individual or group of individuals under a collective persona. But in this instance, the column serves as a forum for multiple individuals—some anonymous, others fairly recognizable by their signed initials—to join in a conversation that tries to define the proper nature and possibilities of friendship as an emotional state for men. The concept of friendship was in the process of transformation throughout the eighteenth century as the rising middle class seized upon it as a social trait that did not depend on preexisting family or religious relations. Because the idea of friendship was being remade during the time, writers debated what it should mean, its rights and responsibilities, and so on. While it is commonplace today to understand friendship partly by the absence of sexual relations, bourgeois dissident writers like William Godwin and Mary Wollstonecraft did not make this distinction. For them, "love" was an irrational and short-lasting, selfish passion, whereas "friendship" was more enduring because it was based on reason and dialogue. Sexual relations could be involved in either case.*

Because friendship might include erotic relations for these writers, scholars have become interested in discussions of "male-male friendship" as a term covering new possibilities for a range of emotional, social, and possibly sexual relations between men. This range is what the "Traveler" columnists investigate. The first column begins with a man declaring his loneliness, in tones similar to what Edgar Huntly might say after the untimely death of his friend Waldegrave. The second columnist, "I. O.," takes this as an opportunity to extol male-male friendship and insist that it is not forbidden by scripture. While I. O. suggests that friendship between a man and a woman is "more refined" than that between men, he illustrates heterosexual friendship by brother-sister relations, not husband-wife ones. Is the writer using the term to remove the odium of relations between men or simply to allow for more room for close bonds between men? The column ends with a reply by "W. D.," who argues for puerile or youthful homosociality, where serial monogamous bonds between one young man and another will be replaced by the more mature man with heterosexual marriage. Is W. D. trying to tell the first traveler that he ought to stop mourning the lost possibilities for male-male relations and "grow up" into respectable domesticity?

The discussion may also have political and social ramifications beyond these emotional questions. The columnists are writing at the time of both their own transitions to middle age (they are in their thirties) and the larger rise of cultural and political conservatism after the revolutionary period. From this perspective, this discussion about lost or vanished emotional possibilities may also suggest a host of other discussions about the passing away of the revolutionary 1790s and the rise of a more conservative spirit in the first years of the new century.

*****

Excerpt from "The Traveler. Number 1." *The Literary Magazine and American Register* 1.1 (October 1803).

I am a man left solitary in the world. I have neither parents, nor wife, nor children, to rejoice in my prosperity, or mingle their sorrows with mine: my friends and associates are few. I am not more than thirty years of age, but my pallid cheek, my museful countenance, and some hairs which have been silvered by an aching head, would declare that I was nearer to forty. In the course of my journey thus far on the stage of human existence, I have not been an inattentive observer of the characters of men, and of passing events. . . . Though I could tell much, yet I am called a silent man: and I must confess, that what I have seen in life, has more disposed me to become a speculative, thoughtful and melancholy man, than a vivacious and busy narrator of facts. I am oftentimes more fond of employing my pen, than my tongue, and have occasionally, through its instrumentality, preserved on paper some sentimental speculation, and the traces of some museful journey. In this propensity I still persevere, and shall probably to the public address several numbers of my speculations and rambles, which shall succeed the one which now solicits their attention.

*****

Excerpt from "The Traveler. Number 2." *The Literary Magazine and American Register* 1.2 (November 1803).

It has been the fate of the traveler to bend over the grave of a friend, to behold the remains of a once amiable, elegant, and high spirited youth deposited in the earth. . . . This event, while it eloquently declared the instability of life and of worldly pleasure, led him to indulge in the following meditation on the passion which had received so severe a wound.

Friendship springs from the most amiable dispositions of the mind, and betokens the absence of those selfish and discordant passions which disgrace our nature. The ancient writers and some of the moderns, have ranked friendship among the number of virtues, and if it be not a virtue, it is something so nearly allied to it, that it can scarcely be distinguished from it. It is a source of a large portion of our happiness; it is the tie of congenial souls. Amidst a world ensnaring and deceitful, where so wild and tumultuous are the passions and pursuits of men, where disinterestedness is seldom found, and where justice often holds unequal scales, how necessary to our peace and comfort is that person who will join us our councils, who will repose in us his confidence, who will be the solace of our solitude, the partner of our prosperity, and the support of our adversity. . . . Let none say that friendship is forbidden, or not encouraged by the scriptures. . . . Religion forbids no rational enjoyment. . . . Religion would never preclude us from one of the sweetest consolations that has ever been discovered for the various afflictions of life. . . . Religion excites us to cultivate every generous and amiable principle, and allows us every indulgence not inconsistent with duty. . . . The examples in the scriptures of the cultivation of this passion by great and good men are numerous. The souls of David and the princely Jonathan were *knit together.* The arm of death could only dissever their cords of love. The instances recorded of their attachment are in the highest degree striking and affecting. When Saul and Jonathan were slain, David seized his harp, and from a soulful of sorrow poured forth his inimitable elegy, pursued with his sighs the spirit of his departed friend, and blasted the mountain of Gilboa in the language of poetical indignation. . . . The example of our Savior, independent of all other instances, gives a sanction to the cultivation of friendship. . . . From the world and the number of his disciples, he selected John, on him bestowed his warmest affections, and admitted him to his free communication.

The silence of scriptural precept concerning friendship, permits no inference to be drawn against its lawfulness. To have made it the subject of divine command would have been absurd, for it cannot be called a duty, and similarity of disposition and co-incidence of sentiment and affection, on which friendship is founded, do not depend upon our choice, neither are they under our will. The propensity in our natures toward this passion is sufficiently strong and operative without the force of a command. The object of our Savior was to inculcate the plain and practiced duties of piety and morality, those duties which are indispensable and impose universal obligation, and which are necessary to our everlasting happiness in the future world.

Let none say that the dictates of friendship are opposed to the duties of universal benevolence, that it lavishes on one object that kindness and affection which ought to be diffused through the whole human race: this objection is certainly unfounded: we may discharge every tender office which friendship demands, and still be observant of the duties enjoined by revelation. . . . Various are the gradations of affection corresponding with the different relations of life, and each contributing its share to that harmony which should reign throughout society. Parental tenderness, filial reverence, brotherly affection, are all limited in their operation, and yet are the subjects of command. The design of Christianity was not to extinguish these, but to regulate them, and to reduce them to their proper dimensions. As the sun is to the planetary system, so love for God, love for men, is the centre, round which all our other affections founded on the world and mortality, should revolve; these are the only restrictions which Christianity imposes upon our impartial attachments, and under these restrictions it excites us to indulge them. It strengthens the ties of Friendship, by holding out to our view immortality. "It revives (says an author) that union which death seems to dissolve, it restores us again to those whom we most dearly loved, in that blessed society of just men made more perfect."

Friendship subsisting between persons of a different sex, is of a nature still more refined that that which prevails between men. A brother feels more tenderness for his sister than he can for his brother. There is in the female, more gentleness, more soft-ened amiableness than men possess: she has more sensibility, more influence upon the heart, more eloquence of persuasion. Man finds in her one who soothes him in desertion, who invigorates his hopes, and impels him to laudable enterprises. . . . she finds in man a provider, a protector, and one who will for her encounter the rough-ness and jarrings of the world from which her nature would shrink.

I. O.

*****

Excerpt from "The Traveler. Number 4." *The Literary Magazine and American Register* 1.4 (January 1804).

Attachment between persons of the same sex

To the Traveler

In reading your remarks in your last number, upon friendship, I could not forbear sending you a few thoughts of my own upon the same subject.

The attachment between persons of the same sex, is called friendship; and perhaps can, strictly speaking, be said only to exist in relation to persons of the same sex. Friendship between man and woman, according to the above definition, must be love. Esteem for one of the opposite sex may influence to numberless friendly offices; but this is not what is meant by friendship. The affection which subsists between some brothers and sisters, is nearer to friendship; still it is distinct, and must be des-ignated by the appellation of fraternal love.

In the course of his life, a man generally feels the attachment of friendship, at dif-ferent periods, towards several individuals of various characters, and dissimilar merit. If he is of a generous and ardent temper, he is, at no period, without some one fa-vored and favoring being, to whom he feels united, by the passion of friendship; yet it is often found that the objects of a man's early attachments, prove, after absence, or the lapse of time, to be such as the heart can no longer cleave to.

I can remember no period of my life, at which, among many whom I loved, there was not one of my own sex, to whom I was passionately attached. While yet an in-fant, I was attached to a good-natured servant lad, who told me stories, taught me to find bird nests, and took me with him to hunt rabbits. At the age of eight, I was pas-sionately attached to a boy of ten. We shouldered our wooden muskets together, and would have died in defense of each other, if there had been any knight or giant who wished the death of either. These bonds were broken by absence: I felt a pang, but immediately found another friend. During the time between the ages of nine and fif-teen, I remember a succession of boys to whom I was sincerely attached, and with whom I had quarrels and reconciliations innumerable. With one I was engaged in reading the achievements of knights-errant; with another, in enacting plays; and with a third in making pictures. From fifteen to eighteen, I had another attachment; though during this period I had at the same time a succession of love affairs, unknown to the objects, and only imparted to my friend, who I recollect was as cold to the charms of the other sex, as he was warm in his attachment to me. This union was broken by my departure for Europe. It was there the same; I immediately found a friend, from whom I was inseparable, and who sincerely loved me.

On my return to America, after an absence of some years, I found some of the persons whom I had formerly loved, but *they* were no longer the same, and certainly *I* was no longer the same. I was pleased to see them, but my heart had again to seek a friend. Is this the picture of friendship, as others feel it, or am I singular in my temper or my fate? Be that as it may, such is the view of friendship, which my experience of life presents, but there is another trait.

I was married, and the passion of friendship was swallowed up in the passion of love. A husband and a father, my heart seeks not away from my own fire-side, a bosom to share its transports, or quiet its tumults. Is my mind less capable of friendship than at an earlier period of life? I think not. Though undoubtedly my eye is much quicker in discerning the blemishes than at that time: yet my heart bounds towards every object which appears to wish its sympathy. I have now a number of persons whose friend I am, and whom I am proud to call my friends; but the sentiment which binds me to them; is not passion. I esteem A, B, C, D, E, F, and G, and I love H, I, and K; but still the *passion* of friendship is swallowed up in the passion of love.

W. D.
[possibly William Dunlap, friend and later biographer of Brown]

K. Charles Brockden Brown, excerpt from "Memorandums Made on a Journey Through Part of Pennsylvania." *Literary Magazine* 1.4 (January 1804): 255–56.

Brown wrote "Memorandums" on the occasion of a journey made by his older brother James to central Pennsylvania (what is now Catawissa, Pennsylvania) to inspect James' recent purchase (in 1801) of 20,000 acres of backcountry land. Although this account is "probably invented" (see Krause, "Penn's Elm," 473–75), the article reflects on settler-Indian conflicts in a finely detailed passage that recalls particular motifs and emphases in Edgar Huntly. *The image of an elm, symbolizing the dispossession of tribal lands and the personification of this dispossession in the potentially vengeful remains of an elderly female, seem to echo the novel. Brown goes on to characterize surviving Indians as witty, resourceful, and seemingly better cultivated than the settlers who displace them.*

Little Turtle, who refers sarcastically and in rhymes to "the unfortunate *affair of St. Clair" in the final paragraph, was a Miami chieftain who in 1791 dealt the U.S. Army the greatest defeat it ever suffered against Native American forces. Arthur St. Clair was appointed first governor of the Ohio territory in 1787 (the year of* Edgar Huntly's *action) and in 1791 led a punitive expedition against tribal forces led by Little Turtle and Shawnee chieftain Blue Jacket. The disastrous defeat he suffered is known as St. Clair's Defeat, the Battle of the Wabash, or The Columbia Massacre.*

Note how Brown extends the Indian "sarcastic humour" he describes, presenting the "savages" in this passage as sophisticated respondents who know how to reverse and mock patronizing stereotypes about their culture, even as they acknowledge and adjust to new commercial and expansionist realities of the nineteenth century. By contrast, the sketch's white settlers hang on to backward and parochial superstitions, desecrate Indian graves, violate Indian hospitality to steal land, and remain ignorant about Indian culture even after centuries of colonization.

*****

Here are still some vestiges of an Indian burial ground, and some peach trees of their planting in tolerable preservation. Having in the afternoon visited J.S. who lives on the western bank of the Catawessy creek, he pointed out to us what he takes to be the traces of an Indian fortification: it consists of a number of square holes, dug at equal distances on the eastern shore, describing a line of several hundred feet; whether these apertures served as intrenchments from which an assaulting enemy might be annoyed, or were subservient to some more complex scheme of warlike operations, or whether they were at all used for hostile purposes, may be left for the sage deter-mination of some future dealer in antiquities.

Some years back a few of the inhabitants, from motives of curiosity, dug up a corpse from the grave-yard. It proved to be a female; she had been interred without a coffin, and was, according to the custom of the Indians, placed in a sitting posture. Care had been taken to provide her with a small iron kettle, some trinkets, and a tobacco-pipe, ready charged in each hand. These equipments were doubtless intended to con-tribute to the comfort and convenience of the deceased on her journey to the land of spirits, and would probably be as efficacious as the tolling of bells, and the firing of guns, over the body of a white man. If this custom of our tawney brethren be repug-nant to our notions of good sense, we should not forget that our own must appear to them equally irreconcilable to reason and philosophy. We were shewn one of the pipes. It is the common clay of European manufacture. The skeleton was preserved for some time by the physician of the town, but the superstitious Germans in the neighbourhood, fearful perhaps that this outrage on the bones of the unoffending squaw might be followed by some tremendous act of vengeance on her part, com-pelled the doctor to re-inter them.

The inhabitants still preserve a large elm on the band of the river, under which the sachems formerly held their councils. I could not contemplate this object with indif-ference. Who that has the feelings of a man, and whose bosom glows with the small-est sense of honour and justice, can view this elm with apathy? Where are now those venerable and veteran chieftains and warriors, who were accustomed to assemble be-neath its friendly shade . . . and who received here with open arms the first white man who came helpless and forlorn among them? Surely they were unconscious that, in a few very few revolving moons, the stranger whom they here cherished and warmed by the council fire; to whom they have presented the wampum of consecrated friendship, and with whom they here smoked the sacred calumet of peace, had come to supplant them in their native possessions, to root out their posterity from the country, and to trample down the graves of their fathers.

These ancient inheritors of the soil reluctantly submit to the discipline and shackles of civilized life, and in general have shewn contempt for our customs and manners; but as their hunting grounds become destroyed, necessity may force them to resort to other means of subsistence.

An Indian being asked by two white men, how he, who gave himself no concern about religion, expected to reach heaven, answered: "Suppose we three in Philadelphia, and we hear of some good *rum* at Fort-Pitt. . . . we set off to get some, but one of you has business in Baltimore, and he go that way. . . . the other wants to make some money too on the road, and he go by Reading. . . . Indian got no business, no money to get. . . . he set off and go strait up to Fort-Pitt, and get there before either of you."

The Indians of North-America are well skilled in this species of sarcastic humour. I remember to have been present at an interview between some of their chiefs and a select number of citizens who had benevolently devoted both time and property to the introduction of useful and civilized arts among the savages. The Little Turtle, among other improvements which he enumerated to have taken place among his people, mentioned that they manufactured considerable quantities of sugar from the juice of the maple. He was asked how they contrived to procure suitable vessels to contain the syrup when boiling. He affected a very grave countenance, as he answered "that the *unfortunate* affair of St. Clair had furnished them with a considerable number of camp kettles which answered the purpose very well." It was known that this chief had headed the united Indian forces in their intrepid attack on the American army, commanded by General St. Clair, and in which the latter were defeated with immense slaughter, and suffered the loss of their camp equipage.

L. Charles Brockden Brown, "Romances." *The Literary Magazine and American Register* 3.16 (January 1805).

In this article on "romances," which in this case means the novel-like narratives that flourished from the Middle Ages to the 1600s, Brown reiterates the need for contemporary forms of art to focus on themes that are relevant for contemporary audiences. Works of the past may have been tremendous achievements, but their usefulness for the modern reader is limited because new historical conditions demand new ideas and modes of behavior. Thus Brown's argument here suggests that there is no unchanging or eternal, transhistorical standard for values, ideas, or behaviors. The lessons of one age may not be useful for another. Like his contemporaries William Godwin and Thomas Paine, Brown remains skeptical about worshipping past forms of art, society, and government.

*****

A tale, agreeable to truth and nature or, more properly speaking, agreeable to our *own* conceptions of truth and nature, may be long, but cannot be tedious. Cleopatra and Cassandra by no means referred to an ideal world; they referred to the manners and habits of the age in which they were written; names and general incidents only were taken from the age of Alexander and Caesar. In that age, therefore, they were not tedious, but the more delighted was the reader the longer the banquet was protracted. In after times, when taste and manners were changed, the tale became tedious, because it was deemed unnatural and absurd, and it would have been condemned as tedious, and treated with neglect, whether it filled ten pages or ten volumes.

Cleopatra and Cassandra are no greater violations of historical veracity and probability, and no more drawn from an ideal world, than Johnson's Rasselas, Hawkesworth's Almoran and Hamet, or Fenelon's Telemachus. In all these, names and incidents, and some machinery, are taken from a remote age and nation, but the manners and sentiments are modeled upon those of the age in which the works were written, as those of the Scuderis were fashioned upon the habits of their own age. The present unpopularity of the romances of the fifteenth and sixteenth centuries is not owing to the satires of Cervantes or of Boileau, but to the gradual revolution of human manners and national taste.

The *Arabian Nights* delight us in childhood, and so do the chivalrous romances; but, in riper age, if enlightened by education, we despise what we formerly revered. Individuals, whose minds have been uncultivated, continue still their attachment to those marvelous stories. And yet, must it not be ascribed rather to change of manners than to any other cause, that we neglect and disrelish works which gave infinite delight to sir Philip Sidney, sir Walter Raleigh, and sir Thomas More, to Sully and Daubigne: men whose knowledge of Augustan models, and delight in them, was never exceeded, and the general vigor and capacity of whose minds has never been surpassed.

The works that suited former ages are now exploded by us. The works that are now produced, and which accommodate themselves to our habits and taste, would have been utterly neglected by our ancestors: and what is there to hinder the belief, that they, in their turn, will fall into oblivion and contempt at some future time. We naturally conceive our own habits and opinions the standard of rectitude; but their rectitude, admitting our claim to be just, will not hinder them from giving way to others, and being exploded in their turn.

M. Charles Brockden Brown, excerpt from "Terrific Novels." *The Literary Magazine and American Register* 3.19 (April 1805).

This short excerpt illustrates Brown's criticism of conventional gothic style and allows us to understand, by contrast, how his own use of the gothic is oriented toward the representation of modern life. Today we generally use the term "gothic" to describe narratives that use the supernatural to excite fear and suspense in their audience. But in this essay, Brown judges such narratives by their motivation, rather than by their form and themes or effect on their audience. Here Brown calls novels that use sensational devices of mystery simply to create suspense "terrific" ones, because they are intended to generate sensations of terror, rather than a sense of excellence. In keeping with his general emphasis on the development of modern forms suited to modern social conditions, Brown criticizes conventional gothic's emphasis on premodern superstitions rather than the anxieties and stresses of contemporary life. As opposed to castles, monks, and superstitions, Brown's version of the gothic, in Edgar Huntly *or his other novels, highlights scenarios and themes that his readers might actually experience: bankruptcy, psychological symptoms of extreme anxiety and stress such as somnambulism, vulnerability to illnesses like the yellow fever, the threat of rape, and so on.*

*****

The Castle of Otranto laid the foundation of a style of writing, which was carried to perfection by Mrs. Radcliff, and which may be called the *terrific style*. The great talents of Mrs. Radcliff made some atonement for the folly of this mode of composition, and gave some importance to exploded fables and childish fears, by the charms of sentiment and description; but the multitude of her imitators seem to have thought that description and sentiment were impertinent intruders, and by lowering the mind somewhat to its ordinary state, marred and counteracted those awful feelings, which true genius was properly employed in raising. They endeavor to keep the reader in a constant state of tumult and horror, by the powerful engines of trap-doors, back stairs, black robes, and pale faces: but the solution of the enigma is ever too near at hand, to permit the indulgence of supernatural appearances. A well-written scene of a party at snap-dragon would exceed all the fearful images of these books. There is, besides, no *keeping* in the author's design: fright succeeds to fright, and danger to danger, without permitting the unhappy reader to draw his breath, or to repose for a moment on subjects of character or sentiment.

N. Charles Brockden Brown, "Somnambulism. A fragment." *The Literary Magazine and American Register* 3.20 (May 1805).

Brown published "Somnambulism" in 1805, but scholars believe it may have been written between 1797 and 1799, in the same period when Brown first wrote Sky-Walk; *or,* The Man Unknown to Himself, *the lost precursor to* Edgar Huntly, *and then published* Edgar Huntly *itself. Given the themes of sleep-walking, a mysterious murder beneath a tree, and a mentally distressed individual hiding in the wilds, whom the unreliable narrator seems to increasingly echo, along with the similarity of the names Norwood and Norwalk and use of "Inglefield" as a character's name, the story seems clearly linked to* Edgar Huntly. *While it can be read apart from* Edgar Huntly, *it also provides an intriguing point of comparison, suggesting thematic decisions Brown may have made in crafting* Edgar Huntly, *since it was possibly written as a draft "fragment" in the process of planning* Sky-Walk *or* Edgar Huntly.

Like Edgar Huntly's *relationship between Clithero and Lorimer's niece, "Somnambulism" begins with a relationship that cuts across class lines, for the narrator Althorpe appears to be less financially secure than Mr. Davis, the father of the woman he desires. The mismatch in wealth seems to be a cause of the narrator's fear that Davis will marry his daughter to another, and thus a factor in the ultimate disaster leading to the death of Davis' daughter in the woods. But while "Somnambulism" contains many elements that appear in* Edgar Huntly, *it does not seem to link them in any overarching, analytical way. Nick Handyside, who seems in some ways like Clithero, does not actually interact with the characters; he remains at the level of a mythic character, possibly nothing more than a campfire fiction to scare urbanites. In addition, the focus of this story involves male-female coupling, which remains in the background stories of* Edgar Huntly.

Unusually for Brown, the story begins with a citation of a medical incident from the Vienna Gazette *that appears to explain the story's mystery even before it unfolds. Although disrupting the conventional sequence of a mystery followed by its solution may seem to weaken the suspense for the reader, Brown's citation of a medical report followed by a story indicates that he is writing a romance that seeks to provide a potential social explanation for facts discovered by a historian (see "The Difference Between History and Romance" for more on this difference). If read in this light, Brown may be suggesting that Althorpe's sleep-walking and mental illness may be the personal manifestation of unequal class relations, either in the older aristocratic regime or the new commercial one.* Edgar Huntly's *precursor,* Sky-Walk, *also emphasizes anxieties about debt and class relations (see this volume's information on* Sky-Walk*).*

Brown was an influence on Edgar Allan Poe, and readers familiar with Poe's pleasure in fabricating European quotations and pseudoscientific hoaxes may well assume that Brown's headnote is similarly dubious, a mere fictional invention. But if this is the case, it would be an unusual use of a fake citation in Brown's work. There actually was a Gazette de Vienne, *a French-language periodical published in Vienna. During the 1770s and 1780s, Vienna was a center of investigation into para-conscious states, most notably Franz Anton Mesmer's research on hypnosis (his therapy of induced hypnotism was often called "mesmerism") and the work of Mesmer's student, the Marquis de Puységur, who in 1784 called induced hypnotic states "magnetic" or "artificial somnambulism." The recognition in this work that the mind seems to have its own internal divisions leads to some of the first records of multiple personality disorder in the 1790s and later nineteenth-century notions of the unconscious. The story's headnote, therefore, may possibly be an accurate account emerging from a center of interest in alternative mental states. Brown's medical friends often culled items from their scientific readings for Brown to use in his fiction. As the editor of a review journal that annotated European publications, and someone who scoured New York and Philadelphia bookstores for French-language materials, Brown may have read such an account in the original. Frustratingly for scholars, however, no archive in either Europe or North America has a copy of the cited issue of the* Gazette de Vienne, *and thus the question of the authenticity of the headnote's medical quotation remains unresolved.*

*****

[The following fragment will require no other preface or commentary than an extract from the Vienna Gazette of June 14, 1784. "At Great Glogau, in Silesia, the attention of physicians, and of the people, has been excited by the case of a young man, whose behavior indicates perfect health in all respects but one. He has a habit of rising in his sleep, and performing a great many actions with as much order and exactness as when awake. This habit for a long time showed itself in freaks and achievements merely innocent, or, at least, only troublesome and inconvenient, till about six weeks ago. At that period a shocking event took place about three leagues from the town, and in the neighborhood where the youth's family resides. A young lady, traveling with her father by night, was shot dead upon the road, by some person unknown. The officers of justice took a good deal of pains to trace the author of the crime, and at length, by carefully comparing circumstances, a suspicion was fixed upon this youth. After an accurate scrutiny, by the tribunal of the circle, he has been declared author of the murder: but what renders the case truly extraordinary is, that there are good reasons for believing that the deed was perpetrated by the youth while asleep, and was entirely unknown to himself. The young woman was the object of his affection, and the journey in which she had engaged had given him the utmost anxiety for her safety."]

———OUR guests were preparing to retire for the night, when somebody knocked loudly at the gate. The person was immediately admitted, and presented a letter to Mr. Davis. This letter was from a friend, in which he informed our guest of certain concerns of great importance, on which the letter-writer was extremely anxious to have a personal conference with his friend; but knowing that he intended to set out from ——— four days previous to his writing, he was hindered from setting out by the apprehension of missing him upon the way. Meanwhile, he had deemed it best to send a special message to quicken his motions, should he be able to find him.

The importance of this interview was such, that Mr. Davis declared his intention of setting out immediately. No solicitations could induce him to delay a moment. His daughter, convinced of the urgency of his motives, readily consented to brave the perils and discomforts of a nocturnal journey.

This event had not been anticipated by me. The shock that it produced in me was, to my own apprehension, a subject of surprise. I could not help perceiving that it was greater than the occasion would justify. The pleasures of this intercourse were, in a moment, to be ravished from me. I was to part from my new friend, and when we should again meet it was impossible to foresee. It was then that I recollected her expressions, that assured me that her choice was fixed upon another. If I saw her again, it would probably be as a wife. The claims of friendship, as well as those of love, would then be swallowed up by a superior and hateful obligation.

But, though betrothed, she was not wedded. That was yet to come; but why should it be considered as inevitable? Our dispositions and views must change with circumstances. Who was he that Constantia Davis had chosen? Was he born to outstrip all competitors in ardour and fidelity? We cannot fail of chusing that which appears to us most worthy of choice. He had hitherto been unrivalled; but was not this day destined to introduce to her one, to whose merits every competitor must yield? He that would resign this prize, without an arduous struggle, would, indeed, be of all wretches the most pusillanimous and feeble.

Why, said I, do I cavil at her present choice? I will maintain that it does honour to her discernment. She would not be that accomplished being which she seems, if she had acted otherwise. It would be sacrilege to question the rectitude of her conduct. The object of her choice was worthy. The engagement of her heart in his favour was unavoidable, because her experience had not hitherto produced one deserving to be placed in competition with him. As soon as his superior is found, his claims will be annihilated. Has not this propitious accident supplied the defects of her former observation? But soft! is she not betrothed? If she be, what have I to dread? The engagement is accompanied with certain conditions. Whether they be openly expressed or not, they necessarily limit it. Her vows are binding on condition that the present situation continues, and that another does not arise, previously to marriage, by whose claims those of the present lover will be justly superseded.

But how shall I contend with this unknown admirer? She is going whither it will not be possible for me to follow her. An interview of a few hours is not sufficient to accomplish the important purpose that I meditate; but even this is now at an end. I shall speedily be forgotten by her. I have done nothing that entitles me to a place in her remembrance. While my rival will be left at liberty to prosecute his suit, I shall be abandoned to solitude, and have no other employment than to ruminate on the bliss that has eluded my grasp. If scope were allowed to my exertions, I might hope that they would ultimately be crowned with success; but, as it is, I am manacled and powerless. The good would easily be reached, if my hands were at freedom: now that they are fettered, the attainment is impossible.

But is it true that such is my forlorn condition? What is it that irrecoverably binds me to this spot? There are seasons of respite from my present occupations, in which I commonly indulge myself in journeys. This lady's habitation is not at an immeasurable distance from mine. It may be easily comprised within the sphere of my excursions. Shall I want a motive or excuse for paying her a visit? Her father has claimed to be better acquainted with my uncle. The lady has intimated, that the sight of me, at any future period, will give her pleasure. This will furnish ample apology for visiting their house. But why should I delay my visit? Why not immediately attend them on their way? If not on their whole journey, at least for a part of it? A journey in darkness is not unaccompanied with peril. Whatever be the caution or knowledge of their guide, they cannot be supposed to surpass mine, who have trodden this part of the way so often, that my chamber floor is scarcely more familiar to me. Besides, there is danger, from which, I am persuaded, my attendance would be a sufficient, an indispensable safeguard.

I am unable to explain why I conceived this journey to be attended with uncommon danger. My mind was, at first, occupied with the remoter consequences of this untimely departure, but my thoughts gradually returned to the contemplation of its immediate effects. There were twenty miles to a ferry, by which the travelers designed to cross the river, and at which they expected to arrive at sun-rise the next morning. I have said that the intermediate way was plain and direct. Their guide professed to be thoroughly acquainted with it.—From what quarter, then, could danger be expected to arise? It was easy to enumerate and magnify possibilities; that a tree, or ridge, or stone unobserved might overturn the carriage; that their horse might fail, or be urged, by some accident, to flight, were far from being impossible. Still they were such as justified caution. My vigilance would, at least, contribute to their security. But I could not for a moment divest myself of the belief, that my aid was indispensable. As I pondered on this image my emotions arose to terror.

All men are, at times, influenced by inexplicable sentiments. Ideas haunt them in spite of all their efforts to discard them. Prepossessions are entertained, for which their reason is unable to discover any adequate cause. The strength of a belief, when it is destitute of any rational foundation, seems, of itself, to furnish a new ground for credulity. We first admit a powerful persuasion, and then, from reflecting on the insufficiency of the ground on which it is built, instead of being prompted to dismiss it, we become more forcibly attached to it.

I had received little of the education of design. I owed the formation of my character chiefly to accident. I shall not pretend to determine in what degree I was credulous or superstitious. A belief, for which I could not rationally account, I was sufficiently prone to consider as the work of some invisible agent; as an intimation from the great source of existence and knowledge. My imagination was vivid. My passions, when I allowed them sway, were incontroullable. My conduct, as my feelings, was characterized by precipitation and headlong energy.

On this occasion I was eloquent in my remonstrances. I could not suppress my opinion, that unseen danger lurked in their way. When called upon to state the reasons of my apprehensions, I could only enumerate possibilities of which they were already apprised, but which they regarded in their true light. I made bold enquiries into the importance of the motives that should induce them to expose themselves to the least hazard. They could not urge their horse beyond his real strength. They would be compelled to suspend their journey for some time the next day. A few hours were all that they could hope to save by their utmost expedition. Were a few hours of such infinite moment?

In these representations I was sensible that I had over-leaped the bounds of rigid decorum. It was not my place to weigh his motives and inducements. My age and situation, in this family, rendered silence and submission my peculiar province. I had hitherto confined myself within bounds of scrupulous propriety, but now I had suddenly lost sight of all regards but those which related to the safety of the travelers.

Mr. Davis regarded my vehemence with suspicion. He eyed me with more attention than I had hitherto received from him. The impression which this unexpected interference made upon him, I was, at the time, too much absorbed in other considerations to notice. It was afterwards plain that he suspected my zeal to originate in a passion for his daughter, which it was by no means proper for him to encourage. If this idea occurred to him, his humanity would not suffer it to generate indignation or resentment in his bosom. On the contrary, he treated my arguments with mildness, and assured me that I had overrated the inconveniences and perils of the journey. Some regard was to be paid to his daughter's ease and health. He did not believe them to be materially endangered. They should make suitable provision of cloaks and caps against the inclemency of the air. Had not the occasion been extremely urgent, and of that urgency he alone could be the proper judge, he should certainly not consent to endure even these trivial inconveniences. "But you seem," continued he, "chiefly anxious for my daughter's sake. There is, without doubt, a large portion of gallantry in your fears. It is natural and venial in a young man to take infinite pains for the service of the ladies; but, my dear, what say you? I will refer this important question to your decision. Shall we go, or wait till the morning?"

"Go, by all means," replied she. "I confess the fears that have been expressed appear to be groundless. I am bound to our young friend for the concern he takes in our welfare, but certainly his imagination misleads him. I am not so much a girl as to be scared merely because it is dark."

I might have foreseen this decision; but what could I say? My fears and my repugnance were strong as ever.

The evil that was menaced was terrible. By remaining where they were till the next day they would escape it. Was no other method sufficient for their preservation? My attendance would effectually obviate the danger.

This scheme possessed irresistible attractions. I was thankful to the danger for suggesting it. In the fervour of my conceptions, I was willing to run to the world's end to show my devotion to the lady. I could sustain, with alacrity, the fatigue of many nights of travelling and watchfulness. I should unspeakably prefer them to warmth and ease, if I could thereby extort from this lady a single phrase of gratitude or approbation.

I proposed to them to bear them company, at least till the morning light. They would not listen to it. Half my purpose was indeed answered by the glistening eyes and affectionate looks of Miss Davis, but the remainder I was pertinaciously bent on likewise accomplishing. If Mr. Davis had not suspected my motives, he would probably have been less indisposed to compliance. As it was, however, his objections were insuperable. They earnestly insisted on my relinquishing my design. My uncle, also, not seeing any thing that justified extraordinary precautions, added his injunctions. I was conscious of my inability to show any sufficient grounds for my fears. As long as their representations rung in my ears, I allowed myself to be ashamed of my weakness, and conjured up a temporary persuasion that my attendance was, indeed, superfluous, and that I should show most wisdom in suffering them to depart alone.

But this persuasion was transient. They had no sooner placed themselves in their carriage, and exchanged the parting adieus, but my apprehensions returned upon me as forcibly as ever. No doubt part of my despondency flowed from the idea of separation, which, however auspicious it might prove to the lady, portended unspeakable discomforts to me. But this was not all. I was breathless with fear of some unknown and terrible disaster that awaited them. A hundred times I resolved to disregard their remonstrances, and hover near them till the morning. This might be done without exciting their displeasure. It was easy to keep aloof and be unseen by them. I should doubtless have pursued this method if my fears had assumed any definite and consistent form; if, in reality, I had been able distinctly to tell what it was that I feared. My guardianship would be of no use against the obvious sources of danger in the ruggedness and obscurity of the way. For that end I must have tendered them my services, which I knew would be refused, and, if pertinaciously obtruded on them, might justly excite displeasure. I was not insensible, too, of the obedience that was due to my uncle. My absence would be remarked. Some anger and much disquietude would have been the consequences with respect to him. And after all, what was this groundless and ridiculous persuasion that governed me? Had I profited nothing by experience of the effects of similar follies? Was I never to attend to the lessons of sobriety and truth? How ignominious to be thus the slave of a fortuitous and inexplicable impulse! To be the victim of terrors more chimerical than those which haunt the dreams of idiots and children! *They* can describe clearly, and attribute a real existence to the object of their terrors. Not so can I.

Influenced by these considerations, I shut the gate at which I had been standing, and turned towards the house. After a few steps I paused, turned, and listened to the distant sounds of the carriage. My courage was again on the point of yielding, and new efforts were requisite before I could resume my first resolutions.

I spent a drooping and melancholy evening. My imagination continually hovered over our departed guests. I recalled every circumstance of the road. I reflected by what means they were to pass that bridge, or extricate themselves from this slough. I imagined the possibility of their guide's forgetting the position of a certain oak that grew in the road. It was an ancient tree, whose boughs extended, on all sides, to an extraordinary distance. They seemed disposed by nature in that way in which they would produce the most ample circumference of shade. I could not recollect any other obstruction from which much was to be feared. This indeed was several miles distant, and its appearance was too remarkable not to have excited attention.

The family retired to sleep. My mind had been too powerfully excited to permit me to imitate their example. The incidents of the last two days passed over my fancy like a vision. The revolution was almost incredible which my mind, had undergone, in consequence of these incidents. It was so abrupt and entire that my soul seemed to have passed into a new form. I pondered on every incident till the surrounding scenes disappeared, and I forgot my real situation. I mused upon the image of Miss Davis till my whole soul was dissolved in tenderness, and my eyes overflowed with tears. There insensibly arose a sort of persuasion that destiny had irreversibly decreed that I should never see her more.

While engaged in this melancholy occupation, of which I cannot say how long it lasted, sleep overtook me as I sat. Scarcely a minute had elapsed during this period without conceiving the design, more or less strenuously, of sallying forth, with a view to overtake and guard the travellers; but this design was embarrassed with invincible objections, and was alternately formed and laid aside. At length, as I have said, I sunk into profound slumber, if that slumber can be termed profound, in which my fancy was incessantly employed in calling up the forms, into new combinations, which had constituted my waking reveries.—The images were fleeting and transient, but the events of the morrow recalled them to my remembrance with sufficient distinctness.

The terrors which I had so deeply and unaccountably imbibed could not fail of retaining some portion of their influence, in spite of sleep.

In my dreams, the design which I could not bring myself to execute while awake I embraced without hesitation. I was summoned, methought, to defend this lady from the attacks of an assassin. My ideas were full of confusion and inaccuracy. All that I can recollect is, that my efforts had been unsuccessful to avert the stroke of the murderer. This, however, was not accomplished without drawing on his head a bloody retribution. I imagined myself engaged, for a long time, in pursuit of the guilty, and, at last, to have detected him in an artful disguise. I did not employ the usual preliminaries which honour prescribes, but, stimulated by rage, attacked him with a pistol, and terminated his career by a mortal wound.

I should not have described these phantoms had there not been a remarkable coincidence between them and the real events of that night. In the morning, my uncle, whose custom it was to rise first in the family, found me quietly reposing in the chair in which I had fallen asleep. His summons roused and startled me. This posture was so unusual that I did not readily recover my recollection, and perceive in what circumstances I was placed.

I shook off the dreams of the night. Sleep had refreshed and invigorated my frame, as well as tranquillized my thoughts. I still mused on yesterday's adventures, but my reveries were more cheerful and benign. My fears and bodements were dispersed with the dark, and I went into the fields, not merely to perform the duties of the day, but to ruminate on plans for the future.

My golden visions, however, were soon converted into visions of despair. A messenger arrived before noon, entreating my presence, and that of my uncle, at the house of Dr. Inglefield, a gentleman who resided at the distance of three miles from our house. The messenger explained the intention of this request. It appeared that the terrors of the preceding evening had some mysterious connection with truth. By some deplorable accident, Miss Davis had been shot on the road, and was still lingering in dreadful agonies at the house of this physician. I was in a field near the road when the messenger approached the house. On observing me, he called me. His tale was meagre and imperfect, but the substance of it was easy to gather. I stood for a moment motionless and aghast. As soon as I recovered my thoughts I set off full speed, and made not a moment's pause till I reached the house of Inglefield.

The circumstances of this mournful event, as I was able to collect them at different times, from the witnesses, were these. After they had parted from us, they proceeded on their way for some time without molestation. The clouds disappearing, the starlight enabled them with less difficulty to discern their path. They met not a human being till they came within less than three miles of the oak which I have before described. Here Miss Davis looked forward with some curiosity and said to her father, "Do you not see some one in the road before us? I saw him this moment move across from the fence on the right hand and stand still in the middle of the road."

"I see nothing, I must confess," said the father: "but that is no subject of wonder; your young eyes will of course see farther than my old ones."

"I see him clearly at this moment," rejoined the lady. "If he remain a short time where he is, or seems to be, we shall be able to ascertain his properties. Our horse's head will determine whether his substance be impassive or not."

The carriage slowly advancing, and the form remaining in the same spot, Mr. Davis at length perceived it, but was not allowed a clearer examination, for the person, having, as it seemed, ascertained the nature of the cavalcade, shot across the road, and disappeared. The behaviour of this unknown person furnished the travellers with a topic of abundant speculation.

Few possessed a firmer mind than Miss Davis; but whether she was assailed, on this occasion, with a mysterious foreboding of her destiny; whether the eloquence of my fears had not, in spite of resolution, infected her; or whether she imagined evils that my incautious temper might draw upon me, and which might originate in our late interview, certain it was that her spirits were visibly depressed. This accident made no sensible alteration in her. She was still disconsolate and incommunicative. All the efforts of her father were insufficient to inspire her with cheerfulness. He repeatedly questioned her as to the cause of this unwonted despondency. Her answer was, that her spirits were indeed depressed, but she believed that the circumstance was casual. She knew of nothing that could justify despondency. But such is humanity. Cheerfulness and dejection will take their turns in the best regulated bosoms, and come and go when they will, and not at the command of reason. This observation was succeeded by a pause. At length Mr. Davis said, "A thought has just occurred to me. The person whom we just now saw is young Althorpe."

Miss Davis was startled: "Why, my dear father, should you think so? It is too dark to judge, at this distance, by resemblance of figure. Ardent and rash as he appears to be, I should scarcely suspect him on this occasion. With all the fiery qualities of youth, unchastised by experience, untamed by adversity, he is capable no doubt of extravagant adventures, but what could induce him to act in this manner?"

"You know the fears that he expressed concerning the issue of this night's journey. We know not what foundation he might have had for these fears. He told us of no danger that ought to deter us, but it is hard to conceive that he should have been thus vehement without cause. We know not what motives might have induced him to conceal from us the sources of his terror. And since he could not obtain our consent to his attending us, he has taken these means, perhaps, of effecting his purpose. The darkness might easily conceal him from our observation. He might have passed us without our noticing him, or he might have made a circuit in the woods we have just passed, and come out before us."

"That I own," replied the daughter, "is not improbable. If it be true, I shall be sorry for his own sake, but if there be any danger from which his attendance can secure us, I shall be well pleased for all our sakes. He will reflect with some satisfaction, perhaps, that he has done or intended us a service. It would be cruel to deny him a satisfaction so innocent."

"Pray, my dear, what think you of this young man? Does his ardour to serve us flow from a right source?"

"It flows, I have no doubt, from a double source. He has a kind heart, and delights to oblige others: but this is not all. He is likewise in love, and imagines that he cannot do too much for the object of his passion."

"Indeed!" exclaimed Mr. Davis, in some surprise. "You speak very positively. That is no more than I suspected; but how came you to know it with so much certainty?"

"The information came to me in the directest manner. He told me so himself."

"So ho! why, the impertinent young rogue!"

"Nay, my dear father, his behavior did not merit that epithet. He is rash and inconsiderate. That is the utmost amount of his guilt. A short absence will show him the true state of his feelings. It was unavoidable, in one of his character, to fall in love with the first woman whose appearance was in any degree specious. But attachments like these will be extinguished as easily as they are formed. I do not fear for him on this account."

"Have you reason to fear for him on any account?"

"Yes. The period of youth will soon pass away. Overweening and fickle, he will go on committing one mistake after another, incapable of repairing his errors, or of profiting by the daily lessons of experience. His genius will be merely an implement of mischief. His greater capacity will be evinced merely by the greater portion of unhappiness that, by means of it, will accrue to others or rebound upon himself."

"I see, my dear, that your spirits are low. Nothing else, surely, could suggest such melancholy presages. For my part, I question not, but he will one day be a fine fellow and a happy one. I like him exceedingly. I shall take pains to be acquainted with his future adventures, and do him all the good that I can."

"That intention," said his daughter, "is worthy of the goodness of your heart. He is no less an object of regard to me than to you. I trust I shall want neither the power nor inclination to contribute to his welfare. At present, however, his welfare will be best promoted by forgetting me. Hereafter, I shall solicit a renewal of intercourse."

"Speak lower," said the father. "If I mistake not, there is the same person again." He pointed to the field that skirted the road on the left hand. The young lady's better eyes enabled her to detect his mistake. It was the trunk of a cherry-tree that he had observed.

They proceeded in silence. Contrary to custom, the lady was buried in musing. Her father, whose temper and inclinations were molded by those of his child, insensibly subsided into the same state.

The re-appearance of the same figure that had already excited their attention diverted them anew from their contemplations. "As I live," exclaimed Mr. Davis, "that thing, whatever it be, haunts us. I do not like it. This is strange conduct for young Althorpe to adopt. Instead of being our protector, the danger, against which he so pathetically warned us, may be, in some inscrutable way, connected with this personage. It is best to be upon our guard."

"Nay, my father," said the lady, "be not disturbed. What danger can be dreaded by two persons from one? This thing, I dare say, means us no harm. What is at present inexplicable might be obvious enough if we were better acquainted with this neighbourhood. It is not worth a thought. You see it is now gone." Mr. Davis looked again, but it was no longer discernible.

They were now approaching a wood. Mr. Davis called to the guide to stop. His daughter enquired the reason of this command. She found it arose from his uncertainty as to the propriety of proceeding.

"I know not how it is," said he, "but I begin to be affected with the fears of young Althorpe. I am half resolved not to enter this wood.—That light yonder informs that a house is near. It may not be unadvisable to stop. I cannot think of delaying our journey till morning; but, by stopping a few minutes, we may possibly collect some useful information. Perhaps it will be expedient and practicable to procure the attendance of another person. I am not well pleased with myself for declining our young friend's offer."

To this proposal Miss Davis objected the inconveniences that calling at a farmer's house, at this time of night, when all were retired to rest, would probably occasion. "Besides," continued she, "the light which you saw is gone: a sufficient proof that it was nothing but a meteor."

At this moment they heard a noise, at a small distance behind them, as of shutting a gate. They called. Speedily an answer was returned in a tone of mildness. The person approached the chaise, and enquired who they were, whence they came, whither they were going, and, lastly, what they wanted.

Mr. Davis explained to this inquisitive person, in a few words, the nature of their situation, mentioned the appearance on the road, and questioned him, in his turn, as to what inconveniences were to be feared from prosecuting his journey. Satisfactory answers were returned to these enquiries.

"As to what you seed in the road," continued he, "I reckon it was nothing but a sheep or a cow. I am not more scary than some folks, but I never goes out a' nights without I sees some *sich* thing as that, that I takes for a man or woman, and am scared a little oftentimes, but not much. I'm sure after to find that it's not nothing but a cow, or hog, or tree, or something. If it wasn't some sich thing you seed, I reckon it was *Nick Handyside.*"

"Nick Handyside! who was he?"

"It was a fellow that went about the country a' nights. A shocking fool to be sure, that loved to plague and frighten people. Yes. Yes. It couldn't be nobody, he reckoned, but Nick. Nick was a droll thing. He wondered they'd never heard of Nick. He reckoned they were strangers in these here parts."

"Very true, my friend. But who is Nick? Is he a reptile to be shunned, or trampled on?"

"Why I don't know how as that. Nick is an odd soul to be sure; but he don't do nobody no harm, as ever I heard, except by scaring them. He is easily skeart though, for that matter, himself. He loves to frighten folks, but he's shocking apt to be frightened himself. I reckon you took Nick for a ghost. That's a shocking good story, I declare. Yet it's happened hundreds and hundreds of times, I guess, and more."

When this circumstance was mentioned, my uncle, as well as myself, was astonished at our own negligence. While enumerating, on the preceding evening, the obstacles and inconveniences which the travellers were likely to encounter, we entirely and unaccountably overlooked one circumstance, from which inquietude might reasonably have been expected. Near the spot where they now were, lived a Mr. Handyside, whose only son was an idiot. He also merited the name of monster, if a projecting breast, a mis-shapen head, features horrid and distorted, and a voice that resembled nothing that was ever before heard, could entitle him to that appellation. This being, besides the natural deformity of his frame, wore looks and practised gesticulations that were, in an inconceivable degree, uncouth and hideous. He was mischievous, but his freaks were subjects of little apprehension to those who were accustomed to them, though they were frequently occasions of alarm to strangers. He particularly delighted in imposing on the ignorance of strangers and the timidity of women. He was a perpetual rover. Entirely bereft of reason, his sole employment consisted in sleeping, and eating, and roaming. He would frequently escape at night, and a thousand anecdotes could have been detailed respecting the tricks which Nick Handyside had played upon way-farers.

Other considerations, however, had, in this instance, so much engrossed our minds, that Nick Handyside had never been once thought or mentioned. This was the more remarkable, as there had very lately happened an adventure, in which this person had acted a principal part. He had wandered from home, and got bewildered in a desolate tract, known by the name of Norwood. It was a region, rude, sterile, and lonely, bestrewn with rocks, and embarrassed with bushes.

He had remained for some days in this wilderness. Unable to extricate himself, and, at length, tormented with hunger, he manifested his distress by the most doleful shrieks. These were uttered with most vehemence and heard at greatest distance, by night. At first, those who heard them were panic-struck; but, at length, they furnished a clue by which those who were in search of him were guided to the spot. Notwithstanding the recentness and singularity of this adventure, and the probability that our guests would suffer molestation from this cause, so strangely forgetful had we been, that no caution on this head had been given. This caution, indeed, as the event testified, would have been superfluous, and yet I cannot enough wonder that in hunting for some reason, by which I might justify my fears to them or to myself, I had totally overlooked this mischief-loving idiot.

After listening to an ample description of Nick, being warned to proceed with particular caution in a part of the road that was near at hand, and being assured that they had nothing to dread from human interference, they resumed their journey with new confidence.

Their attention was frequently excited by rustling leaves or stumbling footsteps, and the figure which they doubted not to belong to Nick Handyside, occasionally hovered in their sight. This appearance no longer inspired them with apprehension. They had been assured that a stern voice was sufficient to repulse him, when most importunate. This antic being treated all others as children. He took pleasure in the effects which the sight of his own deformity produced, and betokened his satisfaction by a laugh, which might have served as a model to the poet who has depicted the ghastly risibilities of Death. On this occasion, however, the monster behaved with unusual moderation. He never came near enough for his peculiarities to be distinguished by star-light. There was nothing fantastic in his motions, nor any thing surprising, but the celerity of his transitions. They were unaccompanied by those howls, which reminded you at one time of a troop of hungry wolves, and had, at another, something in them inexpressibly wild and melancholy. This monster possessed a certain species of dexterity. His talents, differently applied, would have excited rational admiration. He was fleet as a deer. He was patient, to an incredible degree, of watchfulness, and cold, and hunger. He had improved the flexibility of his voice, till his cries, always loud and rueful, were capable of being diversified without end. Instances had been known, in which the stoutest heart was appalled by them; and some, particularly in the case of women, in which they had been productive of consequences truly deplorable.

When the travelers had arrived at that part of the wood where, as they had been informed, it was needful to be particularly cautious, Mr. Davis, for their greater security, proposed to his daughter to alight. The exercise of walking, he thought, after so much time spent in a close carriage, would be salutary and pleasant. The young lady readily embraced the proposal. They forthwith alighted, and walked at a small distance before the chaise, which was now conducted by the servant. From this moment the spectre, which, till now, had been occasionally visible, entirely disappeared. This incident naturally led the conversation to this topic. So singular a specimen of the forms which human nature is found to assume could not fail of suggesting a variety of remarks.

They pictured to themselves many combinations of circumstances in which Handyside might be the agent, and in which the most momentous effects might flow from his agency, without its being possible for others to conjecture the true nature of the agent. The propensities of this being might contribute to realize, on an American road, many of those imaginary tokens and perils which abound in the wildest romance. He would be an admirable machine, in a plan whose purpose was to generate or foster, in a given subject, the frenzy of quixotism.—No theatre was better adapted than Norwood to such an exhibition. This part of the country had long been deserted by beasts of prey. Bears might still, perhaps, be found during a very rigorous season, but wolves which, when the country was a desert, were extremely numerous, had now, in consequence of increasing population, withdrawn to more savage haunts. Yet the voice of Handyside, varied with the force and skill of which he was known to be capable, would fill these shades with outcries as ferocious as those which are to be heard in Siamese or Abyssinian forests. The tale of his recent elopement had been told by the man with whom they had just parted, in a rustic but picturesque style.

"But why," said the lady, "did not our kind host inform us of this circumstance? He must surely have been well acquainted with the existence and habits of this Handyside. He must have perceived to how many groundless alarms our ignorance, in this respect, was likely to expose us. It is strange that he did not afford us the slightest intimation of it."

Mr. Davis was no less surprised at this omission. He was at a loss to conceive how this should be forgotten in the midst of those minute directions, in which every cause had been laboriously recollected from which he might incur danger or suffer obstruction.

This person, being no longer an object of terror, began to be regarded with a very lively curiosity. They even wished for his appearance and near approach, that they might carry away with them more definite conceptions of his figure. The lady declared she should be highly pleased by hearing his outcries, and consoled herself with the belief, that he would not allow them to pass the limits which he had prescribed to his wanderings, without greeting them with a strain or two. This wish had scarcely been uttered, when it was completely gratified.

The lady involuntarily started, and caught hold of her father's arm. Mr. Davis himself was disconcerted. A scream, dismally loud, and piercingly shrill, was uttered by one at less than twenty paces from them.

The monster had shown some skill in the choice of a spot suitable to his design. Neighboring precipices, and a thick umbrage of oaks, on either side, contributed to prolong and to heighten his terrible notes. They were rendered more awful by the profound stillness that preceded and followed them. They were able speedily to quiet the trepidations which this hideous outcry, in spite of preparation and foresight, had produced, but they had not foreseen one of its unhappy consequences.

In a moment Mr. Davis was alarmed by the rapid sound of footsteps behind him. His presence of mind, on this occasion, probably saved himself and his daughter from instant destruction. He leaped out of the path, and, by a sudden exertion, at the same moment, threw the lady to some distance from the tract. The horse that drew the chaise rushed by them with the celerity of lightning. Affrighted at the sounds which had been uttered at a still less distance from the horse than from Mr. Davis, possibly with a malicious design to produce this very effect, he jerked the bridle from the hands that held it, and rushed forward with headlong speed. The man, before he could provide for his own safety, was beaten to the earth. He was considerably bruised by the fall, but presently recovered his feet, and went in pursuit of the horse.

This accident happened at about a hundred yards from the *oak,* against which so many cautions had been given. It was not possible, at any time, without considerable caution, to avoid it. It was not to be wondered at, therefore, that, in a few seconds, the carriage was shocked against the trunk, overturned, and dashed into a thousand fragments. The noise of the crash sufficiently informed them of this event. Had the horse been inclined to stop, a repetition, for the space of some minutes, of the same savage and terrible shrieks would have added tenfold to his consternation and to the speed of his flight. After this dismal strain had ended, Mr. Davis raised his daughter from the ground. She had suffered no material injury. As soon as they recovered from the confusion into which this accident had thrown them, they began to consult upon the measures proper to be taken upon this emergency. They were left alone. The servant had gone in pursuit of the flying horse. Whether he would be able to retake him was extremely dubious. Meanwhile they were surrounded by darkness. What was the distance of the next house could not be known. At that hour of the night they could not hope to be directed, by the far-seen taper, to any hospitable roof. The only alternative, therefore, was to remain where they were, uncertain of the fate of their companion, or to go forward with the utmost expedition.

They could not hesitate to embrace the latter. In a few minutes they arrived at the oak. The chaise appeared to have been dashed against a knotty projecture of the trunk, which was large enough for a person to be conveniently seated on it. Here they again paused.—Miss Davis desired to remain here a few minutes to recruit her exhausted strength. She proposed to her father to leave her here, and go forward in quest of the horse and the servant. He might return as speedily as he thought proper. She did not fear to be alone. The voice was still. Having accomplished his malicious purposes, the spectre had probably taken his final leave of them. At all events, if the report of the rustic was true, she had no personal injury to fear from him.

Through some deplorable infatuation, as he afterwards deemed it, Mr. Davis complied with her entreaties, and went in search of the missing. He had engaged in a most unpromising undertaking. The man and horse were by this time at a considerable distance. The former would, no doubt, shortly return. Whether his pursuit succeeded or miscarried, he would surely see the propriety of hastening his return with what tidings he could obtain, and to ascertain his master's situation. Add to this, the impropriety of leaving a woman, single and unarmed, to the machinations of this demoniac. He had scarcely parted with her when these reflections occurred to him. His resolution was changed. He turned back with the intention of immediately seeking her. At the same moment, he saw the flash and heard the discharge of a pistol. The light proceeded from the foot of the oak. His imagination was filled with horrible forebodings. He ran with all his speed to the spot. He called aloud upon the name of his daughter, but, alas! she was unable to answer him. He found her stretched at the foot of the tree, senseless, and weltering in her blood. He lifted her in his arms, and seated her against the trunk. He found himself stained with blood, flowing from a wound, which either the darkness of the night, or the confusion of his thoughts, hindered him from tracing. Overwhelmed with a catastrophe so dreadful and unexpected, he was divested of all presence of mind. The author of his calamity had vanished. No human being was at hand to succour him in his uttermost distress. He beat his head against the ground, tore away his venerable locks, and rent the air with his cries.

Fortunately there was a dwelling at no great distance from this scene. The discharge of a pistol produces a sound too loud not to be heard far and wide, in this lonely region. This house belonged to a physician. He was a man noted for his humanity and sympathy. He was roused, as well as most of his family, by a sound so uncommon. He rose instantly, and calling up his people, proceeded with lights to the road. The lamentations of Mr. Davis directed them to the place. To the physician the scene was inexplicable. Who was the author of this distress; by whom the pistol was discharged; whether through some untoward chance or with design, he was as yet uninformed, nor could he gain any information from the incoherent despair of Mr. Davis.

Every measure that humanity and professional skill could suggest were employed on this occasion. The dying lady was removed to the house. The ball had lodged in her brain and to extract it was impossible. Why should I dwell on the remaining incidents of this tale? She languished till the next morning, and then expired.———

BIBLIOGRAPHY AND WORKS CITED

In the "Historical Essay" written for the Bicentennial edition of Edgar Huntly *in 1984, Sydney J. Krause noted that "the* Huntly *criticism has grown to be quite voluminous of late" (391); he estimates that there were sixty critical pieces on* Huntly *before 1950 and another ninety from 1950 to 1984. This bibliography concentrates on material published since 1980—that is, the current era of Brown studies. For work on Brown before 1980, see Patricia Parker,* Charles Brockden Brown: A Reference Guide *(Boston: G. K. Hall, 1980).*

I. Writings by Brown

Comprehensive bibliographies of Brown's writings and scholarship on Brown are available at the Web site of The Charles Brockden Brown Electronic Edition and Scholarly Archive: http://www.brockdenbrown.ucf.edu.

A. Novels

Brown, Charles Brockden. *Wieland; or The Transformation. An American Tale.* New York: Printed by T. & J. Swords for H. Caritat, 1798.

———. *Arthur Mervyn; or, Memoirs of the Year 1793.* Philadelphia: H. Maxwell, 1799.

———. *Edgar Huntly; or, Memoirs of a Sleep-Walker.* Philadelphia: H. Maxwell, 1799.

———. *Ormond; or The Secret Witness.* New York: Printed by G. Forman for H. Caritat, 1799.

———. *Memoirs of Stephen Calvert.* Published serially in *The Monthly Magazine*, vols. I-II (New York: T. & J. Swords, June 1799-June 1800).

———. *Arthur Mervyn; or, Memoirs of the Year 1793. Second Part.* New York: George F. Hopkins, 1800.

———. *Clara Howard; In a Series of Letters.* Philadelphia: Asbury Dickens, 1801.

———. *Jane Talbot; A Novel.* Philadelphia, John Conrad; Baltimore, M. & J. Conrad; Washington City, Rapin & Conrad, 1801.

———. *The Novels and Related Works of Charles Brockden Brown.* Bicentennial Edition. Six Volumes. Sydney J. Krause and S.W. Reid, eds. Kent, OH: Kent State UP, 1977–1987. *The Bicentennial edition is the modern scholarly text of Brown's seven novels, plus the Wollstonecraftian dialogue* Alcuin *and* Memoirs of Carwin.

B. Essays and Uncollected Fiction

Brown, Charles Brockden. *Alcuin; A Dialogue.* New York: T. & J. Swords, 1798.

————. *Historical Sketches. Short sections published in the* Literary Magazine and American Register, *1805; most of the project appeared posthumously in the Allen & Dunlap biographies (1811–1815).*

————. *Literary Essays and Reviews.* Alfred Weber and Wolfgang Schäfer, eds. Frankfurt: Peter Lang, 1992.

————. *The Rhapsodist and Other Uncollected Writings.* Harry R. Warfel, ed. Scholar's Delmar, NY: Facsimiles and Reprints, 1977.

————. *Somnambulism and Other Stories.* Alfred Weber, ed. Frankfurt: Peter Lang, 1987.

C. Periodicals and Pamphlets

The three periodicals that Brown edited include hundreds of his own articles and miscellaneous pieces in a variety of genres (essays, short fictions, reviews, dialogues, anecdotes, and other forms) and on a wide range of subjects, from literary and artistic culture to social and political questions, history, geopolitics, and different subfields of science. For a listing of these publications, consult the Comprehensive Bibliography at the Web site of The Charles Brockden Brown Electronic Archive and Scholarly Edition.

Brown, Charles Brockden. *The Monthly Magazine and American Review.* Vols. I–III. New York: T. & J. Swords, April, 1799–December, 1800.

————. *An Address to the Government of the United States, on the Cession of Louisiana to the French.* Philadelphia: John Conrad, 1803.

————. *Monroe's Embassy, or, the Conduct of the Government, in Relation to Our Claims to the Navigation of the Mississippi [sic], Considered.* Philadelphia: John Conrad, 1803.

————. *The Literary Magazine and American Register.* Vols. I–VIII. Philadelphia: C. & A. Conrad, 1803–1806.

————. *The American Register, or General Repository of History, Politics, and Science.* Vols. I–VII. Philadelphia: C. & A. Conrad, 1807–1809.

————. *An Address to the Congress of the United States, on the Utility and Justice of Restrictions upon Foreign Commerce.* Philadelphia: C. & A. Conrad, 1809.

II. Biographies of Brown and Diaries of his Friends Smith, Dunlap, and Cope

Besides the published biographies, an important resource is the unfinished biographical study written 1910–1945 by Daniel Edwards Kennedy, now preserved at the Kent State Institute for Bibliography and Editing. The Smith and Dunlap diaries provide detailed reportage about Brown and his New York circle in the crucial period when Brown was writing his novels. Cope's diary documents Brown's never-accomplished plan, in 1803–1806, to write an abolitionist history of slavery.

Allen, Paul. *The Life of Charles Brockden Brown.* Charles E. Bennett, ed. Delmar, NY: Scholar's Facsimiles and Reprints, 1975 (written 1811–1814). *Allen's unfinished biography is the preliminary version of Dunlap's 1815* Life, *and remained unpublished until the late twentieth century. It prints miscellaneous fictional fragments and other texts by Brown not available elsewhere.*

————. *The Late Charles Brockden Brown.* Edited, with an Introduction, by Robert E. Hemenway and Joseph Katz. Columbia, SC: J. Faust, 1976. *This is a second facsimile edition of the unfinished Allen biography, with additional commentary and information on the circumstances surrounding the influential 1815 Dunlap version.*

Clark, David Lee. *Charles Brockden Brown: Pioneer Voice of America.* Durham: Duke UP, 1952.

Cope, Thomas P. *Philadelphia Merchant: the Diary of Thomas P. Cope, 1800–1851.* Edited and with an introduction and appendices by Eliza Cope Harrison. South Bend, IN: Gateway Editions, 1978.

Dunlap, William. *Diary of William Dunlap (1766–1839): The Memoirs of a Dramatist, Theatrical Manager, Painter, Critic, Novelist, and Historian.* 3 volumes. Dorothy C. Barck, ed. New York: The New-York Historical Society, 1930.

————. *The Life of Charles Brockden Brown.* 2 volumes. Philadelphia: James P. Parke, 1815. *A revision and extension of Allen, above. Together, Dunlap and Allen provide the only texts for the* Historical Sketches, *the complete version of* Alcuin, *and other pieces not available elsewhere.*

Kafer, Peter. *Charles Brockden Brown's Revolution and the Birth of American Gothic.* Philadelphia: U of Pennsylvania P, 2004.

Smith, Elihu Hubbard. *The Diary of Elihu Hubbard Smith (1771–1798).* James E. Cronin, ed. Philadelphia: American Philosophical Society, 1973.

Warfel, Harry R. *Charles Brockden Brown: American Gothic Novelist.* Gainesville: U of Florida P, 1949.

III. Brown and *Edgar Huntly* in the wider context of cultural and literary history.

Axelrod, Alan. *Charles Brockden Brown: An American Tale.* Austin: U of Texas P, 1983.

Bradfield, Scott. *Dreaming Revolution: Transgression in the Development of American Romance.* Iowa City: U of Iowa P, 1993.

Brückner, Martin. "Sense, Census, and the 'Statistical View' in the *Literary Magazine* and *Jane Talbot*." In Philip Barnard, Mark L. Kamrath, and Stephen Shapiro, eds., *Revising Charles Brockden Brown: Culture, Politics, and Sexuality in the Early Republic,* 281–309. Knoxville: U of Tennessee P, 2004.

Chase, Richard Volney. *The American Novel and Its Tradition.* Baltimore: Johns Hopkins UP, 1957.

Christophersen, Bill. *The Apparition in the Glass: Charles Brockden Brown's American Gothic.* Athens: U of Georgia P, 1993.

Dauber, Kenneth. *The Idea of Authorship in America: Democratic Poetics from Franklin to Melville.* Madison: U of Wisconsin P, 1990.

Dawes, James. "Fictional Feeling: Philosophy, Cognitive Science, and the American Gothic." *American Literature* 76.3 (2004): 437–66.

Dillon, Elizabeth Maddock. *The Gender of Freedom: Fictions of Liberalism and the Literary Public Sphere.* Stanford: Stanford UP, 2004.

Ellison, Julie. *Cato's Tears and the Making of an Anglo-American Emotion.* Chicago: U of Chicago P, 1999.

Ferguson, Robert A. "Yellow Fever and Charles Brockden Brown: The Context of the Emerging Novelist." *Early American Literature* 14 (1980): 293–305.

———. *Law and Letters in American Culture.* Cambridge, MA: Harvard UP, 1984.

Fiedler, Leslie A. *Love and Death in the American Novel.* New York: Criterion Books, 1960.

Fliegelman, Jay. *Prodigals and Pilgrims: The American Revolution against Patriarchal Authority.* Cambridge: Cambridge UP, 1982.

Grabo, Norman S. *The Coincidental Art of Charles Brockden Brown.* Chapel Hill: U of North Carolina P, 1981.

Hedges, William. "Charles Brockden Brown and the Culture of Contradictions." *Early American Literature* 9 (1974): 107–42.

Herdman, John. *The Double in Nineteenth-Century Fiction: The Shadow Life.* New York: St. Martin's Press, 1991.

Kamrath, Mark L. "American Exceptionalism and Radicalism in 'Annals of Europe and America.'" In Philip Barnard, Mark L. Kamrath, and Stephen Shapiro, eds., *Revising Charles Brockden Brown: Culture, Politics, and Sexuality in the Early Republic,* 354–84. Knoxville: U of Tennessee P, 2004.

Kornfeld, Eve. "Encountering 'the Other': American Intellectuals and Indians in the 1790s." *William and Mary Quarterly* 52.2 (1995): 287–314.

Larsson, David M. "Arthur Mervyn, Edgar Huntly, and the Critics." *Essays in Literature* 15 (1988): 207–19.

Leask, Nigel. "Irish Republicans and Gothic Eleutherarchs: Pacific Utopias in the Writings of Theobald Wolfe Tone and Charles Brockden Brown." In Robert M. Maniquis, ed., *British Radical Culture of the 1790s,* 91–111. San Marino, CA: Huntington Library, 2002.

Lippard, George. *The Quaker City; or, The Monks of Monk Hall. A Romance of Philadelphia Life, Mystery, and Crime.* [1845] David S. Reynolds, ed. Amherst: U of Massachusetts P, 1995.

Marshall, Ian. *Story Line: Exploring the Literature of the Appalachian Trail.* Charlottesville: UP of Virginia, 1998.

Mogen, David, Scott P. Sanders, and Joanne B. Karpinski. *Frontier Gothic: Terror and Wonder at the Frontier in American Literature.* Rutherford: Fairleigh Dickinson UP, 1993.

Ringe, Donald A. *Charles Brockden Brown.* Revised edition. Boston: Twayne, G. K. Hall, 1991.

Rowe, John Carlos. *Literary Culture and U.S. Imperialism: From the Revolution to World War II.* New York: Oxford UP, 2000.

Rowe, Katherine. "The Politics of Sleepwalking: American Lady Macbeths." *Shakespeare Survey: An Annual Survey of Shakespeare Studies and Production* 57 (2004): 126–36.

Shapiro, Stephen. *The Culture and Commerce of the Early American Novel: Reading the Atlantic World-System.* University Park: The Pennsylvania State UP, 2008.

———. " 'I Could Kiss Him One Minute and Kill Him the Next!': The Limits of Radical Male Friendship in Holcroft, CB Brown, and Wollstonecraft Shelley." In Walter Göbel, Saskia Schabio, and Martin Windisch, eds., *Engendering Images of Man in the Long Eighteenth Century,* 111–32. Trier, Germany: Wissenschaftlicher Verlag, 2001.

Slotkin, Richard. *Regeneration through Violence: The Mythology of the American Frontier, 1600–1860.* Middletown: Wesleyan UP, 1973.

Smith-Rosenberg, Carroll. "Captured Subjects/Savage Others: Violently Engendering the New American." *Gender and History* 5 (1993): 177–95.

———. "Subject Female: Authorizing American Identity." *American Literary History* 5.3 (1993): 481–511.

Strode, Timothy Francis. *The Ethics of Exile: Colonialism in the Fictions of Charles Brockden Brown and J. M. Coetzee.* New York: Routledge, 2005.

Teute, Fredrika J. "A 'Republic of Intellect': Conversation and Criticism among the Sexes in 1790s New York." In Philip Barnard, Mark L. Kamrath, and Stephen Shapiro, eds., *Revising Charles Brockden Brown: Culture, Politics, and Sexuality in the Early Republic,* 149–81. Knoxville: U of Tennessee P, 2004.

———. "The Loves of the Plants; or, The Cross-Fertilization of Science and Desire at the End of the Eighteenth Century." In Robert M. Maniquis, ed., *British Radical Culture of the 1790s,* 63–89. San Marino, CA: Huntington Library, 2002.

Verhoeven, Wil. "Opening the Text: The Locked Truck Motif in Late Eighteenth-Century British and American Gothic Fiction." In Tinkler-Villani, Valeria and Peter Davidson, with Jane Stevenson, eds., *Exhibited by Candlelight: Sources and Developments in the Gothic Tradition,* 205–19. Amsterdam: Rodopi, 1996.

Waterman, Bryan. "*Arthur Mervyn*'s Medical Repository and the Early Republic's Knowledge Industries." *American Literary History* 15 (2003): 213–47.

———. *The Friendly Club of New York City: Industries of Knowledge in the Early Republic.* Dissertation. Boston: Boston U, 2000.

Weidman, Bette S. "White Men's Red Man: A Penitential Reading of Four American Novels." *Modern Language Studies* 4.2 (1974): 14–26.

IV. Discussions primarily of *Edgar Huntly.*

Anderson, Douglas. "*Edgar Huntly*'s Dark Inheritance." *Philological Quarterly* 70 (1991): 453–73.

Bellis, Peter J. "Narrative Compulsion and Control in Charles Brockden Brown's *Edgar Huntly.*" *South Atlantic Review* 52.1 (1987): 43–57.

Berressem, Hanjo. "'To Make Sense of a Random Act of Violence': Tyche, Automaton, and Trauma in Charles Brockden Brown's *Edgar Huntly; or, Memoirs of a Sleep-Walker.*" *Amerikastudien* 45 (2000): 55–72.

Berthold, Dennis. "Charles Brockden Brown, *Edgar Huntly*, and the Origins of the American Picturesque." *William and Mary Quarterly* 41.1 (1984): 62–84.

———. "Desacralizing the American Gothic: An Iconographic Approach to *Edgar Huntly.*" *Studies in American Fiction* 14.2 (1986): 127–38.

Bottalico, Michele. "The American Frontier and the Initiation Rite to a National Literature: The Example of *Edgar Huntly* by Charles Brockden Brown." *Rivisti di Studi Nord-Americani Journal* 4 (1993): 3–16.

Cassuto, Leonard. "'[Un]Consciousness Itself Is the Malady': *Edgar Huntly* and the Discourse of the Other." *Modern Language Studies* 23.4 (1993): 118–30.

Christophersen, Bill. "Charles Brockden Brown, Enthusiasm and the Ghost of William Penn." In Marc Amfreville and Françoise Charras, *Profils Américains: Charles Brockden Brown* 11 (1999): 135–48.

Cowell, Pattie. "Class, Gender, and Genre: Deconstructing the Social Formulas on the Gothic Frontier." In David Mogen, Scott P. Sanders, and Joanne B. Karpinski, eds., *Frontier Gothic: Terror and Wonder at the Frontier in American Literature,* 126–39. Rutherford: Fairleigh Dickenson UP, 1993.

Downes, Paul. "Sleep-Walking out of the Revolution: Brown's *Edgar Huntly.*" *Eighteenth-Century Studies* 29.4 (1996): 413–31.

Gardner, Jared. "Alien Nation: *Edgar Huntly*'s Savage Awakening." *American Literature* 66.3 (1994): 429–61.

Gibbons, Luke. "Ireland, America, and Gothic Memory: Transatlantic Terror in the Early Republic." *boundary 2* 31.1 (2004): 25–47.

Grabo, Norman. "Introduction." In Charles Brockden Brown, *Edgar Huntly; or, Memoirs of a Sleep-Walker,* vii–xxiii. New York: Penguin, 1988.

Hamelman, Steve. "Rhapsodist in the Wilderness: Brown's Romantic Quest in *Edgar Huntly.*" *Studies in American Fiction* 21.2 (1993): 171–90.

Hinds, Elizabeth Jane Wall. "Charles Brockden Brown's Revenge Tragedy: *Edgar Huntly* and the Uses of Property." *Early American Literature* 30.1 (1995): 51–70.

Hinds, Janie. "Deb's Dogs: Animals, Indians, and Postcolonial Desire in Charles Brockden Brown's *Edgar Huntly.*" *Early American Literature* 39.2 (2004): 323–54.

Hughes, Philip Russell. "Archetypal Patterns in *Edgar Huntly.*" *Studies in the Novel* 5 (1973): 176–90.

Hustis, Harriet. "Deliberate Unknowing and Strategic Retelling: The Ravages of Cultural Desire in Charles Brockden Brown's *Edgar Huntly.*" *Studies in American Fiction* 31.1 (2003): 101–20.

Kamrath, Mark L. "Brown and the Enlightenment: A Study of the Influence of Voltaire's *Candide* in *Edgar Huntly.*" *American Transcendental Quarterly* 5 (1991): 6–14.

Kimball, Arthur G. "Savages and Savagism: Brockden Brown's Dramatic Irony." *Studies in Romanticism* 6 (1967): 214–25.

Krause, Sydney J. *Edgar Huntly* and the American Nightmare." *Studies in the Novel* 13.3 (1981): 294–302.

———. "Historical Essay." In Charles Brocken Brown, *Edgar Huntly; or, Memoirs of a Sleep-Walker.* Vol. 4, *The Novels and Related Works of Charles Brockden Brown*, 295–400. Kent: Kent State UP, 1984.

———. "Penn's Elm and *Edgar Huntly:* Dark 'Instruction to the Heart.'" *American Literature* 66.3 (1994): 463–84.

Luciano, Dana. "'Perverse Nature': *Edgar Huntly* and the Novel's Reproductive Disorders." *American Literature* 70.1 (1998): 1–27.

Lueck, Beth L. "Charles Brockden Brown's *Edgar Huntly:* The Picturesque Traveler as Sleepwalker." *Studies in American Fiction* 15.1 (1987): 25–42.

Mackenthun, Gesa. "Captives and Sleepwalkers: The Ideological Revolutions of Post-Revolutionary Colonial Discourse." *European Review of Native American Studies* 11.1 (1997): 19–26.

Newman, Robert D. "Indians and Indian-Hating in *Edgar Huntly* and *The Confidence Man.*" *MELUS* 15.3 (1988): 65–74.

Patrick, Marietta. "The Transformation Myth in *Edgar Huntly.*" *Journal of Evolutionary Psychology* 10 (1989): 360–71.

Pitman, Janet D. "The Wilderness Experience in James Dickey's Deliverance and Charles Brockden Brown's *Edgar Huntly.*" *Ball State University Forum* 23.3 (1982): 73–80.

Schulz, Dieter. "*Edgar Huntly* as Quest Romance." *American Literature* 43.3 (1971): 323–35.

Shapiro, Stephen. "'Man to Man I Needed Not to Dread His Encounter': *Edgar Huntly*'s End of Erotic Pessimism." In Philip Barnard, Mark L. Kamrath, and Stephen Shapiro, eds., *Revising Charles Brockden Brown: Culture, Politics, and Sexuality in the Early Republic*, 216–51. Knoxville: U of Tennessee P, 2004.

Sivils, M. W. "Native American Sovereignty and Old Deb in Charles Brockden Brown's *Edgar Huntly.*" *American Transcendental Quarterly* 14.4 (2001): 293–304.

Slater, John F. "The Sleepwalker and the Great Awakening: Brown's *Edgar Huntly* and Jonathan Edwards." *Papers on Language and Literature* 19.2 (1983): 199–217.

Sullivan, Michael P. "Reconciliation and Subversion in *Edgar Huntly.*" *American Transcendental Quarterly* 2.1 (1988): 5–22.

Toles, George. "Charting the Hidden Landscape: *Edgar Huntly.*" *Early American Literature* 16.2 (1981): 133–53.

Vatalaro, Paul. "*Edgar Huntly:* Charles Brockden Brown's Early American Fairy Tale." *Journal of Evolutionary Psychology* 15 (1994): 3–4, 259–68.

Voloshin, Beverly R. "*Edgar Huntly* and the Coherence of the Self." *Early American Literature* 23.3 (1988): 262–80.

Warchol, Tomasz. "Formal and Thematic Patterns in *Edgar Huntly.*" *Ball State University Forum* 28.3 (1987): 16–24.

Witherington, Paul. "Not My Tongue Only: Form and Language in Brown's *Edgar Huntly.*" In Bernard Rosenthal, ed., *Critical Essays on Charles Brockden Brown,* 164–83. Boston: G. K. Hall, 1981.

V. *Edgar Huntly*'s eighteenth-century context.

A. Irish and Anglophone historical culture and 1790s radicalism.

Bynum, Caroline Walker. *Metamorphosis and Identity.* New York: Zone Books, 2005.

Drurey, Michael. *Transatlantic Rebels in the Early Republic.* Lawrence: UP of Kansas, 1997.

Karkov, Catharine E. "Tales of the Ancients: Colonial Werewolves and the Mapping of Postcolonial Ireland." In Patricia Clare Ingham and Michelle R. Warren, eds., *Postcolonial Moves: Medieval through Modern,* 93–109. New York: Palgrave Macmillan, 2003.

Kidd, Colin. "Gaelic Antiquity and National Identity in Enlightenment Ireland and Scotland." *The English Historical Review* 109. 434 (1994): 1197–1214.

Linebaugh, Peter. "'The Red-Crested Bird and Black Duck'—A Story of 1802: Historical Materialism, Indigenous People, and the Failed Republic." *The Republic* 2 (2001): 104–25.

Smyth, Jim, ed. *Revolution, Counter-Revolution, and Union: Ireland in the 1790s.* Cambridge, New York: Cambridge UP, 2000.

Twomey, Richard. *Jacobins and Jeffersonians: Anglo-American Radicalism in the United States, 1790–1820.* New York: Garland, 1989.

Walters, Kerry S. *Rational Infidels: The American Deists.* Durango: Longwood Academic, 1992.

Wilson, David. *United Irishmen, United States: Immigrant Radicals in the Early Republic.* Ithaca: Cornell UP, 1998.

B. Frontier expansionism and Quaker-Irish-Indian relations.

Brooks, Joanna. "Held Captive by the Irish: Quaker Captivity Narratives in Frontier Pennsylvania." *New Hibernia Review* 8.3 (2004): 31–46.

Camenzind, Krista. "Violence, Race, and the Paxton Boys." In William A. Pencak and Daniel K. Richter, eds., *Friends and Enemies in Penn's Woods: Indians, Colonists, and the Racial Construction of Pennsylvania,* 201–20. University Park: The Pennsylvania State UP, 2004.

Dowd, Gregory Evans. *A Spirited Resistance: The North American Indian Struggle for Unity, 1745–1815.* Baltimore: Johns Hopkins UP, 1992.

Griffin, Patrick. *The People with No Name: Ireland's Ulster Scots, America's Scots Irish, and the Creation of a British Atlantic World, 1689–1764.* Princeton: Princeton UP, 2001.

Harper, Steven C. "Delawares and Pennsylvanians after the Walking Purchase." In William A. Pencak and Daniel K. Richter, eds., *Friends and Enemies in Penn's Woods: Indians, Colonists, and the Racial Construction of Pennsylvania,* 167–79. University Park: The Pennsylvania State UP, 2004.

Hazard, Samuel, ed. *Minutes of the Provincial Council of Pennsylvania, from the Organization to the Termination of the Proprietary Government.* 10 vols. Philadelphia: Jos. Stevens & Co., 1853.

Jennings, Francis. *Empire of Fortune: Crown, Colonies, and Tribes in the Seven Years War in America.* New York: W. W. Norton, 1988.

———. "The Scandalous Indian Policy of William Penn's Sons: Deeds and Documents of the Walking Purchase." *Pennsylvania History* 37 (1970): 19–39.

Richter, Daniel. *Facing East from Indian Country: A Native History of Early America.* Cambridge: Harvard UP, 2003.

Starna, William A. "The Diplomatic Career of Canasatego." In William A. Pencak and Daniel K. Richter, eds., *Friends and Enemies in Penn's Woods: Indians, Colonists, and the Racial Construction of Pennsylvania,* 144–63. University Park: The Pennsylvania State UP, 2004.

White, Ed. *The Backcountry and the City: Colonization and Conflict in Early America.* Minneapolis: U of Minnesota P, 2005.

White, Richard. *The Middle Ground: Indians, Empires, and Republics in the Great Lakes Region, 1650–1815.* New York: Cambridge UP, 1991.

C. Counterrevolutionary backlash of the late 1790s.

Cotlar, Seth. "The Federalists' Transatlantic Cultural Offensive of 1798 and the Moderation of American Political Discourse." In Jeffrey L. Pasley, Andrew W. Robertson, and David Waldstreicher, eds., *Beyond the Founders: New Approaches to the Political History of the Early American Republic,* 274–99. Chapel Hill: U of North Carolina P, 2004.

Davis, David Brion. *The Fear of Conspiracy: Images of Un-American Subversion from the Revolution to the Present.* Ithaca: Cornell UP, 1975.

Fischer, David Hackett. *The Revolution of American Conservatism: The Federalist Party in the Era of Jeffersonian Democracy.* New York: Harper & Row, 1965.

Hofstadter, Richard. *The Paranoid Style in American Politics and Other Essays.* New York: Knopf, 1966.

Miller, John C. *Crisis in Freedom: The Alien and Sedition Acts.* Boston: Little, Brown, & Co., 1951.

Rogin, Michael Paul. *Ronald Reagan, the Movie: and Other Episodes in Political Demonology.* Berkeley: U of California P, 1997.

D. Early American novel and British-democratic novel in the 1790s.

Butler, Marilyn. *Jane Austen and the War of Ideas.* Oxford: Clarendon Press, 1975.

Clemit, Pamela. *The Godwinian Novel: The Rational Fictions of Godwin, Brockden Brown, Mary Shelley.* Oxford: Oxford UP, 1993.

Davidson, Cathy. *Revolution and the Word: The Rise of the Novel in America.* Expanded edition. New York: Oxford UP, 2004.

Kelly, Gary. *The English Jacobin Novel, 1780–1805.* Oxford: Oxford UP, 1976.

———. *English Fiction of the Romantic Period, 1789–1830.* London: Longman, 1989.

Tompkins, J. M. S. *The Popular Novel in England, 1770–1800.* Lincoln: U of Nebraska P, 1961.

E. Sensibility, sentiment, and the gothic.

Barker-Benfield, G. J., *The Culture of Sensibility: Sex and Society in Eighteenth-Century Britain.* Chicago: U of Chicago P, 1992.

Botting, Fred. *Gothic.* London: Routledge, 1995.

Ellis, Kate Ferguson. *The Contested Castle: Gothic Novels and the Subversion of Domestic Ideology.* Chicago: U of Illinois P, 1989.

Jones, Chris. *Radical Sensibility: Literature and Ideas in the 1790s.* London: Routledge, 1993.

Kilgour, Maggie. *The Rise of the Gothic Novel.* London: Routledge, 1995.

Mullan, John. *Sentiment and Sociability: The Language of Feeling in the Eighteenth Century.* Oxford: Clarendon Press, 1988.

Todd, Janet. *Sensibility: An Introduction.* London, New York: Methuen, 1986.

Watt, James. *Contesting the Gothic: Fiction, Genre, and Cultural Conflict, 1764–1832.* Cambridge: Cambridge UP, 1999.

F. Captivity narratives.

Ashbridge, Elizabeth. *Some Account of the Fore Part of the Life of Elizabeth Ashbridge.* In William B. Andrews, et al., eds., *Journeys in New Worlds: Early American Women's Narratives,* 117–80. Madison: U of Wisconsin P, 1990.

Burnham, Michelle. *Captivity and Sentiment: Cultural Exchange in American Literature, 1682–1861.* Hanover: UP of New England, 1997.

Derounian-Stodola, Kathryn Zabelle, and James A. Levernier. *The Indian Captivity Narrative, 1550–1900.* New York: Twayne, 1993.

Derounian-Stodola, Kathryn Zabelle. *Women's Indian Captivity Narratives.* New York: Penguin, 1998.

Ebersole, Gary L. *Captured by Texts: Puritan to Postmodern Images of Indian Captivity.* Charlottesville: UP of Virginia, 1995.

Pearce, Roy Harvey. "The Significance of the Captivity Narrative." *American Literature* 29 (1947): 1–20.

Vail, R. W. G. *The Voice of the Old Frontier.* Philadelphia: U of Pennsylvania P, 1949.

G. Homoerotic relations in the Atlantic world.

Arnebeck, Bob. *Through a Fiery Trial: Building Washington, 1790–1800.* New York: Madison Books, 1991.

Bray, Alan. *Homosexuality in Renaissance England.* London: Gay Men's Press, 1982.

Crain, Caleb. *American Sympathy: Men, Friendship, and Literature in the New Nation.* New Haven: Yale UP, 2001.

Foster, Thomas, ed. *Long before Stonewall: Histories of Same-Sex Sexuality in Early America.* New York: New York UP, 2007.

Godbeer, Richard. *Sexual Revolution in Early America.* Baltimore: Johns Hopkins UP, 2004.

Haggerty, George. *Queer Gothic.* Urbana: U of Illinois P, 2006.

Hallock, John W. M. *The American Byron: Homosexuality and the Fall of Fitz-Greene Halleck.* Madison: U of Wisconsin P, 2000.

Higgs, David, ed. *Queer Sites: Gay Urban Histories Since 1600.* London: Routledge, 1999.

Norton, Rictor. *Mother Clap's Molly House: The Gay Subculture in England, 1700–1830.* London: Gay Men's Press, 1992.

———. *The Myth of the Modern Homosexual: Queer History and the Search for Cultural Unity.* London: Cassell, 1998.

Trumbach, Randolph. *Sex and the Gender Revolution.* Vol. 1, *Heterosexuality and the Third Gender in Enlightenment London.* Chicago: U of Chicago P, 1998.